Born with Wings
The Dragonbound Chronicles, Book 4

by

Bryan Fields

Published by Beasthold Books 2018

Print ISBN 978-1-7324160-0-0
Ebook ISBN 978-1-7324160-1-7

First print and ebook edition July 2018

For old friends who aren't with us any more...

For Margaret Alia Denny, who never gave up or gave in, and in so doing, built a community.

For Mary Dowling, who brought mischief and laughter to those around her, right up to the end.

For Elizabeth Yarrow, who brought music and poetry to every life she touched.

You are loved, and you are missed.

The hidden stars shine forth, and mark the rolling years.
The senseless dead unto, will God their wits restore;
In circles, like attendants, Him they'll stand before.
They'll foot the dance, they'll spread their hands, they'll shout
His praise;
They'll sing their song: "Thou, Lord, us from the dead didst
raise."
Their mortal skins and bones they'll shake off in the earth;
On angel-wings they'll ride, and whirlwind-dust call forth.
  ~ Rumi

Do not criticize God for creating the tiger;
Thank Him for not giving it wings.
  ~ Unknown

<u>Chapter One</u>

Frakking Cat

The last biker jerked hard to the left, trying to dodge his late buddy's tumbling corpse and the assorted bits of motorcycle bouncing and spinning across the ground. His rear tire hit something and fishtailed, spraying dust and clumps of ash into the air. Somehow, he managed to bring the bike to a safe stop. I watched the rear-view monitor as he yanked his helmet off and hurled it after us, along with a volley of foul language and spit. I was sure he would do the smart thing and retreat, but no; he decided to be a team player and make it a total party wipe.

The biker gunned it flat-out and roared up next to us. I yanked the wheel, sending the Interceptor lunging toward him. He must have decided it was time to do something *really* stupid, because instead of swerving out of reach, he leaped off his motorcycle and onto our car. He landed hard, with his face pressed against the windshield and his ass hanging off the Interceptor's bullet-scarred hood.

Up close, this guy was damn ugly. Crude tattoos, yellow-brown teeth filed to points, one cheek covered with gnarled melanoma lesions, and reddish-brown war paint that was probably someone else's blood.

Somehow, he got one leg hooked over the driver's-side mirror. Instead of finding something else to hold on to, he grabbed a rust-covered grenade off his belt and yanked on the pin.

It didn't budge.

He tried again, giving it everything he had. The pull ring snapped. He lost his balance and grabbed onto the hood. The grenade bounced twice and vanished into the dust trail behind us. The biker watched it go, then looked back at me. For a moment, we just stared at each other.

Then I stomped on the brakes.

The biker flew forward, clawing at the hood armor. His fingertips snagged the left-hand gun port. He hung there a moment, screaming, before the hard-packed dirt grabbed his legs and friction dragged him under the front tire.

The Interceptor barely bounced.

I took a quick look at the exterior view monitors, but the area around us was clear. "Where's that dune buggy?" I asked.

Rose pointed to a plume of dust off to our right. "Making tracks hard to the south. Looks like he's trying to flank Nadia."

I clicked on the radio. "Bandit Two, Bandit Two, company coming up on your four-o'clock, one bogey. Can you hold? Over."

Static crackled through a long pause. "Ten-four, Bandit One, but not long. Eric is almost out of juice. He can keep his bullet shield up a few more minutes, but no offensive spells. I'm tapped from repairing the damn tires. I think the last group finally just ran out of arrows, over."

I nodded. "Guess we just have to be Big Damn Heroes and come save the day. Bandit One, out."

I sounded more confident than I felt. The main guns were down to less than four seconds of firing time, with all reserves and backups gone. Drawing from the main batteries—the Interceptor's 'engine'—would give us up to a full minute, but the mains were down to 22% charge. Maybe ninety miles, and we were eighty miles from home, the Devil's Thumb Proving Ground. Get too trigger-happy, and we would be sitting ducks on the side of the road until the emergency solar panels got us charged up again.

Right now, though...I floored it.

"It's a milk run," the cat told us. He stirred two sugar cubes into his coffee and blew on the surface before taking a few delicate laps. "I'd do it myself, but the cargo is fragile. Dimensional transit isn't an option. I need you and your hands. Besides, we're going to need a vehicle and I can't drive."

Sitting in my kitchen, having coffee and a cream cheese Danish while the morning news played in the background, a quick road trip to a parallel version of Earth sounded reasonable. Too bad I forgot the part about no cat ever giving anyone a straight answer.

Frakking cat.

"We were planning on going to Sylvan Faire next weekend, but we can skip it." I waved my butter knife at him. "However, I'm not agreeing to anything until you tell me all about this oh-so-delicate cargo. Anything what goes boom, eats people's faces, or is any manner of contagious, we are in a powerful way of very not interested. I don't mind missing Sylvan Faire, but we're going to Mumbai in two weeks and that is not negotiable."

His ears flicked. "What's the occasion?"

"Miss Aparna is going to be the ringbearer when her birth mother gets remarried. One of the things Manya agreed to before I released the embryos was that if she ever did get married again, we'd tell Aparna I'm her father and set up visitation. That time has come. Now, what's the cargo?"

"Bees," Thirteen said. "Real, live, non-mutated, genetically viable bees. Last month, one of my drones found a good-sized meadow west of

Laramie. The entire area is covered with wildflowers, and I counted at least eight hives. I want to get the three smallest and bring them back to Eldorado Canyon."

I whistled. "That's...amazing. How did they survive the Yellowstone eruption?"

"Beats the shit out of me, monkey-boy. It's enough for me that they did."

Rose smirked. "Any chance someone will get cranky if we take these hives home with us?"

"Slim and none," the cat replied. "That entire region has the same population density as Mars. There's no one living there *to* object."

To be fair, he was right. Up to a point.

The vehicle we'd be using was right where Thirteen said it would be, inside a car dealership's service center in Cheyenne. Most of the buildings over four stories tall had either been destroyed right off or collapsed due to the weight of accumulated ash, leaving piles of broken rubble baking in the sun. The dealership's walls were heavier stuff. They'd stood up to the volcano's fury, and now five feet of compacted, rock-hard volcanic ash covered the building, encasing it like a bug in amber.

Getting in was easy. Rose and Eric changed back to their true forms and carved out a tunnel to the garage door in less than an hour. They turned the tunnel into a ramp while we let the building air out.

This was the first time I'd ever seen Eric in his true form. He had gleaming silver scales and an abundance of piercings, metal bands, and inlaid gems decorating his horns. His wing sails were decorated with knot-work tattoos done in white ink as thin as spider silk. At the base of the spikes running down his neck and back, he had a horse-like mane of wispy white hair. It was braided similar to a dwarf's beard, with gems, charms, and amulets woven into it. He was so Boulder, he could have been sitting on the mall busking for coffee money and no one would have looked twice.

Thirteen's cargo vehicle turned out to be a Liberty Roads Wayfarer motor coach. His best guess was that the previous owner had dropped it off to have the autodrive transponder fixed, right before poison gas and burning ash killed everyone within two hundred miles of Yellowstone. The defective transponder kept signaling Thirteen's reconnaissance drones for close to five years, when the coach's power plant ran out of juice.

While Nadia bent her magic to restoring the Wayfarer's roadworthiness, I prowled through the rest of the service bay. When these folks saw the ash cloud coming, someone managed to lower the garage doors and everyone took shelter in the customer waiting room. That made sense; the signs outside said it had food, water, and a restroom. From the bits of cloth I could see under the door, I guessed they'd tried to seal the gaps with their clothing. But it hadn't been enough. I left the door to their tomb closed and kept walking.

Another garage held cars waiting to be picked up by their owners.

Family cars, people carriers, hatchbacks, sports cars...pretty much what I'd expect to find at a dealership on Earth. I turned around to go back, and my flashlight beam landed on a low-slung sedan covered with sharp-edged, angular armor plates. It looked like a stealth fighter on wheels, a hunting hawk surrounded by pigeons and songbirds.

The badges on the back proclaimed the car to be a Paragon Motors Fer-de-Lance Interceptor. Gouges and pockmarks peppered the front armor faces, and the hood had two good-sized gunports in it. The wheels were still intact, protected by armored hubcaps and cowlings over the wheel wells. Putting air in the tires would be near impossible, so I assumed they were solids. A quick look under the rear bumper revealed three large, rectangular weapon ports set in the underbody armor.

If I were playing *Car Wars*, my money would be on machine guns in front, caltrops in back, and either an oil spray or a minedropper rounding out the rear weapons.

I aimed the flashlight beam through the driver's window, just to be sure there were no bodies inside. Satisfied, I stepped back, and saw four lines of script engraved into the armor under the window:

> *For the Angel of Death spread his wings on the blast,*
> *And breathed in the face of the foe as he passed;*
> *And the eyes of the sleepers waxed deadly and chill,*
> *And their hearts but once heaved, and for ever grew still!*

Okay, then. I guess the previous owner was not a big fan of crystals, tie-dye, and patchouli...

The car's space number on the assignment board held the repair manifest, a key ring, and a credit card-sized item labeled, "Administrator Override and Factory Reset." I took them with me, went back to the main garage, and called out, "I just found a sweet loot drop. Anyone mind if I roll need?"

The Interceptor took off with a silent rush of power, pressing us into our seats. The tires didn't even squeal or kick up excess dirt as we shot forward; that would have been a waste of torque. Still, despite having all-wheel drive, traction control, and automatic emergency steering, I didn't dare take the car over one-twenty. A century of sunlight may have baked the ground hard as concrete, but it was still dirt.

We cleared the top of a small rise and spotted the dune buggy sitting right on Nadia's ass, trying to take out the Wayfarer's rear tires with hand-held spears. I took the guns off standby and targeted the buggy's front left wheel.

"Hold fire! I've got these assholes." Rose released her harness so she could lean out the window. She snarled a spell in Draconic and a sphere of purple nastiness enveloped the dune buggy.

Painweb kills by burning out the target's nervous system. Rose had learned it from Nadia's mother, Aerin. It was now one of her favorite toys, because the target's property stayed undamaged and free for the taking. Well, undamaged by the spell, anyway.

The buggy careened sideways and rolled, tossing debris and chunks of hard earth in all directions. The buggy came to rest on its roof, now crushed in like an empty beer can.

Never buy a roll cage from the lowest bidder.

I stopped next to the wreck and Rose was out the door like a shot. After a quick check to make sure the chassis wasn't booby-trapped, she ripped the driver's door off its hinges, tossed it to the side, and hauled the bodies out onto the road. Rose had called first dibs on these idiots when they jumped us, and she was looking at the corpses the way a kid looks at Christmas presents.

I left her to it and hooked the harvester up to the dune buggy's main power feeds. It drained the charge out of batteries like a siphon in a gas tank; transferring every bit of juice the dune buggy had left to the Interceptor should take no more than five minutes.

Nadia did a U-turn and parked the Wayfarer next to us. She hopped out, stretching and bending until her joints popped. Eric followed, folding his arms behind his head and twisting his back farther than humanoid biology should have allowed.

Thirteen stuck his head out the door. "If anyone needs to pee, the line starts behind me." He disappeared back into the air-conditioned comfort of the coach and shut the door.

Frakking cat.

Nadia snorted. "He could have gone any time in the past two hours. I'm the one who was driving."

"At least you're not wearing a latex body suit and drinking your own recycled water while driving a mile-long earthworm," I said. I needed a bathroom break as well, but relieving myself outside felt like I was peeing in a graveyard. I followed Nadia and Eric into the coach and waited my turn.

Outside, Rose finished her loot search, leaving what was left of the bodies sprawled on the ground. She shook the last bits of marauder guts off her hands and picked up the folded piece of cloth holding the treasures she'd found. A whispered spell and a quick sparkle of magic removed the gore from her hands, clothes, and loot. For the moment, she was the cleanest person in this part of Thirteen's world. Maybe all of it.

Rose set the bundle on the table while she relieved herself. She caught my curiosity about it and called out, "No peeking."

I laughed. "Find anything good?"

"Nothing but a pouch of bottle caps on the first fellow, but his buddy had a dozen different religious symbols inserted under the skin around his heart." Rose emerged from the bathroom and gave Thirteen a mock scowl.

"The next time you come up with some damn fool errand, cat, your plan had better include multiple toilets and bathrooms not filled with cargo. I do not appreciate lack of leg room."

Thirteen jumped onto the dining table. "I'm not fond of it either, but I don't have the luxury of an ass that's too wide to fall in the toilet when we're bouncing down the road."

"I could have an ass that skinny if I wanted one," Rose said. "My ass is not the boss of me! David just likes it this size!"

Outside, the harvester chimed to tell me it was finished. Saved by the bell. I took advantage of the distraction and went outside to pack it away. Rose came out with me and had one more look through the wrecked dune buggy. This time she spotted a hidden compartment in the floor behind the driver's seat. Under a layer of smoked iguana jerky, Rose found two amphetamine gas inhalers and a bottle of Cŵn Annwn.

That item put a smile on my face. It was a supercharged cocktail of adrenaline, endorphins, and essence of badass. It's like drinking thousand-year-old vampire blood out of a Six Demon Bag. Life stood still and let you beat the living shit out of it. It was a miracle of the pre-war world, and for all I knew this bottle was the last one in existence.

Hmm...

I turned the bottle a few times, looking for an expiration date. I found the bottling information, but all it showed was the manufacturing date. The last time I drank a bottle of this stuff it had still been good. Same with the medications I'd gotten from Thirteen. What kind of voodoo could make a product—any product—shelf-stable for a hundred years?

I decided I was better off not knowing.

We reconvened inside the coach. While Thirteen scouted the road ahead, Rose gave the hives a refresher dose of her euphoria gas breath weapon. With the bees too stoned to cause trouble, I set out the pitchers of iced lemon water and cold mint tea I'd made at home. Meanwhile, Eric warmed up some canned beef stew. Breakfast of champions.

At least this time he didn't grease the pot with WD-40.

The cat's timing was perfect; he hopped up the stairs and onto the table just as Eric was scooping the stew into bright orange-red ceramic bowls. Thirteen sniffed it and asked, "Any of those chicken-flavored crackers left?"

"No, you ate them last night." I said. "How does the road look?"

"Not bad. One spot of trouble about thirty miles south. Scavenger gang hit a northbound long-haul trade caravan and lost. I think the goofballs who attacked us were part of the same gang. They just ran across us first."

"I wondered why so many people inhabited this uninhabitable wasteland." I poured him a cup of lemon water. "If we meet up with the caravan, are they more likely to attack us or let us pass?"

"Hard to say." He lapped up the water as fast as he could and waved for more. "Sorry. Moving around that much takes a lot."

I passed him the bowl of stew I'd set aside. "Don't worry about it. Take your time eating. I don't know how to Heimlich a cat."

Thirteen swallowed a mouthful of beef and gave me the finger. "We should avoid the caravan. Both of our vehicles are practically brand new. More than enough incentive for them to try to kill us."

Rose said, "I agree. This close to the end, we should just see it through. I want to shower and have pizzas for lunch."

Nadia and Eric nodded. "Straight through. It's just after eight-thirty. We should be home by ten." Nadia said. She stood up and added, "In fact, I vote we get rolling now. You can finish eating on the road, cat."

The motion passed by acclaim.

Back in the Interceptor, I downed two caffeine pills and plopped a bottle of iced mocha into the drink holder. The juice scavenged from the dune buggy gave us another fifty miles, making Thirteen's valley attainable even if we had a few fights.

Nadia radioed us and said, "Bandit Two to Bandit One. You are clear to take the front door, good buddy."

"Ten-four on the front door," I replied. "Keep your foot on the gas and the bears off your ass. We rollin'." I kept pace with Nadia until she had the Wayfarer up to speed, then pulled in front of her. Southbound and down, good buddy.

Rose stripped her clothes off before reclining her seat as far as it would go. "I need some sunlight. Wake me up if anything exciting happens." She arched her back in a long, attention-grabbing stretch, yawned, and settled into the seat.

Just to be safe, I turned the car's autodrive on. No matter how hard I tried to keep my eyes on the road and hands on the wheel, I'm only human.

David Fraser, by the way. Pleased to meet you. The naked, purple-haired lady lounging next to me is my wife, Rose Drake, and she's not just showing off. Well, she is showing off, but it's out of necessity. She's a Dragon. She's using a spell to take Human form, but some aspects of her biology remain Draconic. Food intake is one. Sunlight is another. Just as we hairless apes need sunlight to make vitamin D, Rose needs sunlight to create the compounds that fuel her breath weapon. End result: my girl sunbathes a lot.

Except that we've been really busy the past few days and haven't had time for quiet lounging around. Hence, Rose getting some sun while the getting was good.

As for me, I needed some music. The car recognized my Earth-made phone as a legacy data/media device and was happy to play music from it, but I wanted to hear something new. The onboard computer was loaded with more than two hundred terabytes of music, most of it bloodthirsty, holy war gospel for Crusaders. I guess the churches on this world were less 'John 3:16' and more 'Ezekiel 25:17.'

The 'Soulful' genre turned out to be similar to our early Blues. It would have been great for late-night drinking bouts, so I skipped it. 'Heritage' encompassed Folk, Bluegrass, and Country-sounding ballads. John Denver and Johnny Cash worked for me, but I really wanted something bouncy, so I kept looking. 'Proud American' was a mix of Sousa marches and World War Two-era Big Band. Not my favorite style, but it was all upbeat pieces suitable for staying awake while driving. I said, "Play random," and the car obliged with a triumphal fanfare.

> *"Oh, they've got no time for glory in the Infantry.*
> *Oh, they've got no use for praises loudly sung.*
> *But in every soldier's heart in all the Infantry*
> *Shines the name, shines the name of Rodger Young!"*

I couldn't help it; I burst out laughing.

Rose cracked one eye open. "What's so funny?"

"That song. It's just funny that the car should pick it." I paused the playback so I didn't have to compete with the brass section. "The version back home is a lot more solemn. It was mentioned a lot in one of my favorite books, Heinlein's *Starship Troopers*. Great book, you should read it. Anyway, I was laughing at the coincidence. Out of all the music in the library, the car picked that one."

She gave me a big fake smile and closed her eyes again. "I'm glad it amused you. Turn the volume down a bit."

"Yes, dear."

Even with the acceptance keeping us in synch both mentally and emotionally, I felt a moment of pure annoyance at having to stay awake and quiet while she napped. It faded as fast as it had come on, but normally it wouldn't have happened at all. I put it down to lack of sleep and started the song again. Quiet this time, as requested.

It's no wonder we were getting crispy around the edges. We'd been up forty straight hours, running on *Bender Mender* spells and various caffeine delivery systems, but the end of Thirteen's so-called 'milk run' was finally in sight.

On Earth, we would be heading for the People's Republic of Boulder, a bastion of urban liberalism surrounded by rock-ribbed conservative ranches and farmlands. Home to the University of Colorado, a mess of solar, aerospace, and climatological research institutes, and the Alferd Packer Restaurant and Grill—the only eatery I knew of named after a cannibal.

Here on Thirteen's world, we were driving on top of three to five feet of volcanic ash, covering a weapon testing range littered with shattered buildings, destroyed vehicles, and Goddess-knows-how-many unexploded artillery shells, mines, and bombs. Logic said we should be safe, but the pucker factor was high.

Half an hour later, I spotted a column of smoke off to the southeast.

Probably the raiders Thirteen had mentioned. It looked like it was coming from somewhere near Johnstown. It was tricky to tell for sure. Aside from being devoid of familiar landmarks, the entire region, from Bozeman to Albuquerque, was as barren as the Black Rock desert in Nevada.

That meant the victorious trader caravan could see the dust we were kicking up. Just to be safe, Thirteen steered us several miles west, well away from any reasonable pursuit by the caravan. Soon enough, we were cruising through the area that should have been the town of Longmont. Here, it was a destroyed ammunition depot, filled with rows of craters and the shells of ruined buildings.

I was glad to find the military engineers of this world had also built their own version of the Diagonal Highway. Even covered in ash, it was a smooth track leading straight into Boulder Valley, and I was pretty sure we wouldn't need to worry about hitting any speed traps around Niwot.

The terrain became more varied the further west we went, but there was still no water and no vegetation. Only skeletal ruins jutting out of a bleak, empty wasteland.

We stayed on the road until we reached a line of razor wire-topped fence sticking out of the ash. Thirteen had warned us there were mines hidden along the fence line, so we stayed well back and headed west.

Several minutes later we came to a gate flanked by two burnt and dented steel towers. Dozens of destroyed vehicles and countless body parts littered the ground around the towers, but the gate was open and the path was clear—except for the six walking cadavers staring at us.

Chapter Two

Souvenirs

"Don't shoot," Thirteen radioed. "The sentry guns will lock on to you and open fire. No spells, either. They react to any energy discharge the scanners pick up."

"What the hell are we supposed to use, man? Harsh language?" I was only half-kidding; the dead guys—well, *mostly* dead—were scuttling back and forth, snarling and hissing at us, but not ready to charge yet.

"Always with the negative waves..." he replied.

Rose slipped back into her clothes and peered over the dash at the mostly dead guys. "Yuck. What happened to their skin?"

"Remember the drug I brought back the last time I was here? It was intended to treat low-level radiation poisoning. These folks overdosed trying to vaccinate themselves against the effects of near-lethal exposure." I snorted. "The stuff worked. It flushed every irradiated cell out of their bodies, liquefying their skin, organs, and fatty tissues. It turned them into walking beef jerky. It's the same thing that happened to Thirteen, just a lot more severe."

Behind the dead guys, red warning lights sprang to life and two Big Freaking Guns folded out of each tower. The dead guys took off, running far faster than I thought possible, but they couldn't outrun energy bolts. With a bright blue light, a heavy stench of ozone, and the crackle of a gigantic bug zapper, all six went from mostly dead to all dead.

Thirteen came back on the radio. "Come on in. I've painted both vehicles as friendly, but I'll stay inside and keep an eye on things until you get here, just to be safe. Head for the canyon mouth and then follow the river."

I took the Interceptor through first since we had at least some level of armor. Even with the cat's assurance he'd switched the guns off, driving between the towers was an anxious moment. Once we were clear, I stopped and waited for Nadia and the Wayfarer. The towers stayed quiet, and we rolled out again.

The walls across the mouth of Eldorado Canyon still stood, but most of the debris I'd seen last time was gone. So was the patch of glass-crusted soil marking Ingrim Thain's last stand. Instead, clumps of long-bladed, bright green grass dotted the canyon floor, thickening to an actual meadow around the doors leading to Thirteen's bunker. Long tufts of ricegrass poked up from behind rocks and crumbling concrete. A handful of waist-high pine trees clung to the sides of the canyon, each seedling surrounded by a small patch of wildflowers. Something flitted across my windshield and I hit the brakes. It was a real, live butterfly. I'd resurrected a handful of them last time I was here; against all odds, some had survived and re-produced.

Yep. Life will find a way.

I parked the Interceptor off the road while Nadia backed the Wayfarer as close to the bunker as she could get. Rose gave each hive a last puff of Dragon Happy Gas and we carried the cloth-wrapped bundles to their new homes.

Once we got the hives in place and removed the cloth wrappings, Thir-teen partially covered the hive openings with leafy fronds from an artificial palm tree. "That will force them into exploration mode," the cat said. "They have to relearn what home looks like. Once they have that down, they'll head out to explore their new environment."

Without thinking, I asked, "You can talk to bees?"

"Of course I can. I'm a cat. I can also read books on beekeeping, dumbass." He flicked his ears back. "Life would be a lot easier if I could talk to insects. I could find out what they need rather than just guessing. I have no margin for error here."

I snorted. "Don't be a Drama Llama. These bees are tough. They survived out there for a hundred years without your help. Have a little faith that they know what they're doing."

He folded his paws under his body, scowling at me. "I didn't accom-plish all of this by leaving things to chance. I'll be watching how the first scouts do and keeping track of the height and spread of the flowers. I have to be careful not to outgrow my water supply. I also have to make sure no scavengers discover this place. Fences and minefields can be breached."

"Well, I'm glad we could give you a hand with your project," Rose said. "I believe you mentioned compensation for helping you?"

The cat didn't move. "I remember you mentioning it. Everyone else is helping out of the goodness of their hearts."

"Because they're suckers," Rose replied.

Nadia glowered at her. "Hey! I'm here for the joy of leaving my own trail of burning wreckage, thank you very much. No reason my mother should have all the fun..."

"How's that going?" I asked.

She grinned. "Better than expected. I loved blowing up all those irre-placeable vehicles. Keeping them functional for so many years must have been an insane amount of work."

Thirteen said, "Whatever your reasons, I do appreciate all of you helping me. Rose, if you want something shiny for your time, I can oblige you. Same for everyone else. Come have a look." He breezed past the quiescent sentry guns, stopped, and glanced back over his shoulder. "Don't worry, I turned the guns and the interior defenses off. You're safe. If the guns were live, they would have burned you down before you parked."

With that comforting thought ringing in our ears, Thirteen led us into the bunker. The maze of steel-walled, submarine-like corridors was just as claustrophobic as I remembered, but that time the main lights had been on. Now, the only illumination came from motion-activated red emergency lights. I ducked a low buttress and asked, "Dining on bats now?"

"Nope. I only eat organic free-range mice raised on a gluten-free diet," Thirteen replied. "They're much better for my colon." He hopped up on the security panel next to a recessed door and keyed in the entry code.

Lights flared on full-strength in the base commander's old office. After our eyes adjusted, Thirteen jumped onto the commander's desk and patted a black steel chest the size of a beer cooler. "Payment, as promised. You will not find this on Earth."

Rose pulled the chest to her and lifted the lid to peek inside. She caught her breath and made a faint crooning noise, her eyes glowing gold and sapphire blue for a moment. She opened the lid the rest of the way, revealing a forest-green, egg-shaped gem big enough to pass for an artichoke.

"The Dejah Thoris Diamond," Thirteen said. "Returned by the Herakles Twelve Mars Mineral Surveyor. Totally non-Terrestrial composition. The color is a result of radiation exposure due to the thin Martian atmosphere. Cutting it took eight years of planning. Afterward, people started calling it the Phoenix Egg, because it glows like a burning coal when you shine ultraviolet light on it. It has something to do with nitrogen in the molecular structure. I'll look up the details if you want." He waited a moment and added, "I trust this is satisfactory?"

Rose closed the chest and nodded. "Oh, yes. A pleasure doing business with you, as always."

"And if you'll check the medical kit on the wall by the front door, you'll find more goodies. Everyone take two vials of RadZero. Drink one now, one in forty-eight hours. Expect your piss to turn bright blue. It will pull the radioactive elements and any damaged tissue out of your system."

Rose picked up one of the vials but didn't drink. "Will two vials be enough?"

"More than enough, but you can take the whole box if you want. I have crates of the stuff."

"Excellent." Rose pulled the first aid kit free from the bolts anchoring it to the wall and stuffed it into her dimensional closet. "I love new investment opportunities."

Nadia stopped in front of a weapons rack full of assorted firearms and tapped one that looked like a semi-automatic Rottweiler. "Why does this pistol have a Bluetooth earpiece?"

"That's not an earpiece," Thirteen said. "It's an optical targeting interface. Denali Arms Myrmidon SG7 smartgun. Touch the trigger and it projects an overlay on your retina showing exactly where the round will hit. Even I can hit a target with that thing. If you want it, you're welcome to it."

A slight smile teased at Nadia's lips. "Does it take fancy ammo, or old-fashioned bullets?"

"Variable configuration chamber, compatible with household nine-millimeter, twelve-mil caseless, and forty-five ACP." Thirteen smiled without baring teeth. "Something to help you in the 'trail of burning wreckage' department?"

"Nope. I'm good there." Nadia found a holster and carrying case in the cabinet under the display and tucked the lot into an empty gear bag. "This year, Geneva is finally going to be excited about one of her Christmas presents."

Thirteen chuckled. "Well, I'm glad to see it going to someone who will appreciate it." He looked at the rest of us and asked, "Well? Anyone else find something they want to take home?"

And just like that, I had a scathingly brilliant idea...

"You're out of your mind," said the cat.

I shrugged. "Maybe, but that's between me and my mind. Can we do it?"

Thirteen shook his head. "No. I can't shift that much mass." He looked at the Interceptor and shook his head again. "Besides, don't you already have a perfectly good car back home?"

"No. Well, yeah, I have a new Mercedes, but this... This is the last Interceptor! A piece of history! It would be a shame to let it fall apart."

Thirteen snorted. "No, it wouldn't. It would be what was supposed to happen. This entire world is dead and decomposing. Let it go. Drop some plasma grenades in the back seat and tell the autodrive to floor it. Send the car out in a blaze of glory if it means that much to you."

"What about that Draconic dimensional closet thingy?" I asked. "I've seen both of you pull all kinds of stuff out of dimensional storage."

"I could handle the total mass," Rose said. "I just couldn't do it all at once. That aside, I don't think I can make the aperture large enough to accommodate it. I'm sorry."

Nadia tapped her foot. "You are never going to get the state to give you a title for that thing, but if you're dead set on tilting at this windmill, I have an idea. Any chance there's a set of silk or satin bedsheets in the bunker?"

"Slim and none," Thirteen replied. "This is a military base. Cotton sheets and maybe a linen tablecloth or two is the best you're going to be able to find."

"Linen will work. Can you show me where they are?"

Thirteen nodded toward the door. "Storage unit, right across the hall. Take a flashlight. Closets don't have emergency lighting."

"Good." Nadia picked up her gear bag and said, "Let's grab it and head back outside."

It didn't sound like much of a plan, but Nadia usually knew what she was talking about. Case in point: while I was fumbling around trying to figure out a cold fusion-powered flashlight, Nadia pulled a quarter out of her pocket and hit it with a spell. The coin flared up like a small star, lighting everything within twenty feet of her as bright as day.

As expected, the bed sheets for the grunts were unusable, economy-level cotton. However, there was a trunk with the base commander's name on it, along with a big damn lock. Nadia's spells couldn't open it, but Eric could. He ripped out the entire lock assembly and tore the lid off its hinges.

"Aha!" Nadia held up a bundle of cloth in a vacuum-sealed bag. "Six hundred thread count Egyptian cotton bedsheets from Milan. I think the commander had a girlfriend."

"And a wife," Thirteen said. "Will that do whatever you need it to?"

"Barring unforeseen issues, yes." Nadia tucked the bundle under her arm, left the coin in the women's bathroom after one last visit, and we followed the cat to the front door.

While Eric and Rose drew the lines and runes for our return portal on the ground, Nadia shook out the top sheet and flipped it over the Interceptor. Once the cloth settled over the car, she said, "Give me a few minutes to get charged up. This spell takes some juice."

"No problem," I said. "I know how it works."

Nadia pushed herself up onto a large, mostly-flat rock and leaned back, looking up at the sun with her eyes closed. "Good. I may have to take Monday off to finish getting all the spells I used back."

"What?" I caught myself and decided to try that again, without sounding like a dyspeptic duck. "You have to memorize your spells? I thought you said you used a mana pool-type thing."

"I did," Nadia said. "It's both."

Now I was really lost. "Both? How does that work?"

She sighed and sat up. "If I tell you, you have to promise to leave me alone until I tell you I'm ready."

"Deal."

"Regardless of species, almost all humanoids who have magical abilities draw on their own life energy when they start out. That's known as innate magic. It's easy to push too hard or use too much and literally burn out parts of your brain. A lot of new mages become former mages that way."

"With practice, mages can learn to gather raw spell energy from ley lines. Over time, they learn to hold more energy and do more spells. That's your mana pool. Innate magic gives you maximum flexibility, but long casting times. It's also easy to run out of gas without warning."

She leaned forward, stabbing at the air for emphasis. "What gamers call mnemonic or Vancian magic is how the pros do it. It just doesn't work the way gamers think it does. I don't forget a spell when I cast it. I just don't have a bullet in the chamber, so to speak. When I study my spellbook, I'm pulling in ley line energy and using the words and symbols on the page to guide that energy into the form of the spell I want."

"When I finish, I can feel the spell...lock into place. It's stored, ready to go, and all it takes to trigger it is a few words and gestures. I can unload several times the total spell energy an innate mage can, I can do it faster, and I can hit harder. The trade-off is not having the flexibility a well-rested, fully-charged innate mage does. Now, pretty please, shut up, go away, and leave me alone."

I sat in the Wayfarer and read the owner's manual.

It took about twenty minutes, but eventually Nadia stood up and cracked her back. She took hold of one edge of the sheet, called out something in Gaelic, and yanked the sheet away.

The damn car was gone.

"Annnd... presto!" Nadia opened part of the sheet out, enough for us to see an isometric image of the Interceptor floating on the surface of the cloth. She changed the angle of the cloth and the image rotated with it.

"Cool. Freaky, but cool. Another one of your mother's spells?"

Nadia shook her head. "No. I learned it from a disreputable Gnomish treasure hunter named Lucky Strike. Not a fellow you could ever trust to watch your back, but very inventive at spells for hauling loot."

"I'll have to send him a thank-you note." I turned to Thirteen and held my hand out, palm facing him. His raccoon-like front paws had fingers and thumbs, but actually shaking hands was out of the question.

Instead, he pressed his palm to mine and gave me a nod. "Thank you for aiding me in this." He looked around and added, "Thank you all. This vastly improves my chances for success here. I won't forget it."

"No problem." I said. "Why don't you come and visit more often? Catch a few Japanese game shows and some overpriced coffee?"

"No, I need to stay here and watch the bees. Make sure they get started well..." He shook his head. "Oh, screw it. Like you said, the bees made it a hundred years without me. They can be left alone a few days." He hopped up on my shoulder. We took our place in the circle, and Rose took everyone back to Earth.

Warm June sun flooded in the windows, dappled by shadows from the pine and aspen trees around the house. Off to the east, down at the foot of the mountains, Boulder hummed like one of the beehives we'd just moved. I took a moment to take it all in—this world, our world, was *alive*, and that was wonderful.

The alarm system on the house was alive, too. I clapped twice and called out, "Janus, stand down! Authorization Mycroft Two-Two-One

Baker."

The household management software confirmed my verbal key code and switched the alarms and motion sensors off. A black-framed photo hanging on the wall changed from a picture of the Maroon Bells to a floor plan of the house and a soothing male voice said, "Good morning, Dave."

"Status, please."

"I am very happy to report that at this time there are no known issues capable of endangering our mission."

Yeah, I know. Cheesy enough to fill a swimming pool. What can I say? I'm a geek with money. I'd also wanted to put a recording on the driveway gate that said, "Dave's not home," but that would pretty much be an open invitation to thieves.

Success has its benefits, one of which was our new house. Initially, I'd wanted to buy the Sculptured House overlooking Genesee along I-70 (the "flying saucer house" used in the movie *Sleeper*), but it wasn't on the market.

The one we did buy was 12,000 square feet of luxury living high in the foothills above Boulder. The neighborhood was a gated community with guards on duty twenty-four hours a day, and it adjoined several hundred acres of open space and hiking trails.

According to neighborhood gossip, the previous owner had decided the guards weren't enough of a deterrent to Boulder's criminal element, so he extended the eight-foot stone walls bordering the neighborhood to enclose the property. He also added a reinforced gate, motion detectors, and a web of laser tripwires. Even after all that, the house still wasn't secure enough for him, so he bugged out and bought a renovated missile silo in Kansas.

My contribution so far was a state-of-the-art household management system, new network wiring, and a dedicated fiber optic Internet connection. Before the summer was out, we planned to add a solar panel system, wall batteries, and a solar water heater. We'd named the house Flagstaff Weyr, and after three months, it was finally starting to feel like home.

Then our cell phones started going off. Nadia and I both had dozens of texts, emails, and voice mails, most asking if we were safe. More than a few said something like, 'I'm doing fine but something happened.' I really wanted to follow up on some of them, but Rose and Eric were sniffing the air, then tasting it with long, forked tongues. Eric asked a question in Draconic, which Rose answered with a quick, emphatic confirmation.

"What is it?" I asked.

Rose opened a window and sniffed the early afternoon air. "Magic," she said. "Everything tastes of primal magic. Raw magic. The first magic. The magic all wonder and mystery descend from. I've never felt it like this, not even at home."

"Is that good or bad?"

Rose frowned, shaking her head. "That depends on who learns to use it."

I really wanted to ask more about that, but first Nadia and I called our folks.

After I assured Mom that Rose and I were fine, she sighed and said, "I'm glad to hear it. Audrey and her family are fine as well, but your father and I... we...changed."

"Whatever happened, you can tell me," I said. "What's going on?"

She took a deep breath. "As near as I can tell, I'm some kind of surfer Elf. I'm all golden blond and graceful. Your father is still mostly himself, just shorter and rounder. And with bigger, hairier feet." She hesitated, and added, "Oh, my boy, we're not human anymore."

"Neither is my wife. Were you expecting that to bother me?"

Mom laughed. "No, but...you know. You never really know somebody until you get turned into an Elf and they have to be seen in public with you."

I couldn't help but laugh a little. "Just remember, no matter what, you're my parents, and I love you. Nothing you say or do can change that. Except for talking in a theater. Pull that crap and I know thee not."

She laughed again. "That's fair. Um, I don't suppose Rose and her friends know what's happening?"

"The world tastes of primal magic, according to Rose. Not sure what that means yet, but I'll let you know if we figure anything out. Take care." I ended the call and posted a quick 'all is well' update on social media. That would have to do for now.

Thirteen stuck his head around the door to the family room and said, "You have got to come and see this."

Nadia had switched to using her message ring. She was facing away from us, but I could see the tension in her shoulders and hear her speaking Scots Gaelic in hushed, urgent tones. She was going to be a few minutes yet, so I followed the cat.

The local network was running a feed from Los Angeles, showing an aerial view of the La Brea Tar Pits. Saber-tooth tiger skeletons were crawling out of the ground, assembling themselves, and attacking anything they could find—which was mostly people. As they...ate...muscles and skin re-formed over their bones. The image changed to downtown New York, showing people scattering as a tyrannosaurus skeleton bashed its way out of the Metropolitan Museum. A mounted cop emptied his pistol's clip into the petrified skull, chipping it a little. Then the hungry bones ate him and his horse.

"Looks like your world just got a lot more entertaining." Thirteen chuckled, an evil sound, like someone dragging rocks across a chalkboard. "Welcome to the jungle, mate."

Chapter Three

World Without End, Amen

"Federal, state, and local authorities are asking everyone to stay home unless there is a compelling reason to be out, such as seeking emergency medical care. At this time, there is a ground stop order in effect for all general and commercial aviation, including national and international flights."

The anchorwoman paused and set her notes to the side. "We'd like to take a moment to remind our viewers that, this time yesterday, we were all just people. We were all driving the same roads, breathing the same air, and hopefully all cheering for the Broncos. We still are all those things today. Some of us look different, yes, but we're the same people underneath."

Three more people joined her. The first was recognizably the morning show's popular meteorologist, a perky, dark-haired woman who was now an even perkier green-skinned Elf. The second person was the affably flamboyant afternoon entertainment reporter. His smile and voice were the same, and seemed to fit his new Gnomish body.

The third person was Denver's favorite retired starting quarterback, now a gold-skinned Elf. More had changed than just his ears and eyebrows; he looked like he was in his twenties again. He finished out the bit, saying, "Remember, folks, we're all on the same team out there. Human or not, we all look good in orange."

Thirteen snorted as they cut to a commercial. "Hey, guys, you forgot to start singing 'Kumbaya' there."

"Laugh all you want," I said. "He can probably do more to calm people down than any politician you care to name."

Nadia came into the family room and flopped next to me on the couch. "It's a good idea. If professional football and NASCAR accept non-Humans, we'll probably get through this with a minimum of riots and torch-bearing mobs."

"Hey, joining a torch-bearing mob is on my bucket list. It always looks like such fun in the movies." The local news switched to the network feed, which was now a bunch of talking heads yapping about ineffective political leadership in a time of crisis. I muted it and asked, "How is your family doing?"

"Geneva turned Drow and Danya's wife, Willow, turned into a Gold Elf. Perfect golden skin, lion's mane of blonde hair, flawless features. They couldn't be happier." She blinked hard and wiped a tear off her cheek. "It figures. The one day when I would actually stand a chance of defying my genetic destiny, and I miss it because I'm putzing around in another universe. Fuck my life..."

I patted her on the shoulder. "Did anyone in your family change? Anyone related to you by blood, I mean."

"No, but..." She picked up her phone and hit speed dial. "Geneva, it's Nadia. Did any of the Llewellyn clan members change? Oh, interesting. Thank you." She set the phone down. "Not one member of the clan, no matter how faint their Elven heritage, changed. About a third of the Humans living in Gilead *did* change, and only ten percent of those became Drow. So, I'd have been immune to it. I guess that helps a little."

"Did they have any idea what happened?"

"Sort of. This is off the record, not for public distribution, need-to-know only. Right after this thing happened, Mother tried to find the person or persons responsible. Normally, whoever it was would wind up with their head sitting on Mother's mantle in a box of cedar oil."

"Eww." Thirteen's ears went back. "That's nasty."

"It's an old custom from back home. Anyway, when Mother started scrying for whoever was doing this, Crom stopped her and ordered her to stand down. The divine powers are allowing these events because Earth is an experiment in free will and this...change...was pure mortal endeavor. One side effect of it is that many limitations on divine intervention no longer apply."

"Such as?"

"Such as divine blessings. The deities can now give devout followers gifts, like the ability to heal. Removing diseases, restoring sight, regenerating limbs...maybe even raising the dead. They don't want to give that up."

I sat back to take that in. "So, the deities of Earth could fix all this, but are choosing not to?"

"Pretty much," Nadia said. "Earth's deities have just been handed history's biggest loophole. Sure, it's an exploit, but it's an exploit humanity created and the gods are going to roll with it."

I stared at her. "Wait a minute—do you mean to tell me the Lord God Almighty, YHVH, the First Cause, the Prime Mover, the Alpha and Omega, the God of Abraham, Isaac, and Jacob, God the Father, who sent His only begotten son to die on the cross for our sins, He who is called I AM, is looking out on the world and saying unto Mankind, 'It's not a bug, it's a feature'?"

"Yep! Functioning as intended, and thank you for stopping by the help desk."

"Holy shit...no pun intended." I ran my hands through my hair and leaned back, closing my eyes and trying to digest this new information.

It sounded insane, but I'd actually stood in Crom's presence a few years ago. I'd even held the spear that pierced the side of Jesus during the Crucifixion. Despite being Pagan, I'd used the blood of Jesus to return people to life. The reality of those events made Nadia's statements much more immediate and tangible for me.

After a few deep breaths, I opened my eyes and asked, "So, any word on how we puny humans created this 'loophole'?"

Nadia shook her head. "Crom told Mother not to look into it. I'm going to take that as the last word on the subject."

While she was talking, Rose, Eric, and Rose's mother Arwydd came in and sat down. I hugged Rose and said, "Nadia, I see why your folks are sitting this one out. I'm thinking we should, too. When a god tells me to stand down, I'm inclined to listen."

"Agreed," Rose said. "If the powers that be wish to see these events unfold, I see no profit in contesting the matter. We should focus on adapting to the new order of things and helping others to do likewise."

I looked out the window at Boulder. Billows of black smoke rose from at least four fires near downtown. Formations of Blackhawk helicopters crisscrossed the sky like busy little locusts, intent on bringing order out of chaos.

We watched the news in silence for a while. It wasn't long until the governor came on. Speaking from the west steps of the state capitol building, he called on all citizens of Colorado to stay calm and accept their neighbor's new beards and pointed ears. At the same time, the newly changed were asked to reach out and renew their connections with their neighbors. It wasn't all holding hands and singing 'Kumbaya,' though; until identities could be confirmed and new forms of identification issued, the newly changed were asked not to travel. At least that restriction was voluntary. For now, anyway.

After the governor finished, they switched to a live spot from the Vatican. The Pope had just released a new Apostolic Constitution, stating that 'spirit transcends flesh' and opening the Church to all the new races.

Back in the US, presidential candidates Clarice Harrison and Gerald Spunkmeyer had released a joint statement that they were suspending their campaigns for a week. The story came with a quick shot of Harrison entering her house in Bethesda. She was Drow, and I could swear one of the Secret Service guys surrounding her was a *Warblade*-issue Troll. The statement said Spunkmeyer had also changed, but he hadn't put in an appearance yet.

Well, at least neither would be able to corner the Human vote.

A little while later the news went to the White House press room. The spokeswoman announced the President was cutting his Pacific Rim summit short and would be addressing the country from Air Force One later this evening. Both houses of Congress were suspending their existing legislative schedules in order to draft legislation protecting the rights of those who had changed.

Order out of chaos.

I nodded at Rose. "That makes sense. Right now, people are scared, but that's all it is. Fear passes. If things were falling apart and society was collapsing into savagery and chaos, I'd say we should try to stop all this. That isn't the case. We still have power, we still have the Internet, and we still have communication. There are police in the street and food in the grocery stores. Let's go with it and see what happens."

"It's also critical no one finds out we know anything about these events," Nadia said. "The Men in Black have already contacted Mother and every other traveler they know about, trying to pressure them for information. I guarantee, absolutely, some people out there want to know how to use magic as a military weapon. Let them figure that out on their own."

All around the room, heads nodded and voices murmured in agreement.

I stood up. "Now that issue is settled, Nadia, can I get my car back?"

"Boys and their toys," she muttered. She grabbed the bedsheet and we headed to the garage. A flip of the sheet and a magic word later, I had my new toy again.

When we bought this house, we only had two cars. A five-car heated and air-conditioned garage seemed to be a bad case of overconsumption. Then I leased a brand-new Mercedes—you know, for summer driving—and parked our big, thirsty Range Rover. Now, the Interceptor filled bay four and we were out of room. Well, technically bay five was unassigned, but that was where we'd put all the exercise equipment we'd had to move to make room for the travel circle.

I snagged the owner's manual out of the Interceptor's glove compartment. It had been printed on hemp-based paper with a leather cover, so it had survived with very little degradation. Sometime during the next few days, I'd have to figure out how to connect a car that wouldn't be invented for a hundred and thirty years to a 110-volt wall socket. In the meantime, I pulled the car's emergency solar cells out of their storage bay and opened the garage door to let the sun do the work.

Outside, I smelled smoke, and not the 'making s'mores around the campfire' kind. There was another column of smoke rising to the northeast. It was close, too—about where the entrance to our neighborhood was.

I set the solar panels down and grabbed the gate remote out of the Range Rover. "I'm going to see what's happening over there. If I'm not back in fifteen minutes, send in the Marines."

"I'm pretty sure Dragons count as Air Force," Nadia replied. She looked at the smoke column and added, "Don't take any chances."

"Roger that." I powered the Interceptor on—and half the controls turned red or started beeping. All the satellites the navigation system recognized were gone, and the ones it could find were providing impossible data. I tried to find a way to switch the alarms off, but the car's computer beat me to it.

"Legacy data systems detected," it said. "These systems are compatible but offer a reduced degree of functionality. Do you wish to utilize legacy data systems?"

"Yes to all!" I said. "Can't you configure all this crap while I drive manually?"

"Reconfiguring active engagement systems. Please do not disconnect primary system power. Manual control active. Please drive assertively."

"Thank you," I muttered. I pulled out and headed down the road. On a map, our house was only a mile or so from the main gate, but the roads curved and looped around several big red sandstone ridges and outcroppings, all part of the same rock bed that formed Red Rocks Amphitheater and the Flatirons. When we moved in, I thought they were a beautiful reminder of the age and majesty of our world; now, they were just a damn nuisance.

One thing my low-speed drive through the neighborhood revealed, though, was that my neighbors were taking no chances. Cars and trucks blocked every intersection and people with rifles and shotguns kept a wary watch on everything that moved. They all nodded and waved me through, but I was on the inside already and the Interceptor could pass for a fancy sports car.

I turned the last corner and slowed to a stop. There was another blockade, this one much bigger than any of the others. Past them, the guard shack at the community entrance was a burnt, smoking ruin.

The people blockading the road held their ground and signaled for me to roll my window down. I had to give the computer verbal approval and disengage two manual locks to do it, but finally I leaned out and said, "Hi guys! Are we expecting a parade or something?"

A grumpy, mid-60's fellow with a 'most likely to enjoy leading a lynch mob' vibe spit tobacco juice and asked, "Anyone know this smart-ass?"

Most of the group shook their heads, but I'd seen one of the guys a few times at the grocery store. We exchanged nods and he said, "I've seen him around. He bought Tom Malone's place. Oh, and his wife is that gal with the purple hair and the gold-leafed car."

"Her name is Rose. I'm David. What happened down at the gate?"

My buddy from the grocery store said, "Looters tried to get in. Cliff, the security guard, tried to hold them off. These guys were green, with big tusks and these...like...Neanderthal brow ridges."

"Orcs," I said. "That sounds like you're describing Orcs."

"That's what I was thinking," my pal said. "I just couldn't bring myself to say it. Anyway, the cops showed up and there was a big fight. The Orcs wound up overturning a police car and setting it and the guard shack on fire. The cops ordered us out of the area, so we pulled back here. We're going to make sure nobody gets in without showing identification."

"Maybe not even then," Mr. Grumpy muttered. "The bylaws say only a natural person can own a home here, and I'm damn sure something that isn't a human being doesn't qualify as a natural person."

I heard several murmurs of agreement, but a good portion of the group looked surprised and offended. I give Mr. Grumpy a tight smile and said, "Oh, really? What about the people living here who had a member of their family change? Are you going to run them out? Where do you draw the line? How long until anyone who's Hispanic, African-American, or Jewish should just start packing?"

That shut down the murmuring and caused a lot of uncomfortable looks. My buddy said, "Come on, Bernie, don't say shit like that. We're down with defending our homes from looters, but you sound about half a step away from white robes and burning crosses. I don't swing that way."

"Joan has horns, hooves, and goddamn tail now," another man said. "She's pretty damn freaked out, but she's still my wife. Are you going to tell me she's not a person, Bernie? What if one of your grandkids changes?"

Bernie ignored the question and glared at me. "We have a right to protect ourselves," he growled.

My buddy cut him off. "We can, and we will. We used to have a good-sized neighborhood watch group. We'll get it going again, beef it up, and look out for one another. But nobody gets to tell me who can live in my house and who I can invite over for dinner."

Bernie sneered. "Oh, please, Kochinski. Neighborhood watch against roaming gangs of subhuman monsters? You and your libtard friends going to give them a time out when they come in and start raping your wives and children? You stupid, ignorant-"

The man standing next to Bernie pushed him back a step and got in his face. "That's enough, Bernie. Merciful Christ, listen to yourself!" He gestured to several other older men, and the group of them took Bernie off to the side of the road. I didn't hear what they said, but Bernie broke down in tears and sank to his knees. The others joined him for an impromptu prayer circle.

While Bernie was getting a reality check, a forest-green hybrid with a photo of Earth from space on the hood turned into the neighborhood. I sighed. So did several of the others on the blockade. The driver parked next to me, facing the other way, and cackled, "Look, everyone! Dave's not home! He's out here, with us!"

No, never using that as a greeting. Ever.

Karma Jones was the guy across the street from our house. A mariju-ana millionaire. He owned a string of legal pot stores and was one of the first federally-approved cultivators in the state. He'd started out in life a little left of Lenin and just kept going, until now he was somewhere right of Reagan, at least regarding money and nutty conspiracy theories. The rest of his mind was subject to change without notice.

He finally noticed nobody else was laughing. "Aw, come on, why so harsh? You guys saw the Dragon, right? Wasn't that the coolest thing ever?"

I looked around to gauge how the others were responding. At least I wasn't the only one looking lost, or the only one to ask, "What Dragon?"

Karma tried pointing toward downtown Boulder and failed, so he got out and pointed toward Longmont. "The Dragon! The chick, man! The naked one! That Dragon!" He stopped and rolled his eyes at us. "Okay, yeah, okay, you weren't there. I was closing early, because, you know, riots are bad for inventory, when this blond chick with red streaks in her hair comes in, pulling her clothes off. Tits to die for, but I told her I don't trade ass for weed. Cash only, you know, and she laughs. Tells me, 'Good for you,' and tosses her clothes at me. Then she sprouts wings and a tail. Says to give the clothes to someone who needs them, walks outside, and *fwoop*! Dragon! She roars, she takes off, and poof! She vanishes right out of the sky! You guys didn't see that?"

Two cars full of pretty women and camping gear pulled in behind Karma's hybrid. Ember leaned out the driver's window of the lead car and waved. "Hi David! Can we get through, please?"

I waved back. "Hi Ember! Rose is at the house. Guys, I know all of these ladies personally. The youngsters with blue hair are my wife's cous-ins, Lara and Zayda. Ember and Harmony are friends of ours, and we're expecting them for dinner. Let them through, please."

A dozen middle-aged guys with guns smiled and moved their cars, sure that the four pretty women they saw couldn't be a threat. Yay for sexist assumptions.

One they had gone, Bernie shook his head at Karma and snorted, "Son, if I'd seen a Dragon, I think I'd remember it. You've been using too much of your own product."

Karma waved the idea away. "Oh, I don't use the stuff I sell. People won't pay for the level of quality I expect. I sell great shit, don't get me wrong. It's all first-rate stuff, but it's not the holiest of holies. Now, the stuff I use? Pure indoor hydroponic cultivation in a totally closed and con-trolled environment. Water and air filtered and balanced. Six decimal points of purity. You can't grow outdoors any more, not with the Feds flooding the air with chemtrails from those black jets. It's all part of their mind control agenda, keeping us from knowing the truth."

I have to admit, I had no response to that whatsoever.

I was spared further brain damage when Arwydd flew over the ridge to the west, flanked by two identical sky-blue Dragonesses. Arwydd slowed to a halt and hovered long enough to drench the remains of the guard post with her blizzard breath weapon. She nodded to the militia and flew off to the north with Lara and Zayda following right behind her.

"Woah..." Karma tilted his head to the side, furrowing his brow. "That's so weird..."

"What is?" I asked.

"The Dragon I saw was red with gold stripes. Or maybe gold with red stripes. I didn't know they came in so many colors. Do you think Dragons can get tattoos? You know, like a flame job on the wings? That would rock."

Off to the side, Bernie buried his face in his hands and said, "Please, Lord, in Jesus' name, make him stop."

In this, Bernie and I were of one accord. Yea, verily.

Chapter Four

A Well-Ordered Apocalypse

"...I therefore urge Congress to pass a bill guaranteeing equal rights to all citizens, both Human and Changed. As a temporary measure, I am issuing an executive order mandating that guarantee be observed and practiced at all levels of the federal government. This order will remain in effect until Congress enacts the appropriate laws. The sooner Congress acts, the sooner my order will be rescinded."

The president paused to gather his thoughts. "We may never know the cause of these changes or be able to reverse them. For now, we must accept these events, and trust that our future will continue to unfold according to the Creator's design. This is not a time for fear, or hate, or bias, though I'm sure we haven't seen the last of these things. As we go forward, remember that we are all Americans. We will get through this, and that we will do it together. God bless you and your families, and may God bless the United States of America."

Rose turned the television off before the talking heads started dissecting the speech. "This is why you people need a monarch. Lawmakers are terrible leaders. 'Send me a bill to sign,' my shapely monkey ass. Just give the orders and let the nobles scream."

Arguing with a Dragon about the merits of a pure oligarchy is a lost cause. The way they see it, those who have the gold *should* make the rules.

"It's not going to do any good anyway," Miriam snuffled. She'd been hiding in Ember's car, terrified someone would see her. She'd always been petite, but now she was barely three feet tall, with hair as pink as cotton candy and the body proportions of a fashion doll. She was not at what I would have pictured when someone said 'Gnome,' but the Dragons insisted that was what she was.

She took another tissue and dabbed at her eyes. "Oh, God, it was hard enough to be taken seriously when I was five-foot-two! I can't even drive my own car now! I'm wearing children's clothes held together with safety pins. It's a damn good thing I don't need glasses anymore because I can't even wear mine now. There's no point in going home, because I'm not going to be able to reach the deadbolt on my own front door! Even if I could get in to my own damn house, I wouldn't be able to get drunk because I'd need a goddamn stepladder to reach the goddamn booze!" She doubled over, sobbing and pounding the couch cushion with her fist.

Ember patted Miriam on the back. "I know it sucks right now, but you've got three Dragons and a sorceress sitting here. You have friends, and we'll do everything we can to help." The arm-long, gold-scaled dragonette perched on Ember's shoulder made a concerned trilling noise and nosed at Miriam's cheek. Miriam had a new friend as well; a gorgeous miniature dire wolf wearing a fluffy pink sheep costume. Well, miniature for me; it was almost large enough for Miriam to ride it.

Miriam hugged her new wolf buddy and shook her head. "It's...there's a bigger issue for me. I work with violent offenders, sexual predators, and worse. I work with the worst humanity has to offer, and I make a difference in their lives. That's who I am. Now? My management isn't going to let me near my own patients, and if I'm unable to work with our population, I can't do my job. At best, I'll be assigned to a low-risk population until I quit. It'll be *a* job, but not *my* job."

"Wouldn't they have to make accommodations for you?" I regretted the question at once, but Miriam just shook her head.

"David, I'm the size of a child, with the sexual characteristics of a porn star. I'm pervert bait. I can sell my house and get one designed and scaled for the new me. I can get adaptive technology for my car. I can tie the state personnel system into knots to keep from being fired. But I can't work with my assigned population. Too much risk. And that would be my position if one of my colleagues walked in like this, male or female. There are no accommodations that outweigh the basic risk factors. I'll have to find another job. It's just a matter of time."

"Could be worse. I mean, look at that Troll gal, Soni." Ember said. "When she was helping us build our critters for the sheep-stealing contest, she was maybe five and a half feet tall. Then, right after dinner, she grows two feet taller, gains a hundred pounds of muscle, and sprouts tusks. She split the seams on her pants and had to have someone cut her corset ties. She was holding her pants up with a bungee cord and keeping her blouse on with a mess of duct tape. One hard bounce and some sweat, and she was going to be all out in the open."

"Sheep-stealing Trolls?" I raised an eyebrow at that, as much as at Ember's train-of-thought method of storytelling.

"Yeah, the Troll bikers. The ones from Wyoming. Rose and I were dancing at their bardic last year."

That tidbit helped me place them. I nodded, and Ember continued.

"This year, they decided to hold a sheep-stealing contest, and they brought all this craft stuff for people to make sheep with. Well, it didn't have to be an actual sheep, just something small and, you know, stealable."

Ember stroked her dragonette behind the eye ridges and it started purring. "I made Jewel, here, and Miriam made Arya. Believe it or not, the stuffed animals coming to life wasn't even close to the craziest bunch of drama last night. This one gal dumped her boyfriend at lunch and switched teams by dinner. Then it turns out the boyfriend had been molesting her since she was fifteen. The Queen had to sit on a dozen guys who wanted to haul his ass into the woods and make him fall down a lot. Anyway, imagine how hard it would be to get people's trust when you're seven feet tall, green, and look like you eat Billy goats and live under a bridge."

"At least then I wouldn't be a security risk to my friends and co-workers," Miriam snapped. "Right now, I'd be afraid one of the drug screening dogs might think I'm a chew toy."

"You're right. That does sound like you're out of a job." Rose stood up and held her hand out to Miriam. "Let's go shopping."

Miriam glared daggers at her and snapped, "Do I look like I want to go shopping?!"

"No. You look like a starving child wearing clothes stolen from rag pickers. That's why we need to go shopping." Rose grinned. "You can ride on my shoulders if you want."

"Bitch!" Miriam was on her feet, kicking and punching Rose as hard as she could. "Don't talk to me like that! I'm a person, damn it, not a toy!" She took a deep breath and stepped back. "I'm not a toy. I'm not a child. Don't ever treat me that way." Behind her, the wolf had dropped its fleecy disguise and was growling at Rose, fangs bared.

Rose met Miriam's gaze and nodded. "Good. Anger is better than despair. Miriam, you are now an adult Gnome. That is your fate, but it's far from terrible. Come back home with me, and I'll take you to shopping so you can get clothes that fit and patterns to make more. If you want to be taken seriously, you're going to have to give up wearing shirts emblazoned with singing fruit."

Miriam sighed. "Damn it. I'm entirely too rational for this crap. I should leave Arya here, though. I hope that won't be a problem."

I rolled my eyes in mock horror. "Start with one talking cat and pretty soon we have a small ark on our hands." I held my hand out for extensive sniffing. "No worries. I'll find some chow for him."

"Her."

I took a quick look. "Right. Her."

Harmony stood up as well. "I'll go with you. I have to report to the Council. The result of these changes is inevitable, but the Ancients will still want to discuss it."

Ember's eyes narrowed and her back stiffened. "What result do you mean?"

Harmony's voice softened, but she didn't look away. "The result you saw with Lara and Zayda. The result you've felt from me all day. The wonder we need is everywhere, and it is strong. Strong enough to fill us in hours instead of years. All day, I've felt our kind going home. I myself could have returned last night. However, I'm not going to."

"Why not?" Ember whispered.

"I have decided not to have any more children," Harmony said. "I like it here, and I'm going to stay a while. That's the rest of what I need to tell the Council."

Ember pulled Harmony into a brief, tight embrace. "Better go, then. You know how the Council loves hearing good news." She managed to keep smiling until Rose, Harmony, and Miriam vanished, but as soon as they were gone, her shoulders sagged and she wrapped her arms around herself. Without looking at me, she asked, "David, can I use your shower?"

"Sure. Do you want fancy, extra fancy, or 'holy shit'?"

She chuckled despite the tears. "Um, 'holy shit' please. If that's okay, I mean."

"Wouldn't have offered if it wasn't." I turned to the panel on the wall and told it, "Janus, show our guest to the master bath, please."

"As you wish, David." Just like that, a string of ceiling lights came on, laying out a path for Ember to follow.

Ember gave me a quick hug and said, "Thanks." Then she punched me in the shoulder. "That's for showing off, Rockefeller." She followed the lights upstairs and out of sight.

Nadia stood up and grabbed Eric's hands. "A shower sounds great right now. We'll be back." They headed off for the guest room they were staying in. As they passed me, Eric's expression was downright troubled, and I wondered if he was pondering what I was pondering.

That's right. Trying to take over the world. Not Earth, though. Rose's world. Dragons have extremely long lives, balanced by an extremely low birth rate. Originally, it took a dragoness around a thousand years to gather enough adoration energy to have a healthy clutch of eggs. With Earth's new level of energy to draw from, a dragoness could conceivably clutch every ten years or so.

This was a recipe for surplus population. Unfortunately, the most basic solution to a surplus population is, and always has been, war. I didn't expect them to get hostile with Earth, but swift and blinding violence against the Humans of their world? Yeah, I could see that.

"If you're quite finished contemplating your navel, toss me the remote. And what's for dinner?"

I handed the remote to the cat. "Depends on who's delivering. We ate all the perishables and most of the canned stuff during our little trip, remember? Although we may have some two-year-old dry kibble."

"Hmm. I didn't know you liked kibble." Thirteen turned the volume back up and started flipping channels.

I left him to bask in the television's glow and headed to the kitchen. As I'd suspected, the only thing I was going to be able to whip together would have to involve canned salmon, Kalamata olives, and cream of mushroom soup. Well, maybe the cat could have the salmon.

"Janus, list restaurants within five miles offering delivery." Janus came up with more results than I expected, which was fortunate. Most of them either didn't answer or had messages stating they were closed. Even the big pizza chains were shuttered.

I found one Chinese place still open, but no one in the owner's family was willing to deliver. I could come pick food up, but it was cash only and three times normal prices. I hung up and dialed an Indian restaurant we'd been to several times.

"Yes, we are open, but closing now," the owner's wife said. "You can have whatever is prepared for only half price, but you must come get it. Cash or credit only. No checks."

"I'll take it all. Give me ten minutes."

The food filled the Interceptor's laundry basket-sized trunk and the passenger seat, not to mention filling the air with cardamom, garlic, and ginger. As soon as I carried the last load out, the owners locked the doors and lowered steel shutters over the windows.

The other businesses in the area were locked up as well, except for the liquor store across the street. The security grates on the windows were locked in place, with a home-made 'CASH ONLY!!!' sign taped to the bars. A red-skinned Orc with a Mossberg 12-gauge was sitting on a stool outside the front door. A sign taped on the wall said, 'YOU DON'T GET STUPID, YOU DON'T GET HURT.'

I drove across the street and parked. I didn't need anything, but I wanted to get an idea of how people were responding to all of this.

The Orc blocked the door, but kept the shotgun pointed at the ground. "Good evening, sir. Cash only means cash only. Please show me your wallet."

"What happens if I wave my hand at you and say, 'you don't need to see my wallet'?"

He grinned. "I kick you someplace funny for implying I have a weak mind. Then I ask again, real nice. Just like this: may I see your wallet, please?"

"Of course." I showed him the bills I was carrying, fanning them out a bit to make them easier to see.

He nodded and stood aside. "Thank you for your cooperation. Enjoy your visit."

I returned his nod and went in. They'd sold almost all of the beer and wine, but I did find five bottles of locally brewed blackberry mead. Not suitable for serving with dinner, and especially not with Indian, but it was great for dessert.

The young lady at the counter was some manner of Elf, but I'd never seen someone like her. Her lips and eyes were pale, glacier blue against skin as white as fresh snow on a ski run, and I swear I saw little sparkles of light when she moved. Her hair looked white on the surface, but changed to a faint, pale blue passing through her ponytail holder. She rang everything up and gave me the total in a Russian accent better suited to a femme fatale wearing a black leather trench coat. When she spoke, I caught glimpses of some very cute fangs.

I handed over the cash and asked, "How are people treating you?"

She counted out my change before answering. "Polite, but of course, I am vampire." She leaned in close and stage-whispered, "No one starts trouble when they see what I have become." She smiled, just to make sure I saw the fangs.

I couldn't help but snicker a little. "No. You're an Elf. I know what they look like, and I have friends who do cosplay. Love the disguise, though."

She shrugged and rolled her eyes as she layered the bottles into an empty box. "Alright, fine. Just don't tell my boyfriend you figured it out. People are more afraid of me than they are of him, and it makes him crazy."

"Sure thing." I scooped up the box and shouldered my way out the door. Outside, I shook my head at the Orc. "Scary looking lady, there. Be careful, man."

He curled his lips back, but nodded. "What can I say? Balls of steel."

I laughed with him and wedged the bottles in among the food containers. I was mostly finished when a passing police car slowed down, turned into the parking lot, and stopped behind my car.

The Orc immediately leaned the shotgun against the wall and sat down again, keeping his hands open and out to his sides. I leaned back enough to look over my shoulder but didn't make any other moves.

The officer nearest me pointed to the Interceptor and asked, "Sir, is this your vehicle?"

"Yes." *Finders-keepers counts, right?* "I'm the only owner this car has ever had on Earth."

"Sir, where is this car registered? I've seen a lot of license plates, but I've never heard of any 'Jefferson Province'."

I sighed. "Just a moment. I need to set this wine down and get my wallet out. May I proceed to do that?" He nodded, and I stuffed the last bottle into a box of foil-wrapped *naan* bread.

As promised, I turned around, got out my wallet, and fumbled with the papers in it. At the same time, I pulled as hard as I could on the magic around me. The influx damn near knocked me off my feet. I stopped pulling, but the energy was making me lightheaded.

"Sir, are you having a problem locating your registration?" The officers might not know what I was doing, but they know something was wrong.

"No, I just straightened up too fast." I handed the officer the registration and insurance card for my Mercedes. "Here you are. I'm sure you'll find everything in order."

The officer showed the registration to his partner. "Wait, this doesn't look right..." He looked back at me and said, "Let me see your license."

I leaned down so I could see both of them. "You don't need to see my license. That is the registration you were looking for." I couldn't help it— I waved my hand in a circle and grinned as they repeated everything perfectly. I followed with, "Everything is in order. I can have my papers back. My cooperation is appreciated. I can go about my business."

Resistance was futile.

I tucked my wallet away as the cops pulled out and noticed the Orc had his back up against the wall with both hands in the air. I waved to him and said, "You kids have fun, now." He nodded and returned the wave as I drove off.

I made a point of sticking to the speed limit and following all traffic laws as I drove home. The Interceptor stood out more than I had expected, so getting Colorado plates on it moved to the top of my 'to do' list. My practical side had a list of reasons I shouldn't be driving this thing in the first place, but I ignored him. That guy is such a buzzkill.

Without warning, a whole host of stuff came on, turning Interceptor's simple, glossy black interior into the cockpit of a 747. I had data displays in places I didn't know existed. At the same time, the car thundered, "Legacy data systems integrated. All systems enabled," loud enough to be heard over a hair metal band.

I jumped, yanking the steering wheel sideways. It wasn't much, but a car seat full of unsecured masala and vindaloo went sideways as well. I got one hand on the curries and steered hard to the left.

Too hard. The food reversed direction and thunked up against the passenger door. The car veered back through the lane and headed across the double yellow line, right into the oncoming traffic lane. At least it tried.

The steering wheel went dead in my hand and the floor pedals froze. By the time the car finished saying, "Collision avoidance active," we were on the correct side of the road and pulling off onto the right-hand shoulder.

After some deep breaths, I made sure the food was intact, turned the system's master volume down, and tapped the switch to resume manual control.

"Manual control is not available at this time. Alcohol vapor detected. Driving pattern indicates possible intoxication. Please state desired destination."

Bloody. Hell.

A lifetime of working with computers told me there was no way I was getting around this—at least, not until I'd learned a lot more about the system. Accordingly, I surrendered to the inevitable and said, "Take me home."

The Interceptor pulled out, smooth as glass. The good part about being on autodrive was being able to pay attention to the world around the car. Everything looked different. With all the data systems active, a heads-up display projected onto the windshield, highlighting people, other cars, traffic signs, the route we were taking, and even wireless networks in the houses and businesses we passed.

Some of the cars had small icons floating over them, identifying things like radio equipment, radar detectors, or, on one luxury sedan, an infrared night vision setup. A Boulder Sheriff's cruiser passed in front of me while I was sitting at a light; the system lit him up in bright yellow, with a 'LAW ENFORCEMENT' tag floating overhead and a lengthy string of equipment icons.

As annoyed as I was at the drunken driving safeguards, I had to admire how well the car was adapting to life on Earth. It did make me wonder what line of work the previous owner was in, though; all the information I was seeing had to come from a serious electronics warfare package, and I couldn't see your average law-abiding citizen needing any of it.

The neighborhood watch was still manning the barricades when I reached our turn. The Interceptor turned in, but immediately hit the brakes. The targeting system lit up the cars blocking the road and the armed people behind them. At the same time, the main guns activated and targeting circles appeared on each of the cars, roughly where the gas tanks would be.

"Deactivate weapons!" I wasn't shouting, really. I was just...being emphatic. I took a breath and added, "Targeting system off."

To its credit, the car didn't decide I really meant to start shooting. The guns clicked off and I was able to open the window. I saw a few new faces, but enough remembered seeing me leave that they just waved me through. Once the cars pulled back to open a path, the autodrive kicked in and we were off again. I didn't even have to park; the car opened our gate and the garage door without prompting and settled down, exactly where it had been when we set off.

Damn. A car that was its own designated driver. Talk about a million-dollar idea...Nah. Maybe later. I got out and hauled an armful of curries into the house. Everyone was back or out of the shower, so we got the car unloaded and dinner set up in no time. Once we finished pouring the mint tea and mango lassi for everyone, I stood up and raised my glass.

"It's always pleasant to have good friends gathered around, and tonight, doubly so. I can't think of any people I'd rather spend the dawn of a new world with. So, to family, both of blood and of choice. May this new world be kinder, gentler, and more wondrous than the last one. So mote it be."

All around the table, glasses clinked as my chosen family accepted the wish and passed it on.

So mote it be.

Chapter Five

Catch the Tale by the Tiger

Blackberry mead is not just a great dessert wine, it's a great wine for hanging out in a hot tub or around a fire pit. We started at the fire pit, but soon enough Ember tossed her clothes onto a lounger and climbed into the hot tub. Rose and Harmony followed and that started a general migration.

Nadia took a detour on the way and teleported to her parents' house in Santa Barbara. She returned with Geneva Rolling Thunder in tow. Nadia's mother, Aerin, has some memory issues due to a gunshot wound to the head. Geneva is Aerin's aide and life manager, as well as nominally serving as bodyguard. She and Miriam have also had an intermittent long-distance relationship for the past two years.

As a Human, Geneva had been Native American, naturally handsome rather than artificially pretty, and looked somewhere between thirty and seventy years old. Her shoulder-length black hair seemed to have an innate immunity to styling products. She could tame it into professional, silky-smooth order for perhaps an hour; much beyond that and it turned back into a windswept river cascading from crown to collar. It had been the one aspect of her life she still struggled to control.

As a Dark Elf, the hair won. The river was now a whitewater tumult, falling unchecked to her waist. Her new features held no remnant of her original face, only sharp, unsparing Dark Elven lines. Her eyes were still familiar, though; the iron-hard, dispassionate, 'It's-just-business' eyes of a House Assassin.

Her old clothes didn't fit her new form, so she was making do with a jogging top and a wrap skirt. Her shoulder holster didn't fit anymore either. She attached a trigger lock to her Glock and passed the whole rig over to me. "Do you have someplace safe to put this?"

"Safe, no, but we can do out-of-sight." I tucked the bundle into an empty side table drawer. "I like the new look. Now you're scary beyond all reason on the outside, too."

"I know. I love it." She smiled and headed outside.

Miriam was sitting by the edge of the fire pit, poking at the dancing flames with a stick. Geneva sat down and said, "For someone who makes her living wrangling psychos, I thought you'd be bigger."

Miriam stiffened. "Don't. I can't handle it right now. And don't tell me how sorry you are for saying it." She paused, then her shoulders sagged and she leaned in to embrace Geneva as best she could. "By the way, nice paint job."

"Thank you. This is actually the second full body make-over I've gone through, and I rather like how I turned out." Geneva stood up and held her hand out to help Miriam up. "I'm cashing in a vacation day to be here, so let's not waste it. There's something I need to talk to you about, but I want to soak a bit first and get a chance to relax." She got undressed and settled into the hot tub with a long sigh.

Miriam turned dark red, but she undressed as well, folding her clothes into a crisp, squared-off bundle. "I've never been comfortable like this," she said. "I just have this small, all-pervading, deep-seated fear of rejection." She slid into the water and made her way to the seat next to Geneva.

I suddenly had an urgent need to get into the water myself. Trying not to think about the source of the problem just made the problem...more obvious. I finally had to just go for it and hope for the best. I draped my towel over the back of a chair and sat down in the tub next to Rose.

"No one is going to reject you," Geneva told Miriam. "Trust me on that. After all, a poorly-hidden erection is the sincerest form of flattery."

Truly, friendship is priceless.

Once the jokes wore out, conversation turned to yesterday's events. Thanks to Ember's obsession with social media, we'd gotten check-ins from all but two of our local friends. About a third of them had changed, which seemed to be on-par with the rest of the world. Mostly Elves, a few Dwarves. One of Ember's ex-boyfriends reportedly became an Orc. He's a guard at the Smith Road Hilton—more officially known as the Denver County Jail—so the new order of things might be good for him.

Some weren't so lucky. Some areas of the country were not responding well to having non-Human citizens. People had been beaten, fired from their jobs, turned away from hospitals and police stations, had their homes and cars burned, and more than a few killed. Children. Entire families. I had to stop reading those stories.

I'd posted a 'we're fine' message on my own social media pages, as well as a message of support for my parents and any friends who had changed. Mom looked amazing as a Gold Elf, and Dad...well, Dad looked like he should be puffing on a pipe full of aromatic leaf while waiting for third lunch to roll around.

Soon after I posted, I got a message from Lorena Norris. She's married to Gordon Norris, the owner of Avalanche Games, and is Avalanche's Vice-

President of Property Development. She doesn't do anything with *Warblade* or any of Avalanche's other established games; her area is new products, such as *Ecophage*, the game my company was developing. Avalanche owned *Ecophage* and Curious Diversions, which made Lorena my boss.

Her message said, "Glad you are doing well. Gordon is fine, I've changed. Have a look."

When we'd met two years ago in Las Vegas, she'd been in costume as a Damazi, a blue half-demon from *Warblade*. Now she was the real thing. The picture she sent was a full-body nude shot. She had all the naughty bits covered, but her horns, fangs, furry tail, and faun legs were on display, right down to the shiny black cloven hooves.

"Anyone who says they can't come in to work because of their appearance better have changed more than I did," her note said. "Show this around as much as needed."

I emailed back, "Yes, Ma'am," and passed the tablet around the table.

Miriam looked at Lorena's picture, took a hefty drink of her mead, and blurted out, "So, when I went to the bathroom before dinner, I called my boss. I told him I'm thirty-four inches tall and weigh eighty pounds. He brought up something I hadn't thought of. Two-thirds of my patients have also changed. They're bigger now, mostly Orcs or even Ogres. Security is being re-evaluated all around. And I was right; I can report for a clerical job in the administration offices, or I can take medical leave and hope my savings lasts long enough for the laws to change. Or, option three, I can quit before they fire me."

"What did you do?" I asked.

"I'm on administrative leave with pay for the next week, while I make up my mind. One last week of dignity before I run off and join the circus. And by that, I mean the clerical side of the Department of Public Health. I'd never disparage an actual circus that way."

Geneva said, "Well, that is as good an opening as I'm going to get. David, is there somewhere Miriam and I could talk privately for a few minutes?"

"Sure." I got out, wrapped up in my towel, and held towels for Geneva and Miriam.

Miriam took the towel but shook her head. "If 'talk privately' means a pep talk, asking me to convert to anything, or doing the mattress mambo, I'm not in the mood."

"None of the above," Geneva said. "This is a serious conversation with life-changing implications and you will have to give it serious and sober consideration. Now, if you want to get your Dark Elf ticket punched after we talk, sure. But that's after."

Miriam crossed her arms, glaring up at Geneva. "Serious conversation...This is that speech you said you weren't going to give me back when we met. You said I wasn't ready. What makes me ready now?"

"The difference is that now, your mind is open to thoughts and ideas you never would have considered. Up until yesterday, you had security and your life had meaning. You were comfortable, and safe. Today, all that security is gone and whole worlds are open for you to explore." Geneva held her hand out to Miriam. "Half an hour. Trust me for half an hour. Please."

"Half an hour?" Miriam took a deep breath and nodded. "I'll give you half an hour. If you really think this talk can make that much of a difference in my life, I should at least hear you out. God, I hate being so rational."

I pointed up the stairs. "Second floor, turn left. Those are the guest rooms, take your pick." They went upstairs and I went to the kitchen for the last bottle of mead. While I hunted for a corkscrew, the phone rang. The nearest Janus panel listed the number as "Private Residence, Mumbai, India.'

I caught the bottle before it slipped completely out of my hands and called out, "Janus, answer phone on speaker! Hello, this is David."

"David, this is Manya."

I set the bottle down and picked up the nearest handset. "*Namaste! Āj keesha mausam hay?*"

"I don't.... are you trying to ask about the weather? Stick to English. You're hurting my ears. Why don't you...never mind that! Aiiigh!!" I heard Manya cover the phone with her hand. When she came back, she said, "David, I need to know: are you alright? It is important."

"If that's a backhand way of asking if I'm still Human, yes, I am." I settled into a chair. "How are things there? Any major troubles?"

"No, none at all. We are all one happy family, doing a big Bollywood dance number around the Taj Mahal while elephants shit rainbow cookies for the tourists."

"Of course. You have to be nice to the tourists. Money alone triumphs, right?"

"Not always." Manya's voice caught, and her voice turned into a guttural growl. "David, we...Aparna is fine, but we...changed. It means many other changes, and... I need your help."

I grabbed a pen and the envelope from the water bill. "Tell me what you need."

"I'm sending you a picture of the new me," she said.

Right on cue, my phone chimed with the new message. I opened it up and jumped back a little.

She was a tiger.

Manya's body was still humanoid, but now she had twitchy ears, green eyes in a feline skull, and coarse, orange and black fur from nose to tail-tip. She still had Human hands, but I bet they had claws. She looked taller and more muscular than she'd been before. I couldn't tell from the image, but I was sure her makeover included nasty, big, pointy teeth.

"David?" It was hard to be sure, but Manya's voice sounded as though she were crying. "Please don't be afraid of me."

"I'm not afraid, don't worry. What does Aparna think?"

Manya was definitely crying. "Aparna thinks my fur is too stiff. She said it was 'pokey.' She also said, 'You don't have enough boobies to be a tiger, Mommy, but you're still pretty."

I laughed. "Well, at least you can buy some conditioner for your fur. What about Aparna?"

"I'm sending you another picture."

This one was Aparna. She looked healthy and happy, smiling for the camera, with a huge pair of rainbow-feathered, parrot-like wings spread out behind her. It looked as though they emerged from her shoulders or upper back. At a guess, I'd say her wingspan would be close to three times her height.

"Those are lovely. How is she doing at flying?"

Manya made a *chuff*-noise into the phone. "David, be serious!"

"I am serious. I want to know if she can fly. If she can, it's going to be a bitch grounding her for being naughty." Before Manya could growl at me again, I asked, "How does Aparna feel about all this?"

Manya sighed. "She's delighted, and yes, against all laws of physics and biology, she can fly. Short distances only. Almost like a long leap or jump. Soon, I fear, she will need much open space and a safe environment. I do not think I will find either in Mumbai."

"I should think not. Have you had anyone look at her wings? An avian biologist, maybe?"

"We just got back from seeing a veterinarian who specializes in exotic birds. The feather colors are very like a scarlet macaw, except that hers span the full color spectrum. The wings most resemble those of an eagle, as do the feathers, except that the feathers have some weird structure on the edges, something normally found only in owls. I don't remember what he called it, but it means she'll fly almost silently."

"There's also a structure where her...where the thumb would be if the wing were a hand, that normally only waterfowl have. It gives her extra lift during takeoff. He had been saying she'd probably only be able to glide on thermals like a condor, but then she...he did not understand how, but she did something to change the shape of her wings. She made them more like a crow's wings, he said. More agile than an eagle's, but they would require more energy. Again, totally against the laws of physics and biology."

In my best Bronx accent, I said, "You know, Doc, I never studied law." Even though Manya couldn't see it, I mimed taking a cigar out of my mouth and wiggling it. Before Manya could jump on me for not being serious, I added, "Have you checked to see if there are any reports of adults with the same physical changes?"

"Our pediatrician contacted the World Health Organization to investigate that question. She told us there have been bird-women in Saudi

Arabia and swan-maidens in Norway, but no matches. Those other women transform into very large birds. A nightingale the size of an ostrich, the doctor said. But no other winged humans yet. Aparna is the first on record. They don't even know what to call her species yet."

"I suppose 'Angels' would have too many religious overtones."

Manya made that *chuff*-noise again. "Aparna is calling herself a Fairy Princess. Doctor Ganaka submitted 'Peri' as a species name. Better than 'Hawk People of Mongo,' I suppose."

"How is Doreen taking all of this?"

"You mean, how is she adjusting to being engaged to a tiger?"

"Um, no. I assumed she was fine with that since you didn't start with telling me the wedding was off."

"Ah. Yes, she is...adjusting. She and my parents still wish us to move to California. I prefer to stay here, but Doreen is correct that we would not have to worry about mobs with torches coming after us in California."

"Are torch-waving mobs a serious threat there?"

"Not yet." Manya's voice caught and she made a loud honking noise. "Sorry. I still don't know how to blow my new nose. Anyway, there are no mobs yet, but there are issues. The temple we were going to use cancelled after we met with them yesterday. The priests did not consider me a demon, but until the law clarifies the status of the Changed, all of us are barred from the temple grounds. The government is working on an emergency declaration that all the Changed are citizens with full rights, but...there is resistance. And the people...David, people who have known me all my life screamed and ran away when they saw me. They called me *rakshasi*, a demon that eats the flesh of men." She started crying again. "Aparna should not have to hear such things said about me!"

"No child should hear such things. How can I help?"

"I must ask you to accept paternity of Aparna. I know, we promised, but without Sharon, a DNA test will show I have no blood relationship. The courts could say I am only a gestational surrogate with no rights."

"You're talking about Sharon's parents, aren't you? What are they doing?"

"Nothing yet. The Oklahoma courts granted them visitation last year, and six months ago the family court here upheld it. We've been negotiating. I offered that they could come get Aparna after her birthday and take her to America for two weeks. The courts approved the agreement, and she has her papers to travel. If they should decide to keep her..."

Aha. The light bulb finally went on. "Okay, I get it. You aren't human now. No blood relationship, plus no rights of any kind, legally, as a non-human. You need me to trump their claim, which would be hard if I've never had any kind of parental relationship with her."

"Yes," she whispered. "I carried her. She is my daughter, in every way but one. More than that, she is all I have of Sharon. I can't lose her." She started crying again,

"Manya... Manya, please, I understand why you're upset, but I need you to tell me the details. I assume you've talked to a lawyer. Tell me what you want me to do."

"You will do it?"

I held my hand up, waving for her to slow down even though she couldn't see me doing it. "Hold on. I'm not saying yes or no yet. I need to know what you're asking for, what I need to do, and when it needs to get done. I also have to talk to Rose, to my parents, and to my lawyer. You need to let me do that. However, I promise you, if I can do what you ask, I will."

Manya breathed out a long sigh. "Thank you. I will send you the details. It is Sunday morning here. I have an appointment before the family court on Tuesday at eight in the morning, Mumbai time. The judge will allow you to attend and testify on video call. Your lawyer will be welcome to attend, and if you wish to hire your own translator, I can give you a list of agencies certified to handle legal proceedings."

"I can see some things haven't changed. How did you manage to get a court date on such short notice?"

"I didn't bribe the judge, if that is what you're implying." She sniffled and gave a little laugh. "I bribed the clerk who sets the docket."

"Go you." I hesitated, trying to decide how to phrase my next question. Problem was, there wasn't a graceful option. "Manya, level with me. Are you in danger? Is Aparna?"

"Aparna is not, but I could be. Many others have also become...partly animal. Some people see us as abominations. Some have been murdered. It is happening in the rural areas, mostly, but even in Mumbai, my money, position, and business connections will not save me if a mob comes."

"It's not just India," I said, "People have been killed here, too, but...anyway. Is there any good news?"

Manya managed a laugh. "Yes, actually. Several major mosques are asking all the faithful who have changed to come before prayers and perform *salah*. Even *djinni* may be accounted good Muslims if they adhere to the teachings and are obedient to God; so also the Changed will be accepted if they can demonstrate their faith. There are also many Changed among the Hindu ascetic orders, and I hope the Babas will follow the example of the Imams."

"I will pray for their wisdom. And I'll call you as soon as I have news."

"Thank you, David. We will be waiting." Manya hung up.

I stood up and saw Rose sitting behind me, wrapped in a big fluffy robe. I asked, "How long have you been there?"

She shrugged. "A few minutes. Everyone else went off to their rooms, so I locked up and came in here."

Normally I would have known where she was and when she entered the room. "I'm sorry. I was a little distracted. How much did you hear?"

"Enough," she said. "Ask me. Not about the little things. Just the important ones."

I sat down next to her on the couch. "Aparna being able to fly is interesting, but at the moment it's a side issue. I need to figure out what I want out of this situation. What's my profit? What's my opening bid, and how much is the minimum I'll accept?" I clasped Rose's hands between mine. "I can't say 'no,' and she knows it. I'd expect her to open low, but she's not offering any incentives at all to me. That makes me think she's hoping I'll just agree without asking for an incentive or any kind of changes to our arrangement."

Rose didn't say anything, but I could feel her agreement. I stroked her hand and continued. "I've stayed out of Aparna's life until now, and I was fine with that. I was fine with telling her who I am and having her call me daddy. But this…"

I lapsed into silence. Inside, I went back and forth between excuses, trying to find a way out of the only decision I could make. Finally, I gave up and stopped fighting it. Resistance is futile. "Fine. If Manya wants me to be daddy, then I'm damn well going to be daddy. I get custody and Aparna lives with us. I won't cut Manya out, but I'm not sharing custody until Manya moves to the US permanently. That's my price."

Rose nodded. "Good."

"How do you feel about it?" I didn't need to ask her how she felt; I could feel her emotions as clearly as my own. I asked anyway. Asking was one of those polite things couples do for each other.

She shrugged. "It hurts, of course. I don't want to deny you this, or keep Aparna out of your life, but seeing the joy between parent and child still torments me. It will hurt, but I will be happy for you. Besides, I've been worrying about what to do with myself once you pass away. If Aparna has children, perhaps I can take one of them under my wing—no pun intended. If nothing else, that would be a reason for me to stay here."

"You need a reason to stay?"

"Not right now, but I will after you die." She shifted in the couch to lean back against me. "I'm sorry to bring it up, but it is going to happen. Looking after your bloodline could be a good way to pass the time, since I don't plan to go home, ever. In fact, I want everyone back home to forget about me and let my story pass into legend."

I stroked her hair, trying to think of something to say. Losing her ability to reproduce had been hard enough, but having strangers constantly praising her for her selflessness was little more than rubbing salt in the wound.

Rose pulled her robe open and pressed my hand against her breast. "If you want to pet me, pet something with nerve endings." Her nipple hardened between my fingers, and she squeezed my hand in hers. "Like that. If you want to make me feel better right now, start with that."

Rose says recreational sex is the one and only aspect of life where Humans are superior to Dragons, mostly because mating in free-fall doesn't allow for it. This is good news for us shaved monkeys, because when it comes time to cheer up a depressed Dragoness, your choices are limited to either a giant pile of gold and gems or Ye Olde Electric Cry of Love. Lather, rinse, and repeat.

With a little repositioning, I was able to apply both hands to the problem area while giving her several solid bites on the base of her neck—it's what Dragons use for foreplay. The last bite sent her into back-arching, toe-pointing, snarling and snapping ecstasy. She shared the wave of orgasms with me, mind to mind, leaving us both gasping.

Once I was able to catch my breath, I turned the lights off and scooped Rose off the couch. Our lovely chaise lounge next to the window was much more suitable for this sort of thing. I settled Rose on the lounge and we took turns busting out the night moves.

Sometime later, Rose paused what she was doing and said, "Someone is out in the open space, probably a mile down on the trail. Six, maybe eight flashlights."

I could see tiny flickers of light, but no other details. "No torches or pitchforks?"

"No."

"Worry about them later, then." I put the mystery night hikers out of mind and focused on Rose. We moved off the lounge, back on for a bit, and wound up pressed up against the patio window. Our minds and bodies were in perfect synch, feeling each other's physical and mental arousal building, until the magic moment happened for both of us.

'Spent' would be a good word for how I was feeling, hovering in that nice, hazy aftermath glow. I braced one hand on the glass and looked out into the night over Rose's shoulder.

A big Orc with dark, reddish skin, bestial features, and nasty teeth leered at me from the other side of the glass. I caught a glimpse of several other figures standing behind him.

Idiot. Security systems don't work if you leave them turned off.

A sledgehammer crashed through the window, shattering it and cracking me on the side of the head.

Chapter Six

Welcome to the New Day

Thankfully, the window took the brunt of the blow and slowed the hammer enough to keep it from killing me outright. It still left me half-senseless on the floor.

Reflexes got the better of Rose. Instead of protecting herself, she turned with me as I fell, trying to catch me. The Orc sucker-punched her in the temple with the butt of the sledgehammer. He followed that cheap shot with a kick in the stomach and another to the side of her head.

Human form, human frailties. Rose dropped, her voice going silent in my mind.

I pushed myself up and lunged, catching the big red guy around the waist and dragging him down to the floor. I managed to land one punch in his gut. Not enough. He twisted like a fish and tossed me into the air like a rag doll.

His friends laughed when I hit the floor again. One clapped and said, "Nice throw, Ronnie."

Ronnie bounced to his feet and thumped his buddy in the sternum, hard. "No names, asswipe, remember? Jesus, try thinking for once."

The distraction was enough for me to clear my head. I risked a quick glance at the intruders, just to get an idea of who I was up against.

The other four guys were Orcs as well, but they were smaller and had greenish skin. There were also two women. The first was one of the smaller, green Orcs, but the other was even bigger than Ronnie and had a wicked set of tusks jutting from her jaw. She was ignoring me and staring at Rose, running her tongue back and forth over her teeth.

I closed my eyes again and gathered as much energy as I could. One person I could control, probably two or three if I pushed hard. Taking on seven would be insane.

First Ronnie, then one or two of the other guys. Peer pressure, right?

Unaware of my cunning plans, Ronnie was busy playing criminal mastermind. He pointed to the stairs and said, "You guys find out who else is here and bring them down. Then toss the place, got it?"

One of the other Orcs reached for Rose's leg. "What about her?"

Ronnie knocked the guy's hand away. "She'll be here. Now get moving." When none of the other guys moved, Ronnie's expression twisted into a snarl. "Unless you all have forgotten who's in charge here..."

The Troll stepped in front of Ronnie and grinned. "Whoever finds the most valuable shit gets her after Ronnie. Move it!"

That did it. The four Orcs grinned back and headed for the stairs.

The female Orc shook her head. "This is not what we talked about. You said we were just going to grab some cash and jewelry and scare them. You never said anything about *raping* anyone!" She looked at the Troll and added, "Zoe, you know...you, of all people, should not be cool with this."

Zoe grabbed the Orc woman's hair and forced her down, onto her knees. "Do you want it to happen to her, or to you?"

The Orc woman scrabbled at the Troll's fingers. "Let me go, bitch!"

I risked another look. Ronnie's attention was on the two women, ignoring both Rose and me.

Now!

I rolled up on one elbow and yelled, "Freeze!"

My spell caught Ronnie and Zoe flat-footed and turned them into statues. The Orc woman's hands and arms were immobile, but she was jerking her head back and forth and trying to say something.

They'd keep.

I opened the drawer where I'd stashed Geneva's pistol, but she must have reclaimed it at some point. Then I remembered she'd put a trigger lock on it—I couldn't have used it regardless. I closed the drawer and looked for anything else useful.

Bingo. The towel I'd used in the hot tub was on the floor next to my robe. I wrapped the towel around my waist and covered Rose with the robe. Next, one at a time, I ordered Ronnie, Zoe, and the Orc woman down on their knees, hands on their heads, fingers interlaced and palms up.

As I worked, I kept glancing up the stairs and listening for any indications the other four guys were coming back. By the time I finished, though, Geneva was halfway down the stairs, pistol out, eyes glowing bloody crimson in the darkness.

I grimaced and gave her a nod. "Did you leave them alive?"

Geneva returned my nod and lowered her pistol. "For now. No promises on how long they stay that way."

Harmony and Eric led the four prisoners out of the guest rooms and down the stairs, followed by Ember and Miriam. All four Orcs were gagged and bound with chains made of glowing gold light. Two were working hard to say something through their gags while one appeared to be alternately praying and sobbing.

The fourth was staring straight ahead, jaw clenched, straining as hard as he could against the magic confining him. That changed when he stepped off the stairs. As soon as he had a clear path to Ronnie, he charged, throwing his shoulder into the bigger Orc's back. Eric and I pulled him back and forced him down to his knees, but not before he'd given Ronnie several vicious kicks.

"Save it," I told him. "The time to be kicking your buddy in the head was when he suggested busting into someone's house and robbing them. You were happy as a pig in shit when he mentioned raping my wife. Now, sit there, be quiet, and pray we send you to jail instead of the morgue."

While Harmony secured Ronnie and the women, Nadia ran down the stairs carrying her purse. She took a steel vial out of her purse, opened it, and rubbed some of the contents on Rose's tongue. That brought Rose around enough to be able to drink the rest.

While she recovered, I asked the room, "Show of hands. How many think we should just kill them now and be done with it?"

Geneva, Thirteen, and Nadia raised their hands.

"Wait," Rose rasped. She sat up on the couch, holding the robe tight. "Did they hurt anyone else?"

Harmony and Eric perked up at the question. Harmony glanced at everyone else before saying, "Only David, and his wounds are not severe."

"Then I claim their lives." Rose stood up and slipped the robe on, belting it closed.

Geneva holstered her pistol. "Is this some ancient tradition none of the rest of us know about?"

"The one wronged has first claim on the offender," Harmony said. "But this is not our world. It does not observe our traditions."

"I'm not going to kill them," Rose said. "Call the police. I want their families to know their shame." Her eyes narrowed and she yanked Ronnie's head backward. "And they will hear it from your own lips, wretch."

Ronnie tried to lunge at her, but the glowing chains tightened around him, freezing him in place.

It only took Rose a few seconds to gather all the power she needed. This time, a small ball of gold light surrounded her hand. The same light spilled out of the prisoners' eyes, lighting up their slack faces.

"Hear these words and be bound by them, from this moment until your last breath leaves your lips. You will confess your misdeeds to the authorities, to your families and friends, and to anyone who asks. You will accept your punishment without attempt to evade or shirk your debt until it is discharged. You will not allow others to lie for you or cover up your actions. The only thing you may not speak of is what we have said here. All you can relate of these events is that we detained you and held you for the police."

I snorted and mentally sent Rose a suggestion. *You know what would really hurt these meatheads? This...*

The corner of her mouth twitched, and the gold light grew stronger. "By these laws are you bound as well: First, you will not, by action or inaction, harm another person ever again, mentally, physically, or emotionally, nor will you allow another person to come to harm. Second: you will help all those who ask for aid if it is within your power to give, so long as doing so does not violate the first rule. Third: you will not allow others to harm, exploit, or take advantage of you, especially if such actions would violate either the first or second rules. The first rule prevails in the event of any conflicts between these laws as I have given them to you. Hear, and obey."

Behind me, Geneva snickered. "Wow. Would have been nicer to kill them."

Rose smiled, but kept her attention on the would-be criminals. "We're going to release you from the spell that created those chains. Stay quiet and do not move until the police take you into custody."

Even with Rose's command holding them in place, Geneva sat behind the suspects until I ushered the police into the house. At that point, she stood up, hands out to her side, and said, "Officers, I am a licensed bodyguard and have a concealed carry permit from California. My firearm is in my shoulder holster and I can provide identification at your request."

One officer secured Geneva's pistol while her partner called for additional units and Mirandized the prisoners. With those details out of the way, he helped Ronnie to his feet. "Sir, put your hands behind your back. Are you carrying any weapons? Knives, guns, anything dangerous I need to know about?"

Ronnie shook his head and tried not to say anything, but Rose's spell won. "Yes, I have a gun. It's in my underwear."

"Do you at least have it in a holster?" When Ronnie shook his head, the cop sighed. "That's a good way to blow your pecker off, and I can show you pictures of people who have done that. Now, slowly, reach in there with your left hand, pull the gun out, and hand it to me."

I could hear Ronnie's teeth grinding, but he stuck his hand down his pants and pulled out a small revolver. I couldn't see how Ronnie would have managed to fire it; his fingers couldn't fit inside the trigger guard.

Ronnie stayed quiet until the cop handcuffed him. At that point, he was in custody, and free from Rose's command to stay quiet.

"Let me go, you little shit magnet!" Ronnie tried to yank his arm out of the cop's grip. When that didn't work, he resorted to kicking and wound up pinned face-down on the floor. Even with the officer's knee between his shoulders, Ronnie kept shouting. "You can't do this to me! When my father hears about this, you're going to wish he'd let you die in a fire. Let me go, dickbreath!"

The officer kneeling on his back said, "You're halfway to getting your ankles shackled already. Keep this up and I will slap a bite guard on your ass. Is that what you want?"

Ronnie grimaced and shook his head. "No, no. Let me up...God, please, let me up!" He must have learned his lesson, because he stayed quiet as the cops walked him out. None of his buddies protested when their turns came, through the Orc woman never stopped crying.

The officer in charge told us EMTs were on the way to examine our injuries and asked that we wait in the dining room while they processed the living room. An hour later, one paramedic with a heavy layer of stubble and a large cup of coffee stuck his head in the doorway. "Any injured Humans? Humans only. Any injuries?"

I held up my hand. "My wife and I need to be checked out. Why only Humans? Non-Humans get hurt, too."

The paramedic sighed. "I need to see your ID and insurance card. No service without both. If you don't have them, I'm leaving."

Rose leaned forward and locked eyes with him. "Why aren't you helping non-Humans?" she asked. "Tell us everything."

She almost didn't need to use magic. The poor guy sagged against the wall, ready to collapse. Geneva got one arm around his shoulders and eased him down on the chair she'd been sitting in.

Rose repeated her command, and with Geneva holding him steady, the paramedic opened his eyes. "No supplies," he murmured. "No information. No training. What's the normal blood pressure for an Elf? What drugs can you give them? What blood types do they have? How bad are they going to sue us if we screw up?"

He looked away, wiping at his eyes. "The CDC. They ordered us to triage calls. Can't waste supplies when we don't have treatment protocols. Even the kids! Tried to ignore the order. We're doing what we can, we all are, but...It's all bad. The calls keep coming. We can't help, but the calls..."

"Enough." Rose stroked his forehead, whispering to him in Draconic. Once she finished, she hit him with a *Bender Mender* spell and clapped her hand over his mouth until he stopped yelling obscenities at her.

"You were too exhausted to help anyone," she said. "You're now fully rested and stone cold sober."

"I should probably thank you, but I'm not sure I want to," he said. He looked around at us and added, "I probably shouldn't ask how you did that, either. Now, let's have a look at those injuries."

While the paramedic worked, Geneva pulled a folded piece of paper out of her purse. "I can't help you with Orcs and Trolls, but for Elves and Dwarves, these are the normal ranges for blood pressure, pulse, and body temperature. This also lists preferred painkillers and antibiotics for Elves generally. Drow react strangely to a few of these, so suitable alternatives are also listed."

The paramedic looked blank. "Drow?"

"Dark Elves. Like me." She handed him the note. "Get this to the closest emergency room and they should be able to get it to the CDC. I'm sure the medical establishment will want to verify all this, but it's a place to start."

"I can do that. How did you get all this together? Someone is going to ask at some point." The paramedic folded the note up again and zipped it into a side pocket on his gear bag.

"Some of my colleagues and I put it together with the help of volunteers from our friends and family," Miriam said. "I'll be the point of contact for it if there are any questions." She handed the paramedic her business card.

He zipped it into the pocket as well and moved to me. "If that's the story you want to go with, I won't argue. I'll get it to someone who knows what to do with it. And thanks for...whatever it was you did to me."

Rose and I were pronounced free of concussion and advised to follow up with our regular doctors. The paramedic left, followed (two hours later) by the remaining officers. Finally, the house was ours again. We covered the broken windows with tarps and duct tape from our camping supplies and called it a night.

Chapter Seven

Cat Chat

The next morning, I found Thirteen reading the newspaper on the kitchen counter, sitting next to three dozen eggs and two pounds of genuine British bangers bundled in butcher's paper marked with an address in Surrey, England.

"Nice," I said. "I take it all this fell off a truck somewhere?"

"No, I took the sausages directly from a refrigerator. If I'm going to steal food, I take food worth stealing. The eggs came from your drug-addled neighbor. He was working on perfecting some kind of cannabis frittata." Thirteen shook himself. "He told me to take what I needed, because the universe would provide for his needs. Something tells me he won't miss them."

"Probably not. I doubt he'll remember talking to you half an hour from now." I took a moment to look into the living room and take in the damage from last night.

"Nice kids," the cat said. "I camped out at the station last night while they were being questioned."

"Who were they?" I didn't want to know, but I felt I should ask.

"Students at one of the local high schools. The guys were all on the football team, and the Troll girl was a cheerleader. I didn't hear anything on the other one."

"Probably not going to be so popular now." I turned the kitchen television to the Sunday morning news and got busy cracking eggs. "I got the feeling they probably weren't good kids to begin with."

"You think? Those kids picked your house because they saw a bunch of naked people in a hot tub. The ringleader planned to add rape to his home invasion agenda. None of the others challenged him on that. They're just lucky you're not willing to get your hands dirty."

"We could have killed them without breaking a sweat and no one would have ever found their bodies. That's beside the point. Turning them over to the police was the right thing to do."

"Just the sort of pudding-brained thinking I'd expect from a Hero." Thirteen snorted. "If someone is a threat to you, take them out before they take you out."

"Sometimes that's what needs to be done," I said. "Last night wasn't one of those times. By the way, what line of work would you say the Interceptor's previous owner was in? I can't believe armed cars were standard civilian issue."

Thirteen shrugged. "Not standard, no, but vehicular weaponry was legal if you had the proper permits and training. High-risk couriers, bonded bodyguards, and corporate security officers all used them. There's not much room for cargo and I didn't see any corporate logos, so I'd go with bodyguard or courier." He yawned and stretched before leaping off the counter.

That line of reasoning made sense. I added milk and chopped dill to the eggs, set them aside, and started shredding potatoes to make some hash browns. Thirteen found a sunny spot and curled up to watch the news.

The Change was still the big news of the day, of course. The anchor was saying, "Due to the lack of current identification with a valid photograph, most non-Humans are currently prohibited from boarding commercial flights and are being asked to cancel or postpone all other non-critical travel plans, even if driving."

The scene shifted to a local Atlanta reporter. "The Centers for Disease Control has issued a request that any Changed experiencing illness or disease report to specific regional hospitals for treatment, due to the complexity of creating disease management protocols for all the new races."

After that, the news cut to a reporter out at City Park. He said, "The entire park area, including the Denver Zoo and the Museum of Nature and Science, is surrounded by a giant wall of redwood trees. In addition, a dense thicket of thorn-laced brambles surrounds the area like a tangle of razor wire twenty feet tall."

"So far, eight such enclosed areas have been identified around the world. In desert regions, the barrier is a hurricane-strength sandstorm. Aircraft and satellite images show the areas covered by a mist or fog, and reports indicate this fog absorbs both radar and laser signals. Some people are able to approach these areas and the barriers will part for them, but no one else has succeeded in getting inside."

The picture changed to a video showing four or five families walking past a blockade and down a path through a patch of brambles. "Authorities in France tried to stop one such group, but both the soldiers' guns and the bodies of the people they were trying to stop became too hot to touch."

That bit made me laugh, and I had to wonder if a classic science fiction geek had suggested it.

A bust of profanity and vulgar personal comments interrupted the rest

of the story. I looked out of the kitchen as Ember raced down the stairs.
She tripped over herself trying to get around the coffee table and went flying headlong onto the couch.

After a moment of stunned silence, Ember pounded her fists into the
seat cushion and screamed, "Everything's gone...psychotic bitch...all
gone..." She rolled onto her side, sobbing into a throw pillow. Jewel, Ember's dragonette, settled on the cushion and nuzzled Ember's cheek, making soft chirping noises.

Harmony sat down on the end of the couch where she could stroke Ember's hair and said, "Our landlord called. The woman in the unit next to
us went crazy last night. Two of her children had become Elves, and she
snapped. The investigators think she killed all three in their sleep. She
went to the garage under the duplex, drained her car's gas tank onto the
floor, and set it on fire. The entire building went up. All the fire department could do was keep it from spreading."

"Blessed Mother..." I closed my eyes and took a deep breath. "I'm so
sorry."

"It's odd for a Dragon to say this, but it's just stuff." Harmony traced
her fingers along the dragon wings tattooed on Ember's back. "The cats
are safe at Kitty Spa, the snakes are at Morgana's, and I put everything of
value into dimensional storage before we left for Sylvan Faire. We will
recover."

"My photo albums. My mom's wooden chest. Harcourt. Those were
of value, too." Ember wiped her eyes. "The rest is just shit."

Harmony smiled and pulled a well-loved, antique Steiff tiger out of
Dragon Mini Storage. "I said, 'everything of value.' It's all safe."

"Harcourt!" Ember hugged and kissed the tiger, then threw herself into
Harmony's arms. I went back to the kitchen. They didn't need my help
for the rest of that discussion.

With the hash browns halfway crisp, I got the bacon and bangers going.
The smells brought people to the kitchen, so I poured the eggs into a skillet
and put the spurs to them. I finished plating just as the last guests took
their seats.

The head of Ember's tiger poked out of her shirt, and Jewel wrapped
around Ember's neck like a golden choker. Ember's eyes were still red
from crying, but she managed a smile and a whispered "Thanks" as our
friends expressed their sympathies.

Miriam looked calm and together this morning, wearing linen pants
and a V-necked knit top clearly designed for her new proportions. Geneva
set two thick phonebooks on a chair seat and Miriam vaulted up to sit on
them.

I stared at Miriam a few moments too long and she arched her eyebrow
at me. "Yes, David, I have cleavage. In fact, I had it before I changed."

"Yes, I'd noticed. I think this is the first time I've ever seen you use
mascara."

Miriam blushed. "Geneva insisted. After we talked last night, I wound up having a phone interview. I need to get my resume updated, because the in-person interview is in Vancouver on Wednesday."

Nadia lowered her fork. "You're interviewing for a position in Gilead?"

"I really can't discuss the details," Miriam said, but she looked flustered and a bit alarmed.

Nadia waved her hand to shoo away Miriam's concerns. "Don't be upset. I pretty much grew up in Gilead. That town needs a good counselor. About a third of the residents are Dark Elven war refugees from my parents' home world. Serious post-traumatic stress issues, all of them. Don't let Josephine lowball you."

"We've been over that part," Geneva said. Her eyes flashed red for a moment, but her voice stayed calm. "Josephine will make a fair offer."

Nadia grinned. "I'm sure she will, since she knows you are Miriam's sponsor." Nadia turned to me and asked, "Are there any rule or policy changes for our office, boss?"

"Yes. Please have Suzanne send out an all-hands email. All personnel should be at work Monday, and we're waiving the lost card fee this week for anyone needing a new ID. If anyone needs a new chair, keyboard, or other accommodation, those issues should go through their team lead. Same with anyone who needs time off to get a new driver's license. Just make sure we have coverage." I leaned back and stared at the ceiling for a moment.

"Ember, Harmony, you're both welcome to stay here. In fact, if I'm right, I may need you to house-sit for us while we're in India."

"You're only going to be gone a week," Harmony said. "Isn't house sitting a little drastic?"

"I'm not sure it's going to be just a week," I said. "Aparna's never met me, I know nothing about her, and I can't see popping in there and taking her away from her mother working out well. If this is going to work, we have to get to know each other. I was thinking we might need to look at a longer stay. I don't know how long."

Harmony shrugged. "I have no objection. I've wanted to look for a new place for a while, but moving a useful amount of wealth to this world is a pain in the ass."

Rose dropped to one knee next to Harmony's chair and bowed her head. "Honored Elder, all my resources are yours in your time of need. I pray you accept my meager assistance-"

Harmony waved at her. "Enough, youngling. Thank you. Your offer is generous, and I will consider it. For now, heed my command and don't address me in that manner again. Ever. Ember, as far as David's offer goes, I'll leave it to you"

"Have you seen the master shower? Hell yes!" Ember fed Jewel a bite of egg and scruffed the dragonette under the chin. "It's going to be a long drive to work, though...you know what? Screw it! My boss is a dick and he sells lousy coffee. Screw him, too. As soon as we finish eating, I'm calling in and telling him to shove it."

"Finally…" Harmony put her arm around Ember's shoulders. "I've told you before: you don't have to go out and work. I can take care of our needs."

Ember hugged Harmony back. "I know. We can have this argument again later, in private. Then we can make up a few times." She winked at me and said, "We accept."

"Thank you, I appreciate it. I'll get you both added to the neighborhood residents list first thing Monday. Maybe second thing. I have to find someone to replace the windows." I finished my coffee and added, "Nadia, you might have to run the shop for a while. I think I'm going to be stuck spending a lot of time talking to lawyers over the next few days."

And I was right. But first, I had to talk to Mom. She took the news pretty well.

Mom pushed her plate away and crossed her arms, scowling at me across the dinner table. "You didn't ask how your father and I felt when Sharon asked you to give her a child we would never see. You didn't ask how we felt when you turned the embryos over to Manya, and let our first grandchild be born on the other side of the planet. Why are you asking our opinions now?"

"I did ask how you felt about it. So did Sharon. What we didn't ask for was your approval. It was a done deal. However, we weren't leaving you out of the child's life. Just me. We just…we never…" I took several deep breaths. "Mom, Sharon and I both knew you would never accept Grace getting to be a grandmother when you couldn't. At the time, Sharon and Manya were planning to stay in Denver. You would have seen your grandchild regularly."

Mom sighed. "Son, I got used to not seeing my granddaughter. If she's in danger, do what you need to do. Grace and Vern be damned. I love Grace to death, but she's always seen Jesus as a white guy with a pickup truck and an AK-47. After Sharon came out, Grace got even worse. She's mellowed since they started going to this new church, but even so, there is no way I would ever accept that woman raising my grandchild."

"So, listen up!" Mom poked me hard in the chest. "I want you to stop being such a fair-minded gentleman, always thinking the best of people and giving everyone second chances. I want you to fight for your daughter's life. Hoist the god-damned black flag and begin slitting throats. Understood?"

I nodded. "Yes, mother." I didn't tell her that Rose had already given me the same pep talk.

After my lunch with Mom, I headed back home and spent the rest of Sunday talking to Alice Hannigan, the family and reproductive rights lawyer Sharon and I worked with for the *in vitro* procedure. I don't know what it is with lawyers, but they seem to like saying, 'I told you so.'

"This is going to be a pain to unwind, David. Situations such as this are why I advised you to hire a gestational surrogate and bring the child to term yourself. At least the paperwork and genetic results from the lab are enough to establish you irrefutably as Aparna's father. The tricky part will be getting the Indian court to take a child away from an Indian mother who is *not* a gestational surrogate and give her to a non-resident American father who has never seen the child in person since her birth and who has no plans to move to India."

"Well, good thing I have a really good lawyer, right?"

She wasn't distracted. "Nice of you to say that. I do my best. Now, I need to know a few things. I need your responses to be truthful and complete, regardless of any embarrassment these questions might cause. First, did you and Sharon Datona ever engage in sexual intercourse?"

I had been expecting this line of questioning, but still didn't like it. "Yes. Several times."

Alice asked more upsetting questions over the next hour, covering our aborted love life, our relationship after Sharon met Manya, and Sharon's death. How she died. Who killed her.

What I was thinking when I killed him.

"Yes," I told her. "I intended to kill Randall. I got his confession recorded on my phone and then I deliberately flipped my Jeep in the middle of the highway. He wasn't wearing a seatbelt and was ejected during the crash."

Alice paused to scribble something on her notepad. She wasn't writing anything; it was her favorite stalling tactic. When she stopped scribbling, she asked, "Why didn't you turn Randall over to the police?"

"He had Rose at knifepoint and would have killed us if I didn't take him out first. But it was more than that. I wanted to kill him myself." I took a breath and tried to keep my voice steady. "I loved her. I'd loved her for years, since we were kids. Randall murdered the mother of my children. Even if they're only frozen embryos, they are my children, and now they'll never know their mother. I can't give them their mother, but I can tell them I killed the man who took her away."

Alice called a break and said she'd call back in an hour. I didn't argue. I poured a glass of Glenlivet and joined the cat watching America's Next Ninja Princess. By long-standing agreement, we didn't discuss the show. I cheered when the competitors cleared an obstacle; the cat cheered when someone slipped and went crashing into the water.

Frakking cat.

I finished my drink and decided I should switch to iced tea. I got up and asked Thirteen, "Want anything from the kitchen?"

"Coffee, please. Two sugars." He jumped onto the side table and set out coasters for both of us.

"Very considerate," I said, when I returned with his coffee and my mint tea. "I have a few friends I still can't train to do that trick."

"Give me some dried salmon and a ten-foot cattle prod. I'll fix them up for you." Thirteen took a sip and made a sound like chains dragging over corrugated steel. He was purring. He took another drink and asked, "Mind if I ask a personal question?"

A policewoman from Tacoma leaped off a swinging telephone pole half a second too late and missed her landing net. She slammed into the padded wall framing the landing zone and careened into the water under the obstacle. I winced in sympathy for her and said, "You can ask."

The cat actually looked uncomfortable. "I know things are different here, but back home, in the old days...it was just the Republic and India as the only two superpowers. We weren't friends. I'm trying to accept your outlook on things but...Mother Bastet, how could you hand your own flesh and blood over to a curry-eater?"

I scowled at him. "I don't like the sound of that term. It's obviously intended to be disparaging, so please don't use it. I don't care if you're prejudiced, as long as it's in the privacy of your own mind."

Thirteen snorted. "Easy for you to say. They didn't eat your cousin with a side of minty yogurt sauce. Why do you think they call it 'Persian rice'?"

I shook my head. "Look, I admit I don't know what India was like on your world, but here, most Hindus tend to be vegetarians..."

"Good grief! Can't you recognize a joke when you hear one?" He lashed his tail and looked away.

I said, "As a matter of fact, I can. It's just that I'm trying to get along with Manya, and, frankly, at this point, my daughter is Indian by culture if not by ethnicity. You're hitting a little close to home."

"Do you honestly think I'd be cracking jokes if one of them *had* eaten my cousin?" Thirteen shook his head. "I'm sorry I offended you. That wasn't my intent. I thought I was sharing a joke with a friend."

Damn cat sure knows how to lay down the guilt trip... I sighed and held my hand out. "I'll make you a deal. Stop saying racist crap and I'll answer your question."

"I'm doing my best," he growled. "I've never eaten Indian food before, but I ate it last night. It was pretty tasty. I'd even be willing to eat some of it again. That's a big step for me. You should be happy."

"You should be nice. I have a motorized water pistol, and I'm not afraid to use it."

"And I can crap in your hot tub, but what would that accomplish?" Thirteen sat through three more contestants falling into the water before he spoke again. "I apologize. I will...mind my language. I'm just curious why you didn't get someone more...local...to carry your child?"

"Because I didn't do this for me. I did this because Sharon asked me to help her get pregnant. It's the one thing Manya couldn't give her. As for giving away my flesh and blood, Sharon's original plan was that I wouldn't have a place in our child's life. Manya and I stuck with that because, if

Sharon had died after Aparna was born, the situation would be the same. Manya would have adopted her at birth and would have custody of her anyway."

Thirteen made a *hrrumph* noise, but nodded. "I suppose, if you put it that way, I see the logic of it. I trust you made sure she had the means to raise a child?"

That made me laugh. "Manya's family is wealthy beyond the dreams of avarice, and at the time, the pittance I was making as a database administrator wouldn't have dented Aparna's clothing and toy budget. She has servants, cooks, housekeepers, drivers, and a kitchen staff to do the grocery shopping. If she wanted to find a cobra in the bathroom one morning, the poor thing would be brought in on a satin pillow."

Conversation stopped as a tiny young woman with yellow and orange striped hair stepped up to the starting line. The announcer said she was four foot ten, weighed one hundred pounds even and worked as an aerobics instructor. She took off as though shot out of a cannon, bouncing back and forth between footholds, leaping up to grab an inch-wide ledge with her fingertips, and shimmying along it like a neon squirrel. She kept the pace up across the spinning balance beam and up the thirty-foot rope to the finish line, ending her run half a minute ahead of the next closest finisher.

We both applauded her run. Thirteen said, "That was art. Poetry. I can't understand why your world stopped holding the Olympian Games in the nude."

I snorted. "Aren't nude gymnastics a little wild and crazy for the Republic?"

"You'd be wrong. We were the heirs of Rome and Sparta. We had women in combat two thousand years ago and still executed criminals by crucifixion. We were tough enough to handle a few exposed genitals every four years."

"Were the winter games held in the nude too?"

"We didn't do winter games. Skiing and ice skating are entertainment, not athletics." He coughed and added, "Look, I can't promise I can overcome a lifetime of mistrust. I was a soldier, and India was the enemy. But I owe you, so I'll treat it like the Olympian Truce. No fighting, no disrespect, no intentional insults. Will that work for you?"

I nodded. "I think it will." I reached out and touched palms with him. As I did, I realized he hadn't quite been honest with me. I waited until the next commercial break and asked, "So tell me: how well do you speak Hindustani?"

Thirteen didn't look at me, flinch, or bat an eyelid. "I don't."

"Bullshit." I chuckled at him. "I just figured you out. Your hands should have given it away. The process took months, you said. No government spends that kind of time and expense on a single soldier. Armies produce soldiers by the thousands. Your unit photos were of individuals,

56

all of whom had unique enhancements. You and your friends were spies."

He still didn't move. "I never liked that term."

"Intelligence operative. Whatever. Your job was to be sneaky and learn things."

"*Semper Vigilo*," he said. "'Always Watching.' And we were. The Sapient Nonhuman Espionage Division. 'For all have SiNED and are reborn to glorious purpose'."

"I'm sure your countrymen would have been thankful to you and the others for your service," I said. "Regardless, you weren't a common foot soldier. You were an operative. And you are damn well fluent in Hindustani."

One ear flicked. "No, I'm not. 'Hindustani' isn't actually a single language. It's more of a regional spectrum of language dialects. That detail aside, I speak Hindi, Urdu, Marathi, Bengali, and Tamil. Now, why are you asking?"

I smiled. "Because I'm calling in that favor you owe me."

The cat sighed. "Oh, balls..."

Chapter Eight

Trust, but Verify

"Tell the court, sir, if the child was so important to you, why have you not visited before now? Why this sudden interest?"

I smiled at the camera and pretended the question didn't bother me. "I have visited before, in point of fact. Rose and I were present for Aparna's birth. Nor is my interest sudden. I've always thought of Aparna as my daughter, but it was Sharon Datona's desire that I have no active role in her life.   Until now, I have respected her wishes.   However, these...changes...that we've all experienced pose a potential threat to Aparna's safety. Her mother and I agree that this is the best course of action."

I waited while my translator relayed my response. I would have preferred to have Thirteen translate, but getting the court to accept a talking cat seemed unlikely at best. Instead, I waited and made a note to myself about learning how to say, 'My hovercraft is full of eels' in Hindi.

Manya's lawyer started to ask another question, but the judge told him to wait. The judge made several notes and asked, "I have a doubt, Mr. Fraser. Tell the court, is it your intention to take the child Aparna to America with you at any foreseeable future time?"

"Yes, Your Honor. My parents would like to meet her and get to know her. I have not had a chance to speak with Sharon's parents, but our families have been friends since before Sharon or I were born, and I would be willing to give them a chance to meet their granddaughter."

"You would, eh?" The judge tapped a sheaf of papers and held it up for the camera to see. "Are you aware Vernon and Grace Datona have filed a petition to have your claim rejected? The only parent they wish the child to have is their daughter."

I said, "Sharon is deceased, Your Honor. I am the only living biological parent. If the Datonas have a valid claim because Sharon is Aparna's biological mother, my claim is also valid, and my status as her father trumps theirs."

"You are understanding, sir, the girl Aparna is not human?" More tapping of papers on the desk. "You accept this?"

"I think a lot of people in Boulder are going to be envious when they see her soaring off Flagstaff Mountain without a hang glider." I smiled and chuckled. "I think Aparna's change is a wonderful one, and I can't wait to see what happens with her."

The judge nodded. "Very well." He waved at Manya's lawyer and said, "Proceed."

"Thank you, Your Honor. Mr. Fraser, in your opinion, is Manya Patel unfit?"

"No."

"Are you aware that the child Aparna cannot legally hold dual citizen-ship?"

I shook my head. "I know India doesn't recognize dual citizenship. I have already discussed Aparna's status with the US State Department and, assuming the court grants my petition, I will be asserting Aparna's Amer-ican citizenship, if for no other reason than her own safety."

"Mr. Fraser, why bring up the child's safety?"

I sighed and glanced to the side for a moment. "I trust Manya, or I wouldn't have agreed to her carrying my child. However, as the court noted, she is no longer Human. Some people fear these changes, and the Changed. I fear someone might harm Manya, or Aparna, for what they have become. Until Indian law fully protects the Changed and the people of India accept them, I believe it is in Aparna's best interests to have a recognized, Human parent."

"Nothing further, Your Honor."

The judge declared a ten-minute recess. I made a bathroom run and fixed coffee while my lawyer talked to Manya's lawyer about the next phase of the hearing.

The attorney representing Sharon's parents was another old friend from Oklahoma, Paige Novella. Her parents thought her name was a real knee-slapper, so they named her younger brother Christian. There had been only one decent movie theater in the area back when we were grow-ing up, so Sharon and I had seen Paige and Christian at least once a week, often more. We didn't get along back then; Christian had a hard time read-ing comic books and Paige had delusions of Antebellum charm and class. None of that had changed since the last time we met.

According to my mother's gossip grapevine, there was a rumor Paige had been involved with a fellow attorney named Rudy Turner, until he'd decided to propose. I guess going through life as 'Paige Turner' must have been a deal-breaker.

When we reconvened, Paige introduced herself and said, "Your Honor, I must disclose on the record that Mr. Fraser and I are childhood friends. I also knew the deceased, Sharon Datona, while growing up. My clients retained me due to those relationships and are comfortable I can advocate for them without conflict. Mr. Fraser and Ms. Patel have already agreed to my services."

The judge nodded. "So noted for the record. Proceed."

Paige smiled. "Mr. Fraser...David...is it true, yes or no, that you were a suspect in the death of Randall Marbuck?"

You bitch... I smiled and said, "No, that is not true."

"Really?" Paige waved a stack of papers at the camera in her office. "I would like to enter the contents of file attachment one into evidence, Your Honor. This is the police report on Randall Marbuck's death—"

I leaned into the camera. "Randall *murdered* Sharon! He hid in my car, held a knife to Rose's throat, and threatened to kill both of us. I recorded his confession and then rolled my car. Randall wasn't wearing a seat belt. He was ejected and crushed. My *only* regret is that I didn't get to rip that degenerate bastard's cock off and *feed it to him!*"

I was up and out of my chair, fists clenched and heart pounding. The judge was shouting for calm, and Paige's mouth was flapping open and closed like a beached catfish.

I sat down again and said, "Your Honor, I apologize, but I brought Sharon's murderer to justice. For her parents to insinuate that somehow makes me unfit is an outrage. It's an insult to Sharon's memory. However, for our daughter's sake, if the court wishes, I will keep answering."

"Only a moment, please." The judge pulled up the police report and scrolled through it. While he did, I glanced at Rose and nodded. Rose wrapped a dark blue scarf around her hair and darkened her skin before scooping up the cat. Thirteen gripped her hands in his paws and they both vanished.

The judge closed the lid of his laptop. "I do not believe this line of questioning is pertinent. Move along, counsel."

Paige's accent slid a hundred miles further south as she batted her eyes at the judge. "Yoah Honah, we believe Mr. Frazhahh's run-ins with the laaaw are cause for concern..."

Thirteen erupted out from under one of the spectator's benches and raced across the lawyers' desks, knocking laptops, microphones, and stacks of files to the floor. He leaped onto the judge's side table, kicked over a carafe of chai, and scattered all the file folders onto the floor before racing back to the spectator's seating. In the midst of the commotion, I heard a quiet, intense burst of hissing and growling in the background audio. Rose was taking out a little insurance policy, by commanding the judge to approve the petition to reinstate my status.

The shouting and commotion filled the audio feed for several seconds, continuing even after Rose and Thirteen reappeared next to my couch.

Rose lurched to the side and vomited into a trashcan. "Never...again..." she coughed. "I'll fly coach before I let that cat take me anywhere again!" She staggered off to wash up and change clothes while I took care of the messy stuff. Meanwhile, the judge ordered a half-hour recess to allow the computerwallahs to get everything working again.

60

Once the trashcan was clean, I washed up myself and checked on Rose. She was sitting on our bed, brushing her hair while watching her financial news channel. I sat on the bed and asked, "How are you doing?"

"I'm fine. I think the problem was shifting twice so close together. I didn't feel sick until we got back here." She squeezed my hand for a moment. "Please tell Thirteen I'm sorry for yelling at him."

"I'll let him know." Lingering with a naked Rose sounded like a great idea, but the recess wouldn't last forever. I got up before my resolve gave out and went back to the living room.

The feed from the courtroom camera was back, but we were still recessed. Thirteen was sitting on the table, reading the file he'd snagged from Manya's lawyer.

I unplugged the system microphone, just to be safe. "Rose says she's sorry for yelling at you. The return trip was rougher than she expected, apparently. Find anything interesting in there?"

"Apology not needed, but still welcome." Thirteen set one bundle of pages aside. "And yes, some interesting stuff. Her lawyers drew up contingency plans in case you ask for full custody, try to remove the girl from the country, take refuge in the American Embassy, or kidnap Aparna and flee somewhere within India. They consider asking for full custody the most likely."

"What's the plan?"

The cat flipped through several pages and pointed at one section. "Manya's final offer is to ask for one month-long visitation per year, with her coming to your home, input into lifestyle decisions and religious upbringing, neither party to pay child support, stipulation to a mutual agreement that neither of your spouses will attempt to adopt Aparna, and you and Manya are both listed as Aparna's parents on the amended birth certificate."

I whistled. "That's interesting. What are they afraid of?"

"Mmm...You're married now, and Manya has no official standing as a person. If you claim she was just a gestational surrogate and that Rose intends to adopt Aparna due to being unable to have children, they think you'll probably win full custody with no visitation."

I sat back to ponder the information. "Thank you, I appreciate it. Let me know if you see anything else." I turned back to the computer, but Thirteen held up one paw.

"David, your friend, Manya...her emails make it clear she's rejecting a number of negative attacks on you. Nude pictures of Rose. Former neighbors accusing you and Rose of molesting children. A complaint you drove a former employee to kill himself by jumping off the roof of a casino. She's being a decent person."

I smiled. "Thank you. I want to be one as well." I turned the microphone back on and waited for the court to resume.

The judge started by addressing Paige. "Counsel, you are not to bring up any allegations of wrongdoing against Mr. Fraser, unless he has been tried and convicted of an actual crime. It is not allowed. With that in mind, do you have any items of merit on which to proceed?"

Paige turned dark red. "I do not."

"Then your client's petition is dismissed without prejudice. If you find items with merit, you may refile."

"Yes, Your Honor." Paige pasted on a smile and added, "Well, bless your heart, David. It's just your lucky day, I guess."

"It was wonderful to see you again, Paige." I glanced at her perfectly styled blond hair and said, "After so many years It's nice to see you've stayed true to your...roots."

She smiled wider and her voice just dripped sugar sweetness. "Well, you take care now, David. Words can't express how special it was to see you again."

That, by the way, was how you say 'Screw you and the horse you rode in on' in Southern polite society. Sweet tea with just a touch of hemlock.

After a hurried consultation, Manya's lawyer rose and said, "Your Honor, if there is no contest, the petitioner requests summary judgment in our favor..."

"Very well," the judge said. "Petition of plaintiff is granted. David Fraser is recognized as the father of Aparna Datona-Patel and is awarded custody. Mr. Fraser, do you wish Sharon Datona to replace Manya Patel as the child's mother?"

Even under her fur, Manya looked stricken and pale, hands shaking and clasped in front of her.

I shook my head and replied, "No, Your Honor. Sharon would haunt the crap out of me if I did that. Please continue listing Manya Patel as Aparna's mother. Nor am I asking for Aparna's name to be changed."

The judge nodded. "Very well. Will you be coming to India to collect the child?"

I looked at Manya in the monitor and almost changed my mind. Almost. "Yes, Your Honor. My wife and I already had a trip to India planned in the next few weeks, and I want to bring Aparna home with me as soon as possible. Manya's comments about the uncertainty of her status and the risks to her personal safety convinced me that would be in Aparna's best interests."

The judge said, "The court agrees," and Manya rushed out of the room.

Much discussion later, we all agreed Aparna should have a chance to get to know her new family members in a known and comfortable environment. Therefore, Grace and Vernon would be coming to India as well. Manya and Doreen even invited them to the wedding since Aparna would be having a prominent role in the ceremony.

That gave us several weeks between the wedding and Aparna's birthday for her to get to know us. Manya's parents, Rajesh and Ananya, offered to let all of us stay with them instead of at a hotel. Grace and Vernon would take Aparna first. When their two weeks with her in Oklahoma were up, I would fly out to Tulsa and bring her back to Boulder. After that, Aparna would live with us full-time.

At 11:20, the judge ended all discussion and read off his rulings on the various issues and petitions, including several we hadn't gotten to yet. Most of the rulings came down to "the discretion of the father." In other words, my decision.

I couldn't figure out what the rush was until I remembered the time zone difference. Mumbai was twelve and a half hours ahead, not twelve even. It was almost noon there, and the judge was hungry.

Lunch alone triumphs.

Manya called soon after court recessed. "David, can we discuss joint custody? Please, just tell me what I must do."

I said, "You said Doreen wants the two of you to move to California. So do your parents, because of their investments. California and Denver are close enough for joint custody to work. Remember, we're doing this for Aparna's well-being. If you won't move for your parents, or for Doreen, do it for Aparna."

"I can pay to fly her back-"

"No. You said she could be in danger in India. You said you don't have rights as a person or as her parent. None of that has changed in the last five minutes. You can come to Boulder and have visitation, or you can move to America and we can talk about joint custody."

Manya muffled her phone, but I could still hear her sobbing. When she came back, she asked, "Is there no other way? I can't come back. It's...too painful. What if I moved to England? I know people in London..."

I closed my eyes, clenching my fist. "We already went through this. With our lawyers, I might add. It's decided." I took a deep breath. "I'm not going to keep you from seeing her or try to get Aparna to forget you. But you asked me to protect her, and I'm going to."

Manya was silent for a time. "I know," she whispered. "But I had to ask. I just...I don't want to accept the answer. I'll...I'll get there, don't worry."

"I know. I can't imagine how much it hurts right now, and I'm sorry I have to do this to you."

"I know. It's the right thing, but I...never mind. Goodnight, David."

When I hung up the phone, Rose took my hand and hauled me out to the hot tub. We cuddled in silence a while, until I whispered, "Thank you for making sure the judge ruled for us. I don't know how this is going to play out, but this was the key to everything else."

Rose nuzzled my shoulder and let her long, forked tongue trace over the skin of my neck and down the middle of my chest. "I've always known how you felt about Sharon, and I couldn't help but like her myself. Of course I'm going to do what I can to help." She sat up and wagged her finger at me. "We have a lot to do before we leave for India. To begin with, we have to go get that car taken care of as soon as that office opens. I don't like being pulled over. You just tell me what needs to happen and I'll make sure the person we talk to takes care of it."

"I doubt it will come to that," I said. "I'm just going to say it's a home-made prototype that's ready for street testing. It obviously doesn't look like any other car on the road, so why would they argue?"

Rose leaned back up against me. "Just let me do it. Trust me, the best way to deal with any government agency is to mind control everyone until you get what you want."

"I'll try to keep that in mind." I kissed her and let my hands roam a little. "Still, how hard could it be?"

Chapter Nine

The Dragon is Always Right

The woman behind the counter at the Boulder County Department of Motor Vehicles raised her eyebrows at me and leaned back, putting a little extra distance between us. "So, you didn't actually buy this car from anyone, it's not a kit car, and it's not put together from several different salvage vehicles. You, yourself, built the entire vehicle, from scratch. Is that correct?"

I nodded. The nameplate on the front of the counter said her name was Chokka; I made a note in case I needed it later. "That's correct," I said. "Henry Ford and Enzo Ferrari did it. Why shouldn't I?"

"I'm not making any comments about your abilities, sir." Chokka tapped on her keyboard and frowned. "Mr. Fraser, the fact you built the car doesn't eliminate the taxes and registration you owe. Now, was the chassis obtained from an automotive manufacturer?"

"No. I created it with a rapid prototyping printer."

"That's one of those 3-D printer things?" Her eyebrows went up. "And it can just...make...a steel car chassis?"

"The details are proprietary." I pasted a smile on and asked, "Is there some issue I need to know about?"

"Well, the first issue is that your car has to be assigned a Vehicle Identification Number. You're going to need to fill out a request form and provide a written account of how you came to possess the car and submit it to the Department of Motor Vehicles, along with receipts for all your parts and materials and your records of the assembly process in order to document the source of the parts you used and your ownership of them. I can give you the exact statute number for reference if you'd like."

"Sure, why not..." I took the forms Chokka passed me and tried not to look alarmed. "I think I can provide all that. Is there anything else?"

"Yes. All assertions you make in this process are done under penalty of perjury." She leaned forward and beckoned me to lean in as well. "I think you should know, sir: an investigation doesn't have to prove where you actually got the car; they just have to prove you lied about it."

I sat back and sighed. "Point taken. Okay, all of that about building the car was a bunch of BS. The truth is, this cat I know lives on a parallel version of Earth. He took me there so I could help him run an errand. I found the car on his world. There's no bill of sale because the previous owner died in a nuclear war a hundred years before I found the car."

Chokka shook her head. "So, it's an abandoned vehicle? Well, okay sir. That's fine. You can put that story down if you want, but it won't reduce the fees you'll owe. It will also need to pass an emissions test. If it doesn't pass, we will not issue a registration."

"No worries there," I said. "It's an electric vehicle."

"Well, then, you need to get the car certified as exempt. Be sure to put that down." Chokka smiled and asked, "So, are you trying to start a new car company or something?"

I waved that idea away. "Oh, no. I might license it to someone, but I'm not running a company like that." I stood up and asked, "Any idea on how long all this normally takes?"

"I couldn't tell you. This will involve title and lien searches, stolen vehicle queries...who knows what. It could take some time. Obviously, the more documentation you provide, the faster you'll get through this."

Thirteen hopped up on the counter, snickering. "If that's the case, you are screwed." He was still laughing as I picked him up and waved goodbye to a wide-eyed and staring Chokka.

Rose was sitting in front of the corner coffee shop reading the morning Wall Street Journal. She shook her head without looking up at me. "I told you to let me take care of it."

"It's not that bad," I said. "I just need to find receipts for every component of the car and photographs of me building it. Or I can tell them I got it from my good friend the talking cat. At least I can produce him when they ask for proof."

"I doubt you can make me talk, however." Thirteen shook himself and sniffed the air. "I'm going to get some coffee. You want anything?"

"Chai latte, please. Need a hand with it?"

"No, I'll be fine." He slipped into the coffee shop as someone was leaving and leaped up on the counter. Nobody seemed the slightest bit surprised by a talking cat ordering coffee. Thirteen paid with bills taken from a pocket inside his drover's hat and sat there chatting with the barista while she fixed our drinks. I expected the cat to teleport back to the table with the drink carrier, but instead the barista held the door open for him and delivered everything to our table.

"I love the way the world is now," the barista gushed. "My boyfriend's mom in India sent us pictures she took of flying tigers—flying tigers! How cool is that? Just working here I've met Elves and Dwarves, and this smokin' hot sex-demon chic, and now a talking cat! This is so awesome!"

"A sex demon? That's a new one." Rose grinned and asked, "Seen any Dragons yet?"

"Yes! The first day of the Change." The barista pointed to a table inside the shop. "This woman came in, had a hot chocolate, and then dumped a mess of cash out of her purse onto the table. Then she walked over to the pot store. I was stuffing her cash back into the purse when I saw her walk into the middle of the street, bare-ass naked! And then..." She paused, shaking her head and trying to find the right words.

I said, "Let me guess—*fwoop*, she turned into a red and gold Dragon, roared, took off, and vanished in midair?"

"Yes! Did you see it? Wasn't that amazing?" She stared up into the sky, eyes slightly glazed and hands shaking.

"No, I just heard about it." I took Rose's hand and gave it a squeeze. "But, as a friend of mine once said, this sky wants Dragons."

The barista nodded. "Oh, yeah. Dragons rule. And she was really cool. Let me get a selfie with her and everything. I just wish one would track down whoever murdered that girl in Cheesman Park. I know it's not a very karmic thing to say, but I have no problem with someone like that becoming Dragon chow."

"Sorry," Rose said. "Dragons don't eat junk food. What about roasting the murderer into charcoal?"

"I'd go for that, sister. Well, I have to go back to work. Just wave at me if you need anything. See you, kitty." She scruffed Thirteen behind the ears and went back inside the café.

"A murder in Cheesman Park? When did that happen?" I'd been too busy the past few days to pay attention to anything not Aparna-related.

"Late Sunday night," Thirteen said. "No official details yet, which makes me think the circumstances are on the horrific side." He scratched behind his ear and asked, "Are you suggesting we investigate?"

"Not a chance," Rose said. "We leave for India in a week and you have to prepare to become the father of a child who doesn't know you. Leave it to the police. That's their job. Besides, the last thing you need right now is any kind of legal trouble. Do you want me to have to call Aparna and tell her Daddy can't come to India or his bond will get revoked?"

I nodded. "You're right." I looked through the sheaf of papers Chokka had given me and gave up. "I have a scathingly brilliant idea. Let's do it your way."

"I have a scathingly brilliant idea of my own," Rose said. "You need to learn Hindi and you have a week to do it in. So, you and the cat come home with me. The time distortion will give us six months on the other side. Plenty of time for us to give you an immersion course."

The idea appealed to me. "Manya's been teaching Aparna English, but being able to speak Hindi would mean a lot." I nodded to Rose and said, "Let's do it. How long will it take to get the car registered?"

"Not long at all," Rose told me. "By the way, this time I'm doing the packing. You suck at it."

She was right, of course.

Chapter Ten

Mumbai

The first rule of travel in India may be 'there's always room for more,' but 'don't fly in during monsoon season' should run a close second. Our nice, heavy, American-built and British-operated 777 was shaking like a belly dancer's hips as we emerged from the clouds and turned onto the vector for final approach to Chhatrapati Shivaji International Airport.

Being a creature naturally able to fly under her own power makes Rose a terrible airline passenger. She can see rising and falling columns of air, pressure gradients, wind currents, and a bunch of other weather conditions. She kept up a steady stream of non-step muttering about everything the pilots were doing wrong. At least she was doing it in Draconic; the rest of First Class was just annoyed instead of freaked out.

As we dropped lower, the wind evened out and the plane stopped shaking and lurching as much as it had been. Outside the window, tight, uniform rows of cookie-cutter apartment buildings raced by, interspersed with the teeming, organic chaos of slum neighborhoods. A few of the apartments showed signs of damage; by comparison, whole swaths of the slums lay in smoking ruin, charred to the ground. I caught a few lightning-fast glimpses of people sifting through the wreckage, and we were down. The local time was 12:40 in the afternoon, with temperature and humidity both in the low nineties, heading for one hundred.

The new international terminal had been under construction the last time we were in India. The old Sahar terminal was a claustrophobic gerbil run of endless queues in nightmarish heat, accented by a distinct lack of bathrooms. T2 was a freaking museum with glass-walled jetways, gorgeous artwork, marble surfaces, and soaring columns supporting a vaulted ceiling patterned after a peacock's feathers. Once off the plane, it was more or less a straight shot through the terminal to the outside world – no more leaving a trail of breadcrumbs or marking up the walls with chalk to help you find your way around.

That's not to say we didn't have bureaucracy to deal with. Paperwork alone triumphs. However, even those obstacles weren't bad. The flight crew had passed out the forms we needed before landing, and getting through immigration took about five minutes. Being in First Class, we had the advantage of deplaning ahead of everyone else, but even so, I'd half-expected to need either bribery or mind control to get through that fast. Or maybe we picked a guy who was just phoning it in, who knows.

All the carousels in baggage claim were going full-tilt, surrounded by hundreds of our fellow travelers. We didn't stop. Instead, we pushed through the chaos and went right on to the customs station for foreign nationals. Each of us had an overnight bag, but nothing else. My clothes were all in Rose's dimensional storage closet, and Rose hadn't brought any clothes at all beyond what she was wearing.

What she did have was a stack of pre-paid credit cards, each one having a five *lakh* balance—that is, half a million rupees, or eighty thousand American dollars. Why bring a packed suitcase when it's easier to buy what you need when you get where you're going? Yes, new outfits would mark her as a tourist, but she's six foot one with metallic purple hair. You could dress her out of your most *desi* maiden auntie's closet and she'd still look American.

Several of our fellow international travelers just waved their passports at the customs agents, who passed them through without running their bags through the x-ray machine. And yet, we got stopped by the one guy there who didn't get the logic of traveling light. To him, not having luggage was suspicious. I would have loved to point out that we'd gotten off the plane instead of hijacking it, but I made my Wisdom check and kept my mouth shut.

After a dozen variations on "Only these are all your cases?" and much harrumphing, Rose ran out of patience. Her eyes flashed red as she growled an order at the customs officer. His expression went blank and he passed us through, muttering "Welcome to India."

Once free of further Imperial entanglements, we hit the prepaid taxi ticket counters and booked our ride. I'm not sure why, but the people who designed the T2 terminal seemed to have forgotten about air conditioning this area. Or maybe it was and India just overwhelmed the machinery every time the outside doors opened.

Stepping through the terminal doors and into the hot, soggy Mumbai air was everything a refreshing splash of ice-cold water isn't. The pickup zone held a throng of hire car and limo drivers, all holding up signs showing the names of the people they were picking up. Not that it mattered; none of them were looking for us.

On our first trip to Mumbai four years ago, it took us a week to learn how to behave in public. This time, we were ready. We waved off any touts offering discount taxi rides immediately, repeating *"Nahin, chalay jo!"* ("No, go away") like a mantra. An unsanctioned taxi (or a private car masquerading as a taxi) might have been less expensive per mile, but those scenic routes and extra fee scams got expensive fast.

The new terminal came with a new highway, the Sahar Elevated Access Road, which whisked us away from the airport and south into the city proper. Our driver's English was very good, so we had a lovely time talking about the Change, people's reaction to it, and how much our driver hated driving anyone who wanted to talk about cricket.

During a lull in the conversation, Rose leaned forward and looked at the decorations and family pictures adorning the dashboard. "There's a picture missing," she said. "Did one of your children change?"

He shook his head back and forth and said, "Yes. She is beautiful, something from a fairy tale. Three days after the changes, two men beat another driver because of his son's picture. I hid my daughter's picture and sent her to my brother in London."

"My daughter changed as well," I said. "So did her mother and I fear for them both. That's why we came."

"Do you believe...do you think what happened was the will of God?"

My chest tightened. I really didn't want to think about the information Nadia had relayed from Crom, especially if it was true. I leaned back in the seat and shrugged. "How could it be otherwise?"

At least that thought kept the driver occupied until we reached Manya's apartment in Lower Parel. Manya's last email warned us to expect 'some extra security' due to threats the family had received. I had assumed that meant an off-duty cop or two. I was wrong.

The taxi got a visual inspection by two armed guards and a German Shepherd before we could drive to the building entrance. A door attendant and three gorillas—not literal gorillas, just big guys in suits—met us there. Our driver put our luggage on a cart while the door attendant asked for our identification. Before dealing with him, I tipped our driver fifty dollars and said, "I will pray for your family's happiness and safety."

He nodded and clasped my hand. "Thank you. Blessings to your family as well." He drove off, and heavy steel gates closed behind him, sealing us off from the chaos and overcrowding of the streets.

The door attendant checked our passports, comparing our faces and arrival information to the details on the guest list. He called Manya to let her know we were here, and only after she talked to me to confirm my identity did he give us our guest key cards. They were good for the floor the Patels lived on, the parking garage, and the clubhouse. One of the gorillas rode up with us, ostensibly to make sure our cards worked.

Rajesh, Manya's father, met us at the elevator. "Welcome, welcome! So glad you could be here!" We embraced, and then he bowed to Rose. "I must speak with your husband for a moment. It is...a private matter. For men. Please..." He gestured her toward the apartment door where Ananya was waiting.

If he knew what I was, his cock would wither and drop off, Rose thought to me. Outwardly, she smiled and said, "Of course. I'll wait for you inside." She joined Ananya and closed the apartment door behind

70

them. The gorilla stepped back into the elevator and went back down-stairs, leaving us alone in the foyer.

Rajesh clasped his hands together behind his back and said, "You have broken my daughter's heart. You are here to rip Aparna away from the only family she knows, and your presence casts a shadow of grief over my daughter's wedding with the anticipation of this separation. All this, you do to keep my beloved grandchild safe. I can welcome you for that, and forgive you for doing what must be done."

I looked down, shaking my head. "You would do anything for Manya. I would do anything for Aparna. I couldn't live with myself if Sharon's parents got custody and I could have stopped it but didn't. They are not evil people, but I've never liked them."

"Nor have we. We loved Sharon, but her parents..." Rajesh threw his hands in the air. "I have not forgotten how they treated Manya when Sharon died. They were vile to her, and now I must welcome them into my home! I must bow to those I would spit on. How can I do this?"

I said, "The same way I will: by knowing that, in the long run, it is for the greater good. Every day they spend in your home, they will know your family more and more. It's easy to wrong someone you don't know. You will have a month. Use it well."

"Yes, yes, most certainly. I will do what is needful." Rajesh leaned closer and whispered, "But what if they betray our trust and try to keep her?"

I'm not sure what I meant to say. Something reassuring, I suppose. Sharon's parents harming Aparna didn't seem likely, but the idea of them treating Aparna the way they'd treated Sharon filled me with sudden anger. My fingers clenched, remembering the weight of steel in my hand. I said, "I hope it never comes to that. But if it does, trust me, I will respond with Kindness."

Rajesh's brow furrowed and he shook his head, but his confusion was understandable; he's never met my sword. "Ah, well then...thank you for the reassurance. Shall we rejoin the ladies? Manya is in her apartment, consulting the wedding planner. She will join us when they are finished."

I looked around. Aside from the elevators and a maintenance closet marked 'Custodial,' the foyer only had two doors leading off of it, and one of those belonged to the Patels' apartment. "I thought Manya was living with you?"

"In a way," Rajesh replied. "We own one of the penthouse suites. Manya owns the other. This building went up six years ago, but when the notes came due after three years, only eleven of the one hundred twenty-eight units sold. The investors cut their losses, the building partnership collapsed, and our firm bought the controlling interest from the last lienholder for less than one hundred rupees *crore*."

I nodded, trying to do the math. "One billion rupees...twenty million dollars and something? Did I figure that right?"

"It is close enough. We do not need to operate it for profit, and the companies I do business with have been able to make residence here available to many of their senior executives as part of their compensation packages." Rajesh lowered his voice and put his finger across his lips. "In many cases, the executives have put their mistresses up here, instead of their families. I approve of this, because it means they will not risk forgetting to pay their rent." Rajesh chuckled as he opened the door and ushered me into their reception room, where Ananya and Rose were waiting.

It wasn't as nice as the 'Forest Lord' Legendary-level suite at the Trove in Las Vegas, but that was built by people who lost hundreds of thousands of dollars per hand. The Patels had to actively make money with their investments, which was a little harder. Still, they'd managed to do quite well for themselves. They had half of the two upper floors, giving them ten thousand square feet on each floor. They'd decorated with modern furniture that replicated the styles from the days of the British Raj, accented with classic Indian art and authentic Victorian antiques.

Just behind the decorations, though, lurked the latest consumer technology. Rajesh turned a candlestick sitting on a side table in the reception area, and the landscape painting over the mantle turned into a serious young woman spouting financial gibberish in an earnest and upbeat British accent as columns of letters and numbers raced by on either side of her face. The paint on the television's casing and trim exactly matched the color and grain of the antique frame around it.

Ananya ran her finger across a sepia-toned photo of old Bombay City and it changed to a familiar household management interface—they used the same system I had at home. Ananya tapped the floorplan and sent a page for the staff to report to the reception room. When she finished, the interface went back to looking like a Victorian photo. The way they had integrated technology into the décor gave the place a 'Steampunk Kipling' vibe. I liked it.

What I really didn't like was the servants assembling so we could be introduced. The Patels didn't have domestic employees; they had honest-to-Cthulhu *servants*. Most were from *dalit* families—what used to be called 'untouchables.' They smiled and bowed, but vanished as soon as they were dismissed.

Looking at them, I felt a harsh mental shearing, running from my left ear down my spine. I winced and muttered, "Sorry, cramp from sitting too long." I pretended to work it out while I tried to settle the actual issue, which was Rose and I having a mental and emotional conflict over the servants. The pain was the acceptance forcing us, none too gently, to a compromise. It only took a matter of seconds, but I was relieved when we reached a resolution. In this case, Rose allowed that having servants was an outmoded concept for modern Earth culture, while I allowed that I was being a cultural imperialist and judging rather than accepting and celebrating our differences.

Damn, being held to my own values sucks.

An hour or so later, Manya and Doreen came in. Manya looked amazing with her orange and black fur contrasting against the embroidered green *shalwar khameez* she was wearing. Doreen was wearing something dark blue, but I didn't pay attention to her. My attention focused on the little girl holding Manya's hand.

Aparna Hyzenthlay Datona-Patel, my daughter, might well have been the whitest child in all of Mumbai. She had Sharon's creamy Irish skin tone and blazing red hair; I couldn't see anything of myself in her face, but I saw Sharon and my mother both. She was wearing a green dress the same shade as Manya's; it took me a moment to realize both dresses were a match for Sharon's eyes. I also realized I adored this little girl more than I'd ever thought possible.

Aparna's wings finally registered. Manya's pictures hadn't done them justice; they towered a foot and a half over Aparna's head and spread out behind her like a cloak. The tips of her primary feathers would have drug along the ground, but she kept them canted at an angle to give them clearance.

I stood up and pressed my palms together, but I went blank for a few seconds. Rose gave me a mental nudge and I finally remembered to say, "Namaste."

Manya and Doreen replied in kind, but Aparna shook her head. Manya knelt next to her and, in English, said, "My jewel, this is David. Remember what I told you. Please use your good manners."

"No! You're the one who made Mommy-ji cry!" Aparna stomped and glared at me. "I have Mommy-ji, and Doree, and Angel Mommy! I don't need you. I hate you, now go away!"

She was speaking Hindi, but thanks to Rose and Thirteen, I understood her all too well. Less than a minute together and she'd already ripped my heart in half. I guess that proved how important she'd become to me.

Family alone triumphs.

Chapter Eleven

Never Work with Children or Animals

"Aparna! You do not mean that."

"Do too." Aparna hid her face in Manya's skirt and pointed at me. "Eat him, Mommy-ji!" Behind her, Doreen was struggling not to laugh.

I sat down on the floor and asked Rose, "Could you get the album out of my carry-on?" She nodded, and I looked back to my little girl. "Do you know who I am?"

She peered around Manya's thigh. "Go away."

Rose handed me the photo album I'd schlepped halfway around the planet. I patted the cover and asked, "Aparna, did your mommy tell you about her friend Sharon?"

She looked up for Manya's approval and said, "She's my Angel Mommy. She's dead."

"Yes, she is." I held up the photo album and opened the cover. "She and I were friends when we were children. My mother took these pictures as Sharon and I were growing up. I thought you might like to look through it. If you wanted, I could tell you about what was going on when the pictures were taken."

Aparna stepped back again, but she did ask, "Can I, Mommy-ji?"

Manya glanced at Doreen, got a nod from her, and nuzzled Aparna's ear. "I want to see them as well, my jewel. Can we look at them together? Maybe at the dinner table?"

"Yes!" Aparna took off running and sailed over the table to grab the chair with the best light. Manya and I sat on either side of her, going through some of my happiest childhood memories.

Swimming at Disney's lakeshore recreation area. Disney the town, I mean, not the Mouse Empire. Picking blackberries in a thicket big enough to hide a mobile home. The time a friend's father took a group of us to hunt arrowheads in a freshly plowed field. Supposedly, the field had been used as a campsite for the survivors of the Trail of Tears. Whatever the truth of that, each of us came home that day with at least a dozen arrowheads, hide scrapers, or spear points. I still had mine on display in my office.

While Aparna was engrossed in the pictures of Sharon as a teenager, Manya slipped away for several minutes, returning with a black and red DVD case. The sight brought me half out of my chair without my realizing it.

Well, if she can watch it, I can. I sat down and gave Manya a nod.

Manya stroked Aparna's hair and said, "My jewel, there is something I want you to see. Can you bring the book to the couch, please?"

Aparna nodded. "Yes, Mommy-ji!" She trotted across the room and plopped down on the couch, then ran back to get the photo album. "Did you buy a new movie for me?"

"No, my jewel. This is...older than you are."

"Seven years," I said.

Manya took a ragged breath. "Yes. Just so." She didn't move to open the video case; merely held it in a white-knuckled death grip.

I waited a moment, but she still didn't move. "Manya, do you want me-"

"No."

I nodded. "When you're ready, then."

Aparna leaned forward and poked at the DVD case. "Whats is, Mommy-ji?"

"It's Angel Mommy. The last picture I took of her, and..." Manya's voice broke. "And the only video of her."

"I wanna see."

"I know, my jewel." Manya wiped her eyes and gave Doreen's hand a quick squeeze. "It just makes me sad. I loved your Angel Mommy very much."

Aparna threw her arms around Manya's neck. "She knows you do. Can I see the picture?"

"What picture?" I aked. "I thought her last picture was the one from RenFaire.

"She wanted to show Grace how much weight she'd lost. I took this an hour before...we lost her." Manya opened the DVD case and handed the picture to Aparna.

Aparna looked the picture over. "Hm. That's how she always looks. But she has wings now." She handed me the picture and went back to looking at the album.

I raised my eyebrows at Manya; she shook her head and tapped her watch. *Later.* I nodded and turned the picture over.

Sharon was wearing ripped jeans and a white halter top, pulled up to show off her stomach. She had lost over a hundred pounds, and was a week away from her last physical before implanting our embryo.

It hurt seeing her so happy.

"Mommy-ji, can we watch the movie now?"

"Of course, my jewel." Manya loaded the disk into the DVD player and sat back down. "I was going to save this until you were older, but...maybe this is a good time."

"Can I press play?"

"Yes." Manya took Doreen's hand. "Go ahead."

The television lit up with the image of a woman in a scrub outfit and mask sitting next to a microscope. She waved a gloved hand at the camera and said, "Ready?"

"We are rolling," Manya's voice answered. "This is Dani, our wonderful embryologist, and today's the day we get to see the kids. Over to you, Dani!"

"Alright, then, up on this monitor, please." She flicked a switch on the microscope, and the monitor lit up, showing a cluster of little black dots on a grainy background. "All the embryos are at the blastocyst stage, of course, and these are the ones that made the 4AA rating. Congratulations, folks, you have fourteen embryos, all ready for vitrification."

Sharon leaned in, hair hidden under a surgical cap. "Can we get closer?"

Dani said, "Of course, just a moment."

While she worked on the microscope, my younger self said, "Manya, why don't you let me hold the camera? You two should get the first look." The screen went black for a moment, then returned showing Manya and Sharon holding hands and taking turns looking through the microscope. On the monitor, the image focused on a round, impossibly delicate cluster of cells.

Aparna jumped up and pressed her face to the television. "Is thats me?"

"I don't know," Manya said. "I like to think so."

"Me too," Aparna said. She waved and said, "Hi me!"

"Sit back down, my jewel. We can't see through you."

Back on the screen, Dani said, "I really hate doing this, but it's time for me to be incredibly insensitive and throw you out of the lab. So, if you want a last look, now's the time."

Sharon asked, "Can we watch the freezing?"

Dani shook her head. "No, I'm sorry. It's really, really delicate and, for the safety of your embryos, we have to minimize distractions."

"Well, fine, just pull out a reason I can't argue with." Sharon sighed. "It's just...nah, it's silly."

"What? Believe me, it's not silly."

"I...I wanted to sing them a lullaby before you dropped them in the liquid nitrogen."

Even through her mask, you could tell Dani was smiling. "You're not the first. Go ahead."

Sharon shook her head. "No, never mind. I'm too verklempt right now, anyway." She touched her fingers to her lips and caressed the image on the monitor. "Sweet dreams, little ones."

The picture went black. When it came back, a burly guy in a kilt was hoisting a twenty-foot section of tree trunk to his shoulder. As he stood for a moment, panting, Sharon leaned into frame, pointing over her shoulder. "For the record, this was just what I needed today. You know the best thing about the caber toss? If the wind comes up, he can't use his hands to hold the kilt down."

The man started trundling forward, steps coming faster and faster, until he roared like a bull and heaved the caber into the air. It struck well away from him and toppled forward to cheers from the crowd. The man bent over, hands on his knees as he gulped air, and just as Sharon had predicted, a gust of wind sent the back of his kilt flapping.

"Woohoo!" Sharon clapped and cheered, bouncing from foot to foot. She looked back at the camera and added, "Please tell me you got that!"

Manya's voice answered, "I did, I did. Didn't you promise me you were giving up guys, though?"

Sharon laughed. "I said I was giving up sleeping with anyone but you. I never said I was giving up leering and thinking naughty thoughts."

The video cut to a bull elk escorting his harem through an intersection in the middle of Estes Park, right in front of our car. Offscreen, Sharon said, "So much for the natural world being free from patriarchal oppression."

My younger self said, "No, no, you're missing everything." The image swung to show me driving, pointing out the windshield. "All of his ladies know about each other and are fine with the situation. They're poly."

Oblivious to our laughter, the last two does hopped up on the sidewalk and scampered after the bull. Sharon waved goodbye to them as the recording stopped.

"My other mommy was pretty," Aparna declared. "And she has my hair!"

"Yes, she did," Manya said. "Your eyes are the same color, too." She stroked Aparna's hair and whispered, "OK, let's watch. She's going to sing for us."

The picture focused on an old friend from my SCA days. Lady Vivien was tuning her harp while Sharon watched, wide-eyed.

"...sound is dulled if you use the pads of your fingers. You have to keep your nails just right to get the correct sound." She ran her fingers over the strings, and the harp rang out with clear, crystalline notes. "Nylon or gut is softer. They work better for some pieces, but wire strings have a precision not found with other materials."

"Wow..." Sharon nodded, but I could tell she was feeling overwhelmed. She glanced at one of the nylon-strung harps near her and asked, "Yours doesn't have the little...thingies...on the strings. What are they for?"

"The sharping levers?" Lady Vivien nodded and tucked her tuning key into a pocket on her harp bag. "They didn't come into use until the mid-

Eighteenth century, early Nineteenth. This is a replica of the O'Ffogerty harp. The original is from 1670, so the levers would be...inappropriate."

Elizabeth, Lady Vivien's wife, sat down next to her, brushing back a strand of silver hair. "Sharon, why don't you tell us what you want us to play? Otherwise this is going to turn into an Arts and Sciences collegium."

"Um, right, sorry. I've just never seen anything like this before. You know, Oklahoma and all that..." She took a deep breath. "I was thinking about a song my grandfather used to sing for me when I couldn't sleep. 'The Parting Glass.' Do you...know it?"

Several of the others in the room snickered, but Lady Vivien just nodded. "Yes. A lovely choice."

Elizabeth unrolled the bundle she was carrying, revealing a Native American-style flute adorned with an ebony crow. "Do you mind if I join in?"

"Not at all."

"Thank you." Elizabeth pointed to the patio doors. "Keep an eye out there. This morning two foxes were sitting on the deck watching while I practiced. I'm hoping they come back."

"That's all I need..." Sharon muttered. "A bigger audience." She pulled her hair back and nodded.

Elizabeth began first, setting a slow, plaintive tempo. Lady Vivien matched it, somehow making the harp sound like wind rustling through ancient trees. At her nod, Sharon took a deep breath and began.

> *Of all the money that e'er I had,*
> *I spent it in good company*
> *And all the harm that e'er I've done,*
> *Alas, it was to none but me.*
>
> *And all I've done for want of wit,*
> *To memory now I can't recall*
> *So fill to me the parting glass,*
> *Good night and joy be to you all*

One of the other musicians added a gentle tattoo on a bodhrán. Sharon's eyes lit up and her voice became stronger.

> *Oh, all the comrades that e'er I've had*
> *Are sorry for my going away*
> *And all the sweethearts that e'er I've had*
> *Would wish me one more day to stay*

The guy sitting next to the drummer came in with a set of uilleann pipes, shifting the tempo up. The lullaby became a celebration. Sharon rolled with it, changing to full-blown Catholic Choir Girl mode.

But since it fell into my lot
That I should rise and you should not
I'll gently rise and softly call
Good night and joy be to you all!

Fill to me the parting glass
And drink your health, what e'er befalls
I'll gently rise and softly call
Good night and joy be to you all!
Good night and joy be to you all!

In the hush that followed the music, we heard claws scrabbling on the wood of the deck. The camera swung around and focused on the bright-eyed, bushy-tailed spectators peering in at us. We watched each other in silence for a long moment, then the foxes bounded away into the night.

Sharon blew them a kiss. "Good night, and joy be to you all," she whispered.

The playback stopped, and the television screen went black.

Manya and I were both in tears. Aparna, however, was delighted. She went back to flipping through the photo album while we regained our composure. Once the snuffling stopped, I caught Manya's attention and whispered, "Now?"

Manya closed her eyes and nodded once, squeezing Doreen's hand.

I said, "Aparna, my mother made this album for you to keep. She wanted you to have these pictures of your mother, Sharon."

"Angel Mommy!" Aparna jumped up and down. "She's the one who gave me my wings. She told me they were just like hers."

"I...well, I'm sure they're the kind she would like." I took a moment to think about what to say next. "Aparna, you are very lucky little girl. Most kids only have one mommy and one daddy..."

"I'm going to have *three* mommies!" she crowed. "I get to carry Mommy-ji and Doree's rings."

I had to laugh. "Yes, Bugbear, you have three mommies. And a daddy. Me. I'm your father."

"Whats is bugbeers mean?"

I tousled her hair. "A bugbear is a magic creature that you remind me of."

Aparna turned to Manya. "Is he *really* my daddy?"

"Yes, my jewel. He is."

Aparna started tapping her fingers together, looking terribly serious and intense. When she looked up, she pointed at Rose and exclaimed, "Is the purple lady my mommy too?"

Manya stiffened a little. "I suppose...if she wants to be."

Rose smiled at Aparna and said, "I can't have children, but I can be another mommy for you if you really want me to be."

"Uh-huh." Aparna nodded and laughed. "*Four* mommies *and* a daddy! I'm gonna' get so many presents!" She jumped off her chair and grabbed Doreen's hand. "Come on, Doree, help with my wishes list!"

Doreen laughed and followed Aparna back to her playroom in Manya's apartment for an intense session of reviewing possible birthday loot.

Manya leaned forward, putting her elbows on her knees and burying her face in her hands.

"Well," I said. "It's a start. It's something we can build on."

Manya didn't look up. "David, I figured it out. Sharon's parents were the only others with that photo. I hate them right now! They're monsters! I want to rip their throats out with my teeth! Show them what a *real* tiger mother can do..."

"Let's call that 'Plan B'," I said. "Blessed Mother, you're a banker. I bet you don't even have a plan to get rid of the bodies."

Manya looked up at me, scowling. "And I suppose you do?"

"I wouldn't exactly call it a plan..."

"Don't look at me," Rose said. "I told you, I don't eat junk food."

Manya looked back and forth at both of us, then leaned back, shaking her head. "Rama preserve me," she muttered. "You're both mad."

"Fringe benefit of being Americans," I said.

Her voice dropped. "In point of fact, wiseass, I *do* have a plan to get rid of the bodies. It's just...not a good one. I kill them, call the police, claim self-defense, and hire a really good lawyer. I'll either be acquitted, or executed as a monster."

I clasped her hands between mine. "Manya, do not think like that. Focus on living and taking care of Aparna. Giving up and going out in a blaze of glory is easy, but you can't afford to do it. You need to live and fight battles you can't even dream of yet. Killing Sharon's parents won't bring her back, and you can't do Aparna any good if you're dead or in jail."

"You know what they said about me...what they said to Sharon! To her face! I want to kill them for that alone. How can I let them take her?" Manya's shoulders tensed and the claws tipping her fingers pressed against my palm, but she didn't draw blood. "What if they won't give her back?"

I said, "That's my problem now. But Aparna would be better protected if we both were in America and you had a high-paying job."

Manya's tail lashed from side to side and her ears flicked back. "Maybe you didn't get the memo," she growled, "but I'm a demon now! How can I run a company looking like this?"

"Stop snarling, for one." I got out my tablet, brought up the picture Lorena had sent out showing her new self, and handed it to Manya. "For another, accept that you aren't a special snowflake. She changed at least as much as you did, but business is business."

"Whuff." Manya shook her head. "Who is she?"

"My boss. Lorena Norris, V P of Property Development for Avalanche Games."

Manya's ears went up and her eyes widened. "*That* is Lorena Norris?" She closed the picture and looked at the email itself. "The address is the same, but..." Her voice trailed off and her eyes narrowed. "I suppose you're going to insist knowing her is just a coincidence? That she didn't send you to convince me to sweeten the deal?"

"What deal?" I shook my head. "Never mind. Doesn't matter. I don't know anything about any deal. I had no idea you knew Lorena or had been talking business. Someone forgot to send me that memo."

"That's my fault," Rose said. "I'm the yenta who introduced them to each other. I didn't tell you because Lorena asked me not to. You're not part of this project."

I nodded. "Not a problem. I know how she is."

"I still don't believe it," Manya growled.

Rose looked over the top of her paper. "He's telling you the truth, Manya. I also think you might want to have another look at whatever offer she's submitted. You'll find I was right."

"About what?" Manya asked.

"That she can't afford to build to spec. She needs existing buildings she can convert as she needs them. That shopping mall you're stuck with fits her needs better than either of you realize." Rose folded her paper in half. "I was also right that your usual contacts wouldn't be able to find another buyer who wants the mall structure itself, and you can't sell just the land without taking a loss. When you look at Lorena's offer, you need to think long-term. Think partnership. You can absorb the short-term loss, help Lorena make her little project work, and unlock some terrific profit potential."

"Bollocks..." Nevertheless, Manya's brow furrowed and she scratched out several notes. Eventually, she set the pen down and sighed. "It might work. I'd have to do more projections, but, frankly, I don't see the point. Honestly, who's going to do business with me? Your friend represents a gaming company. No one cares if she's odd-looking. The people I work with don't do business with demons that eat human flesh."

"Well, that's their own fault," Rose said. "They're losing a tremendous share of the market by being so picky."

I said, "All of this is a clever means of getting away from the more important issue. Manya, you need to move to California, and not just because it means getting to see Aparna. If being taken seriously is an issue, you obviously have no idea what 'rakshasa' means in America."

"A flesh-eating demon by any other name..." she muttered.

"That's what it means here," I said. "In America, most folks have never heard of rakshasas, and most of those who have learned it playing D&D. I'm sure you have plenty of business suits, right?"

"None," she snapped. "They don't fit any more. Besides, I have a tail now."

"Make a hole," said Rose. She waggled her index finger in the air and lengthened her nail into a talon. "I can do it if you want."

"You don't poke holes in a six thousand-dollar suit," Manya said. "Especially without a good reason. What would it accomplish?"

"Do you know what Americans say when they see a gorgeous tiger-woman in a six thousand-dollar designer suit?" I didn't wait for Manya to answer. "They say, 'Damn, that tiger must be loaded'."

"Money doesn't solve every problem, David." Manya tapped herself on the chest. "Money can't make me the person I was."

"No, but it can make being the person you are now a lot easier." I stood up. "Let's go shopping. Rose needs some local clothes and you need some new suits. Are there any good tailors in the area?"

Manya nodded. "Yes. I know someone. She is happy to work with me, but the last time I went out, a crowd gathered. It was almost a riot. My bodyguards requested I not go out again until the wedding."

Rose snorted. "You don't need bodyguards. You have me." She looked at me a moment and turned back to Manya. "Us. You have us."

Manya's right ear twitched. "Well, let us pray that will be enough."

We took two armored Escalades, each with a driver and bodyguard. The traffic was fairly light—well, light for Mumbai—so we travelled the whole three miles to the tailor's store in a comfortable twenty minutes. I was surprised at how flexible Aparna's wings were; she folded them close to her body and just sat down. Her wings wrapped around in front of her, fit through the upper and lower portions of the seatbelt, and looked none the worse for wear when we got out of the cars.

The shop turned out to be in a partially-renovated building originally built in the late 1800s. Half of the structure was covered with tarps, scaffolding, and advertising for the coffee shop that was moving in.

Madeline, the tailor, was a British expatriate, so Manya insisted Aparna speak English during our visit. Aparna had no interest in Manya's plain black ensembles, but the outfits Rose was looking at were all bright colors, vivid embroidery, and shining metallic accents. Aparna was all over them.

I picked out a few plain cotton *kurtas*—long-sleeved tunics made for the climate—and two embroidered silk ones in forest green and midnight blue. I was contemplating what else I wanted when Rose emerged from the dressing room.

This time she'd gone for a traditional sari in scarlet and gold silk, with hand-stitched embroidery in metallic threads along the hem, cuffs, and neckline. I pulled the *kurta* I'd just been looking at back off the rack; it was gold, trimmed with a darker scarlet and lined in purple. It should work for the wedding.

Aparna came out wearing a child's version of Rose's sari. I couldn't help but sigh and stare, overwhelmed by just how damn cute my little girl was. Doreen came out after Aparna, trying in vain to secure Aparna's shoulder wrap.

The back of Aparna's outfit was open, and her wings kept pushing the shoulder wrap away when Doreen tried to arrange it. Aparna slipped from Doreen's grasp, spun out of the shoulder wrap, and grabbed on to Rose's hand. "Buy me this one, Rasa-ji! We look pretty together!"

Rose flinched away from Aparna, averting her eyes. She shook her head and leaned toward Aparna once more. "Say that again, little one."

"Buy me this dress, *pleeease*! We can be so pretty together!" Aparna clapped and jumped up and down.

That time, I heard it as well. Aparna was using the imperative form, but she didn't have enough magical energy behind it to get past Rose's mental defenses.

She does not know how to gather or control her energy, Rose thought to me. *She's doing this with instinct alone. With proper training, most Humans aren't going to be any challenge for her to control.*

Aparna tugged at Rose's sleeve. "Rasa-ji, I'd like it very much if you would buy this dress for me." This time, she was putting all the energy she could summon into forcing Rose to agree.

Looks like Daddy's Little Girl might have a career in world domination ahead of her. Rose looked over to me and winked. *What should I wear to her coronation?*

Chapter Twelve

Daddy's Little Angel

I knocked on the door to the fitting room and called out in English, "Manya, something just came up. We need to talk as soon as you're available."

"Now is a good time," Manya replied. "Come on in."

She was standing in front of a three-panel mirror while Madeline measured and pinned a suit coat to fit. She already looked damn good, even with one suit arm hanging loose.

I pulled a chair over near the mirror and sat down. "Have you noticed Aparna getting her way a lot more often since the Change?"

Manya's ears twitched. "No more than usual. Though, to be fair, she gets her way a great deal. Why? Am I spoiling her?"

"I doubt it, but...she's not just cute. She can control minds. She's not very strong yet, but she'll get there. To make matters worse, she already knows she can do it."

Manya asked, "Madeline, could we have a moment?" Madeline nodded and closed the door behind her.

Turning away from me, Manya slipped out of the partially pinned jacket and hung it on a rack, then did the same with the white dress shirt under it. She was wearing a black sports bra, and when she twisted her shoulders, muscles moved under her fur like waves on the sea.

Manya pulled another chair over to sit next to me. "Yes, we've noticed. She's always been charming and charismatic, but this ability is far beyond that. Aparna can enthrall total strangers, and they do what she asks of them. She only asks the things a child is supposed to ask, but what if that changes?"

"Oh, it's going to change. Imagine that power in the hands of a teenager..." I rubbed my hands together while I tried to sort out my thoughts. It didn't help, so I went to the window and looked out on the flood of color and motion filling the street.

Swarms of scooters and tuk-tuks raced by, dodging luxury SUVs, overburdened bicycles, and family runabouts held together by duct tape and good will. It was like watching fish racing around a coral reef...or blood, flowing through the body.

Out on the sidewalk, a guy in his twenties was running a food cart, selling plates of *pani puri*. People on scooters would drive up onto the sidewalk, pay with one hand and grab a plate with the other, then zoom off with the plate balanced on their lap.

A man who had to be over eight feet tall walked up to the cart, holding the lid to a food cooler. He had thick, grey skin, a beer gut that probably weighed more than I did, and the head of an elephant. His shirt had been stitched together from three normal-sized ones, and he wore a sheet wrapped around his waist instead of pants. I couldn't hear what he said, but the cart owner loaded all the servings he had ready onto the cooler lid. Full up, the giant fellow turned and walked off.

Behind me, Manya said, "What about the Datonas? If they take her..."

I turned around, shaking my head. "They won't. I won't allow it."

She snorted. "What if they don't give her back?"

"We'll get her back. By hook or by crook." I walked to the door of the dressing room, but paused before I opened it. "Manya, Aparna is a beautiful, charming little girl, and I want her safe as much as you do. We will not allow anything to happen to her. That includes allowing her to grow up being a monster."

Manya growled, a full-throated, proper growl matching any you'd hear from a big cat in a zoo. The sound rushed through me, stopping me in my tracks and freezing my hand on the door handle. It only lasted a second or so, but if Manya had attacked, I would have been a sitting duck.

She didn't attack. She had her head bowed, eyes closed, hands clasped around her muzzle. Tears carved dark furrows in her fur, and her breathing was harsh and ragged.

I stayed where I was and asked, "Is there something else I need to know?"

Manya didn't look up. "The staff, the ones calling me *rakshasi*. They call Aparna a *devi*, a divine spirit. One of my housekeepers is Muslim. She moved here from Iran. She calls Aparna a *peri*. I have no doubt what Sharon's parents will call her. And all of them call me a demon. I fear for what they might decide to do, for a demon cannot be the parent of an angel."

"Manya, don't get obsessed thinking about what might happen. The fact is, we don't yet have enough information to know what Aparna is. She might be an angel, but she might also be nothing more than a little girl who has wings. There's no reason to panic." I kept my gaze locked with hers, though that old saw about no one winning a staring match with a tiger kept running through my head. "Now, regardless of any other factors, the best thing for Aparna is for you and me to get along and live as close together as possible. Enough stalling. I want an answer. Will you move to California to go to work for your parents?"

Manya blinked. "Do you swear—*swear!*—that you will allow joint custody of Aparna if Doreen and I come to America?"

"No." I held up my hand to forestall her response. "I intend to maintain full custody until you and Doreen finish getting settled in California and we have a concrete situation to work with. Right now, there are too many 'ifs' in the air. I also want to see how Vernon and Grace do at holding up their end of the visitation arrangements."

"Assume you are satisfied with the situation and all parties are behaving to your satisfaction. Will you allow it?"

I said, "Manya, you would never let yourself get nailed down like that, and neither will I. I want you to be in Aparna's life, and to have a much greater role than Vernon and Grace. That promise I will give you. Now, please, focus on getting through the wedding. Have a good time, make some great memories, and when you get back, take your time finding the right place in California. Can you do that?"

"For Aparna, for Doreen...yes. You win. I will go to California."

"Good. Thank you." I lowered my voice and stepped toward Manya. "If you want Vernon and Grace out of Aparna's life you need to stand back and let them screw up first. Just like in football. Wait for them to jump offside and then let the referee nail them. Or the court, in this case."

"I understand the strategy, David. I just find it frustrating." She picked up her white dress shirt and shrugged back into it. "Tomorrow morning Doreen and I are doing *Haldi*. It's kind of a spa day. Girls only. Rose is welcome to join us, but you might want to find something you and the Datonas can do with Aparna. Get to know her better."

"That sounds wonderful. I'll talk to the Datonas." I opened the door and nodded to Madeline. "Sorry about interrupting your work."

Aparna and Rose were sharing a leather wingback chair by the front window, working on a picture in Aparna's *Celestial Dream Pony* coloring book. From the number and color variety of the crayons in Rose's hair, I guessed they were working on a pretty prancing pony party picture.

Nope. One pony only, but her wings and Aparna's had the same color pattern. I said, "Wow, she's pretty. Who is that?"

"She's Spectrum Blaze." Aparna stopped coloring and frowned at me. "Are you sure you're my daddy? 'Cuz my daddy would know that so we can play Pony Palace Tea Party. Spectrum Blaze likes mint tea with strawberry jam, and Firehoof has chai with cream and hay scones. And Mrs. Mullatagawny-"

"Mulligatawny," Doreen said.

"That's what I said! Mullatagawny!" Aparna looked back at me. "Mrs. Mullatagawny is a big black cat with glasses and a pointy hat with flowers and she's runs the library in Hyppolitan. She drinks magic cream that smells like roses and she knows everything."

I smiled. "Most librarians do know everything. What do you drink at the party?"

Aparna rolled her eyes and let out a massive forced sigh. "I don't get to drink anything. I'm not a pony." She shook her head and went back to coloring.

I pressed my lips together and nodded. How could I not have known that? I decided to wander off and check out the refreshment table.

As soon as I had turned away, Aparna sighed again and announced, "Mommy-ji was right. Boys are dumb."

I poured myself a cup of chai and tried not to laugh out loud. *Yep, that's my progeny over there, giving me that rash of shit. Welcome to parenthood.*

Rose snickered. "Yes, but some can be taught neat tricks. That's why we keep them around." She switched to a deep violet crayon and started coloring the sky around Spectrum Blaze.

"That's not the color of the sky in Hyppolitan," Aparna complained. She looked over her shoulder at Rose and added, "It's pretty, but it's not right."

"I'm not doing the sky in Hyppolitan," Rose said. "She's visiting some friends somewhere else."

"Ohh..." Aparna nodded, then twisted in the chair and climbed over Rose to look out the window. Across the street, a food cart vendor was shaving ice off large blocks and packing the shavings around sticks to form giant, ice-cold lollypops. Aparna looked at Doreen, then at me. In precarious English, she said, "Daddy-ji? Can I has mango *gola*, peas?" She pointed to the food cart, where the vendor was pouring syrup over the packed ice.

I didn't feel any magical influence, but I had nothing against the idea. "A *gola*, huh? In America, we call those snow cones or snow balls." I looked at Doreen and asked, "What would you and Manya normally say? I don't want to...you know, start off with conflicting boundaries."

Doreen raised an eyebrow, but said, "Sure. She loves them. We get *gola* a lot. Just be careful crossing the street."

"No argument there. Indian drivers may not have invented the idea of pedestrians being worth points, but I can tell they've embraced it." I stepped outside, and the assault of heat, color, noise, motion, humidity, and smell stopped me in my tracks until I adjusted to it.

There's a well-known video game based on getting a frog across progressively nastier sections of roadway; maybe you've played it. I was facing a live-action version of it. When we came here for Aparna's birth, Manya had joked that the problem with giving driver's licenses to people who believed in reincarnation was that personal safety wasn't a high priority for them.

The trick, as it was explained to me, was to wait until fifteen or twenty people were ready to cross and set out with them, walking at a brisk pace in the middle of the group. The other option was to watch the traffic, run fast, and hope for the best.

I went with the crowd option. The great thing about being in the middle of a city of twenty million people is that someone is always going the same place you are. I decided to follow right behind a middle-aged fellow in a Western suit and orange turban.

Doing it right means moving as part of a wave, presenting the drivers with a wall they can't push through or shove aside. I did something wrong, and the scooter on my right jumped between me and the fellow I was following. I stepped back on instinct, and one of the blue and silver air-conditioned taxis surged past me. I dodged another scooter and jogged forward enough to join several women in walking in front of an oncoming bus. The driver slowed enough for us to get out of his way and into the relative safety of the middle of the road. But now traffic was coming from the left with no sign of stopping.

A six-wheeled yellow lorry decided to cut across traffic to make a left turn, creating a gap in the flow. I dashed the rest of the way across, and never have I been so happy to be standing on a sidewalk.

I turned around to make sure no one was down in the traffic or injured, and there, at the far end of the block from the tailor's shop and until now hidden by the tarps covering the store renovation scaffolding, was another *gola* stall.

Damn. If I got myself killed in this traffic because I didn't bother asking someone where else I could buy a snow cone, I'd become a joke meme on the Internet as fast as my friends could put one together.

The vendor nodded and waved at me, calling out, "Very good sir, *gola* is most cold. Very refreshing, very refreshing."

Five mango *gola*, plus an empty water bottle filled with mango syrup, came to eighteen hundred rupees. The price listed on the cart menu was two *gola* for three hundred. It was too hot to haggle, so I paid with two thousand-rupee notes and scored an urchin to help me carry the cups back to the shop. This time I stayed right next to my erstwhile guide and made it across the street without issue.

Aparna said, "Thank you!" in between slurping and ice-chewing. I had to admit, after being outside dashing through the traffic, the *gola* was indeed most maximum refreshing.

By the time the adults finished theirs, Aparna had slurped her way through the extra syrup, passing through sugar high and into instant, nearly-comatose sleep, draped across Doreen's lap.

As delightful a child as she was, Doreen, Rose, and I sat in silence, not moving unless we had to for fear of waking her up. In that quiet, we all heard Manya's cell phone ring in the other room. We didn't hear her answer it, but we did hear her voice turn sharp, almost hostile.

Manya emerged from the fitting room in her street clothes and put her phone on speaker. "I emailed you directions days ago. I wrote out all the phrases you would need, gave you the name of the taxi service, and even emailed you photographs of which stand to use and what kind of taxi to take. Did you even try to use them?"

Vernon Datona *hrrumphed* into the phone. "Did you really think we would use a taxi operated by the Indian government? I don't let my own government spy on me, kitty-cat; there's no way I'll ever let *your* government do it. I thought I was supporting a free-market independent businessman! Instead, some guy jumps in the cab and tries to charge us two hundred bucks for a road use permit. I smelled a scam, so I refused."

"Then the driver pulled into an alley and this thug in khaki comes up, claiming to be a cop! He demanded five hundred or he'd arrest us for not paying the taxi fare. We had to pay him off to get our luggage back! None of this would have happened if you had sent a car to pick us up in the first place. We got kidnapped and robbed by a couple of your sand-ape buddies and it's your fault!"

Manya's ears went flat against her skull. "You're talking a lot of racist shit for someone who's lost and doesn't speak the language. Do you want my help or not?"

Vernon panted into the microphone while he thought it over. "Fine. I... apologize. I'm angry and I've just been robbed! Now, please, send a car for us. We're at some weird freaking castle being used as a train yard."

Manya rolled her eyes but kept her voice level. "Are you at Chhatrapati Shivaji Terminus?"

"Chatty-party what? No! The sign says we're at, um, U-N-E-S-C-O? Un Esco? Why in God's name is this sign in Spanish?"

Manya stared at the phone. "Look again. Does the sign say, 'UNESCO World Heritage Site'?"

"Yeah, yeah, UNESCO. Yes, we're standing next to it. The sign, I mean."

"Very good," Manya said. "Go inside the main terminal and look for a booth advertising pre-paid air-conditioned taxis. Buy a ticket from them. If you do that, you will have a nice cool ride and be at the apartment in less than an hour. If you want us to come get you, you will be sitting outside in the sun for at least an hour, then another hour driving to the apartment. What is your preference?"

In the background, Grace said, "Vernon, just give up and do it the pussycat's way. Get the blessed taxi and let's get out of here before we pass out and our luggage gets stolen."

Vernon snapped, "I'm already out five hundred dollars because of her! I'm not throwing good money after bad!"

"Has the heat in this little corner of Hell melted your remaining brain cells? I'll have you know, Vernon Osgood Datona, if I get killed for my sneakers then abducted and raped by terrorists, I swear by our precious Lord, one of them damn holy cows will come in to my bed before you do. Now hang up the phone and get a damn taxi! Lord God Almighty..."

Vernon covered the audio pick-up so we couldn't hear the rest of the exchange, but when he came back to the phone, all he said was, "We're getting a taxi. See you at your apartment."

Manya hung up and put the phone away. "We should go. I don't want them in my home while I'm not there."

Doreen lifted Aparna into Manya's arms and whispered, "Our home."

"My parents gave me this one. I had no say in it, but it's mine." She nuzzled Doreen's cheek and said, "Our home, we will find together. In California."

Doreen stiffened. "Don't tease me," she whispered. "Don't say that unless you're serious."

Manya said, "California..."

Doreen pulled Manya close, burying her face in Manya's shoulder. She didn't say anything, but her tears left tracks in Manya's fur.

Chapter Thirteen

Family Time

"I suppose you're going to say her transformation is...what? Simple genetics? Garbage DMA suddenly becoming active? Sunspots?"

"It's Dee-ENN-Ay," I said. "And yes, DNA might be an issue. We don't know enough to say anything is or isn't a possible cause."

"Exactly my point," Vernon jabbed his finger at me for emphasis. "You can't prove it wasn't the guiding hand of the Lord Almighty blessing this child with the form and might of Heaven's most holy servants."

"I can't prove it wasn't the Flying Spaghetti Monster touching her with His noodly appendage, either. That doesn't mean I think it's a credible explanation."

We both stopped talking as Aparna hurled herself down a water slide, riding a thin foam toboggan. Grace was right behind her, riding in the next lane and whooping like a rodeo champion hoping to make it the full eight seconds. Vernon and I were at the bottom, tasked with taking video and getting pictures suitable for plastering over all known forms of social media.

Today was just my lucky day. I was focused on Aparna and tracking right with her, keeping her in frame like an expert, when she went over the last hill of the water slide. Her wings opened when she hit the top of the hill and she sailed into the air, dropping the toboggan.

Vernon dropped his camera and lunged forward, calling out, "Whoa, there! I got ya, I got ya!" He stepped closer, then back and sideways, reached up and caught Aparna under her arms. He puffed his breath out and said, "Oh, little girl, don't scare me like that."

One of the kids swarming the water park picked up the camera and held it out to Vernon. "All good, Uncle! Very strong case, very wise." The kid was right; only a few scratches marred the waterproof case.

"Um, thanks..." Vernon set Aparna down, snagged his camera, and managed to tip the kid and help Grace out of the pool all at the same time.

"See, Daddy? I told you I could fly!" Aparna shook her wings, sending water in all directions and making the kids around us squeal and laugh. "Did you see me?"

"Sure thing, Bugbear. I was making a movie of it to show everyone when we get home." I kept the video rolling and turned to the Datonas. "Good catch there, Vernon. How's your camera?"

He shook his head and rubbed his back. "Fine, fine...too damn old to be playing running back. Aparna, darling, if you're going to fly like that, let us know ahead of time and your daddy can catch you. His back is expendable."

Aparna stared at him. "Daddy, what did Grampa say?"

"He said he wants me to catch you next time." I turned off the camera and, in English, said, "How about trying that lazy river for a bit? Something nice and restful?"

"Sounds delightful," Grace said. "Any chance I could get a nice big glass of brandy to go with it? Something like about a Mason jar would do me right now."

"Probably not until we get back to the apartment." I patted Aparna's shoulder and switched to Hindi. "How about riding the lazy river current for a while?"

"Everyone has to ride!" Aparna took her grandparents' hands and hauled them off in the wrong direction. Being the only person in our group who could read the signs, I took over navigation and led the way through the crowd.

Aparna sprawled across an inner tube from some giant construction truck and spread her wings out. The tips dangled in the water, but, like the rest of her feathers, they simply refused to get wet. Water could get caught between her feathers, but it never soaked into them. I decided not to think about it right now; I stored the movie camera in one of the zippered pockets of my cargo pants and plopped my backside into a tube painted with bright yellow flowers.

The last time I went tubing, it was along the Yampa River near Steamboat Springs. We saw eagles, a ton of deer, and even a black bear shoving rocks around looking for snacks. I chuckled, shaking my head at the slow, meandering current pushing us along. *If Aparna likes this, she is going to love the real thing.*

For that matter, one of the largest water parks in the world was a little over half an hour from my house. We should be able to have some fun there...

Aparna made it through one whole circuit of the river before deciding we needed to do something else. We piled out of the water and waited while Aparna shook her wings out. The feathers might not get wet, but there were a lot of places in there for water to hide.

Once her wings were settled, Aparna pointed across the park and tugged on Grace's hand. In her best English, she said, "Gamma-ji, *gola* get us, yes?"

Grace knelt and said, "Oh, darlin' I can't understand a thing you're saying. You're asking for a cola, right?"

Aparna nodded. "*Gola*, yes."

In English, I said, "Grace, she's not saying 'cola.' She's asking for a *gola*. It's a glass of shaved ice with syrup poured over it."

"Oh..." She nodded. "Kind of a soda-flavored Icy-Cup?"

"Same sort of thing." I knelt next to Aparna and said in Hindi, "That was good asking, but try this..." I switched to English and added, "May I have a *gola* please?"

She bounced up and down and rushed through, "May hai half a *gola* peas!"

"Close enough for that new service station outside Spavinaw," Grace said. "Let's get us some *golas*!" I had to give Grace credit; she was making a legitimate effort to get close to Aparna and embrace India, even to going swimming in her street clothes like most of the other park attendees.

Aparna led the way, following the whirring of the ice shaver. This booth was in with a group of snack vendors, all of whom were far cleaner and better organized than the street vendor I bought from yesterday.

The *golawallah* wiped syrup drippings and melted ice off the counter top and waved Grace forward. In English, he called out, "Welcome, auntie, how may we serve you today?"

Aparna flexed her wings enough to get some lift and floated up to hover at Grace's shoulder height. Also in English, she chirped, "Watamelow *gola*, peas, sir."

The *golawallah* nodded, then leaned over the edge of the counter to look at Aparna's feet, dangling in mid-air. "Yes, watermelon," he muttered.

Grace took a phrasebook out of a plastic bag and flipped to the last page. She tapped Aparna on the shoulder and said, "*Pairah. Buhoomi.* Um...*boo-mi*. Understand?"

Aparna giggled. In carefully enunciated English, she said, "Feet. Feeeeet. Ground." She dropped with a dramatic "Ungh!" and pointed at her toes. "Feet on the ground!"

"That's my girl." Grace put the phrasebook away and said, "Right, then, sonny. Make it two of them watermelon *golas*. Vern, you get you something different so I can have a taste."

Vernon shook his head at the menu but didn't ask for help. "Hmm...I guess just...make it something an Indian would order. Typical Indian, I mean." I guess he got what he wanted; his turned out banded in orange, rose milk, and lime, the colors of India's flag.

I spied a drink stand selling bottles of imported American root beer for three hundred rupees—ten times as much as a normal *gola*. Sure, there's a locally produced version for sale all over the place, and for a lot less, but I can taste the difference between the two. I bought three bottles, tucked two away for later, and found a stall where I could get plain *malai kulfi*, a thick ice cream made of buffalo milk. Normally it's served as kind of a popsicle, but a little more money got mine served in a tall glass. I got some looks as I poured the root beer over the *kulfi*, but, hey, I'm just another crazy American, right?

While we ate, Grace and Vernon huddled together with their guidebook and debated where to go next. They were set on going to one of the landmark Catholic cathedrals in the city; the only debate was over which one.

I stayed out of it and enjoyed my float. Truth be told, it was almost too much for me, but Aparna mooched a good portion of it—and that was after downing her entire *gola* and half of Grace's syrup. As skinny as she was, I had to think stuff like that levitation trick consumed a lot of energy. It did help explain how in the name of Isaac Newton she could fly, though. One more item for her new pediatrician to look into when we got back home.

Vernon and Grace were still arguing when Aparna announced the need for a bathroom trip. Grace went with her. When they returned, Grace's eyes were wide and her smile was fixed in place. "Vernon, I'd like us to take Aparna home now. We've had enough excitement for one day."

Vern snorted and shook his head. "What are you talking about? We were going to the cathedral-"

"We are going to be here a full blessed month! We can see it another day." Grace took the satchel Vernon was holding and rooted around inside it, muttering about needing to pack a bottle of hand sanitizer.

While Grace was digging around, a Muslim woman and her two daughters came out of the restroom. All of them wore bright blue trouser and tunic ensembles with swim cap-like headcloths. Mom left the girls with her husband and tapped Grace on the shoulder.

"Just a blessed..." Grace turned around and froze a moment. "Well, hi there. Lor-*dee*, that is some swimmin' suit."

The Muslim woman smiled and nodded, but I got the impression she didn't understand English. It hardly mattered, though; the woman opened her handbag and offered Grace a sealed package of antiseptic wipes. In Hindi, she said, "I saw you, back there. Please, take these. I always bring extra."

I smiled and nodded to her and asked Grace, "Do you want me to translate that?"

"Nope, I think I got it right enough." Grace took the package and pulled the woman into a hug. "Thank you and God bless you for your generosity."

I did a quick translation and looked over to the woman's husband. I pressed my palms together and gave him a brief bow. He returned it, but still looked uncomfortable until his wife rejoined him and the family went off for more fun with the water rides.

"Why did you thank him?" Grace pulled a wipe out of the package and scoured Aparna's hands and her own. "She's the one who was showing us some kindness."

"Because it's not appropriate for me to talk to his wife," I said. "I

94

translated what you said and made sure to say you had said it."

Grace shrugged and tucked the wipes into the satchel. "Alrighty, then. Still, time we were going. Is there any place in this entire human anthill of a city where we can get a blessed hamburger? One made of beef?"

"Steak would be nice," Vernon muttered. "Cows gotta' die sometime."

I said, "There's a mall with some American restaurants near Manya's apartment. I'm sure they'll have something you like."

"Hope so. I hear sacred cow is good eating."

I smiled and called Jaidev, our driver, to come pick us up. He knew what to expect; the seats were already covered with towels over a plastic tarp. Aparna's feathers were dry, but our clothes weren't, and these were leather seats.

The drive to the Palladium Mall was long enough for us to dry off and for Aparna to give Grace a detailed introduction to who was who in *Celestial Dream Pony* world. I paid attention as best I could; after all, I would need to know all this stuff when she came to live with us. It wasn't easy, though. As an Alpha Geek, I can maintain a minimal level of interest in almost any subject just out of a basic level of politeness, but those frakking ponies were getting on my last nerve by the time we arrived.

The mall took Aparna's mind off the ponies, at least. Every store we passed had something in the window to fascinate her. I finally promised to buy her an American treat before we left, just to get her moving.

Parenting skillz. I haz dem.

One of the restaurants was as 'suburban American' as I could have asked for. Vernon and Grace sighed and smiled at the familiar tables, booths, wall décor, and music. That came to a screeching halt when they looked at the menus.

"Now, what kind of fool puts cottage cheese on nachos? Cheese and spinach fajitas? Christ Almighty..." Vernon shook his head and glared at me. "You said we could get a burger here, smart ass."

"You can." I showed him the menu page. "Barbequed bacon burger, chicken teriyaki, spicy grilled chicken..."

"Those are chicken sandwiches, not burgers. Even under the 'Beef' section, it says 'carabeef' or 'buffalo'." Vern thumped his knuckled against the menu page. "They aren't talking American buffalo, um...whadda' you call them...bison! No sir! I studied before we came here. They're buffalo, all right—water buffalo! Not really cattle, not really beef."

"I said you could get a burger, and you can. I never said the meat came from a cow." I let him fume and looked back at my menu. The barbecued pork ribs sounded enticing. I looked to see what they came with and saw a footnote in English, Arabic, and Hindi: 'Customers please be aware our pork ribs are not *halal*.'

I snorted. *Geeze, ya think? Next, we'll need a notice saying a bucket of fried chicken isn't vegetarian...*

Grace waved Vernon's complaints away. "Well, I am getting fajitas.

Chicken is chicken. Aparna, sweetie, do you know what you want?"

"Uh huh." Aparna fixed Vernon with a stern look and said, "You shouldn't eat meat. Animals have souls. Eating them is wrong." Of course, I had to translate that little gem.

"Oh, Christ almighty..." Vernon lowered his menu, scowling. "You know something? People like meat. Meat tastes good." He waved at the vegetarian items on the menu and said, "Real Americans don't eat pretend meat made from mixed vegetables. We eat meat. Real meat. Cut-up pieces of dead cows. And it is *good*. Do you understand that, little girl?"

Aparna nodded. In English, she said, "Uh huh. That's why you're so fat." She went back to looking at the children's menu while Grace and I tried desperately not to laugh.

Vernon turned purple and started to stand up. His hands were white-knuckled and shaking. I thought he was going to lash out at Aparna, but he stopped, took a deep breath, and sat back down. Under his breath, he muttered, "Americans eat beef, little lady, and as God is my witness, I will make you an American."

Once things were calmer at the table, the waitress came over for our orders. I decided on the amazingly non-*halal* pork ribs. Vernon tried a water buffalo burger and even admitted it wasn't as bad as he had expected. Despite her comments about meat, Aparna tried bites of all our dishes and liked everything but the coleslaw served with my ribs.

When we finished, Jaidev got the car from the valet while I paid the bill and the ladies visited the nice, clean, Western-style bathroom.

While we waited, Vernon looked at the restroom sign and sighed. "Prob'ly better drain the lizard while we're here."

"Sure," I said. "I'll watch your stuff. At least you don't have to balance it while you squat."

He snorted and headed for the restroom.

As soon as he was out of sight, I took his phone out of his satchel. Way back in my wage slave days, I used to run the security training class on how to avoid social engineering hacks, mostly because I was very good at carrying out social engineering hacks. The first time Vernon unlocked his phone in my presence, I learned his password started with a capital letter, had seven characters, and ended with three numbers, of which the second was the smallest and the third was the largest. My first guess was 'John316'.

Bingo.

The rest was easy. I connected to my private server, installed a cute little keylogger, set up a back-door administrator account, and had the phone back in his bag in under a minute.

I had no reason to think Vernon and Grace were planning anything nefarious where Aparna was concerned. They were making an effort to have fun and bond with her, were coping with India moderately well, and were mostly being pleasant people. So, why the nagging feeling something was afoot?

Because Vernon said he was going to turn Aparna into a meat-eating American. You can do a lot in two weeks, but changing the dining habits of a lifetime? Not likely. That takes longer. A lot longer. If he was planning something, I wanted to know about it.

Preparedness alone triumphs.

Chapter Fourteen

Making Nice

What a delightful child. Aparna fell asleep five minutes into the drive home and stayed asleep while I carried her to her room and tucked her into bed. The first portion of the wedding started tonight, and a good nap was essential.

Tonight was the first dinner between the two families. Doreen's family turned out to be my kind of weird; her parents ran a used bookstore in San Diego, her brother worked for a Las Vegas-based company developing a commercial space vehicle, and both sisters were literary agents at competing firms in New York. All of them supported the marriage, at least outwardly, and didn't hesitate to embrace Manya as one of their own.

Both brides looked amazing. Doreen's skin had a golden hue and Manya's fur was smooth, sleek, glossy, and vibrant. This wasn't a fancy-dress occasion, but they were wearing high-end Western-style gowns in complementary shades of blue and green.

Grace and Vernon stayed quiet most of the meal, until Doreen's mother said, "Manya, I have to ask: what did you use on your fur? It looks lovely."

Manya chuckled. "Thank you. This is so embarrassing... I talked to four different hairstyling salons and they all turned me down. The last one made a point of saying they didn't work on animals. I was so angry my claws left gouges in the reception desk. When I calmed down, though, I thought that might actually be a good idea. I did some research and finally found a professional stylist for show dogs."

I held up my hand. "Sorry if this sounds really patronizing, but, India has dog shows?"

"Yes, we do. I know it's hard to believe, what with India being a lowly cultural backwater, but we do have dog shows." Manya snorted. "Another legacy of British rule. They established kennel clubs all over when they were in charge. Anyway, as I was saying, I found a stylist. She showed up with a crate of hair-care products for dogs and some items used for horses.

Humiliating, but it worked. I'll never be soft and fluffy, but...I can at least look nice." She laughed. "The only problem is that washing my hair is a two-person job now."

Grace gave Manya a big, friendly smile and said, "Well, then, it's just so lovely you've found someone else who can help you with such things. You know, it's just so fortunate you have a managerial position. Why, I can't see how some poor soul at a fast food joint could have continued working after this kind of...event. Well, not without some kind of full-body hair net, anyway. Lord almighty, could you imagine that?"

Manya's claws flexed as though she were strangling someone, but she kept her voice pleasant. "That is so true! You are quite right—it would be a disgrace to look away and leave another of the Changed to face discrimination and hardship when we can help them. Daddy-ji, I think we should look into supporting entrepreneurs making tools and equipment to accommodate the Changed in the work place. What do you think?"

Rajesh ribbed his chin. "It is possible. What sort of tools or equipment were you thinking of?"

"Well, sanitary uniforms for food workers, for one." She wiggled her fingers in the air, showing off the claws on the tips of her fingers. "Gloves for claws and talons, to prevent accidental cuts and scratches."

I said, "Clothes in the right size and proportions would be a blessing, especially for laborers and construction workers. I saw one fellow a few days ago who was a humanoid elephant. His outfit had been stitched together from several sets of normal clothes. I'm sure he would be grateful for something in his size."

"Certainly we can do this," Rajesh said. "There must be people working on such things already. If we backed them...yes. Long investment, I think, but worthwhile return."

Manya pressed her palms together and bowed toward Grace. "Thank you for your concern for my fellow Changed. Very Christian, very Christlike, to think of those less fortunate. What is the verse, on clothing the one who is naked?"

I said, "Matthew twenty-five, verses thirty-five and thirty-six. I always liked that passage."

Vernon snorted. "Aren't you supposed to be one of them tree-hugging Druids or some shit? Didn't think you all put much stock in God's Word."

I smiled. "I put stock in compassion, no matter what the source. Feeding the hungry and clothing the naked, paying your taxes, repaying anger with kindness—I try to live that way because I think it makes the world a better place, not because someone ordered me to."

Grace took Vernon's hand and patted it the way you'd flatten a ball of pizza dough. "Now, now, boys, let's not get carried away during this joyous occasion. Our Lord celebrated the wedding feast at Cana, and we would be poor examples not to celebrate this one. How about it?"

Rose nuzzled my ear and whispered, "Are you sure I shouldn't eat him?"

I nodded at Grace and gave Vernon a small salute with my glass. Out of the corner of my mouth, I whispered, "Not yet. That's still Plan B."

"Oh, fine." Rose downed half a dozen chicken *pakora* while no one was looking her way and filled the empty bowl with butter chicken. "You know, if you can get them on the water, I can make it look like a shark attack."

I kissed her on the temple. "Do I get to shout, 'Release the Kraken'?"

"As long as you're not taking your pants off when you do."

"Deal."

After dinner, the party moved out onto the balcony for chai, sweets, and a view of the sunset over the Arabian Sea. The daily monsoon had been and gone, leaving the air cool and fresh (by Mumbai standards, anyway). The breeze coming in off the sea set all the hanging vines into motion and sent wisteria petals swirling among the tables.

Aparna drifted off next to a half-eaten bowl of rice pudding. This time Manya carried her to bed. Rose and I decided to take advantage of the moment and bid everyone a good night as well.

The time difference between Mumbai and Denver was on our side for once, so I called my parents. I updated Mom on the latest events and emailed her a stack of pictures, mostly of Aparna being cute. She sent a few more photos of herself and Dad for me to print up and give to Aparna. I promised her I would and said goodnight.

My next call was to our house, which Harmony answered. "No major issues so far. Everyone has been friendly, and we signed up for the neighborhood barbeque next month. By the way, I'm paying for a row of trees just inside the wall. All of them are native pine species already sprayed with a pine beetle repellant, along with native flowers and a small water feature intended to attract birds. I think you'll like it."

"I thought Ember was just going to do a little gardening?"

"She is," Harmony said. "I'm having all this done by professional landscapers. It really is the sort of thing servants are best suited for."

"You've been talking to Rose, haven't you?"

"Constantly." Harmony chuckled. "David, I've watched your world discover mathematics, economics, trade goods, surplus income, banking, accounting... Even before these things, some had much and some had nothing. A lot more nothing than much, actually. Servants have always existed, in every time, place, and culture. You can change a person's economic status, but you can't change an economic system, and it's the system you're uncomfortable with. You want to believe you can help people, or move them out of their circumstances, and thus make the world better. You can't do it. You can fix a person, but it makes no difference to the world. There are always more to take that person's place. If you're going to rescue people, do it to make yourself feel better, not because you think it will change the world."

"Thanks for the pep talk," I said. "What brought this on?"

"Rose said you were upset about the condition of the locals. I thought you'd appreciate some perspective."

"Absolutely. Anything else going on?"

"Nothing with us. You've gotten several calls from someone...just a moment..." Harmony set the phone down for a moment and I heard paper rustling. "Here we go. Steve Nelson. He's the campaign coordinator for a woman named Vivian Davis. She's running for Attorney General and he wants to talk to you about doing some campaign ads for her. How do you two know each other?"

I couldn't say anything for several long seconds. "She's...ah...well, she's the psychotic bitch District Attorney who wanted to prosecute me for killing Randall. Rose finally had to mind control her to get her to back off. Not just no, but hell no."

"Fair enough. I'll let him know."

After I hung up, I turned the lights off and went out on our patio to join Rose. She was naked, leaning over the railing and looking out at the waters of the Arabian Sea. "Sorry about Harmony," she said. "I didn't intend for her to lecture you."

I caressed her curves and planted a kiss on the base of her neck. "I think I can forgive you. So, what's on your mind? Or are you just out here to scandalize the neighbors?"

Rose kissed me back. "Actually, I was thinking of going out for sashimi. I'm feeling peckish."

I looked around the deck and into the bedroom. "We're forty floors up and have no open space. There's not much room to change in the bedroom, and I doubt the patio would support you. Or am I missing something?"

"I've been practicing," Rose said. She stepped back several paces, took a deep breath, and sprinted for the edge of the patio. I lunged for her arm and missed as she leaped over the railing. She cleared it easily and dropped out of sight.

By the time I looked down, Rose was in her true form, an amethyst Dragon some fifty feet long. Our patio was over four hundred feet up, and she had fallen at least half that distance before finishing enough of the transformation to be able to fly. She pulled up well clear of the ground, but still clipped the roof of another apartment building, crushing the side of an air conditioner and sending a cluster of satellite dishes flying. She appeared unhurt, and I watched her skim over trees and buildings until she vanished in the darkness. I had a strong drink and went to bed.

Rose returned an hour before dawn, happy, tired, and reeking of fish guts. She took a quick shower, toweled mostly dry, and perched on the edge of the bed wearing jade-green skin and a smile. I love the 'alien dancing girl' thing, so we got to breakfast a little late.

Today's activities started with packing and driving across town. Since the wedding was starting at 10:30 in the morning, everyone (including

Manya and her parents) had rooms at the hotel.

The wedding party skipped the traditional henna decorations on the brides (how are you going to paint henna on a tiger, anyway?) as well as the *barat* (the groom's arrival on horse- or elephant-back), but the *milni* dinner was most maximum needful. Tonight was also going to be a *sangeet* party, with the emphasis on music and dancing rather than conversation. Even though many of Manya's family members spoke at least a reasonable level of English, and quite a few of Doreen's friends and family had been learning standard Hindi as well, socializing would be tricky.

Our job, in online gaming parlance, was tanking the boss. Rose and I, along with one of Doreen's cousins and his girlfriend, had the joy of sitting with Vernon and Grace. It was a crappy way to spend a wedding dinner, but no one wanted to give the Datonas a chance to cause a scene.

Once the staff cleared the dinner plates, Rajesh and two women I vaguely remembered as being Manya's cousins took over the center of the room. Switching between Hindi and English, Rajesh said, "Welcome, all, welcome! I especially want to welcome our friends who have travelled all the way from America. We love Americans here, except that every time my Internet goes out, I have to talk to some guy from Topeka. Calls himself 'Deepak from Jaipur,' and his Hindi is just terrible."

I wasn't the only one rolling my eyes, but one of the benefits of being the father of the bride was getting to tell bad, embarrassing jokes and still get a laugh.

Unfortunately, the laughter convinced Rajesh to go for two. "I hear our American friends talking about not eating local food, and only drinking bottled water. They are afraid of getting the Delhi Belly. Well, to be fair, I tried American food once, and just the opposite happened. I got the Manhattan Tunnel traffic jam. It took a week until the subway was running again."

Oh, yeah. Great choice for a dinner joke.

Rose leaned forward, locked eyes with Rajesh, and hissed a brief command in Draconic under her breath.

Rajesh blinked and shook his head, then waved the two women forward. "Yes, yes, Moving on. I'd like to introduce two of my nieces, Jaina and Janya. They are both dancers, and have appeared in, oh, a dozen Bollywood movies at least by now. They are here to teach a few simple dance steps. It is not *sangeet* without dancing." He laughed again and vacated the floor.

Jaina and Janya didn't have to convince Rose to join them; she was out of her seat like an arrow shot from a bow. I was a bit slower, but I've learned not to argue with Rose about dancing. I just relaxed and followed her lead as best I could.

It's traditional for the bride and groom's friends and family to put on choreographed dances, play music, or sing during the *sangeet*, but modern Hindus and Westerners aren't always willing to do such things. Not an issue here; Jaina and Janya even managed to get Vernon out on the dance floor. Turns out, he's not too bad.

Once we made it through the Bollywood dances, one of Doreen's cousins announced we'd be doing a few rounds of country line dancing. Doreen took Manya's arm and said, "Come on, I'll show you some easy steps. I've been doing this for years."

Manya laughed. "So have I, dear heart. Denver *is* a cow town, remember?" Nonetheless, she followed Doreen onto the dance floor and let her lead.

For the first time since they arrived, Grace and Vernon were in their element. Vernon had the advantage of being the only person at the party wearing real cowboy boots and blue jeans, so he stepped up and went to town, showing the kids how it was done. And, damn, the man could dance.

Aparna loved the line dancing, aside from a spot of confusion over why everyone was shouting 'Buuuulll-*shit!*' during *Cotton Eyed Joe*. Sadly, her silk slippers didn't make much noise when she stomped and kicked with her grandfather. She tugged on Vernon's sleeve between songs and asked in English, "Gra'pa, when we going to Oaksahoma, would next to boats forget me?"

Vernon tried to parse it out, then shook his head and said, "I'm sorry, sweetie, I just don't understand what you mean."

Aparna heaved an overwrought, dramatic sigh and said, "BOATS, like them. Your boats." She pointed to his boots and stomped her feet. "Boats! For get me boats!"

"Boots," Vernon said. "Bo-o-o-o-ts. Not boats. You want boots like these?"

"Yes," Aparna declared. "I want butts like yours!"

Those magic words cut across the dance floor like a knife, bringing everyone to a silent, staring halt. Manya covered her mouth with her palm and turned away, shoulders shaking with laughter.

Vernon turned a dark red. "Well there...um, yes. Yes, we can get you boots like this. We'll make a regular little cowgirl out of you."

Aparna threw her arms around his waist and hugged as tight as she could manage. "Thank you, Gra'pa-ji!"

Vernon stroked Aparna's hair and his expression softened. For the first time since he'd arrived, there was something in his eyes other than anger and hurt over losing Sharon. For the first time, I saw love there.

Maybe this thing will work out after all.

Chapter Fifteen

Here Come the Brides

Sadly, the front desk was punctual with our wake-up call. Rose snarled and lunged for the phone, but I beat her to it, meaning the nice woman from the front desk got a 'thank you' instead of a profane death threat. I ordered five English breakfast platters (eggs, bangers and mash, bacon, toast with butter and marmalade, sautéed mushrooms, and fried tomatoes) and we got a fast shower before room service arrived.

After the dancing, the singing, the more dancing, the dancing after the dancing, and the oh-we-forgot-these-dances dancing, I would have loved to sleep in. Instead, I had extra coffee while Rose changed clothes four times. She eventually settled on an Elven gown in several shades of scarlet silk, accented with gold ear dangles, necklace, and wrist cuffs, all done in a delicate, lace-like filigree. Once she was settled, I picked my outfit to properly accessorize her.

According to Manya, Vedic astrology holds that the most auspicious time to start the ceremony was half past ten. The most auspicious time to grab a seat with a good view, however, was a bit less clear, so we headed up to the hotel's rooftop garden an hour early.

At the appointed time, Aparna came skipping out of a break in the foliage, scattering rose petals behind her. Rajesh, his brother, and two of Manya's male cousins emerged, carrying Manya on a gilded *doli*. Her sari was scarlet silk, with lotus flowers embroidered on it in gold thread, but most of it was hidden under the mass of gold jewelry she was wearing.

Rose perked up and sniffed the air. I felt a rush of greed go through her, but she made no overt move to stuff Manya into her hoard pile, so I let it pass.

Across the garden from Manya, one of Doreen's nieces emerged from between two small trees, this time scattering lotus petals. Doreen's father was already waiting at the *mandap*, so her mother walked her down the aisle. Rajesh helped Manya out of the *doli*, and Ananya joined him, both holding Manya's hands. Doreen's parents did the same for her.

Once in Hindi and again in English, Rajesh said, "Normally, this would be *kanyadaan*, the giving of the bride, and a piece of our heart would go with her to her new family. But, we do not give her away this day. We welcome the one she loves, as a new daughter to our family."

Doreen's father still needed to work on his Hindi, but it was good enough. "Parents have hopes for their children. Good lives, happy lives, spent with those they love. We welcome the one our daughter has chosen and will love her as a daughter of our family."

Manya and Doreen placed garlands around one another's necks. Manya recited a passage in Sanskrit, which Doreen repeated in English:

"Today we come before our families and our friends to declare our love and acceptance of one another. We enter this union willingly and without reservation. Our minds and hearts are in harmony, flowing together as water in a river. As Heaven has provided us to one another, let us grow together, become old in years, and fulfill our dharma, one with the other, always."

The priest followed their declaration by reciting several Vedic passages, all in Sanskrit, asking for blessings of harmony and prosperity on the marriage. He also did a number of small ceremonies I couldn't see much of, culminating in Manya and Doreen anointing one another's forehead with dark red *sindoor* powder, marking one another as married women.

Wedding rings aren't part of the Hindu ceremony, but they were a tradition Doreen had insisted on. She placed her ring on Manya's hand and said, "Now there will be no sadness, for you are the joy in my heart. Now there will be no rain, for you are shelter and warmth to me. Now there will be no pain, for your touch soothes me and makes me whole. As we go from here and enter into the days of our togetherness, peace and happiness will follow with us, so long as we both shall love."

Manya slipped her ring onto Doreen's finger and froze, eyes wide. "Oh, no..." she said. "That was so beautiful I forgot what I was going to say."

Aparna leaned forward and said, "Mommy-ji, you say 'I love you too'!"

Manya couldn't keep a straight face, which looks really odd on a tiger. She took a deep breath and said, "I love you, too." The guests laughed and applauded.

Next, Manya and Doreen held their hands over a small fire while the priest poured rice into their palms. They let the rice fall through their fingers into the flames, then walked around the fire seven times while the priest pronounced another blessing in Sanskrit.

When the last circuit of the fire was finished, the brides fed each other pieces of rose-flavored candy while trying not to get powdered sugar on each other. As they did, both fathers stood up and clapped, shouting, "You may kiss your bride!"

This they did.

The reception was on the other half of the hotel's roof, under a tall white awning that caught the sea breeze and sent the cool air swirling across the tables and dance floor. There was no assigned seating this time, so Rose and I snagged a table next to the railing. We'd done our time with the Datonas; now we wanted to meet new people.

Manya and Doreen took to the dance floor to start the party off with a romantic dance, but the DJ had other ideas. He opened with *Eye of the Tiger*. Everyone froze for a second, until Manya nodded and laughed, inviting everyone to laugh with her. Her laughter might even have been genuine, but her 'get on with it' gesture was clear and emphatic. This time the DJ put on the song Manya and Doreen had picked, *The Power of Two*. Not a traditional romantic dance song, but it fit their relationship like a glove.

When the next song started, I offered my hand to Rose, but Aparna grabbed it. "Rasa-ji, can Daddy-ji dance with me?"

Rose laughed. "Of course, little one. As long as you promise not to wear him out." She all but pushed us out onto the dance floor.

I can dance to the music the DJ was playing just fine, but all Aparna knew how to do was either bounce a lot while waving her arms, trying to dance Bollywood-style. I tried to match her style as best I could, but I felt like I was doing a drunken version of the world's worst 'dad dance.'

Oh, well. It made my little girl happy, and hearing her laugh made me happier than I would have ever believed.

Parenthood alone triumphs.

Chapter Sixteen

Homeward Bound

"First thing I do, I'm getting a huge, fat, greasy hamburger. With *mounds* of bacon." The speaker grunted and sighed. "No one mentioned we'd have to eat Indian food the whole time. I just don't get how those people can stand the stuff."

"I know," a female voice said. "I'm going to have a word with that travel agent. She should have told us what India was really like. The smell, the traffic, the crowds... And those kids! They should have been in school, not swarming in the streets and begging for change everywhere. The government should do something about their parents."

"I thought the schools were on summer vacation, like ours are." He sounded genuinely confused by the idea.

"Of course not," the woman said. "India is on the other side of the world, remember? It's the middle of winter there. That's why we went in July."

"Are you sure it was winter? It was a hundred degrees and rained constantly."

I put my face in my hands and sighed.

The idiots were behind me, in economy. It was four in the morning Mumbai time and most of the passengers were sleeping. This fact didn't seem to have occurred to these two, and their voices carried all the way up to first class.

British Airways had been kind enough to provide each first-class seat with a set of slippers, pajamas, and a set of noise-cancelling headphones, so everyone up here but me was sound asleep, including Aparna. I had tried the headphones right after we took off, but they actually made the environment too quiet.

The headphones weren't the only issue. Despite banging around India with the Datonas for a solid month, the idea of letting Aparna spend two weeks alone with them still bothered me enough to make sleep impossible.

Even catching up on paperwork from the office hadn't been enough to knock me out. I closed that folder and brought up the latest report from the keylogger I'd loaded on Vernon's phone.

So far, he'd been boring and predictable. News updates from his friends, corny jokes, and daily Bible verses from assorted mailing lists. He also had some text messages to a men's issues ministry group, mostly concerned with having impure thoughts about one of the maids on Manya's housekeeping staff.

Well, it's a human reaction, at least.

Aparna's name came up three times this past week, all concerned with activities at Still Waters, the New Life Fellowship's compound north of Tulsa. Furniture and clothing accommodations for her wings, finding a good English-as-a-Second-Language tutor for her, and making sure that she'd have a vegetarian option for her meals there. All three requests had been approved and provided without any argument.

I made a note to find an ESL tutor in Boulder. I should have thought of that before now. I'd already taken care of the other two issues.

The church also had a bunch of topical mailing list servers. Church service announcements, wedding and funeral notices, news items…I skimmed through the listings, but found nothing pertinent to Aparna. The 'Outreach' list had the most activity, sometimes thirty messages or more per day. All of the church's activities fell under 'Outreach,' and most of them constantly needed volunteers or donations of some kind. Day care staff, caregivers for sick or homebound members, collecting usable women's business clothes for something called 'Steps to Success,' female contractor needed for repairs at the New Life Residential Shelter, and dozens more along those lines.

There was also one transcript of a sermon by Reverend Harper Wren, talking about how Christians should respond to the Changed. Her sermon concluded with, "The Lord has reached down and touched many among us, bringing forth mighty signs and wonders. These are not strangers, but our own family members and loved ones. Whatever these changes mean has not yet been revealed, but we must not assume these are marks of sin and wickedness. Give no heed to those voices calling you to turn from your flesh and blood, for all have sinned, and all are welcome in the fellowship of Christ."

I went back to the top and read the sermon again. That sounded a lot more reasonable than I had expected. It didn't even sound like the kind of church Vernon and Grace would attend.

The idiots in economy picked that moment to start spreading the stupid again. "Another thing that pisses me off about India—they're still sucking up to the British. One good nap and the Limeys are home, but they stick Americans with a thirty-hour flight. How fair is that?"

I shook my head. *Figures. We have magic capable of turning people into humanoid elephants, but there's still no cure for stupidity.*

Rose opened her eyes and sat up, snorting. "Oh, yes there is," she muttered. She leaned out of her seat so she could look down the aisle into economy and said, "You two! Until we land, don't speak unless you are spoken to!"

The woman's voice stopped in mid-sentence.

Rose smiled at the smattering of quiet applause from the other passengers. "Happy to help," she murmured, and settled back into her seat.

I set the headphones back in their little alcove, leaned back, and the next thing I knew we were coming in to Heathrow. Four years ago, getting to Mumbai and back had involved running around finding our terminals, gut-wrenching stress over making it to our next flight, and a pile of drama from our fellow passengers. Not this time.

We deplaned first, along with a handful of other VIP club flyers, and a dedicated chauffeur drove us across the airport to a hidden, unmarked lounge. I would have loved to go out running around Old London Town during our layover, but our visas didn't allow us to enter the UK proper. Instead, we hung out in quiet, air-conditioned luxury and ordered dinner from one of the restaurants in the terminal.

Aparna looked at my steak and gave me an accusing look. "You're not going to eats a cow, are you Daddy-ji?"

I nodded, trying not to laugh. "Yes. I like beef. Americans eat cows, my dear. We respect cows for all they provide, but here, they aren't sacred."

She wasn't buying it. "It's wrong."

"No, it's just different. I've eaten meat all my life, and so did your mommy Sharon. Even mommy Manya eats meat now; she just sticks to chicken."

Aparna shook her head. "Eating meat is fine for Mommy-ji because God turned her into a tiger."

Our concierge presented Rose with the six salmon fillets she's ordered. "Ma'am the salmon does not travel or reheat well-"

Rose downed the first fillet whole. "That's fine. There won't be any leftovers."

This was Aparna's first exposure to Rose's appetite. Her eyes got wide and she shook her finger at Rose. "Slow down, Rasa-ji! Chews your food or you gets tummy ache! Even Mommy-ji don't eats so fast."

"I'm bigger than Mommy-ji," Rose said. Still, she cut up the rest of the fillets and ate them in a more Human fashion.

While Aparna watched Rose, I watched Aparna. It had taken most of the month to get her to accept the idea of living with me. Well, maybe 'accept' was being generous... Just because we hadn't had a screaming hysterical tantrum in a week didn't mean she'd accepted the idea.

Whatever the reason, she was quiet now. I let her eat, then read to her until she fell asleep. I let her nap until we had to check out of the suite and catch our flight to Chicago.

Just before takeoff, Vernon slipped into first class and tapped me on the shoulder. "Don't forget, she's coming with us when we get to Chicago. Her tickets don't say 'Denver' on them."

"Don't worry, Vernon. You'll get your time, as agreed." I stood up and offered him my hand. "This past month was tough on everyone, but it showed me both of you are making every effort to be proper grandparents to Aparna. I hope you're satisfied that I'm taking my role seriously as well."

He shook my hand. "Hmm...yeah. You're not bad, for a liberal and a Godless heathen. Don't worry; we'll enjoy our two weeks, and when you come get her, we'll be waiting."

We ended our happy little moment with a nod and he took his seat. Soon the plane was racing down the runway and up into the bright British sky.

I made the most of our time on the flight, even coloring a picture of Berrymint in Aparna's *Celestial Dream Pony* coloring book. I got a gold star from Aparna for staying in the lines. Everything was fine until we reached Chicago.

Rose and I said our goodbyes to Aparna in the international arrival terminal. She and the Datonas were headed for Terminal Four, while Rose and I were going to Terminal Three. I gave Aparna one last hug and managed to keep it together until she was out of sight.

Good thing about arrival terminals: everyone is in such a hurry they don't notice things like a grown man crying. I'd spent four years pretending she was someone else's child, and she'd shredded that illusion in our first day together.

Rose waited, aware of my emotions but holding her own in check. Once my initial anger and sadness faded, she said, "Don't worry. We'll watch them. If anything happens, we can get her back from anywhere in this world."

I sighed and pulled her close to me. "I know. Grace and Vernon are being normal grandparents. I can't imagine they'd allow anything to happen to her."

After a quick restroom stop to wash up and regain my composure, Rose and I made our flight without issue. Half an hour after takeoff, Rose went to use the restroom. Normally this isn't a significant event, but this time she took a lot longer than normal. I didn't want to interrupt her, so I passed the time looking through the photos I'd taken last night. Aparna had insisted on having a going-away tea party with me, Manya, and Angel Mommy. She'd set a place for Sharon and insisted we all tell her what we'd been doing. But no tears. There's no crying in Hyppolitan.

After she returned to her seat, Rose leaned over and whispered, "I couldn't find a level spot to balance the obsidian for scrying, but I did get a crappy image using the sink. They're on the plane, waiting for boarding to finish. Aparna was coloring. She looked fine."

I smiled and patted her hand. "That helps. Thanks." It actually did help; I relaxed enough to sleep until we started our descent into Denver.

Normally, seeing the mountains always made me feel better, because they meant I was home. It was after ten at night, though, so instead of the familiar peaks of the Front Range welcoming me home, it was 'Blue Mustang,' the giant blue stallion statue outside Denver International.

Several years back, some wag had nicknamed the horse 'Blucifer' and the name had stuck. During the Change, it had gained a halo of flame, along with flaming eyes and hooves. It had also developed a disturbing habit of turning to glare at anyone who got within shouting distance. No one had yet ventured any closer.

At this point, even the demon horse was a welcome sight. I waved as our taxi drove past and said, "Good to see you, big fellow."

The horse's head snapped around, staring right at us. He didn't make any threatening moves, but his gaze followed us as we drove down Peña Boulevard.

Oh, yeah. Home sweet home...

Our driver was kind enough to drive through a late-night burger place so we could get dinner. We finally got home just after eleven. Harmony and Ember were waiting up for us, but they retired and left us to eat. News, catching up, and unpacking could wait until tomorrow. Rose and I took a nice, hot shower and collapsed into bed.

Home alone triumphs.

Chapter Seventeen

Fox and Coyote

A week after we got back from India, I woke up to an empty house. According to the notes on the refrigerator, Thirteen was off talking to a beekeeper in Nederland, Harmony and Ember were at the vet for a kitty checkup, and Rose was at her belly dancing group. Apparently, she had also polished off our last carton of eggs. Oh, well. I didn't feel like cooking breakfast anyway. I powered up the Interceptor and headed downtown.

The People's Republic was a little diner a block east of the Pearl Street Mall. It didn't have a drive-through, but it did have a chorizo-filled breakfast burrito omelet that was downright sinful. I ordered three, (two wrapped to go), and found a table.

On top of the other errands I wanted to run today, I needed to buy some more eggs. Between Rose and Harmony, our household's food consumption was on the order of a small village. Thankfully, some friends of ours owned a farm east of Eldorado Springs. They usually had a good supply of fresh-laid eggs; I pulled out my phone and gave them a call.

"Stone Toad Farm, this is Wiley."

"Wiley, it's David. How are you set for eggs this morning?"

"We got a couple. India leave you hungry for duck eggs Benedict?"

"Terribly. I need six dozen if you have them."

"I can do five dozen at the moment. Coming down soon?"

"I'll be leaving as soon as I finish breakfast, if that's convenient."

"I'm awake and have pants on, so we're ready for company." He coughed and cleared his throat. "Any chance I could ask you for a favor?"

"Ask away," I said. "I took the morning off to run some errands, but they can wait."

"There's a friend of ours staying at a bed and breakfast a couple blocks off the mall. I was going to pick him up in a bit, but it would help us out a lot if you could swing by and give him a ride down here."

"No problem," I said. "I'm at People's Republic now. Email me the details and give me half an hour."

"Will do. See you when you get here."

I set my phone aside and picked up a discarded newspaper. The lead story was the three-state manhunt for Colby Green, primary suspect in the Cheesman Park killings. Five women had been ripped apart in the past month, despite heightened police patrols and a massive neighborhood watch program. The break in the case had come a few days ago, when a possible sixth victim was saved by a chance encounter with a guy looking to avenge his little sister's honor. Big Brother was in Special Forces, and a few punches had sent the scumbag serial killer running.

The sidebar had an interview with Vivian Davis. She'd become Drow in the Change, which delighted her to no end. The article stated she'd been dating Colby Green, and was shocked—shocked, I tell you!—at his duplicity and viciousness.

I folded the paper and tossed it to the side, just as my breakfast showed up. As I ate, the information from the paper kept rolling around in my mind. Tracking this bastard down and killing him would be a pleasure...

Yeah. *Now* it would be a pleasure. Previously, it had been a nuisance I was glad not to be involved with. If I had gotten off my ass and done it before we went to India, four women would still be alive.

Some Hero I was.

Well, he's not going to see another dawn. Whatever it costs, I will find him...

"Excuse me, are you David Fraser?"

I looked up. A guy in his mid-twenties was standing by the table. Worn-down boots, patched cargo pants, and a sweat-stained canvas boonie hat in a desert camouflage pattern. He had a bedroll tied to a black nylon gear bag slung over his shoulder and a carved wooden walking stick suitable for use in a 'wandering wizard' costume. Long hair and medium beard, both clean and in good order. One lens of his glasses was solid black, and I saw burn scars around the edge of the dark glass.

I raised an eyebrow. "Do I know you?"

"No, but Wiley told me you were eating breakfast here. I was ready to go anyway and thought it would save us both time if I ran over here. I recognized you from some pictures on their social media page." He held his hand out to me. "Fox."

"David Fraser, but you knew that already." I shook his hand. "Just 'Fox'?"

"Well, Wiley has 'Coyote' all kinds of spoken for."

"That he does. Have a seat. Can I buy you breakfast?"

"No, I already ate, but thank you." He looked at the stacked to-go boxes and grinned. "Although, maybe I should, if the food is that good."

"It is that good. However, after reading the morning news, I've lost my appetite." I scooped the rest of my omelet into one of the to-go boxes and stood up. "I'll have the rest for lunch. Let's get you down to the farm."

Fox nodded. "Sounds good."

He followed me out to the car and somehow made his pack fit under his feet. "Nice car. What year is it?'

"2076, I think. I picked it up somewhere around the year 2150. I'm not actually sure what the exact year was, though."

Fox shook his head and grinned. "Alrighty, then."

I let him be skeptical; I just pulled out and threaded through downtown Boulder's maze of one-way streets until I could turn south on Broadway.

Fox spent the time contemplating the assorted informational overlays marking the people, cars, and buildings around us. After we passed an unmarked police car festooned with information icons, he asked, "You weren't kidding about this car being from the future, were you?"

"Nope."

"Uh huh." Fox scratched his ear. "Wouldn't that create a paradox and blow a hole in the space-time continuum?"

I chuckled at that. "Points for being the first person to ask that. No, it's not a paradox. This car isn't from one of our possible timelines. Our world and that one diverged a long time ago."

Fox dismissed whatever concerns remained with a wave of his hand. "No biggie, then. As long as my stuff doesn't blink out of existence, I'm cool."

"Fair enough. How long have you known Margot & Wiley?" The banter was fun, but I really didn't want to go too far down that path.

Fox rolled with it. "Five or six years on the Alpacalypse forums, but this will be the first time meeting them in person. I'll be here a few months while Margot recovers from her hip replacement." Fox caught my blank look and added, "She tripped on a prairie-dog hole trying to corral one of their alpacas and Paris accidentally body-checked her into the livestock gate. She's more mobile now, but she's also under orders not to go near any large animals."

"Ouch. That would be why they have that 'inherent dangers of working with llamas' disclaimer posted." Paris was their herdsire, a four hundred-pound male llama. I shook my head at the image. NFL quarterbacks don't take hits like that. "I've been out of the country for the past month. This is the first I've heard of her being hurt. I take it you're a llama-slash-alpaca wrangler?"

Fox nodded. "I grew up on an alpaca ranch outside Bartlesville, Oklahoma. It belonged to my mother's great-aunt Esther. At least, it used to belong to her. When I enlisted, the family arranged for some guys from her church to take over working it for her. It was all going great for a year or so, but then she had a stroke. She never woke up. When the family started arriving at her house for the funeral, the Sheriff was waiting for them. Said the family was welcome to be there for the service, but the land wasn't ours any more. Aunt Esther had signed everything over to her church a week after I left for basic training. 'A bequest to Jesus,' she called it."

"How much did your family lose?"

"Eighty acres, two houses, a hundred and some-odd alpacas, two dozen llamas, and several bank accounts. Six million or so all told. My mother's family had been working that land since 1889. The original sod farmhouse was rebuilt in 1910. My grandfather rebuilt it again in the Sixties. It had cinderblock walls filled with concrete, and a tornado shelter in the basement, all reinforced with railroad irons driven to bedrock. Generations of work, gone, just like that. All nice and legal, too."

"Blessed Mother...what kind of church could do that to someone? Did they at least make some token effort at trying to help someone with all that?"

"Oh, yes." Fox said. "They have a day care center, a retirement home, a food bank, and an online business selling yarn made from the alpaca fleece. They also offer job training scholarships for battered women, give life skills classes, and sponsor people into drug rehab programs. A lot of their members live in mobile homes, so one of their biggest community service projects involved digging up the pasture and burying a bunch of Quonset huts to use for public tornado shelters."

"Doesn't sound too nefarious," I said.

"I wish it was. It would be a lot easier to be pissed off at them if they were being hateful psychotic jerks." Fox sighed and shook his head. "Aunt Esther would have seen through something like that in a heartbeat. Funny thing is, she was always worried one of the kids would sell the ranch off after she died. Keeping Still Waters in the family was an obsession for her."

I looked sideways at him. "Still Waters? Are you...no, wait a moment." I pulled into the next available parking lot and stopped. "Is the church you're talking about run by a Reverend Harper Wren?"

"Yeah, the New Life Fellowship. Should I be worried that you know her name?"

"My daughter's maternal grandparents are members of her church. They're taking Aparna to summer camp there next week." I sighed and drummed my fingers on the steering wheel. "I hadn't been concerned about it but running into you like this is setting off all kinds of alarms for me. I can believe six impossible things before breakfast, but one of them isn't that our meeting was coincidence. If you're involved with some master plan or acting under orders, especially divine ones, I'd like to know the truth, now."

Fox grimaced and scratched the side of his jaw. "Sorry. No secret plans here. I'm just an out-of-work alpaca jockey. If you're on a mission from God, I didn't get the memo."

"I've done the 'mission from God' thing already, and someone else can save the world this time. My daughter has just become part of my life, and I intend to focus on that." I checked for traffic and pulled back onto the road. "I am officially out of the Hero business."

"I don't know much about Heroes," Fox said, "But I do know you don't get to choose when you retire from that life. If your little girl is the one who needs a knight in shining armor, are you really going to sit back and leave it for someone else to do?"

I glared at him for a moment. "You just had to go and notice that detail, didn't you?"

"It is a big one." Fox sighed, looking out at the mountain peaks off to the west. "Any human-caused disaster is more than a single event. It's more like a room full of dominos. The more that fall, the more dominos they tip over, so on and so on, until the whole thing cascades out of control. The Hero's job is to stop the dominos from falling in the first place. The earlier the Hero gets involved, the easier it is to break that chain."

Like killing Colby Green when I should have. Like killing Randall when I should have.

"I'm familiar with the theory," I said. "The hard part is knowing which domino needs to be stopped. Most of the time you can't tell until after it falls."

I pushed the self-recrimination aside and turned the Interceptor into the farm's driveway, passing a cottonwood stump carved into the likeness of a pipe-smoking toad. Nacho and Frito, the resident Australian Cattle Dogs, raced around the corner of the house and down the edge of the drive-way, driving a few stray ducks and a curious goat out of the parking area and back into the safety of the repurposed carport running along the side of the large barn. I parked next to a maroon Caddy I didn't recognize, and we presented ourselves for inspection.

The dogs sniffed at me and moved on, giving Fox a more thorough going over. Nacho settled down to watch us from under Margot's pickup while Frito raced off, sounding the intruder alert.

"I hear you, I hear you...hang on." Wiley came around the corner of the house, shooing three ducks toward their enclosure as he tried not to trip over them. He was either the skinniest Santa Claus you could ask for, or the cuddliest mad scientist this side of Miskatonic University. "Morning, gentlemen."

"Morning, Wiley." I gestured to Fox and said, "This one came over to the restaurant and found me. Fox, Wiley. Wiley, Fox."

"Aha, the 'paca-man himself. Welcome to the jungle." They shook hands and Wiley continued, "Let me get David taken care of, then I'll show you to your bunk. Once you're settled, we can go up the hill to the Thunderdome and I'll introduce you to the Ding-Dong himself."

Fox cocked an eyebrow. "Ding-Dong? Wild doorbell, or a free-range snack cake?"

116

"Paris, sorry. When we got him, his name was Rama, which became Rama the Llama, then just Rama Llama, and finally Rama Llama Ding-Dong, but it turns out he isn't a Hindu and the 'Llama' bit was redundant, so we cut the name in half."

I shook my head. "So where did 'Paris' come from?"

"Miriam named him that because his face can launch a thousand spits."

"Sounds like something she'd come up with." I glanced toward the house. "I just heard about Margot. How is she doing?"

Wiley shook his head and held up his hands to forestall further questions. "Not taking visitors, but thanks for asking. She just got back from therapy and isn't feeling social. Physically, her profile is nominal and all variables are within expected parameters. Feel free to pass that on."

"Will do. Let us know if you need any taxi services or errands run; Rose and I are usually available."

"I'll keep that in mind. Let's go get your eggs." Wiley waved and led us to the smaller barn. Nacho and Frito cruised behind us, ready to nip at our heels if we strayed from the path.

The smaller barn had better insulation and air flow than the large one, so it housed the farm's refrigerators and most of their merchandise. Wiley loaded up the eggs before pointing out several shelves of cheeses. "You should try some of the hard cheese. This batch turned out almost like aged parm. Ricotta, mozzarella, and some blue stuff that'll give Stilton a run for its money. Still no luck on the feta, but we just traded two goats for a mountain of processed lamb if you're in the mood for gyros. Even got a few sets of ribs if you want to take a shot at crown rack of lamb."

I held up my first and middle fingers to signal *missio*. "Enough, enough, I give! Half a wheel of the neo-parm and five pounds of the lamb. Rose loves gyros. Damn, man, you could sell a fifty-year-old mainframe to an Internet start-up."

Wiley laughed. "I have. How do you think we bought this place?"

My purchases filled the Interceptor's micro-trunk, even with the duck eggs travelling on the passenger side floor. I gave Frito a quick scruff behind the ears, telling her, "Just you wait...yes, just you wait...I can't wait to see you try to nip at Aparna's heels. You're going to be a frustrated doggie."

Frito gave me a "wanna' bet?" snort, shook herself, and bounded off to nudge a humungous Flemish rabbit back to its designated patch of greenery. Wiley watched the dog run and asked, "Really think your daughter can outrun those two if they decide she needs herding?"

"Outrun, no, but I'm betting she can sure as hell outfly them." I pulled out my phone and brought up a picture of Aparna from the wedding. "She'll be with Sharon's parents until the end of the month. I thought the farm would be a good place to bring her. She's lived in a high-rise apartment all her life. Petting goats will be good for her."

"Maybe start with the rabbits. The goats might decide to nibble on those feathers. How is she at flying, actually?"

"We're about halfway to gliding," I said. "She can jump long distances if she gets a running start. Her muscles are still developing."

Wiley nodded. "Found a spot for flight practice?"

"Not yet. I was thinking about an indoor skydiving place, or finding out where people go to learn hang gliding." I raised my eyebrow at him and asked, "Got some place in mind?"

"Well, the alpacas get most of our range land, but we left a bit for the goats." Wiley gestured to the northeast and led us through the big barn. "It's fenced off, but on the north side of the barn is a meadow. It's about an acre and a half, not too steep a slope, mostly covered with grass, and you got the barn between it and the road. No one can see you but the 'pacas. And they are well out of spitting range." He ushered us through a sliding door and out into the meadow. "Think this'll work?"

I jogged up the slope until I reached the property line. Other than the occasional small cactus, the slope looked perfect. It was certainly a lot more private than an indoor skydiving place.

I made my way back down to the barn and gave Wiley a thumbs-up. "Looks great, exactly what I was looking for. I'll have to bring Rose out to look it over, but I'm sure she'll approve."

"Wise policy." As we went back out through the barn, Wiley asked, "Coming to the circle tonight?"

I shook my head. "Hadn't heard about it, but I'm probably going to be busy. Something special going on?"

"We've been holding weekly rituals, raising energy to bring the Cheesman Park Killer to justice. Tonight we'll be focusing on this Colby Green fellow specifically. Nothing to harm him, of course, but to keep him from hurting anyone else and see that he receives justice for his actions."

"Justice is a good goal." I swallowed the self-recrimination and nodded to him. "If we can make it, we will."

"Good. We always raise more energy when Rose is dancing."

Dragon magic in action. "I'll let her know." We shook hands and I bid Wiley and Fox farewell. Once I was back on the road, I engaged the auto-drive and said, "Home, James. Play something bloodthirsty."

The car picked the Mars movement from Holst's *The Planets*. I stared out the window and daydreamed about bloody redemption.

<u>Chapter Eighteen</u>

Fighting Monsters

"Once again, this has not been officially confirmed, but at this time we believe that Colby Green, the accused Cheesman Park Killer, is dead. He was shot and killed, that is, reportedly shot and killed, during a daring hostage rescue operation. This was the scene about an hour ago at this house on the 2100 block of-"

Ember paused the news broadcast and pointed at one of the frozen figures. "There. Her. I think she was the one in the middle of all the girl-friend-stealing drama at Sylvan Faire. I don't remember seeing her with wings, though. Is she the same race as your daughter?"

"No, Aparna's wings have feathers." I hit 'Play' and lowered the television volume. As the paramedics lifted the bat-winged woman's gurney into their ambulance, I said, "I think she might be a Succubus. Which could be interesting. If she's an actual demon, I mean."

Rose nuzzled my ear. "No wonder you like me to take that form..."

I kissed her back, and would have kissed her some more, but Ember interrupted our snuggling.

"Whoa, cool! Mage in the house!" Ember ran the broadcast back several seconds to the start of another helicopter shot. A good portion of the basement looked to be on fire, and black smoke was pouring out of several broken windows. An injured Drow woman nearly fell off her own gurney trying to twist around enough to point at the house. Apparently, the fire department wasn't responding fast enough for her; she made several emphatic gestures and pointed at the house, sending a jet of water through one of the basement windows. Moments later, two figures in black tactical gear stumbled out of the smoke-filled doorway. As paramedics surrounded them, the Drow woman fell back and let herself be loaded onto the ambulance.

When the video ended and they switched back to the live feed, Vivian Davis was preening next to the reporter. I got up and went into the kitchen. Ember didn't need to be burdened with my issues. I poured myself a glass of tea and headed for my office.

Thirteen yawned at me from the windowsill. "Someone is trying to message you. You forget to set your 'Away' status."

"Cats do computer support now, too? Let me guess—you toy with your customers until they beg for mercy and then format their hard drives?" I sat down and unlocked my system. Sure enough, I had a pile of messages waiting. I ignored most of them and brought up an email from Grace. They'd taken Aparna to Kiddie Park in Bartlesville, and Grace wanted me to see how much fun my little girl was having without me. I wrote a nice letter thanking her for the pictures. As an afterthought, I added that I hoped Aparna enjoyed the rest of her stay with them.

"Your daughter really is having fun," the cat said. "And Sharon's parents really do love her."

"I hope so. I want her to have a healthy relationship with them." I sent the email and reached for my tea, but there was a cat in the way. I sat back and asked, "Is there something else I need to know about?"

Thirteen nodded. "I tried to shift her the night before last. Just a test run as a precaution. I couldn't do it. She was...fixed in place. I can't explain it, and that worries me."

"You can still keep an eye on her, right?"

"Of course. That isn't a problem. Moving her is." The cat tapped his claws on my desk and hissed under his breath. "I can stay by her, but if things go bad, I'm not going to be able to rescue her. Rose may not be able to teleport her, either, so you're going to need to adjust your plans."

"Easy enough," I said. "I don't have a plan yet. Just options. Indecision is the basis of flexibility."

"Nice. Did you come up with that yourself, or read it in a fortune cookie?"

"Fortune cookies?" I snorted, waving at the bookshelves lining the walls of my office. "Why doesn't anyone ever assume I have the education and insight to distill complex concepts into simple epigrams? I mean, I've been to college, I'm very well read, I have an elegant sense of humor-"

"You have a massive collection of buttons from all the conventions you've attended..."

"Oh, dear. My secret is out." My email dinged and displayed a new batch of emails asking for money. "Good grief. How do all these people keep getting my email address? I've changed it three times in the past year."

The cat flicked his ears at me. "You have a fan club now?"

"Not exactly. This fellow helped us out with that demoness in Las Vegas, and as a reward, I gave him four million dollars. The problem is I didn't make his family sign a non-disclosure agreement."

120

Thirteen's paw twitched, producing a dried catnip stem out of thin air. He clenched it between his teeth like a cigar and added, "It just doesn't pay to be nice to people, if you ask me."

"The person I was nice to isn't the problem," I said. "Boudreaux is going to school and living like a college student. It's Jeanne, his sister, who won't keep her mouth shut. I've told her I can't solve the world's poverty issues, but it's like talking to a freaking wall. She acts like wealth is something I should atone for. Honestly, I'm about ready to file for a restraining order."

"Why don't you?"

"Because Heroes don't do things like that." I snorted. "Not that I'm much of a Hero anymore. Not after sitting around and looking the other way while that rat bastard werewolf murdered five women."

"I didn't know you were responsible for finding and punishing this world's evildoers," Thirteen said. "Doesn't someone have to murder your parents while you're walking home from the opera for you to get that gig?"

"Be serious," I snapped. "I could have prevented those murders, and I didn't."

"Oh. I didn't realize you were the only person who could possibly have done anything at that point. Do you have any idea how arrogant that sounds?" He picked up the remote and turned my office television on, flipping to a news channel. As usual, the headlines were filled with assaults, murders, war—an unending cacophony of misery. Thirteen waited until the next commercial and said, "Well?"

"Well what?"

"Well, which of these wrongs is enough to motivate you to action? What about that bombing in the street market? You could have Rose scry for terrorists planning an upcoming action and turn them in. Or kill them yourself, whatever."

I took a deep breath. "I am not going to start hunting people down for what they 'might' do. Colby Green had already killed one person. That was more than reason enough to act."

"Oh, you need reasons before you can act. What about that child prostitution story? I'm sure there are plenty of repeat offenders in the Denver area alone."

"I'm not a masked vigilante," I said. "I can't save the world, I know that. I'm not an idiot. I was talking about taking out one person, not launching some damn fool idealistic crusade."

Thirteen muted the television. "I'm glad to hear that. You missed an opportunity, but that doesn't invalidate who you are. Besides, you didn't just wake up one morning and decide to become a Hero. You people— Heroes—are forged in pain and loss. Heroes are the good that comes out of tragedy. You needed Sharon's death to find your purpose. Well, Colby Green was the kind of evil that could awaken someone else to their purpose."

"I don't disagree with any part of that," I said. "I'm still disappointed in myself for ignoring the issue."

The cat turned the volume back up. "It's still a self-indulgent waste of time. Are you still going to the drumming thing tonight?"

"I don't know if the drumming is still going on." I pulled up the social media page Wiley maintained for the farm. "Hmm, yep. 'We will be drumming and dancing to raise energy for the healing and recovery of those damaged by these criminal acts. We will also be collecting donations of cash, unworn casual clothing, and unused plush animals for the Boulder Police Department's Victim Advocate Program'."

"Voodoo for Victims," Thirteen said. "Sure, why not. You people never cease to amuse me."

"It's not Voudoun," I said. "It's Western Metaphysical/New Age Eclectic Paganism, often with a veneer of quasi-Celtic symbols and iconography."

"Fine. Naked Voodoo. Do these people like cats?"

"Are you kidding? They're Pagans. You'll be lucky if people don't get into a fight over who gets to adopt you."

I wasn't far off.

All five of us rode to the drum circle in the Range Rover, with Thirteen sitting in the back between Harmony and Ember. We set up our camp chairs just outside the dancer's ring, along with a large, comfy pillow on top of a folding stool for Thirteen. He hadn't even gotten settled on the pillow when the first would-be savior appeared.

"Oh, wow...love the hat and bandanna look. Is he yours?"

I didn't recognize the woman, but I could tell she had at least two other cats. One black, one orange. "Thirteen is our houseguest," I said. "He comes and goes at will. He is a cat, you know."

"Are you looking for a forever home for him?" The hope in her voice was almost palpable.

"Oh, he has a home, out in Eldorado Springs. He's just hanging at our place for a bit." I had to give six more people the same speech before the drumming started. All the while, Thirteen basked in the adoration and deigned to accept the various nibbles and treats people offered to him as tribute.

Margot made the trip from the house to the fire circle under her own power and took her seat to much applause. She waved the applause away and said, "Yes, the rumors are true. I can, once again, walk and chew gum. You may alert the media." She sat back and gave everyone a 'carry on' wave.

Wiley started a brisk, crisp rhythm on his doumbek. Another drummer matched the beat on a large, carved wood djembe. Rose and Ember joined several of the other dancers in a *zagareet* (that 'lalalalala' trill belly dancers make) as they shimmied into the dance ring.

Rose had turned her skin my favorite shade of green for the occasion. She and Ember were both wearing clothing and jewelry we'd brought back from India, and they looked spectacular in the firelight.

The first dance was just a warm up, getting everyone relaxed and ready to focus on raising energy. The drummers stretched while the dancers rehydrated and hit the bathroom. I grabbed some sliced melon and spent some time catching up with friends I hadn't seen for a while.

Wiley stepped up to the fire, drumming out a brief, staccato salute. "Pray attend! Mommy, Arthur wants to know where you wandered off to. He was waiting outside the bathroom for you."

Across the fire from Wylie, Ember knelt on the ground next to a toddler. She was smiling and singing a song from a children's television show. Young Arthur looked unsure whether to giggle or cry. So far, giggle was winning.

Mommy's friends recognized the boy and brought Mommy back from searching the barn. She scooped Arthur up in a fierce hug, voice and hands shaking. Ember helped her to her seat and kept Arthur distracted while Mommy calmed down. Even with the crying and carrying on, Ember stayed calm and cheerful... exactly the response I'd want in someone taking care of Aparna.

I smiled and mentally shared my idea with Rose. She approved.

Once calm was restored, Ember came back to our little section of the circle and took a long drink out of her water bottle. "Wiley has too many neat toys in his office," she muttered. "I think it should be classified as an attractive nuisance."

"I wouldn't expect anything different," I said. I waited for her to finish another drink and asked, "Would you be interested in a job? Free room rent is part of the benefit package."

She laughed. "What, live-in maid? That isn't really my style."

"I have a housekeeping service already, you might have noticed. No, I had something much more important in mind."

Ember raised her eyebrows. "Like what?"

"Aparna's nanny. Or governess, if you like that title better."

"You're kidding."

I shook my head. "Not at all. I was watching you, and you did great with Arthur. The past month to the contrary, I do have a day job, and I'd feel a lot better doing it if I knew you were looking after Aparna. And, trust me; I will pay you a lot more than the coffee shop did."

Ember nodded slowly. "Free room and wages...okay. We can talk. But, if we do this, I want one more thing."

"Which is?"

"I want to be able to use your shower. Not when you're in it, of course, just when it's available."

I didn't hesitate. "Agreed." We shook hands to seal the deal. I added, "You are going to love Aparna. I know every parent says the same thing, but, really, she's an absolute angel."

Bad choice of words.

Chapter Nineteen

Southern Hospitality

Forty-five minutes from touching down in Tulsa, I got a text message from Vernon. "Engine crapped out in Ramona. Waiting for help. My friend Tyson lives near the airport, will pick you up. Wearing a hunting vest and Kenworth hat."

Bloody. Hell.

I only had an hour between arrival and my return flight. They were supposed to have Aparna through the security line and be waiting in the terminal when I arrived. There was no way I could pick up Aparna, get back to the airport, and get through security again.

Sure, I could have driven down and picked her up, but driving from Denver to Tulsa takes ten to twelve hours on a good day. Too late now, regardless. I messaged Vernon back saying I'd look for Tyson, saved the expense report I'd been working on, and started shopping for a new return flight.

The best I could get was standby for a flight leaving at midnight. Traveling all night with a cranky four-year-old was right out. Tomorrow at ten in the morning would be much better for all concerned. I booked two seats and reserved a two-bedroom suite at a hotel near the airport. They even offered a vegetarian option with their complimentary breakfast bar.

As soon as the jetway was connected and the door open, I thanked the crew and jogged for the terminal. Thankfully, I made it to the giant revolving door at the terminal exit without having to do hurdles over anyone's luggage. Several people were waiting on the far side of the "Do Not Cross This Line" warning on the floor, but only one was wearing a blaze-orange hunting vast.

Tyson appeared to be in his mid-seventies, tall and spare. He had the dark, weathered look of a life spent working outdoors and bone-white hair in a vintage crew cut. Other than the orange hunting vest, he might have been dressed for church—black slacks, dress shirt, and narrow black tie.

He looked like he'd just shaved (with a straight razor, I bet) and smelled like English Leather. He looked me over and said, "You've grown a bit since I saw you last, but you probably don't remember me."

I chuckled and shook his hand. "I do, actually. You...ah...you own a stable and board horses, right? Sharon and I came out to ride a few times."

Tyson nodded. "Used to own, more like. Sold it six years ago. I'm surprised you remember the place."

"I remember because Sharon always made the trips memorable, truth be told." I chuckled, shaking my head. "She was obsessed with getting the guy who saddled our horses to crack a smile. He was always so polite and serious, and it made her crazy. She dug up every dirty joke she could find. She even flashed him once. All he said was, 'You should put on sunscreen' and kept on adjusting her stirrups like nothing had happened. I don't know how he put up with us."

"Ben..." Tyson's cheek twitched. He shook his head and cleared his throat. "His name was Ben. He, ah, well, he passed away last year. Fell asleep watching football, just never woke up."

"I'm sorry to hear that," I said. "I wish I'd had a chance to know him better."

"Thank you. He was one of the best men I've ever known." Tyson cleared his throat again and asked, "How much luggage you got?"

I nodded and went with the change of subject. "None. Since we were supposed to fly back at once, I just brought my laptop so I could work on the plane."

"Guess that's what happens when you make plans." He nodded at another revolving door (big enough to accommodate someone pushing a luggage cart) and said, "Car's parked out here."

As we crossed to the parking structure, a taxi blazed past us, then slammed on the brakes and screeched to a halt at the passenger drop-off. Tyson just kept walking. I shook my head and followed.

He led me to a gleaming early-Eighties model soft-top Jeep. It smelled of sunlight, soap, and Carnauba wax. I took a moment to admire the car and said, "This is gorgeous. Do you do car shows?"

Tyson unlocked the passenger door and held it open for me. "Thought about it a few times, but it seemed like bragging. Ben always wanted..." He stopped talking and shrugged. "Doesn't matter." He got in, started the car, and drove to the exit in silence.

While we waited in line at the parking lot tollbooth, I got three twenties out of my wallet and held them out to Tyson. "Normally I'd offer to buy you dinner for going to all this trouble, but since I can't guarantee how Aparna will be once we pick her up, I can at least pay for parking and buy you gas."

He waved it away. "Nope, keep your money. I'm doing this as a favor for Vernon."

"Coming to meet me was Vernon's favor. Now I need to ask you for one. Aparna and I are going to need a ride back into town. I got us a hotel room for the night. Aparna's a good kid, but I want her rested and happy when we get on the plane tomorrow."

"Well, in that case, thank you kindly." Tyson took the cash, paid the attendant, and we were on our way.

I checked my phone for any updates, but Vernon hadn't sent anything since his original texts. I sighed and asked, "I don't suppose Vernon gave you their exact location, by any chance?"

"Yup. I even know how to get there. But you can keep an eye out if you want. You see me getting on a road going to Joplin, you let me know."

I chuckled. "I'll do that."

I stayed quiet until we turned off the 11 west and merged onto the northbound 75. "If you don't mind my asking, am I remembering correctly that Ben was Native American?"

"He was an Indian, if that's what you mean. Osage. Not full-blood, but close."

"I'd wondered, but I was always too intimidated to ask him. He was never rude or hostile or anything, just...formal, I guess. Like there was always a wall between us."

Tyson nodded. "He was just being careful. He didn't want to give anyone reason to, well, get upset about anything. Being around kids, I mean."

Aha... "Um...if I'm wrong, I apologize, but...you two were together?" It made sense, but I didn't want to upset him if I was misinterpreting everything.

"Well, 'together' is a nicer word than 'faggots,' so, yeah." He looked sideways at me for a moment before returning his attention to the road. "But I guess that doesn't matter to a godless bleeding-heart liberal like you, right?"

"It doesn't make me think any less of you, and it wouldn't have stopped me from bringing Aparna for rides if the stable was still open." I shook my head. "For what it's worth, if our coming to the stable caused you any grief, I'm sorry. Being gay around here can't be easy in the best of times."

"Not your doing, for one thing. Not gay, either. Never liked that word. I loved Ben, and that was it." Tyson sighed. "Twenty years we were together, and I miss him every day."

We lapsed back into silence until we reached the exit for Ramona. Tyson pulled into a parking lot to check his directions while I messaged a status update to Rose and Nadia. He noticed the two names and raised his eyebrows at me.

"Nothing like that," I said. "Rose is my wife and Nadia is Vice President of the company I own. She's managing the office and likes to know where I am in case our boss calls. She's actually more worried about me than Rose is, because she'd be taking over if anything happened to me."

Tyson chuckled. "Damn. If she's going to be watching your ass like that, maybe you should go ahead and sleep with her." Something must have showed on my face; he broke out laughing and added, "Guess that piece of advice is a little late."

I rubbed my face and looked out the window. "Nadia and Rose hooked up one night in Vegas and invited me to join in. It had nothing to do with my charm and good looks, trust me. It was just a mix of loneliness and vodka." Well, in Nadia's case it was actually a mixture of pot and catnip, but that would take too long to explain.

"Nice to know someone else is doing their part to destroy traditional Christian marriage. Thought Ben and I had to do it all by ourselves." He chuckled again and pulled out onto the road. "Anyway, they're parked behind a service station with one of them big green dinosaurs in front of it. Should be up ahead here."

The gas station was long-closed and appeared to have been a head shop in its last incarnation, but the vintage Sinclair dinosaur was easy to recognize, even with the sunglasses, leis, and bright red Hawaiian shirt it was wearing. We drove around to the back and saw three guys who looked to be in their twenties poking around under the hood of an SUV. I looked around for Vernon, Grace, or Aparna, but they were nowhere in sight.

When I got out of the car, a guy with greasy blonde hair and a Dallas Cowboys shirt straightened up and tucked a big Maglite flashlight into his belt. His hands didn't look dirty, but he still grabbed a cleaning rag and wiped his hands. "Are you David?"

I nodded. "Yes. Any idea where my daughter and her grandparents are?"

"They went to the diner down the block to use the bathroom." Cowboys Fan looked at his buddies and said, "Guys, want to give us a hand with all this?"

The other two nodded and all three put on latex gloves, even though their hands weren't that dirty. Cowboys Fan opened the SUV's liftgate and stepped back. I looked to see how much luggage there was. Other than a roadside emergency kit, the cargo area was empty.

Before I could turn around, he cracked me across the back of the skull with the Maglite.

It staggered me and hurt like hell, but I didn't fall. He hit me again, this time across the temple. Everything went blurry and the ground punched me in the face. I stared at the blood spattering on the pavement, and for a long moment I couldn't remember who I was or what was going on. I knew I was in danger, and tried to crawl under the SUV. Cowboys Fan kicked me in the ribs, leaving me with trouble breathing and a terrific view of the spare tire.

"Hey! What are you doing?" I heard a crackle of electricity and Tyson shouted, "How do you like that, ya' rat bastard?" From under the SUV, I had a great view as one of the thugs stumbled away and fell face-down on the concrete, convulsing. I could hear Tyson and Thug Two grappling, but when I tried to move, black spots covered my vision and my lunch went everywhere.

Cowboys Fan paused in mid-kick and snarled, "Real cute, faggot!" He charged at Tyson, clubbing him with the Maglite. Tyson hit the ground. A small stun gun bounced out of his grasp and rolled away. Cowboys Fan planted his boot on Tyson's neck and pounded on his head with the flashlight.

I flinched at the sound. *Get on your feet, or you are both going to die.* I grabbed the SUV bumper and levered my way out from under it. As I did, Thug One stumbled back to his buddies and all three took turns stomping on Tyson's head and chest. He wasn't moving or saying anything.

I closed my eyes and looked away a moment. *Sorry, man. You didn't deserve this.*

The bastards were still kicking Tyson's body and laughing. Well, if I couldn't save him, at least I could avenge him. I rolled up on my knees and opened the emergency kit, looking for anything I could use as a weapon. All I found was an air pressure gauge and three roadside flares. I took the flares, but stood up too fast. The world spun and I fell against the side of the SUV. I focused on breathing and tried to get my balance.

Even though Tyson wasn't moving, Thug One and Thug Two grabbed him by the shoulders and hauled him to his knees. Cowboys Fan drew a .38 revolver, stuck the barrel of the gun into Tyson's mouth, and said, "One last thing for you to suck on, fudgepacker."

Rage and adrenaline cleared the fog out of my mind. I charged as Cowboys Fan fired. I hit him too late, but I still got credit for the sack. I landed on top of him and the gun bounced under Tyson's Jeep. Cowboys Fan got both hands on my throat, squeezing hard. I scraped one flare against the pavement to light it and shoved the burning end six inches into his eye socket.

So much for his trying to choke me.

Thug One seized a handful of my hair and drove a screwdriver into my back. The remaining flares slipped out of my hand. He pulled me to my knees and tried another kick to the ribs. He missed. I lunged and snagged his waistband. My punch missed his crotch and his knee broke my nose.

Damn, it's getting hard to breathe... I felt one of the flares against the side of my knee. I grabbed it with my free hand, ignited it, and stuffed it into his pants. *Goodness gracious, that has to hurt.*

Thug Two scrambled out from under Tyson's Jeep, holding the pistol. Thug One rolled off to the side, screaming and clawing at the flare. Thug Two gaped at him, wide-eyed and frozen.

I wiped blood off my forehead, gulping air and waving the last flare as threateningly as I could. Then I remembered my magic sword. I tossed the flare to the ground and summoned Kindness.

A surge of energy from the blade got me up and moving. Thug Two fired and missed. I sliced his gun hand off with one swing and opened him like a trout on the follow-through. Thug One, crotch still smoking, was crawling toward the street. He wasn't going to go far; probably just to the nearest hospital. I could talk to him there. *I got a lot of questions for you, bub.*

The world got blurry and I couldn't remember why I'd been so angry. I leaned against Tyson's Jeep and tried to remember what I needed to do now. I knew it had something to do with my phone. I had to...*man, it's hard to breathe.*

Flashing lights and loud sirens. Good. Blue uniforms. I saw Jake and Miranda waving at me. I staggered toward them. I'd missed them so much after they died...

Drop the sword? Sorry, I can't. No swords on my loot table...

At least the cops were nice enough to shoot me in the lung that already had the screwdriver in it.

Chapter Twenty

Down, but not Out

Waking up in a hospital sucks, but it's better than not waking up.

I wasn't intubated, but I was wearing an oxygen mask. The right side of my chest was a general pool of ache with occasional spots of throbbing pain, all made worse whenever I inhaled. Probably had something to do with all the bandages and gauze encasing my ribs. On top of all that, I was handcuffed, shackled to the bed, and I could see a uniformed cop sitting outside the doorway. The clock told me it was nine-thirty; the window told me it was night.

Sharon was standing in the corner of the room, wearing the same tank-top and jeans outfit she's died in. I smiled and waved. Her wings did look like Aparna's...

A nurse bustled into the room, pushing a computer on a rolling stand right through Sharon. She vanished, and the nurse gave me a big smile. "Glad to see you back with us, sir. I'm Thankful, and you should be, too. You're in the ICU at St Francis Hospital in Tulsa. You were airlifted to our trauma center earlier today. Now, let's have a quick look at you."

"Did you see...no, never mind."

"See what, sir?"

"I thought I saw a friend of mine. She was killed a few years ago."

"Well, maybe you had an angel watching over you today."

I nodded. Yeah, maybe." *And maybe I can still see the honored dead...*

"If she's still here, you two can talk after I leave. Let's get your blood pressure..."

Along with the usual poking, prodding, measuring, and squeezing, she asked if I knew my name, the date, where I was, and so on. I answered as best I could; hospitals liked it when people cooperated. For a reward, I got a wonderful, glorious, life-saving drink of ice water. I kept it down, so Nurse Thankful was happy to let me have more when her duties took her through the room. She even turned the television on and left the call button/remote within reach.

Sharon didn't come back. That was fine. Aparna needed her more than I did.

In between Nurse Thankful's visits, I stayed quiet and got caught up with Rose. She was angry and frustrated but doing her best to stay calm. She'd already spoken with the police in Tulsa and Bartlesville about Aparna and sent them a copy of my custody papers. I promised Rose I'd behave and take it easy while the acceptance did its thing. Aside from forcing our emotions into synch, it also healed me far faster than anyone at the hospital would expect. Or believe, for that matter.

An hour after I woke up, a doctor cruised through and checked my physical responses as well as the answers I'd given to Nurse Thankful's questions. Once that was out of the way, he said, "Well, you are an inexcusably lucky individual. Two bullets passed through you without hitting anything important, one grazed your right lung, which was also perforated by a screwdriver. The blunt-force trauma to your skull resulted in concussion and a nice lineal skull fracture, but no brain swelling so far. You also have a mess of bruises and small lacerations not worth mentioning individually. You managed to avoid any other bone fractures or broken teeth, which I personally find both astounding and unfair."

The doctor closed the tablet he's been reading from and shook his head. "I'm not sure why, but those wounds aren't nearly as bad as you deserve them to be. Frankly, if it were my place to question God's will, I'd be damn pissed with our merciful Lord and Savior's choices where you're concerned. All in all, regardless of my assessment of your character and moral deficiencies, I'd say you got off light. You are still looking at a significant amount of medical care, but you have good insurance and seem to be responding well to treatment. In my opinion, your odds of a successful recovery are excellent."

"I'm glad to hear that," I said. "Would it be possible to get a phone in here? I'd like to call my wife and let her know I'm alive."

The doctor shook his head. "I called your wife and updated her before I came in here. You may rest assured I treated her with all due courtesy."

"Why can't I speak with her?" I didn't need to, of course, but it would look odd if I didn't ask. "I also need to talk to the police. I think my daughter's grandparents are trying to kidnap her. They were supposed to be at that gas station, and I think they sent those idiots to kill me. Please, I need you to call the police and get someone down here as soon as possible."

The doctor snorted. "Way ahead of you, son. There are two policemen waiting to speak with you. You aren't officially under arrest—yet—but don't think about running. Between the morphine, the concussion, and the catheter, running would be tricky anyway."

"Not to mention the handcuffs and leg irons," I said. "Do you treat all your assault victims this way, or am I just special?"

"Son, you gutted one of those boys like a trout," he replied. "But don't worry. We are sworn to heal all who come to us, and we will do just that. Now, why don't you just sit back and exercise that right to remain silent?" He gave me the kind of look usually reserved for toilet paper stuck to the bottom of one's shoe and walked out.

I refrained from giving him the Impudent Finger and counted to ten, silently and slowly. This wasn't the best position to be in, but at least I was alive. *Remember that, and don't make things worse for yourself.*

There was definitely no love from the police. Detectives Danes and Albion were both in Bad Cop mode as soon as they walked in. Danes did the introductions, followed by, "David Fraser, you have the right to remain silent-"

I sat up on my elbows, pushed all the energy I'd been able to collect into the imperative form, and hurled it at them. "No. I'm the victim, not the suspect. There's no reason to arrest me."

Danes shook his head. "Right...you...you're the victim."

Albion's face went blank. "No, no need at all."

A wave of dizziness and nausea damn near sent me into the dry heaves. I took a deep breath and risked pushing again. "Get me some water and take these shackles off. Then you can ask your questions." I collapsed back onto the bed. The effort left me seeing double and gave me a nosebleed, but the handcuffs came off and I got my water. Plus, gauze rolls for my nose. Getting my phone was an unexpected bonus.

"Please understand, restraining you was just a matter of reasonable caution," Danes said. "Three people dead, one badly injured, and you covered in blood while waving a giant sword. We couldn't take chances."

"That's fine," I said. "Officer safety, you can't be too careful, I get it. I don't care. I need to find out where my daughter is." I gave the detectives a recap of the custody situation. "I have a copy of the visitation agreement in my black satchel. It was in the back seat of Tyson's car. I need the satchel and my laptop as soon as possible, please. And my clothes."

Albion said, "The vehicle is still being processed for evidence, but we can see about having those items returned to you. Your clothes had to be cut off and are no longer wearable. I'll see if our victim advocate program can find some donated items that fit you. When you're well enough to be released, that is."

"I spoke with your wife and she said she was arranging transportation down here. She also told us about your daughter. Tomorrow morning, two sheriff's deputies and an investigator from Osage County child services are going out to this church camp to get her. We'll update you when we know more." Danes left his card on the table next to my bed. "My cell number is on the back. Call me if you have any questions or if you remember anything you need to add to your statement."

"I'd like to get my sword back as soon as possible," I said. "Leaving blood on it is bad for the blade."

Albion snorted. "That isn't going to happen, Mr. Fraser. You killed two men with it. It's evidence now. You can petition the court to have it returned, but it's not likely to happen."

I sighed and nodded. "I know. I had to ask, though." I slumped back onto my pillow and did my best to look despondent. It must have worked; they murmured apologies and left, taking the officer guarding the door with them.

Once they were out of the room, I snagged my phone and started to call Rose. I made it halfway through the phone number before she appeared in the middle of the room, Thirteen perched on her shoulder. He gave me a nod and vanished again. Made sense. Visiting family members were one thing, but a cat would attract a lot of attention. Not as much as the Spielbergian storm clouds we'd get if Rose portalled here via her home plane, but a lot.

I waved at Rose and said, "Hi honey. Sorry I'm late, but I have a really good excuse."

"Not for long." Rose kissed me thoroughly and we held tight to one another for a long moment. I felt her drawing in a vast amount of energy, right up to the limit of what she could hold without changing form or increasing her body mass. Once she was fully charged, she looked at my eyes and shook her head. "Nosebleed, broken blood vessels, and your irises have a silver sheen to them. You put too much energy into a spell and got mana-lashed. Keep it up and you'll turn your brain into egg salad."

"I had to convince the detectives I was the victim. I guess I overdid it."

"No kidding. You have to be careful. The imperative form helps keep you safe, which is why I let you use it, but you can't push yourself like that. Lay off the magic for a few days and you'll feel much better."

"Well, if one spell is all I can do, at least it's a useful one."

"It's not quite all," Rose murmured. She looked out the door and mind-controlled the nearest nurse. "David is checking out," Rose said. "Get all this stuff unhooked so he can leave."

"No, just remove the catheter. I can pee on my own, thanks." I tried to sit up, but the nurse pushed me back onto the bed, tossed the sheet back, and clamped on to my Old Fellow with ice-cold, shrinkage-inducing talons. She had the catheter out in moments. Rose hit her with a *Retcon* spell and sent her out of the room.

I salvaged what dignity I could and asked, "Have you had any luck finding Aparna?"

Rose took my hand. "No. Not since this afternoon. When I saw her, she was fine. Vernon and Grace were with her. She looked tired, but not like she'd been crying or anything." She gave my hand a squeeze and added, "They were talking about you not showing up at the airport. Grace thought it might have been due to an accident, but Vernon was thinking you had some evil scheme in mind. We need to get you out of here."

"Later. Now I need to stay here. The police expect to find me in bed and they expect me to be injured. They're sending a couple of officers to the compound to pick up Aparna in the morning. I don't want to rock the boat." I caught a glint in Rose's eye and added, "Yet."

Rose narrowed her eyes, scowling at me. "Vernon and Grace tried to have you killed. They're out of second chances. Nadia has your car stored with that silk bedsheet spell, Eric and Harmony are fully loaded with combat spells, and the rest of my family is ready to tear that compound apart down to the last brick. We plan to hit them at three in the morning and flood the area with euphoria gas-"

I leaned up and kissed her to stop her from talking. Bad idea. Searing pain lanced through the side of my chest and I couldn't breathe in. Collapsing back onto the bed made things a bit easier, but not enough. *Hmmm—so this is what a fish dying on a riverbank feels like...*

Rose hissed something horribly profane in Draconic and put her hands on my chest. Her chanting changed to a continuous, didgeridoo-like drone. The pain in my chest got worse, until everything went black.

I woke up to glorious, pain-free breathing. Rose was trailing her fingers down the middle of my chest. She said, "I fixed your lungs. And your skull. The rest isn't critical. Why don't you like my plan?"

"I'm not ready to cry 'Havoc' and let slip the dogs of war yet. I'm sure it would work, but I'd like to get out of this without having to find out if you can cast *Retcon* on a global scale."

She snorted but settled down. "Fine. What's the first step in *your* cunning master plan?"

"It was going to be hot, steamy, hospital recovery sex, but everything hurts too much for that." I settled for a kiss and added, "Besides, there's something to take care of first."

Rose raised an eyebrow. "More important than your health? I doubt it."

"Trust me, it is. One of the three guys who jumped us is still alive somewhere."

"He's as good as dead." Rose stood up and headed for the door.

"Wait!" I sighed and waved for her to come back to the bed. "I don't want him dead. Not yet, anyway. I want you to find him and convince him to confess everything. The truth, the whole truth, and nothing but the truth."

"If I just kill him, all they have to go on is your version of events." Rose threw her hands into the air. "Why complicate things?"

"If he dies, there will always be questions about what happened. If he confesses, confirms my statement, and implicates Vernon, then I'm cleared and Aparna's safe." I gripped her hand and gave in to all the desperation I'd suppressed since I woke up. I had to show her how critical this was to me.

Rose took in my desperation. Smelling it, tasting it, weighing my need against her instinct and desire. And to her, it really *was* simple. Few problems remain problems once you burn them to ash. I didn't argue; I just did my best to convince her this problem was one she couldn't solve with claw and flame.

After many long seconds, she nodded. "I'll take care of it, but, really, you people need to develop truth spells." She pulled her scrying bowl out of Dragon Mini-Storage, followed by my sword-cleaning kit. "There. That should keep you out of trouble while I take care of this bastard."

"Thank you," I said. I summoned Kindness out of the evidence lockup and grimaced at the condition of the blade. The bloodstains were set, sticky to the touch, and smelled terrible. I apologized to the sword while I wiped her blade down as best I could with a piece of linen. I followed that up with a silk cloth soaked in a Dwarf-made sword cleaning oil. That stuff was amazing; it cut through the blood, fingerprint powder, and Goddess-knows what else the police used, leaving only gleaming steel.

I was cleaning the last traces of blood off the sword's tang when a small Hispanic woman in scrubs and a lab coat walked into the room. "All taken care of," she said. She dropped a personal property bag into the chair next to the bed and stripped the scrubs off before changing back into Rose.

"Any problems?"

"None at all. Well, none for me. The guy who attacked you is in a world of trouble." She took her regular clothes out of the bag and got dressed again. "He's two floors down, chained to his bed. A minister who claims to be able to heal stopped in to see him this afternoon, but refused to use his gift if it meant he had to touch another man's naughty bits. Mister Great Balls of Fire was somewhat put out."

"I bet. You know you're in for a bad day when the healer refuses to *Lay on Hands* because touching your junk would be an alignment violation."

Rose snickered. "He was actually ready to talk before I got there. I didn't even have to push him very hard to get the confession flowing. The prospect of going through life with a penis that looks like a lump of charred marshmallow is a terrific incentive to purge your soul."

Despite the fact I had inflicted the injury in question (or perhaps because of it), I flinched at the visual. Still...he made his choice back in that parking lot. "What did he say?"

Rose snorted. "All his life, religious teachers told him homosexuals were evil. He signed up because he didn't want to miss a chance to, as he put it, 'waste a couple fags'."

"Vernon told him I was gay?" It didn't matter either way; I'd stopped being afraid of that word a long time ago. What bothered me was Vernon selling Tyson out when they were supposed to be friends.

Rose leaned back in her chair, shaking her head. "He said it wasn't Vernon. One of the associate priests told those three goons you were a gay friend of Sharon's and reminded them the Bible says gay people should be stoned to death. I guess they decided shooting you in the head would be close enough.”

“Charming.” I sighed and rubbed my temples. I had no qualms about killing in self-defense. Not anymore. When someone tries to kill you, you’d best kill them right proper first. But murdering for the thrill of it...there’s a special place in Hell for people like that. “At least his confession will give the cops all the probable cause they could ask for.”

I gave Kindness one more pass with a clean piece of silk and sent her back home, hanging on the wall of my office. Without thinking, I stood up to go to the bathroom, and the world decided to spin in place. Rose caught me before I fell. She ignored my protests and helped me into the bathroom. I took care of business while she tucked the blood-smeared cleaning cloths into the biohazard receptacle. I did better on the way back to bed; it helped that the room decided not to spin around this time.

“I’m going to get something to eat,” Rose announced. “You just stay put and get some sleep. It’s almost midnight.”

“As you wish.” I found the television program guide and picked a cooking show to lull me into slumber. “It might be uncharitable of me, but, deep down, I really hope Vernon decides to ignore the court order and resist arrest. That would just make my day.”

I should have known better. Never give the Dungeon Master ideas.

Chapter Twenty-One

Cunning Plans 101

"What do you mean, 'she's gone'? Did your people even search for her?"

Danes bristled at me. "Mister Fraser, the officers on-scene called in two more units and went through every building out there. There was no sign of your daughter, or the grandparents, or their car. The associate pastor said the Datonas left three days ago. It's a church, not a prison."

I reminded myself that punching cops was a bad idea and unclenched my fists. "I'm sorry, detective. I'm sure the officers who went out there did their best. It's just...I'm sure she's there. Her grandparents know there's going to be a search for her and for them. If they get caught, they're losing visitation and probably going to jail. They don't want that. They're hiding somewhere they feel safe, and that church is the most likely spot."

"With all due respect, Mister Fraser, I'm not a post turtle and this isn't my first time dealing with an abducted child." Danes flipped open his notebook. "So far, we've issued a national missing child alert and put out descriptions of Aparna, her grandparents, and their car. We are also in the process of obtaining search warrants for their home, telephone records, bank accounts, and credit card activity. We've also reached out to the media and requested they help get the message out."

Danes flipped the notebook closed. "Beyond that, we've got state and municipal resources mobilized and are in touch with agencies in all neighboring states as well as the FBI child abduction team. That's a lot of law enforcement for what could be an elderly couple forgetting what day their visitation ends."

"I'd like to believe that's all this is, detective, but I don't buy it for a second." I gestured to my injuries and added, "Not when they sent three goons to kill me."

Danes all but rolled his eyes. "There's no solid evidence the grandparents were involved with the assault. The one survivor implicated someone else when we questioned him. If it turns out the grandparents were involved, we'll deal with them. Until then, these are two separate cases."

"Are you blind?" I pounded my fist on the rolling table, sending some silverware and trash left from lunch flying. "Vernon messaged me to meet him there! He had to call Tyson to ask him to drive me! Do you seriously believe he just happened to send me to the exact location where those guys were waiting?"

"Mister Fraser, I don't *believe* anything. The question is what I *know*. And right now, I don't know enough to reach any conclusions...or rule anything out." Danes gestured at the black satchel he'd left next to the bed. "I did you the courtesy of bringing your laptop, as you requested. I'd appreciate it if you did us the courtesy of assuming we know what we're doing and are trying to help you." He turned and left the room, closing the door behind him.

"Didn't you say you wanted to keep the police on our side?" Rose scooped up the scattered debris and dropped it back on my lunch tray.

I flopped back on the bed, rubbing my temples. "I do. But he has to see Vernon set this up! I get that he doesn't want to jump to conclusions, but he could at least admit it's a reasonable suspicion!"

"Yes, it is. It's not the only possibility, though. What if a stranger took Aparna, killed the Datonas, and used Vernon's phone to trick you?" Rose spread her hands and shrugged. "It's not likely, but that's the point. He's just trying to do his job, and we have a lot of unknowns here."

"Yeah..." Fragments of some quote about 'known unknowns and unknown unknowns' flitted around my head, trying to distract me. I squished it, only to have it replaced by a more disturbing thought. I sat up on my elbow and asked, "Was Aparna at the church compound when you scried her?"

"No, she was in a car with Grace and Vernon. They were sitting in a restaurant parking lot with trays of food hanging from the car windows. The menu had an entry on it for a 'tender-*lion* sandwich,' if that helps any."

I chuckled. "Actually, that does. I know exactly where they were. The restaurant has had that spelling error on their menus for sixty years or so."

"Well, let's see where they are now." Rose pulled her obsidian scrying bowl out of dimensional storage again and took it into the bathroom. She said, "Give me fifteen minutes, and make sure no one tries to get in here," before blowing me a kiss and shutting the door.

"No problem," I said. I glanced at the television again and sighed. Cooking shows weren't going to give me anything useful. Instead, I snagged my laptop and pulled up the feed from Vernon's phone.

Well, that was interesting...three days ago, all the incoming traffic dropped to almost nothing. I found several messages about the phone being reported lost or stolen, followed by the messages sent to me claiming the car had broken down.

Well, I suppose the phone being stolen might count as a kind of plausible deniability, unless there was something more incriminating in his emails. I searched the messages I had archived, looking for anything that might be a code word or phrase, but the text remained obnoxiously unsuspicious. I closed the laptop again and went back to watching cooking shows.

Rose shook me awake an hour later. "The good news is I'm sure she's at the church with Vernon and Grace, because I can't find her or them anywhere else. The bad news is I can't actually see them. The entire site has some kind of anti-magic barrier around it. It's nothing I've ever seen before and nothing I do can even dent it." She sat on the bed and wrapped her arms around me. "David, I'm worried. I...I think it's some kind of divine intervention. If those people have one of your gods on their side...we may not have a chance."

I nodded. "Maybe not. I'm still going to try, though. I have to."

We cuddled in silence for a while. Inside, we were working the issue as only the Dragonbound can. We came up with and discarded a dozen reasonable ideas and twice that many insane ones, all without speaking.

Click.

Just like that, a big piece of this made a lot more sense.

Rose already knew what I was going to say, but I said it anyway. "I'm not so sure having a god on their side matters. If divine intervention against ordinary people was legal, I'd be dead already. Or we could have someone looking out for us, too. Either way, it's just the us and our friends against a few hundred of them."

"Good," Rose said. "We have them outnumbered."

I laughed. Then I doubled over, gasping and holding my chest. Rose reached for me, but I waved her off. Once I could breathe without wincing, I asked, "I thought you said you fixed my lungs?"

"I did fix them," she said. "I also patched your broken ribs back together. What I didn't fix was the bruising and tenderness in the surrounding tissue. You wanted to look injured, remember?"

I nodded. "Right. Being in pain is a good thing. I keep forgetting that."

Rose cocked her head to the side. "What could be good about feeling pain? If I hadn't fixed you as much as I did, you'd have more pain than you know what to do with. Those wounds could have killed you."

"Pain means you're still alive, my love." I smiled and patted her hand. "It means we foiled Grace and Vernon's evil scheme...this part of it, at least."

"Yes. Now we just have to figure out the rest of their plan, starting with why they'd want you dead in the first place. Obviously it's part of a plan to gain custody, but that takes more time than they would have. As soon as you died, Manya would just swoop in and take Aparna back to India."

"Well, there is at least one other option if that happened. You could take Aparna to Colorado. My parents would have as much standing to ask for custody as Grace and Vernon."

Rose shook her head. "I already checked on that for your mother. Allison said it isn't really an option. I didn't adopt Aparna and my name isn't on the custody order. I could be arrested for kidnapping her. Yes, it's possible I could get Aparna back to Colorado. But if I failed, I don't think your parents would get a fair hearing here. Your parents have rights, but they aren't Human anymore. Allison did say the one thing in our favor is that we have plenty of money. We can afford a lot more lawyer than Vernon and Grace can."

Another piece fell into place. "Not with a nice big church backing them and tons of sympathetic donors with deep pockets." I snorted. "They'll probably have some bleached blond Stepford Wife with too much makeup sobbing, 'Save this little angel from the demon trying to rip her away from her loving grandparents.' The actual truth and things like Aparna's wishes wouldn't matter."

"So they make sure you're killed under suspicious circumstances, file for custody, and use public outcry to keep Manya and your parents from having contact with Aparna." Rose got up and went to the window, looking up at the sky. "I suppose it's a reasonable plan. We're probably totally off-target, though."

"Certainly a possibility," I said. "At least it covers the goals we know about. We can't scry for more information so...I'm going to have to go in."

Rose whipped around, eyes narrow and glaring. "Not a chance! They know you. They'll be expecting you to try something stupid and they'll be looking for you! You barely survived one attack by these people. You're not waltzing in there and handing yourself over to them so they can do it again. I'll go."

I stood up, then reconsidered and sat down again. "No. That anti-magic field would leave you trapped, assuming it didn't dispel your shape change as soon as you walked in the front door. What do you think they'll do if they catch you in your true form? They'll see you as a monster and kill you without a second thought."

"Humans have tried before," she snapped.

I nodded. "Yes, and you won those fights. How would they have gone if you had no magic at all?"

Rose didn't say anything, but we both knew the answer. I pressed on. "At least if they discover me, their prejudices are actually on my side. I'm rich, I'm white, and I'm male. I'm at the top of their social pecking order. They have to try to convert me at least twice before they think about killing me. Maybe three times if I promise to write them a big check."

"Be serious."

I wiggled my eyebrows and waved an invisible cigar. "I can't be Sirius, he's a character copyrighted by J. K. Rowling."

Rose crossed her arms. "I will hurt you until you cannot leave this place for weeks, if that's what it takes. You are not walking up to them and handing yourself over for slaughter."

"Believe it or not, I'd prefer to *not* get killed doing this," I said. "Why not help me come up with a clever disguise or something?"

"Because any disguise I could do for you would have to survive the anti-magic field on the property," she replied. "I don't do wigs and makeup."

I threw my hands up. "I know that! But what if you're wrong about it being an anti-magic field? What if it just protects them from scrying? Or if it's just a barrier around the property, and everything is normal once you're past it? Did you test either of those ideas?"

Her brow furrowed. "I tried to break through it and couldn't. I already know it isn't just a simple scrying barrier. I'd have to be next to it to test anything else."

"Then I'd say we have the first step in our response plan. Let's not worry about any other details until we know what that field is and what it can do."

Rose snorted. "I don't need to worry about any of it. In fact, I'm half-tempted to tail-whip your ass into a coma and take care of everything myself. I'll wake you up once I have Aparna back."

A light bulb went on in my head and I started laughing. "My dear, I just had a scathingly brilliant idea..."

Chapter Twenty-Two

Faking It

"This is insane."

I nodded. "Probably. Will calling my mother interfere with the spell?"

Rose shook her head. "No. Call her if you want. Just leave me alone. I'll let you know when I'm finished." She turned around and went back to painting Draconic runes on a naked, featureless, roughly humanoid body. It looked like a life-size Ken doll made of Silly Putty.

I looked away and dialed Mom's cell phone. "Mom, it's me. I need-"

"It's about time you called, young man. Are you alright? Where's Aparna? I tried calling Rose and keep getting voice mail-"

"Mom! Stop! I need you to listen to me for a minute."

"I beg your pardon? Who raised you to interrupt your mother that way?"

"You did. You always yelled at me if I let you distract me from telling you important news. Now let me get through this." I tried to think of the best way to put it and decided to just lay it out. "Rose is going to make it look like I had complications from my injuries. According to the charge nurse, it's easy for gunshot wounds to the chest to throw a clot and send the patient into a coma. That's going to be my cover story, and I need you to go along with it."

I'll give her credit for not hanging up on me. She said, "Alright, mister, you have about a minute to explain yourself." It was the same tone my sister and I used to hear right before Mom grabbed a wooden spoon and dished out some spankings.

"Mom, someone sent those thugs to kill me. Maybe it was Grace and Vernon, maybe it wasn't, but it was someone. If whoever it was thinks I'm on the edge of dying, they won't be expecting me to try to break in to the church. That will make the next part a lot easier."

"I see. And just how are you going to pull this off?"

I glanced over my shoulder. Rose was chanting in Draconic. As she did, the runes vanished, one by one, absorbed into the...body. Each rune changed it, morphing it to look more and more like me. It was like watching the face-melting scene in *Raiders*, but in reverse. I shuddered and looked away. "Rose is creating a simulacrum of me."

"A what? For pity's sake, speak English."

"A double, Mom. A living body that looks like me but has no mind or memories. We're going to leave it here in the hospital so no one knows I'm gone."

"Ohh..." She paused for a moment. "Is it something like that robot thing in that movie? *The Last X-Wing*?"

"*The Last Starfighter*, maybe?"

"Whatever. The one about the guy in a trailer park who learned to fly a spaceship by playing video games."

I chuckled. "The Beta Unit, yeah. That's the idea. Only this is living tissue, not a robot."

"Well, good. It's not a completely stupid idea." Mom sighed. "I hope the hospital and the local police are in on your plan. Did you at least have that much sense?"

"Mom, we don't know who we can trust. We don't know who might be a member of the church, or be willing to sell us out. So, no, we're not telling anyone, and neither are you."

She drew in a ragged breath. "Fine. I can be worried and distraught if it helps you pull this off. But I want you to promise me—*promise me!*—that you are going to go in, grab Aparna, and get out. No heroics."

My hand clenched on the phone. "No heroics...unless lives are in danger."

"I guess that'll have to do." Her voice caught. "Son..."

"I'll be careful, Mom. That I can promise."

There must be a leaking pipe somewhere; my cheek was wet. I coughed and brushed the offending moisture away. "Now, if I do manage to get arrested, deny knowing anything. I'll take the heat for being a total loser who let his mother think he was gravely injured and might never wake up."

"Then don't get caught." She sighed, and I could picture her shaking her head. "God, you're an idiot. You must have gotten that from your father, because you sure as Hell didn't get it from me. Good luck. I love you, son."

"I love you, too. And Dad, and Audrey." For some reason, the word 'goodbye' stuck in my throat. "See you soon." I ended the call and pressed my forehead against the cool glass.

Rose came up behind me, wrapping her arms around my chest. "Everything is ready. Grab whatever you're taking and let's go."

I pulled the battery out of my laptop, waited a few seconds, and slid it back in. Anyone trying to boot it up now would have to get past the hard drive encryption. I left it on the side table and stuffed my phone in my pocket. "Ready."

Rose touched her fingertips to the middle of my forehead and trailed them down the side of my face. Her touch left my skin tingling, and I couldn't suppress a shudder as the magic spread through me.

She moved my head from side to side and nodded. "Not my best work, but it'll do for now."

I followed her to the door, pausing to look back at the thing in the bed. "Take care of my face," I whispered. "I'm going to want it back."

Nobody looked twice at us as we left the hospital. A few minutes of brisk walking in the oppressive afternoon heat brought us to a nearby diner. The Interceptor was waiting in the parking lot, now sporting a brand-new set of Oklahoma license plates. "Getting those took Eric five minutes," Rose said. "No questions asked."

"Yes, I get it. Mind control works. I hereby promise to let you handle all government interactions in the future."

Rose patted my cheek. "At least that beating knocked some sense into you."

Nadia and Eric were both having something deep-fried and smothered in sausage gravy. Nadia tossed me the Interceptor's keys and said, "Nice face. What's the plan?"

"First, I'm having a plate of that," I said. "Then, road trip and some research. We'll have a better idea then."

"Sounds reasonable," she said. "I take it you aim to misbehave?"

"Most grievously. We just don't know exactly how yet."

"Sounds like one of Mother's plans," Nadia said. She handed me a stack of papers topped with an Oklahoma driver's license. "All this is bull, so take care of business fast. Your cover will come apart like toilet paper in a blender if the cops take a close look."

"Trust me, I don't plan to linger." I looked at the driver's license and noticed something missing. "There's no name, address, or picture."

Nadia snorted. "Of course not. We don't know what your disguise is going to be yet. Once you're settled on an identity, Rose will lock in the details and complete the spell. That will update all the appropriate databases and you'll be ready to go."

"Damn it Nadia, I'm a meat shield, not a spell-chucker. I don't think that way." Thankfully, the waitress arrived and saved me from embarrassing myself further.

While we ate, Rose, Nadia, and Eric discussed the anti-scrying barrier and what tests would give them the most information. The whole conversation was over my head, so I tuned it out until Rose elbowed me in the ribs. I gave her a blank look and asked, "What? Did I miss something?"

Nadia pointed her fork at the television on the wall behind me. "You're on the news."

Yep. The word was out. I was officially comatose due to a blood clot working loose from my damaged lung. I guessed someone in the police department decided to call the press before calling my family. I'd love to have words with the police department's public information officer when all this was over.

I slid the remaining portion of my lunch over to Rose and stood up. "Back in a minute," I muttered.

"Don't go overboard checking out the new you," Rose said. "Besides, I didn't change anything below the shoulders." She and Nadia shared a look and started laughing.

"Anyone who would be in a position to notice is looking too close." I headed for the bathroom before that conversation went further downhill. I held my breath as I opened the door, and let it out in a rush when the place turned out to be empty. Privacy beat courtesy and I snagged the stall.

As promised, everything looked normal and functioned without issue. I finished up and reached to unlock the stall when the bathroom door opened. Two guys came in and occupied the urinals, talking about work while they did their thing. From the sound of it, they were both about as tall as I was. The view under the stall showed the one closest to me was wearing steel-toed boots and denim jeans.

Come on, David. No reason this should get ugly. I opened the stall and saw myself in the mirror for the first time.

Crap.

I was now a clean-shaven MBA-type with a tidy executive haircut held in place by a judicious application of styling gel. Instead of a cast-off set of sweats blazoned with the name of a famous evangelical university, I was wearing a raspberry dress shirt with a patterned gray and silver silk tie. I didn't know anything about shoes, but I was willing to bet I was wearing Italian loafers.

The guys finished their business while I was washing my hands. I gave them a nod and moved to one side to give them room. There was no reason for them to take a dislike to me, but stranger things had happened.

One snorted and elbowed his friend in the ribs. "That's a...real nice shirt there, buddy. I can never find anything in that color."

"Neither can I. My wife picked it out." I tossed my soggy paper towels into the trash. "She found out where my boss gets his. I thought she was full of shit, but bonuses don't lie."

"Nice for you, but our boss wears NASCAR T-shirts."

"Don't show up in anything from the wrong team," I said. They chuckled and nodded. Tension broken. Two steps got me to the door and I held it open for them. "After you."

They both muttered, "Thanks," and went back to their meals. I was already forgotten.

146

Our table was cleared and there was a nice pile of cash sitting on top of the bill. I picked up my phone and said, "The Interceptor can only take two. Did you already get a car, or did you still need one?"

"We're heading home," Nadia said. "Some of us have a dear friend in the hospital who needs our thoughts and prayers."

"I'm grateful for your support," Rose told her. "I'll email you when we find a hotel."

"Sounds good." Nadia pulled Rose into a tight hug and whispered, "I'm so sorry. Let me know if there's anything we can do to help."

Rose's brow furrowed. "What do you mean? We just spent an hour-"

"Meaningless social pleasantry!" Nadia exclaimed. "Something people say when they don't know how to respond to personal tragedy."

"Yes. Right." Rose shook her head. "I knew that. I just got distracted."

Nadia opened the Interceptor's passenger door and held it for Rose. "Don't worry. We'll be ready. I'll need a few hours in the morning to get the spells I used back, but I plan on starting early."

"I'll do my best to keep him out of trouble until you're ready." Rose turned to Eric and took his hands, touching her forehead to his. In Draconic, she said, "Wind to your wings, heat to your flame."

Eric answered in Draconic as well. "May the sky open before you. Fly free, always."

Formalities concluded, I got in the car and powered it on. "In case anyone was wondering, I have no intention of getting myself killed."

Rose slid into the passenger seat. "I know. But if it happens, know I will find Aparna. I'll take her somewhere safe. Then I'm going back. And when I'm finished with them, nothing will grow from that soil for a thousand years."

I nodded. "Fair enough."

We headed out in silence.

Chapter Twenty-Three

Bartlesville

Before leaving Tulsa, we pulled into a drive-through car wash with a door that came down over the entrance. While we were out of sight, Rose turned the Interceptor into a 1977 Pinto with mismatched body panels and a bunch of 'Gas, Grass, or Ass'-type bumper stickers. She redid the two of us to match the car—twentyish, road-weary, and running on fumes.

Dinner came from a truck stop diner outside Bartlesville. We stayed quiet, watching to see if anyone noticed anything amiss with our illusions. Our waitress gave us the same cheerful treatment everyone else got, and a group of cops gave us only cursory glances as they walked past our table. I guess we passed.

Securing a low-rent motel room without showing identification took a combination of cash and mind control. We napped, watched the news, and waited. I kept looking at the clock, willing time to move faster. My head knew we needed information, but my heart wanted to charge in with all guns blazing. I settled for pacing and staring out the window as the hours crawled by.

Rose passed the time curled up on the couch, meditating on her hoard and trying to drown out all the tension and anxiety I was mentally inflicting on her. I didn't blame her; I didn't want to be in my head, either.

When three in the morning finally arrived, it was almost a physical relief. I reached out to shake Rose's shoulder, but she was already up and moving. She grabbed her sack of magic testing supplies and shoved me out the door as gently as possible.

Most of Bartlesville looked like something from a fifties-era television show, usually brick-fronted cinderblock fronted with plate glass. None of the stores or offices were open, of course, and no one else was out except the cops. I made a point of going a little too fast and slowing down for them, just because driving too carefully sets cops off as much as driving fast and reckless does. 'Fly casual' seemed like good advice.

It worked. They ignored us.

The main entrance to the Still Waters compound was a rolling livestock gate with an intercom, video camera, and an ID-card reader. I'd hoped the property itself would be fenced with simple barbed wire, but no such luck. They'd used a heavy, woven-wire fencing, five feet tall and strung between wooden posts. The stuff was livestock anti-climb fencing, with gaps big enough for a nose to get through, but not a hoof. Getting myself over it would be tricky and take more time than I was comfortable spending (especially if someone was shooting at me).

We kept driving, looping around to the north and coming back on the far side of the ranch. The Interceptor's electronic warfare gizmos showed no radio transmissions within a mile, no stray Wi-Fi sources, and nothing odd about the section of fence we parked next to.

Standing on the side of the road with the car lights off, I could tell where the road was and not much else. Fireflies darted and swirled out in the pasture, and a partial moon made a valiant effort to pierce the thin cloud cover. I stepped on the grass along the shoulder, and my foot went straight down into a soggy layer of muck at the bottom of a drainage ditch.

Rose shook her head. "Just...wait until I finish what I need to do. There's no point in trying to cross the fence until then."

Mud and slimy water squished out of my shoe when I stepped back on the road. Kicking the side of my shoe against the Interceptor's rear wheel dislodged more mud. Hopefully no leeches had latched on to me; I couldn't see well enough to tell.

While I patted my leg down to make sure I didn't have any unwanted hitchhikers, Rose set out a row of quartz crystal points on the Interceptor's hood. One by one, she cast different spells on them and tossed them over the fence.

Some glowed, some gave off tiny sparks of light, others showed no effects at all. All but one of the glowing crystals winked out as soon as it crossed the fence line. I heard them land in the grass, so they hadn't been destroyed. That was at least a little reassuring.

After several minutes of staring into her scrying bowl, Rose looked up and shook her head. "Nothing is getting through that shield. Even the stones with tracer spells on them are blocked. Message spells and location magic are just as useless. If you go in there, you won't be able to call for help."

"What about the disguise?"

"Time to find out." Rose scooped me up, put me over her shoulder, and did a running long jump over the fence. I managed not to shout anything, profane or otherwise, which was something of an accomplishment by itself.

At the same time, the Alpha Geek part of me was saying, *"Better. Hotter. Snarkier."* and making cheesy bionics noises. That guy could be damn annoying sometimes.

The Six Million Dollar Dragon and I landed a good twenty feet past the fence line. The illusions Rose had cast on us vanished in mid-jump, but her form remained human. At least the field didn't dispel all forms of magic.

After she set me down, Rose pulled her scrying bowl out and focused on it. For a moment, I thought we were in luck, but then she shook her head. "Totally blocked. Nothing in, nothing out." She tucked the bowl away and said, "Try pulling in enough energy to power the imperative form."

Normally, this should be easy. I focused, opening myself to the energy around me, and found nothing. I knelt, placing my hands on the ground, and reached for the power flowing through and from Mother Earth. Again, nothing.

Even though I couldn't draw energy, Rose and I were still bound by the acceptance. She used it like a set of jumper cables, filling me with enough magic to power two, possibly three spells. Then she cut the feed.

The power Rose had given me vanished, leaving me as empty as I'd started. I looked at her and shook my head. "I couldn't hold on to it."

"That's fine. I didn't expect you to." She held out her hand and the stones she'd thrown into the pasture leaped into her hand.

"Finished?"

"Almost. I just have one more test to run." Rose handed me a thin wire bangle bracelet, the cheap, pot-metal kind usually found at convenience stores and head shops. "Think of your mother, whisper a short message, and then break it."

"Um, Okay. Ah...let's see...Mom, Rose and I are fine. I love you." I tried to think of something else to say, but Rose mimed pulling something apart. I decided that would have to do. I gave the bracelet one solid yank with both hands and it vanished. No lights, no sound, just...not there anymore.

Rose let out a puff of air. "Good. At least that worked. Let's head back to the hotel."

"Do we have a plan yet?"

"Pretty close. Oh, and I want pizzas."

I meant to vault over the fence this time, but even if I cleared the wire, my landing spot would have been back in the muck. The thought of leeches and a possible broken leg convinced me to swallow my pride and let Rose ferry me across again. The one upside to being out in the back end of nowhere at Oh-Shit-Thirty in the morning was that there was no one standing around with a camera and an Internet connection.

Rose redid our illusions and we headed back into Bartlesville proper. This time we didn't even see any police cars, just a rig hauling a fat tank of gazzoline. We followed it to an all-night convenience store without being attacked by wasteland marauders in assless chaps.

150

The trucker held the door for us, nodding to Rose and saying, "Evening, miss." Rose was so pleased, she let him get his pizza slices before she bought the place out.

Back at the hotel, Rose polished off four pizzas before I'd downed three slices. Even though I'm used to her appetite, it was still intimidating to watch. While I finished eating and cleaned up our trash, she pulled one of those big, red, rolling Craftsman tool cabinets out of Dragon Mini Storage and started going through the drawers.

She set out a dozen white china bowls about the size of sake cups, a cut crystal carafe, and a rolled-up leather case holding a dozen shiny steel pokey-stabby things. They looked like something a Klingon dentist would use. It wasn't until she started putting small measures of rich, vibrant inks into the bowls that I realized the stabby things were tattoo needles.

For some reason, that thought was actually less comforting.

I waited for her to finish setting everything up before asking, "Am I getting new ink?"

"Only temporarily." She hooked her thumb toward the bed. "Get undressed and lie down on your back. It's fine if you go to sleep. I'll have to knock you out anyway once I get started."

"Fine." I pulled my clothes off and found a comfortable spot on the bed. "Just don't do anything too crazy."

Rose opened one of the tool chest drawers and removed a quill pen made from a reddish-orange feather that glowed like molten steel. She twirled it between her fingers and said, "Don't worry. I will do only the needful. Only the most maximum needful."

She dipped the quill into one of the ink pots and began drawing faint guide marks on the bottoms of my feet. It didn't tickle nearly as much as I expected, and I was asleep before she reached my ankles.

Years ago, during one of our summers in Spavinaw, I caught an episode of *Kung Fu* on one of the Tulsa stations we didn't get very well. The picture was fuzzy, the audio full of static, and the station had way too many commercials, but it pulled me in like a V8-powered vacuum cleaner. The episode revolved around the story of a great teacher who dreamed he was a butterfly. When he woke up, he didn't know if he was a man dreaming of being a butterfly, or a butterfly dreaming he was a man. I was about ten years old, and that story was profound enough to shake my whole worldview.

This time, it was my turn to dream I was a butterfly.

But I wasn't flying around. I was perched on a leaf, wrapping myself in a cocoon. The only thing I could move was my head. I was spraying silk out of my mouth, coating myself with thick, fibrous goop. I tried to wake up, but couldn't. The silk just kept pouring out, wrapping all the way up my body, around my wings, and finally encasing my head.

Then, I melted, because that's what you do in cocoons. And that was the last thing I remembered.

I awoke to nothingness – no physical feeling, no light, no sound, and no awareness of my body. I could feel Rose's presence, though. I focused on that and thought, *"What happened?"*

Don't move, she replied. *Don't try to speak or open your eyes. Your mind doesn't know this body yet. If you do too much too fast, you could reject it. Just stay still and let yourself settle in. I'm going to wash the ink off you now. Let me know when you feel that.*

Rejecting my body sounded like a really bad thing. I tried to focus on remaining still, but I couldn't tell if I was successful or not. Even the bed I was laying on failed to register. It had to be there, obviously, but there was no sense of it, not even pressure against my back.

The first sensation I felt was a faint whisper of breath across my lips. I couldn't tell if it was moving in or out, but it gave me something I could use to measure how much time was passing.

My toes reported for duty in a burst of pins-and-needles tingling. It didn't hurt as much as feel odd, as though they were floating in space with nothing connecting me to them. Without thinking about it, I tried wiggling them. I couldn't tell if I was successful, but Rose said, "Yes, they work. Give the rest of you a chance."

Hard advice to follow.

Not long after that (at least, I think it wasn't long), the air moving past my lips started going somewhere. I still couldn't feel my chest, but I could feel pressure rising and falling somewhere between me and my toes. Then more sensation, this time in my ears. That had to be my heartbeat.

You know that falling feeling that hits right before you go to sleep? It washed over me, hard and fast, as if I'd been shoved out of an airplane. And, just as in a dream, I couldn't move or make a sound. I couldn't feel any wind, but I heard one roaring around me, drowning out the screams I couldn't make. The ground had to be coming up. I'd be nothing but a grease stain. Pavement pizza. Wet cleanup with bone fragments in aisle three...

Whumph. I had a body again. From the smell, I was still in the same room. The coarse weave of the bedsheets was the same, as was the worn-out pillow.

Rose was still with me, too. She patted my hand and said, "You're doing great. I think integration was successful, but I want you to keep your eyes closed. Don't try to talk yet, either. I'm going to lead you to the bathroom now. I want you to focus on walking. If you feel yourself starting to fall, don't try to fight it or grab anything. I will catch you."

She had to help me sit up, but once I was on my feet, walking was easy. She still kept both hands on me, just to be safe. I wondered for a moment how I was going to aim at the toilet with my eyes closed. It turned out to be a moot point; she had me sit down to take care of business.

I tried to stand up when I finished, but Rose stopped me. "Hold your horses. You need to get cleaned up first."

That didn't make sense. Even in this condition, I think I would have noticed if I'd done anything more than pee. Well, then again, maybe not. I nodded and fumbled for the toilet paper.

"Here." Rose guided my hand to the roll. "Don't stand up. Just...lift yourself up on one cheek."

Oh, please. I know how to wipe my-

Oh, SHIT...

I dropped the toilet paper and lurched to my feet, fumbling between my legs for a penis that wasn't there. According to my fingers, I was now the proud owner of a brand new, low-mileage, factory-issue vagina.

That, as they say, was a real eye-opener. Literally. Big mistake. The room lights seemed bright as the afternoon sun. Blocking them with my hand helped. Between blinking and squinting, my sight improved enough for me to visually verify the input from my hands. I had lady parts now. Grabbing the wall for balance, I lurched past Rose and staggered to the mirror over the sink.

My new body was skinny to the point of looking underfed. Fish-belly pale, with short, stringy copper hair and an A-cup bust. I was just a bit closer to pretty than to plain, and apparently hadn't been to the dentist or worn a bra in a long time. I had three rainbow-winged butterflies tattooed on my left forearm, a skunk on my right breast, and a generous helping of freckles.

I turned around so I could look at the mirror over my shoulder. My backside was as underwhelming as the rest of me and—of course—I had a tramp stamp. It said "Angels Are Real" in big, black, Ye Olde English block letters. There was also a big Gothic cross between my shoulder blades.

I sagged back against the counter and asked, "Okay...just...what the hell?" My voice came out low and rasping, perfect for a heavy smoker. Perfect fit for this body, too.

"I'm assuming the church leaders are smart enough to check out anyone who comes in," Rose said. "They're relying on that anti-magic field to protect them by revealing any intruders, which it will. If you go in relying on an illusion, you'll be caught at once. Any man they don't know who wants to join the church in the next month will be watched, in case he's you in disguise. They might even prepare for the possibility you'd disguise yourself as a woman. However, there is no way David Fraser could disguise himself as *this* woman. They have no experience with this level of magic and no reason to think it's possible. It's your best shot."

I looked back at my reflection, then down at my broken, well-chewed fingernails. "Fine. I see your point. It's just...no offense, but you made me a skank."

"That means everyone will be surprised at how nice you clean up. By the way, just for the record, I made your boobs that size for your protection. If you had anything bigger, you'd be too busy playing with them to get anything done."

OK, fine, maybe she had a point.

Rose pushed me out of the bathroom. "There are two burritos in the bar fridge. Eat one, then start walking. Pacing back and forth is fine. Don't pop your hips like that. Just walk."

I walked. Back and forth, front door to toilet. At first, I was too unsteady to walk unsupported. Six or seven laps later, my inner ear remembered what it was supposed to be doing. It felt good to walk at a normal pace, without tottering or grabbing something for support.

Meanwhile, Rose dug through her wardrobe for clothes that might fit me. Talk about a lost cause. Rose is six foot two with a gymnast's muscles. The new me was five feet tall—okay, fine, four eleven—and weighed a whopping eighty-seven pounds. Rose's clothes made me look like a toddler playing dress-up.

I don't know exactly how big Rose's extradimensional warehouse was, but it had to be at least the size of a house. She's pulled an amazing variety of items out of it, including camel saddles, lace-up moccasins with the back feet of a bear attached to the soles, and a vial of instant cockroaches (just add water). Yet, with all that stuff filling all that space, the best she could come up with was an Elway jersey that fit me like a nightgown and a short, bright scarlet robe with matching front-laced bustier. I skipped the bustier and belted the robe on over the jersey.

Eventually Rose gave up and grabbed her purse. "I'm going shopping. Eat the other burrito if you get hungry. Don't open the door to anyone until I get back."

"I'll be careful, don't worry. Have fun storming the castle." I threw the deadbolt behind her, crawled into bed, and started flipping channels. The mere idea of watching the news caused my heartbeat to speed up and made it hard to breathe. Shopping channels, reality shows, reruns of television shows originally filmed in black and white—all of them either annoyed me or raised my anxiety level.

Eventually I found a nature show with a bunch of fuzzy baby animals that were busy cavorting and doing fuzzy baby animal stuff. That I could live with. I pulled my arms and legs inside the jersey and hugged my knees to my chest as hard as I could.

I've always been big enough to dissuade most troublemakers from starting anything with me. The magic of the acceptance had given me added muscle mass and terrific tone, not to mention the endurance of a marathon runner. The new me didn't have any of that.

Even assuming I could find Aparna and convince her to escape with me, there was no way I'd be able to get past anyone who objected to us leaving. I'd already failed miserably at doing push-ups and arm curls while holding a phone book. Not even the Tulsa phone book, mind you—the bloody Bartlesville phone book! In this body, I couldn't beat up an angry kitten. Kindness wouldn't be any help, either. Even assuming I could manage to lift her, the sword was almost as tall as I was. Using her was out of the question.

Yesterday—or the day before, I couldn't remember—I'd taken a beating, gotten shot, killed two guys ten years younger than I was, and hospitalized a third. Now, I was terrified to walk out the door of the hotel room. I could be robbed, beaten, murdered...raped. I mean, sure, all guys know it could, and did, happen to men. *Other* men. We never think it could happen to us. It could never happen to *me*.

Yeah. The benefits of White Male privilege. In my case, it was even worse. I had Rich White Tough Guy Male privilege. Up until a few hours ago, I'd been playing the Game of Life in god mode.

Rose's reasons for making me this way were dead on, but I was not prepared for this. I didn't know how I was going to get in the church. I didn't know what I was going to do. I didn't know who I was supposed to be. I didn't even know what my new name was. And I most certainly did not know how to be a woman.

I hugged myself tighter, breathing hard. *You'll learn. Every woman you know is strong and capable. You can be as strong as they are...*

I banged the back of my head against the wall. *Good grief...I'm mansplaining to myself!*

That was it for the motivational speech. Fear won.

Outside, shadows lengthened, the sky turned dark, and there was still no sign of Rose. I stayed curled up, rocking back and forth under the covers, jumping at every sound. When I finally fell asleep, I dreamed I was a princess locked in a tower, praying for the fearsome dragon to protect me from all those asshole knights on the other side of the drawbridge.

Chapter Twenty-Four

Meeting Neesy

"Yo, Sleeping Beauty. Rise and shine."

Rose dumped a bag of clothes onto the bed and set another sack on the tiny side table in the corner. "Sorry that took so long. I had to go to Tulsa to find what I wanted. There's also some sesame chicken and cashew beef for you."

"That sounds great." It took me a bit to get out of bed; my arms and legs were filing angry protests over sleeping curled up. On the good side, I felt better both physically and mentally. The yawning pit of helplessness and terror I'd fallen into earlier was gone. I was still nervous and concerned about how this was going to play out, but it was a reasonable level of concern, not blind panic.

The fuzzy baby animal channel was now showing an infomercial about Jesus' teachings on real estate investing. I guess I missed whichever gospel contained the sermon on flipping houses using someone else's money.

I went to turn the television off, but Rose said, "Find something for background noise. Doesn't matter what. I doubt anyone is listening to us, but I don't want to take the chance."

A little paranoia sounded healthy right now. One of the Tulsa channels was showing a *Gilligan's Island* rerun. Well, mindless comedy sounded healthy too.

After I finished eating, we sat on the bed and went through the clothing Rose picked out for me. Most of it was second-hand, thrift store specials. Well used, but still serviceable. My new summer wardrobe consisted of two pairs of denim jeans, seven assorted rock concert t-shirts, three sets of underwear and socks, a pair of worn sneakers, and a fringed leather jacket only one size too large for me.

The jacket was the only near-new item. According to the label, it was handmade by a Lakota artist from the Pine Ridge Reservation. It was black bearskin suede with brown, Western-style leather trim on the yoke and sleeve. There were two layers of fringe, brown and black, running down along the yoke and around the waist. The neckline and forearms had rows of bone hairpipe capped by sterling silver beads laced into the outer shell. Both checkbook-sized inner pockets could be zipped closed, and there was a well-hidden document-sized pocket running down the back, between the shoulders.

The thing was ridiculously gorgeous. It even made me look good. I did some fashion-model turns in front of the mirror, shook my head, and took it off.

"What's wrong?" Rose asked. "Don't tell me you don't like it. It looks great. I may get myself one when all this is over."

"It's great," I said. "That's the problem. I look like a crackhead dressed in stuff I stole from a donation bin, but I have that jacket? It doesn't make sense."

Rose gave me a blank look. "What's a crackhead? Oh! Like a butt crack, right? A person with their head in their ass?" She paused and scratched the back of her neck. "Hunh. Humans aren't flexible enough to do that, though. Not if they want to walk afterward."

"That's not what it means. A crackhead is someone with a bad drug addiction. One so bad it destroyed their life." I waved the question away. "Never mind that. My point was that everything else about me says I'm broke. Probably homeless. That coat is out of my price range. People will think I stole it."

"There's no reason to assume you were always poor. Why does it matter anyway? You aren't going in there to apply for a mortgage, David. You're rescuing your child, probably fighting your way out, and hopefully killing whoever sent those punks after you."

"I know. And while we're on the subject, who the bloody hell am I? I'd also like to know how I'm supposed to fight my way to freedom when I can't punch my way through a sack of cotton candy."

"Right." Rose dumped another sack on the bed and handed me a zip-top baggie full of cash and papers. "Let's start with who you are."

I went for the driver's license first. "Huh...you named me after the Loch Ness Monster?"

"Look again. It's Neesy, not Nessie. With a long E. How long have you been speaking this language?"

"Long enough. I think this girl needs glasses. Alright, then. Neesy Rae Avalon. Twenty-three years old. She's from Spavinaw?"

Rose nodded. "It seemed like a good choice since you know the area. Since you haven't been there recently, Neesy's records show she moved to Miami four years ago. It's big enough for people not to know each other."

"Good plan," I said. "Wrong city, though."

"What?"

"My-am-EE is a city in Florida. The one in Oklahoma is My-am-UH." Her glare just made me snicker. I held up my hand and added, "Don't worry, people get it wrong all the time. And you're not the one who has to know that little detail, I am. So, what does Neesy Avalon do for a living?"

"If I had time to change the records, I'd make her a maid. Make you clean houses for a few days..." She narrowed her eyes and shook her head, feigning outrage. I wasn't worried; if she really were pissed, her eyes would be glowing red. And she'd be ripping people's hearts out with her bare hands.

Neesy's employment history only showed two jobs, both as a day care staff assistant. I had to assume that involved a lot of diapers and singing dinosaur videos. High school diploma, but no college. Few skills and fewer prospects.

The rest of the papers turned out to be a grade transcript from high school, a lame letter of recommendation from Neesy's last employer, and a dozen pages of overwrought, angst-ridden teenage love poems from a guy named Arn.

I stopped reading halfway through the first poem. "I think my eyes will bleed if I read any more. Where did you find this stuff?"

"Mother has some minor research demons on retainer at a dead letter repository in New York. They find some wonderful material."

Research demons. It made perfect sense; that poem was a vision of Hell. For a moment I wondered if Rose would get a joke about daemons and search term formatting. Then I remembered the last few times I'd tried telling her computer jokes and gave up on the idea. I set the papers aside and asked, "What else did you pick up?"

"Just a few essentials. Handbag, security wallet, pepper spray, toiletries, ratty stuffed animal—might be a kangaroo—and a greasy bag of really ancient hard candy I pulled out of the bottom drawer of a desk locked up in that storage place down the road. I wouldn't eat them, but Neesy would have candy."

"Okay," I said.

"The security wallet is the most important thing. You're alone, defenseless, and don't have a place to live, so you have to protect your cash." She handed me a lacy black garter. "Should be the right size. Try it on."

The garter turned out to have pockets inside the lining. Useful, I admit, but it looked too large for Neesy's legs and I couldn't see any way it would fasten to a belt. "Any special instructions for putting it on?"

"Yes. Your foot goes through the hole in the middle and then you pull up."

"Aha. Thanks—this thing doesn't have an instruction manual."

"You never read them anyway."

Even the top of Neesy's thigh was too skinny for the garter to have much tension. "It feels loose."

"Good. You've got a lot of stuff to keep hidden."

She wasn't kidding. Twelve hundred bucks and change (mostly in tens and twenties), the letters, Arn's crap poetry, and one of those credit card-sized survival tools went into the pockets. Once everything was in place, the garter didn't feel like it was going to fall off my leg anymore.

Thirty-four dollars, my new driver's license, and a stack of family photos went into a metallic gold, imitation leather clutch wallet that was probably older than the *Gilligan's Island* episode we weren't watching. The wallet and everything else went into a worn leather carry-on bag. The pepper spray holster clipped to one of the bag's D-rings.

"I think you're ready to go," Rose said. "So, what's the plan?"

My eyebrows shot up. "I was about to ask you the same thing. You came up with this disguise and all this stuff for it, I assumed you had a plan to go with it."

She snorted. "You said the first two parts of your plan were to convince everyone you were near death and to get into the church using a disguise. Those two things I know how to do, so I took care of them. Didn't you put any thought into the rest of the plan?"

"Of course I did! Part two is 'find Aparna' and part three is 'get both of us out alive'."

Rose's eyes turned red. She closed them, looked away, and took a deep breath. I stayed still until she let it out. When she looked back at me, her eyes were darker, the reddish-black hue of metal beginning to heat. Without raising her voice, she said, "I really want to punch you right now. And I don't have a problem with hitting girls."

"I'll come up with something," I said. "This was just a...failure to communicate."

She handed me my phone. "Get on it. I'm taking a shower."

I listened to the shower running while I flipped channels, looking for something either distracting or inspiring. The best thing on was an awful reality show about people no one could stand to be around going on blind dates and abusing each other over drinks. The good side of things was that they were making each other miserable instead of involving two innocent people whose only crime was being lonely. I promptly tuned it out.

The only idea I had that even resembled a plan was walking in the front gate and applying for a job. When I drove Fox out to Wiley and Margot's farm, he had mentioned the church having a day care center for members out at Still Waters. Well, Neesy had child care experience. It was a long shot, but it was better than no shot.

Rose emerged from the bathroom wrapped in a towel. "Well?"

"I have the basics of a plan. The church has a day care and Neesy has experience changing diapers. I'm willing to bet the staff also helps with the summer camp thing they're doing. I'd at least have a chance to get close to Aparna."

"That's better than I expected. It might even work." As she spoke, I felt the last of her anger slip away. It was a relief to watch her eyes turn blue again. Then she asked, "How are you getting in?"

"I can walk in. That's not an issue. The tricky part is landing the job since I can't use the imperative form."

"I can help you there." Rose took my arm and pointed to the butterflies tattooed on it. "Each of these is a spell. Just touch one of them and will it to release. The one farthest from your hand is *Binding Word*. It's more powerful than the imperative form, but the more people you use it on, the shorter the command has to be. For one person, seven to ten words. Four people or more, keep it to a single word."

"The middle one is *Don't Get Involved*. It's your best option for making an escape. If you use it, get out fast. The anti-magic field will dispel it in six or seven minutes. Ten minutes at most."

I nodded. "Trust me, when the time comes to leave, I will be hauling ass."

"Good." Rose tapped the third butterfly. "These tattoos don't hold combat spells well, but you can't go in defenseless. This is *Song of Dreams*. Everyone in the immediate area takes a nice long nap. Totally non-lethal, safe for use on civilians and children."

"That could be useful. What about the skunk?"

Her face went blank. "If I tell you it is just decorative, will you accept that answer?"

I took her hand. "Yes. If you want me to accept that, you don't need to say it." I didn't know why she wanted to lie to me, but I wasn't going to put her through the shame of actually doing it.

Rose didn't say anything, so I waited. It seemed forever until she said, "I will not tell you that. In this form, by my design, you are weak. Some could see you as prey. If that happens, if someone tries to...violate you, they will die in agony."

I kissed her. "Thank you for thinking of me. I'll do my best not to need it. Now what about this cattle brand over my ass?"

"It's keeping your ass looking so skinny," she said. "That's your anchor. Keep an eye on it. The anti-magic field shouldn't be able to affect it, but if it does—if the tattoo starts fading—you might only have a few hours."

"When it vanishes, I change back?"

Rose nodded. "Be sure you're either naked or wearing something with a lot of room when it happens. You can dispel it if you need to, but once you do, it's gone."

"I'll try not to need to, then." I stretched, listening to my back pop. "Anything else I need to know?"

"Yes. You forgot the cross on your upper back."

"So I did. Please enlighten me."

"It's a healing spell. It will trigger automatically if you sustain a significant injury."

"Define significant."

She shrugged. "A crossbow bolt to the knee would do it. As would a severe head injury, significant blood loss, or loss of total body volume."

"Total body volume? Like, if something takes a bite out of my ass?"

"More like running over your foot with a lawnmower. The spell wouldn't replace your foot, but it would halt the bleeding and suppress shock." She leaned forward and took my hand. "Keep in mind, this spell will not fix you. All it does is keep you from dying."

"Very thoughtful." I sighed. "I hope I don't need to use it."

"They tried to kill you once already. Don't ever forget that."

"I don't intend to," I said.

"You better not." She sighed, her grip on my hand tightening. "Now, if something goes terribly wrong and I need to get you out, I won't be coming in as a human. I'll do my best to minimize casualties, but no promises. If I can't get to you, though, we're going with my plan. I'll have to shift home for a few hours, but I will be back. I will be bringing friends and we will be coming in force. We'll send out a signal to guide you to whoever will be flying you out. If you don't come to us, we will stop at nothing to find you. That could mean a lot of collateral damage, so find your ride as fast as you can."

"I'll do my best. What's the signal?"

Rose shrugged. "I don't know yet. I'll think of something geeky. You'll know it when we use it."

"Make sure it's really geeky, then." I rubbed my eyes and checked my phone for the time. "I need to do some research for a few minutes, and I may have some scrying targets for you."

"I'll be here if you need me," she said. She changed the television to her financial network and leaned back in the bed, radiating happy excitement. Of course, for Dragons, it was practically a twenty-four-hour porn channel.

I was missing a lot of details with my plan (such as it was), and I needed to fill in the blanks. I started by doing searches on everything I could think of concerning Harper Wren and the New Life Fellowship's activities. An hour later, I was still searching. The one thing I had learned was that the church had a for-profit side. It was wholly owned by the church but had a separate management structure. I found a bunch of financial and tax information that made no sense to me; I emailed the link to Rose with a note asking her to look into it. If something was amiss, she would find it.

I was down to looking at social media postings by church members when I found what I needed. It was a blog entry by a woman who had come to the church as a victim of domestic violence. In her post, she talked about seeing Still Waters for the first time from the back seat of a police car, wearing borrowed clothes and wishing she could wash the dried blood out of her hair. She'd decided to leave her husband to rot in jail instead of bailing him out and needed a place to stay. The shelter at Still Waters had a room available, and the police officer was driving her to it. She went on to join the church's Steps to Success program, which taught her basic office skills, what to do in an interview, and provided clothes she could wear to an office.

That was my road in.

My phone said it was almost four in the morning. I got Rose's attention, explained my brand new cunning plan, and asked, "Can you scry for the best person to talk to about getting in to this program?"

"Don't be ridiculous. At the very least I need to have a unique quality specific to a single person to be able to find someone." She tapped the middle-aged woman's picture. "I'll start with her. If we're in luck, she'll have a connection to the person you need."

It took an hour and involved six different people, but Rose was both skilled and tenacious. Once she found the right person, it took another twenty minutes to work out a viable plan. Ten minutes and two *Bender Mender* spells after that we were on the road.

We didn't talk much. Rose drove while I rehearsed my story, looking for flaws and loose ends that could trip me up. When that stopped being enough to keep me from fretting about all the things that could go horribly wrong, I prayed.

The sky was getting light when we reached the right part of town. My target should be in position by now, so it was go time. Rose found a secluded spot behind a hair salon, parked, and took a moment to make sure no casual passers-by would see us. We kissed and said our goodbyes silently. I stepped back from her, set my jacket and bag off to the side, and said, "I'm ready."

"I'm sorry," Rose whispered. "I wouldn't do this for anyone but your daughter."

Then she kicked me in the stomach.

I dropped to my knees. She followed the kick with a flurry of punches to my face, chest, and the side of my head. While I threw up, she tore my shirt and left multiple finger marks on my breasts and ribs, yanked my hair, and kicked my inner thigh twice.

I pushed myself up, panting and blinking, trying to focus on her. She stood still, right in front of me, and waited. When I could only see one Rose, I smiled and whispered, "I love you." Then I punched her in the groin as hard as I could. I might as well have been punching a rhino for all the reaction I got. I cradled my hand, knuckles bleeding from scraping against the zipper on her jeans.

Rose knelt next to me. "That should be enough. Stick with the plan. I'll be nearby in case someone comes along and totally cocks things up."

I managed a nod. "Guardian...angel..."

She turned away, wrapping her arms around her chest. "Get going before I change my mind."

I nodded again and stayed quiet.

Getting to my feet was a bitch, but I made it. I grabbed my gear and half-ran, half-stumbled down the alley. Rose wrapped a *Don't Get*

Involved field around the car and drove off. I didn't look back, and neither did she.

Courage alone triumphs.

/setpref godmode false

The little diner didn't open until six, but the morning crew was already at work doing setup and prep. I leaned against the corner of a building, trying to catch my breath before crossing the road.

An SUV braked hard, even though the light was still green, and the guy driving called out, Hey, baby, need a taxi? We can work something out if you need some cash..."

Great. I've been in the world as a petite woman for ten whole minutes and some asshole is already hitting on me. I straightened up and let him get a good look at my injuries.

He turned pale and floored it. Asshole.

I crossed the road as fast as I could limp. Too fast, as it turned out. My foot caught on the curb, sending me sprawling across the sidewalk and headlong into the diner's faux stone exterior. Pain lanced through my head and red-black blotches filled my vision.

Oy, that's a lot of blood.

I got my bag open enough to grab one of my shirts. Putting pressure on my new cut caused more blotches. I celebrated by throwing up. At least I hit the sidewalk and not myself. Or my stuff.

Rose was on the job. I couldn't see her, but I knew she was there. I felt a warm tingle and the worst of the pain faded. I was still messed up, but I could think and move now. I stumbled to the door of the diner and banged on it with my free hand.

A woman called out, "Sorry, honey, we don't open for another half-hour."

Crap. I moved to one of the windows and knocked harder. Saying anything was out; I felt ready to throw up again.

This time someone turned to wave me away from the window. Moments later, they had the door open and people came rushing out. I turned away from them just in time. Big hands held my shoulder and pulled my hair out of the way until I finished vomiting. The big hands picked me up and carried me into the diner.

The gentleman carrying me was football-player big, bald, and wearing a dress shirt and tie. I blinked at him and said the first thing that came to mind. "Were you in that movie about the guys on death row?"

He laughed. "No, miss, I wasn't, but a lot of people ask me that. My name is Chris. I'm the manager. Now, hang on. I'm going to set you down." He lowered me into a booth, careful not to move too fast. Once I was down, he said, "Stacy, sit with her and make sure she doesn't fall over. I'm going to call the police."

Stacy put her arm around me, then quickly fixed my bra and put the torn part of my shirt back into place. Another woman brought one of those tubs used for bussing tables and set it in front of me. She followed it up with a glass of water and a draped a damp, slightly musty towel over my chest.

As soon as Stacy and I were alone, I locked eyes with her and said, "You need to use the restroom. Call Rachel Red Elk over and tell her to watch me while you run to the toilet."

Maybe Stacy already had to go; she sounded sincere enough. Stacy made sure I was stable, slid out of the booth, and kept her hand on my shoulder while Rachel took her place. When I heard the bathroom door open, I hit Rachel with her own set of orders.

"You want to talk to your sister about me. You're going to call her, tell her about me, and tell her I need her help. You are going to use the most persuasive arguments you have. You are sure I'm the kind of person the Steps to Success program was intended for. If you know of anything else you can say to convince your sister to take me into the program, you will say that also."

Rachel stared into space several seconds before blinking and shaking her head. "Wow, sorry about that. I just zoned out for second there. So, do you have a place to stay?"

"No, I...owww..." My stomach contracted into a tight little ball of pain and I doubled over. This time I managed not to throw up, at least. Rachel patted me on the back and made sympathetic noises until the spasm passed.

"No, I don't. The place I was working in Miami shut down. When I couldn't pay my part of the rent, my roommate kicked me out." Something tickled in my throat, starting a painful bout of coughing. Once I was breathing normally again, I managed to swallow a drink of water. It helped my throat and managed not to provoke my stomach.

"Do you know anyone in Bartlesville?" Rachel asked. "Or did you want to call your family and let them know where you are?"

"I'm in Bartlesville? No. I mean I wasn't sure where I was," I told her. "This guy driving a pickup was getting gas and talking on his phone. I heard him say he was heading in to Tulsa. When he went inside the store,

I climbed into the bed and hid there. The guy stopped behind a store a few blocks from here to take a leak and I decided that was far enough. I hopped out of the truck and tried to run, but he caught the strap of my bag and yanked me back. He said I owed him cab fare and ripped my shirt open. I managed to punch him in the balls and ran like hell."

From her expression, I got the feeling Rachel really wanted to slap a load of sense into me. I nodded and looked down at the bruises flowering on my arms and chest. "Yeah. I know. That was damn stupid and I'm lucky to be alive. I feel like such an idiot."

She put her finger under my chin and lifted my head so she could look in my eyes. "Make better choices next time."

Maybe I looked sufficiently sad and remorseful; Rachel didn't say anything else. She sat with me until the police and paramedics showed up. Thanks to Dragon magic, the cut on my scalp had stopped bleeding and I was free of concussion. The paramedics decided I didn't need stitches, so I got some gauze wraps while I gave my statement. The officers were sympathetic, but 'a middle-aged white guy in a light blue pickup' wasn't enough of a description for the police to do anything with. They promised to 'keep an eye out' and left.

By that time, I was feeling almost normal. Everything was at a manageable level of hurting. The paramedics told me to see my regular doctor and call 911 if I passed out, then they left as well. Since I didn't have any more official responsibilities, I went to the bathroom to wash up and change into a clean shirt and jeans.

Rachel found me while I was finishing up. "Neesy, I brought someone who wants to meet you." She stepped back from the door, adding, "This is my big sister Taylor. Her church has a shelter for battered women and I know they have a bed open. She also does a program to help women find jobs. I told her about your situation and she's willing to help you. Taylor, this is Neesy Avalon. I'll leave you two alone."

I waved and said the lamest thing I could think of. "I'm very pleased to meet you, ma'am."

Taylor rolled her eyes a little, but her smile didn't waver. "I appreciate your manners, Neesy, but, please, don't call me that. I'm running out of my thirties fast enough as it is." She looked me over, checked my arms for needle marks, and grimaced at my tattoos. When she finished, she asked, "Why should I help you? Give me a reason. Convince me."

That was not a question I'd prepared for. A tangled mess of responses leaped to mind, most the sort of thing I'd expect to see on a resume. I shoved them aside and went into gamer mode. Neesy was a character I was playing. She was a student, searching for a teacher, and this was the admissions test. *Annnnnd...GO!*

I shrugged and ran my fingers through my hair. "I don't think you should," I said. "I want help. I really do. I want to be more than this. But there are other people who can be more than I ever could and I think you should help them."

"You don't think you're worth helping?"

"I do, but...It's like, there's a big pie, and all the help out there in the world is in that pie, and everyone wants a slice. But you only got so many slices, and not enough to go around. But then the people who get that pie, they can help make a cake that is all the good in the world, so my piece of pie should go to someone who can make the cake bigger."

"Well, that is an answer I've never heard before, I'll give you that." Taylor looked me up and down again. "Let's try a different question. If you were going to give yourself some advice about what happened to you last night, about the choices you made, what would it be?"

I chuckled. "Wear a heavier coat, maybe. I feel like I should say I'd talk myself out of it, but that'd be a lie. This could be a chance for me to...like I said, to be more than this. And I want that. I want..."

I had to turn around and hide my face for a moment. I was using these people, plain and simple. It might be for a good cause, but I've never accepted the idea that the end justifies the means. What Rose and I were doing was wrong. For a moment, I thought about calling the whole thing off.

Suck it up. Aparna is on the other side of her. Find her weakness, exploit it, and hate yourself later.

When I turned back around, I stopped slouching and met Taylor's eyes directly. I put as much confidence as I could into my expression and voice. "It's hard to believe in myself right now, but I am trying as hard as I can. If you can teach me skills to get a decent job and show me how to get my life together, I'm ready to learn. I want whatever help you can give me. And I'm sorry, but I can't tell you what advice I'd give myself last night, because it would depend."

Taylor raised her eyebrows. "On what?"

"On what answer will convince you I'm worth your time and energy."

That answer almost made Taylor laugh. She covered it up and asked, "What will you do if I say no?"

I shrugged. "Then I'll find someplace else to crash and look for another way to make something of myself. But as bad as I've screwed up so far, that could take years. Not to mention costing millions of dollars and thousands of lives. I'd rather do it this way."

"Well, if helping you get on your feet will save millions of lives, it'll be worthwhile." Taylor opened the bathroom door and held it for me. "I'm glad you still have a sense of humor after the morning you had. Get your things and we can go."

"A sense of humor is about all I have left," I said. Just to be safe, I did a quick inventory. Everything was in place.

On the way out, Chris handed me one of the diner's breakfast specials in a to-go box. "You take care, miss. Come back and see us anytime."

"I'll do that," I said. I exchanged hugs with Rachel and Stacy, making a mental note to do something for them once this was over. There was no reason an eccentric customer couldn't leave a generous tip.

While we drove, Taylor went over the rules for living at the shelter: No loud noises, weapons, fighting, smoking, alcohol, or drugs. No entering another resident's room without permission. Any visitors had to be approved in advance by Taylor and by the Steward's office. Curfew was ten during the week, midnight on weekends. No overnight visitors. If you made a mess, you cleaned it up. Chores in the shelter rotated weekly. Not doing assigned chores three times or breaking any of the other rules merited a warning. Three warnings and I would be out. Everything seemed reasonable; just the basic rules of living in a group.

"Please remember that the shelter is owned and funded by the New Life Fellowship church," Taylor said. "You aren't required to attend worship services, but you're welcome to, of course. It would be good for you to make new friends and get to know people. Speaking of which, our church is open to all races. Some people are bothered by that, but the Bible doesn't say Jesus only came to redeem one group of people. It says 'whosoever,' so that's what Sister Harper teaches."

"I'm fine with that," I said. "I was bummed that nothing happened to me. It might sound vain, but I would have been so stoked to wake up...you know...beautiful. I kept hoping there would be another wave, or that I was just late getting started."

We made a left turn and I spotted the gates of Still Waters coming up on the right. Taylor didn't mention it, though; instead, she pointed to the opposite side of the road. "We put in a new parking lot last year. Sixteen hundred covered spaces topped by a community garden. Every family that donates time gets a share of the harvest."

There were quite a few more cars than I expected. That was troubling, since I hadn't even seen the parking lot when Rose and I drove past in the middle of the night. It couldn't be helped, though; I'd just have to roll with it and hope it was only crowded during the day shift.

As we turned into Still Waters, I got a good look at a beautiful but solid-looking house set off to the right of the entrance. A low stone wall topped by an ornate iron fence ran around the yard, and the whole area was shaded by oak and black walnut. It had to be the house Fox's aunt lived in; my money was on Harper Wren living there now.

Taylor slowed the car down and pointed to the pasture on the far side of the main parking lot. "See that tall grass over there? Stay out of it. Some feral dogs dug their way into the pasture a few weeks ago and killed one of our crias."

"Killed what?"

"A cria. Baby alpaca. The herdsire killed one of the dogs and drove the others off, but we've seen the pack nosing around a few times since then.

168

Anyway, the ranch hands set up a mess of coyote leg traps out there in the grass. So, unless you got an excess of toes, stay away from there."

"Uh, no, I like my feet the way they are."

Taylor laughed. "There's signs posted too, in case you forget."

We passed the sanctuary and parked in another covered lot next to the offices. First stop on my tour was the Steward's office ('Steward' being a polite euphemism for the Director of Security Operations). Fingerprints, photos, guest resident ID card, and information on 'getting-started loans' (Borrow cash on the finest terms!) to pay for clothing, a computer, classes outside the church, or a one-way bus ticket home (or at least to someplace a relative could pick me up).

The Steward himself was a squat, burly fellow named Russell Gates. He went by Rusty because being called 'Russell' was more annoying than a lifetime of 'Rusty Gates' jokes. He was Human, but even before the Change, people thought he looked like a Dwarf (the fantasy kind, not a little person). He certainly had the personality for it.

As it turned out, he was also the facilities manager, the IT manager, and sharper than I expected. He caught me checking out his data and telecom cabling schematic for the main building and his eyes got narrow. I looked down, but my geek side betrayed me. The privacy shield covering his keyboard caught my eye for a moment. He noticed that, too. I kept my gaze fixed on my feet and stuck with 'yes, sir' and 'no, sir' when I had to answer a question, but it didn't help; I'd already made him curious. Or suspicious, which was pretty much the same thing.

Before he handed me my ID card, he tapped it on his desk several times, glaring at me like I'd just eaten a kitten or something. "You'll have to come back for a new picture, once you're cleaned up and those bruises fade. Assuming, of course, you are still here. I'm getting a very strange vibe off of you, Miss Avalon. People running from something aren't calm. You are. People running from something check the corners for threats and glance under the desk for signs of someone hiding. You looked at my map of the ranch and then you looked down to check out my desk when you saw I'd noticed. Care to explain yourself?"

Stalling would never work with this guy. I met his gaze and shrugged. "Um, well, I'm not running *from* anything. I got stupid and someone beat the snot out of me for it. And I was looking at your map for a 'you are here' sign. I don't like feeling lost. When I came in, I didn't see you at first, so wanted to get an idea of where things were. Then I realized you were here, and I didn't want to seem rude, so I stopped looking at it. Then that sneeze guard on your keyboard caught my attention. I was trying to figure out why you would have one. Looking at it seemed to make you mad, so I thought I should just stare at the floor and not get into more trouble."

Rusty stopped tapping my card. "It isn't a sneeze guard. It's a screen to prevent people from seeing which keys I'm pressing and using that information to guess my password."

"You can do that?" I looked down again, shaking my head. "I'm sorry. That was a dumb question. You wouldn't be using it if that wasn't something you were worried about."

"Do you know what makes a password strong, Miss Avalon?"

"Lifting weights and eating spinach?" Amazing how easy it is to giggle in this body. I stifled the urge to bite my nails and added, "I'm sorry, I'm just all kinds of nervous. No, I don't know how to do that. I never used a computer much. If I needed to learn, is that something you could teach me?"

Gates managed to turn his scowl into a grimace and said, "Sure, I can do that." He passed me my ID card and I followed Taylor into the hall. Behind us, I heard a sigh I knew very well. Instead of seeing me as a threat, I was now listed under PICNIC—Problem In Chair, Not In Computer. For my purposes, that was a much better list to be on.

Taylor led me to a security door monitored by a video camera and had me try my badge. It worked like a charm and let me into the Steps to Success office. The left-hand wall had a rack of dresses, pants suits, and nice-but-not-fancy shoes, along with a 'before and after' photo gallery. Each woman had photos for 'First Day in the Program' and 'First Day on the Job.' It was a good-sized collection, especially considering how big the town was.

Taylor's desk and three smaller work areas took up the other wall. Each work area held a phone and a computer that had been mid-range ten years ago. None of them even had an operating system that was still being supported.

Something must have showed in my face. Taylor laughed and said, "Yeah, they're crap, but that's why I keep them. All they're good for is going to job sites and writing resumes. You can't play games on them and nobody would bother stealing them."

We got my 'before' photo taken, with my torn shirt, dried blood all over my face, and flowering bruises on full display. Taylor also took my measurements, since odds were that nothing on hand was going to fit skinny little me.

The next step would normally be having me spend a few hours doing different aptitude tests. Instead, Taylor led me to the door in the back of the room. My badge worked here as well, and the door opened to reveal...stairs leading down. Just like the description at the start of almost every dungeon adventure I've ever played through.

With one hand on the hilt of my imaginary sword, I started down the stairs...

Chapter Twenty-Six

Now What?

Well, there wasn't a ten-foot by ten-foot room full of Orcish bandits waiting for me at the bottom of the stairs. Not that I was actually expecting to find such a room, mind you; It's just ingrained reflex after a lifetime of gaming.

What I did find was an open, welcoming space being used as a living, dining, family, and television area. The walls were a light, powdery blue, mottled with lighter and darker shades to give them a textured look. The ceiling was open, done in darker blues, with the load-bearing supports painted bright yellow. The furniture had nothing in common except for looking comfortable and being dark enough for stains not to show.

One corner held a television, with two curved sectional sofas and a dozen or so floor pillows arranged in front of it. A woman wearing a tank top and jeans was sitting on the floor watching a game show while cleaning a disassembled assault rifle of some kind. She didn't look at us. Taylor didn't react to either her or the rifle, so maybe that rule about 'no guns' had some loopholes in it.

Other than the couches around the television, the living area was laid out as a collection of small nooks, allowing privacy without isolating anyone. Brilliant idea; it would be a great way to set up one of the conference rooms back home.

Focus, idiot. You don't work in an office. Now pay attention!

The corner farthest from both the kitchen and the television held a cluttered office desk topped with a decent workstation, several security camera monitors, and rows of wall shelving crammed with books. The woman sitting at the desk tucked a bookmark into the thriller she was reading and smiled at me.

Taylor said, "Neesy, this is Ofelia. She's one of our counselors. If you have a problem, bring it to the counselor on duty. There's always someone here, day or night. The counselors are here to help you if you need it, but they also run things when I'm not here."

I said, "Pleased to meet you," and stuck my hand out just from reflex.

Ofelia ignored my hand. "Welcome to the Spa. Um, we don't do a lot of touching in here. No offense; it's just that some of the women who come through here get jumpy about physical contact. So, do you have any psycho stalkers or bomb-throwing exes I need to be watching for?"

"Neither," I said. "I hitched a ride in the wrong pickup truck and the owner kicked my ass. And yeah, I know I was lucky. I just...need a chance to get my act together."

"Neesy will be staying with us until she gets settled," Taylor said. "She's also joining the Steps program."

Ofelia unlocked her desk and handed me a neon pink keyring. "You're in room C. Fran and Sara, the women in A and B, are both off at work. I'll introduce you to them later." She nodded toward the woman working on the rifle. "Kaitlyn here is in room D. She's your next-door neighbor. She's taking classes at the gunsmithing school, so don't be worried if you see her with a rifle or shotgun. She also doesn't talk much. If you say something and she doesn't answer, don't take it personally."

I gave her a smile and a half-hearted wave. "Nice to meet you, Kaitlyn."

Without interrupting her work or looking at me, Kaitlyn said, "Just K."

Before I could stop myself, I replied, "As you wish," in a gentle, slightly British voice. Damn that inner geek...

K lowered the rifle to her lap and looked at me. Something passed across her face—memories, emotions, dreams; I couldn't be sure. Then she smiled, nodded at me, and went back to work cleaning her rifle.

Ofelia pulled me into the kitchen. "That's the most interest she's taken in someone for the last six months," she whispered. "We've all tried to get through that wall of silence she lives in and failed. I can't believe you just reached her without trying. I mean, it's just-"

"Inconceivable," K said, her voice carrying from the front room.

"Yeah. I guess that's one word for it." Ofelia started down the hall but paused when she noticed my grin. "Did I miss something funny? Is this some kind of joke I should know?"

I didn't have to fake looking lost. "Um, no, not really. Haven't you ever seen *The Princess Bride*?"

"No," she said. "But I've heard all about it. It has witches, promotes sorcery and torture, and it makes fun of Biblical marriage. I'd never watch such a horrid thing. *That* would be inconceivable."

Back at the front desk, Taylor snickered. "Well, K, I guess that word means what you think it means after all."

"I'm not saying you all can't watch it. I'm saying I won't watch it. Your souls are your problem. I and my house will follow the Lord." Ofelia moved down the hall and pointed to the next door on the right. "Bathroom and shower. The door doesn't lock and don't try to block it closed. There's a biohazard trash bin in there. Anything with bodily fluids on it goes in there, not in the normal trash. That includes used tissues. This is the laundry area. You wash your stuff on Thursday unless there's an emergency or you make a mess. That's clothes and bedding both. Your room is the last one on the right. A and B are on the left. They're both bigger than yours because they're for families."

"Thank you," I said. "I'll try not to be here too long. Right now, I just want to take a shower and get into some clean clothes."

"Well, I'll just leave you to that, then. There are towels and bathrobes in your room." Ofelia went back to her desk, leaving me to enter my new quarters alone.

I hadn't expected much, but the room turned out to be nicer than the one Rose and I had been using the past few days. Other than the lack of a window, it could have been one of my old dorm rooms. Bed, dresser, television, bar fridge, hotplate, microwave, and a small table with two chairs, suitable for eating and doing homework. One cabinet had a small safe built into it, which I resolved to look at later. I tossed everything on the bed, stripped off my blood-stained clothes, and headed for the shower.

No one had mentioned a time limit, so I scrubbed until the rinse water was free of blood or dirt. Once I was clean, I took a moment to just stand there, savoring the feel of the water across my skin. It felt so good I didn't want it to stop.

It did, of course. All good things and all that. Back in my room, the mirror showed an impressive catalog of bruises—at least, it did until I hung a towel over it. It wasn't just the bruises, it was this body. Looking at it—I couldn't think of Neesy's body as 'myself'—made me feel like an exceptionally perverted voyeur. I dressed fast and got my meager possessions put away. I kept a hundred bucks in twenties out, stashing the rest of my cash and what's-his-name's poetry in the safe. The little stuffed kangaroo (or whatever it was) went on the bed, snuggled under the covers.

The breakfast Chris had given me when I left the diner was still kind of warm. Eggs, sausage, hash browns, two big fluffy biscuits, and a container of sausage gravy. Breakfast of champions. I warmed it up a bit and took my time eating, pondering what to do next.

Looking for Aparna right off sounded good, but charging in never went well. If I screwed up being Neesy, they'd be extra paranoid about any other new arrivals.

I'm also supposed to be injured and scared. Staying inside would be the most logical thing for someone in that frame of mind to do. That wasn't an option either. I needed information.

Well, if I was going to be living here for a while, wandering around and getting to know the place was reasonable, right?

I spent a moment brushing my hair, trying to look a little more presentable and less like a Dickensian street urchin. The hair put up a token fight before falling into place. When it did, though, it made a huge difference. Neesy looked...sensible. The concert t-shirt and jeans looked comfortable rather than rebellious or lackadaisical. All in all, Neesy seemed to be a quiet, stable person. I wished I knew as much about working with children as she seemed to.

Just pretend you're Ember and do what she would do.

Sage advice.

Ofelia looked surprised when I came back to the main room. "Well, I must say, I hadn't expected you to be out and about for a while. You're looking nice. Are you feeling better?"

"Thanks. I'm actually sore all over. Everything hurts too much for me to lie down. I thought maybe I could go out and just look around the church. Is that allowed? I have my badge."

"Of course you can look around! This isn't a prison." Ofelia rummaged through a file folder and produced a map of the church buildings. "We're here, and all this area is church administration. Covenant Center takes up these three buildings. It's a retirement community, but you're welcome to go over for lunch or dinner. Most of the church staff eats in the cafeteria over there. They also have a little convenience store that carries basics for the residents who are homebound, and a shop that sells...well, items that were left behind."

"Left behind?" I didn't have to feign my confusion. "Left behind by whom?"

"By residents who have taken their places in Heaven, dear."

"Ah. That kind of 'left behind'..." Changing the subject sounded like a good idea, but all I could come up with was, "Isn't there a day care center here too? I thought I saw something about that."

"Taylor said you didn't have children."

I shrugged. "I don't, but that's the only work I've ever done. I thought I could apply for a job there."

Ofelia circled a spot in the main office building. "The day care is here, but I know they do background checks on everyone before hiring them. I mean, I'm sure you can pass; it's just that they might need some time before they could hire you."

I shrugged again. "At least I can get things started. Maybe I could work for free and let them see how I do."

"Well, if that's God's plan for you, I'm sure the way will be opened," Ofelia replied. Her wide eyes and forced smile made it clear she thought I was wasting my time. She was probably right, but that little detail didn't matter. Neesy might be used to people treating her with veiled contempt and disapproval, but I'm not.

I leaned forward, wrapping my arms around her shoulders for a brief, tight hug. "I know you said people here didn't like touching," I told her. "But it means so much to have someone like you believing in me and being supportive. Nobody's ever cared about me like that before."

Ofelia stiffened and pulled away, her face turning dark red. I hadn't reckoned on her being that averse to touching people. I wanted to annoy her, not trigger a personal issue, so I released her and stepped back. She went for her industrial-size bottle of hand sanitizer, slathering it all over her arms. I muttered "Oh, I'm sorry," grabbed the map off her desk, and slipped out the door as fast as I could. I'd find a way to apologize properly later.

Rushing over to the day care still seemed rash, but it was all I could think of. At least Neesy had a reason for going there first.

The day care was empty, but I heard children laughing and excited caterwauling coming from outside the building. It sounded like recess, so I headed outside. Maybe I'd get really lucky and Aparna would be just a quick hop over a short fence...

No such luck. The playground had an eight-foot fence around it and four adults watching the mob. Aparna was easy to spot. There were other Changed kids, but she was the only one with wings. That aside, she looked like a normal four-year-old, wearing blue jeans and sneakers. She was sitting by herself next to the fence, sticking her hand through it and petting a big Shepherd mix. The dog had black fur, gone to grey around the muzzle, with bluish-grey spots and patches all over. He looked like the negative image of a Dalmatian.

I actually took two steps before my brain kicked in. Walking away was the right thing to do, but I couldn't just leave while Aparna was right there in front of me. I glanced around and noticed an old walnut tree with a nice shady spot not far away. It offered a good view of the playground, so I found a comfy spot and sat down.

Aparna seemed to be enraptured, and the dog either liked the attention or was too mellow to make an issue of it. She looked healthy, if not happy, and none of the kids seemed to be picking on her. It looked a lot more like she was rejecting them. Regardless, there she was... For a moment I seriously considered popping the spells Rose armed me with and charging in like a petite berserker.

I pushed the thought aside. She didn't belong here, but I didn't know enough about the church to risk it. Reason and logic demanded I get an idea of what kind of response I'd have to deal with. Maybe Neesy should spend a lot of time looking around her first day or two...

"Excuse me, miss, was there something we could help you with?"

I started like a frightened rabbit and looked up. One of the day care teachers was standing next to me, arms crossed and tapping her foot. I scrambled to my feet and said, "God, you scared the snot out of me."

"You seemed pretty distracted. I called out to you twice before I came out here. Doing some deep thinking?"

"Um, kind of. I was thinking about the kids I worked with in Miami. I'm really missing them, I guess. My last job was helping at a day care, and

I wanted to apply here, if there were any openings. It's really the only job skill I have." I did my best to sound hopeful and nervous

She shook her head. "We don't have any openings right now. Do you live in town?"

"No, I...I don't have a place right now. Of my own, I mean. I just moved into you all's battered women's shelter. My name's Neesy. Neesy Avalon."

"Tuesday Wells. I run the day care center. Just so you know, around here you should tell people you're staying at the Spa. The staff knows what you mean, and it's better not to use that other term to refer to it."

"Oh, crap...sorry! I mean, I'll remember next time." I clapped my hand to my forehead and sighed. "I shouldn't have come here so soon. I got the bejeezus kicked out of me this morning, I'm not thinking straight, and now I'm screwing this up. Can you just...pretend we never met and let me try asking for a job again tomorrow? Or the next day? I'm not this hopeless, I promise."

"I can't do that," Tuesday said. "If God sent you here to meet me, you have to roll with Heaven's schedule. So, tell me how you would try to reach a kid who didn't want to interact with anyone."

I had to think a minute, but that seemed to be what she wanted to see. Finally, I said, "Well, I'd try asking about superheroes, comic books, video games, cartoon shows, whatever they might be interested in. If they like to read, I'd try to find out about that. I've done pretty well with girls talking about *Celestial Dream Ponies*, since they're pretty popular. If none of those ideas work, I'd have to see what the child likes to do when they have free time."

"You wouldn't talk to them about the Bible? This is a church, you know."

I shook my head. "Not unless they spent their free time reading the Bible. I'd want to make a personal connection with the child, not convert them. That can come later."

Over in the playground, one of the adults rang a bell and called out for the kids to come back to class. The teachers rounded up the children and herded them toward the classroom door. Aparna lingered at the fence, petting the old mutt until one of the teachers came to get her personally. She had to be coaxed to her feet, and even then she shuffled along, head down and wings slumping. The teacher didn't pull or drag her, but had to keep touching her arm and encouraging her to keep up all the way back to the classroom.

Something must have showed in my face. Tuesday grimaced and said, "That poor little girl...just breaks your heart... Her mother passed away just after she was born, and now she may lose her father too, poor thing. Not that he'd be missed..."

I bit back my first response. Instead, I asked, "Why would you say that?"

Tuesday looked around and lowered her voice. "I'm not one to spread rumors, but in this case...he's a horrible person. He lured the poor child's mother into a life of idolatry and perversion. One of his sick friends actually murdered her during a ritual. Anyway, that girl's grandparents have been fighting to protect her all her life, and they finally got the court to allow them visitation. Just as soon as they had her, they came here and asked for protection."

"Does her father have custody?"

"Oh, of course. If the father wants custody, he gets it in this country, especially if he's rich. Which this guy is." She glanced around and lowered her voice. "What I heard was that he intended to sell that little angel to another pervert. The grandparents think this other man abused their daughter when she was a child. Heck, he probably indoctrinated the father into molesting children, too. Well, word got around about this sale and some brave young men went off to stop it from happening. They just wanted to send the father away or convince him to turn to Jesus. Instead, that monster killed two of them and maimed a third. Thank the Lord the police showed up and shot him like a rabid dog."

"Oh, god, that...oh, god!" I put my hand over my mouth and turned away so she couldn't see my face until I got my emotions under control. Picturing a peaceful mountain meadow didn't help. Nor did any of the meditation techniques I've learned over the years.

Tuesday stepped up next to me, oblivious to how close I was to saying 'screw it' and letting Rose's family scour the entire compound down to bare rock. She tentatively put her arm over my shoulders and whispered, "I'm sorry! Did I touch on...something private? I didn't mean to upset you." She paused, pulling back for a moment before gingerly patting my shoulder. "Did something...happen?"

In for a penny, in for a pound. I nodded, still looking away from her. "It's not something I like talking about," I said. "I just...need a moment." Inside my head, Rose quelled the rage like a heat sink for emotions. She didn't extinguish it, only made sure it wouldn't lead me to doing anything stupid.

At least Tuesday didn't pry. "You poor thing. If you want, we can go to my office. You can cry all you need to there."

I turned around and met her eyes. "I don't cry about it anymore. All that's left is rage and hate. Nobody wants to see that." I turned away again, hugging my arms to my sides. "Now I've scared you off, too."

"No, you haven't, not at all!" Tuesday caught my arm, just enough to get me to stop walking. When I didn't flinch, she put her arm around me and pulled me toward her. I didn't fight it.

As she helped me inside to her office, I murmured, "Look, I know you have to follow the rules, but if there's anything I can do to help with that little girl, just let me know."

Tuesday pulled me into a hug, patting my back. "Well, I can't see you being some kind of criminal or terrorist. God brought you to us for a reason, and I'm sure we can find something you can help with around here. Give me some time to work on it."

"Thank you," I said. I sat down and pulled a handful of tissues out of the box on her desk. "Can I tell you something? Something private? I just...I have to say it to someone."

"Of course."

I looked up and met her eyes. "That girl deserves a good life. A good home. Loving parents. And I will do whatever it takes to make sure that happens."

Tuesday went pale. "Jesus wept..." she whispered. "All that anger in your eyes..."

"It's not anger," I said. "It's love."

That was the truth of it. Love. Love can do great things. Terrible things. Wonderful things. Love makes you mighty. Love is stronger than fear, despair, or death.

But wrath is good, too.

Chapter Twenty-Seven

Sister Harper

"It'll take some time to get your background check done, but I don't expect any problems. I'll have to take you to get fingerprinted at some point, too. We have a few days for that." Tuesday stretched in place, turning from side to side until her spine popped. "Uhf. I've needed a new chair for a few years. Asking for one feels like I'm being selfish, though."

I smiled and nodded, not saying anything. The background check would probably shred what there was of Neesy's cover. It couldn't be helped, though; refusing would have aroused immediate suspicion. It didn't really change anything, just added a bit more urgency.

I was so wrapped up in planning my next move I missed what Tuesday was saying until she waved her hand in front of my face. I jumped back, wide-eyed and staring. "Hunh? What?"

"I was asking if you wanted to go get lunch. The Shepherd's Rest is having a taco bar today. That's the cafeteria over at the retirement home. Do you have any cash with you?"

"Some, yeah...well, sure. I don't have any food waiting back in my room or anything." I checked my pocket to make sure the twenties I'd stashed were still there. "I'm good. Lead the way."

The daycare kids were getting their lunches out as we passed by the classroom. I didn't see Aparna, but I had no time to look, either. We met up with a group from the church offices who were also heading to lunch and Tuesday introduced me as we walked. I got to retell my tale of picking the wrong truck bed to stow away in, and they all made sympathetic noises.

I'd barely gotten my plate for the taco bar when K pulled me out of the line, dragging me over to a steam table holding wrapped burritos and tamales. "Get these. Costs less and reheats better." Without waiting for a response, she dived in and loaded her plate.

I wasn't really in the mood for overdosing on burritos. However, she was right about the prices. A starving waif with no prospects would do well to stock up. I loaded my plate and even splurged on two plastic containers of guacamole. The cashier smiled at my haul and asked, "You want a Coke with that?"

"Sure."

"What kind?"

It took me a moment to remember what 'Coke' meant in these parts. I smiled and said, "Dr. Pepper."

K took charge of my pile of spare burritos. "I'm heading back to the Spa. I'll tuck these in the fridge for you." She took off before I could think of a reply.

Tuesday waved me over to a table, and I got to tell my story once again for a new group of people. This time I downplayed my injuries while emphasizing that the police had no way to find my attacker. They made sympathetic noises and promptly forgot about me as the conversation turned to the three goons Vernon recruited to kill me.

According to everyone in the room, all three were altar boys with spit-polished halos. Obviously, this was a terrible tragedy and a miscarriage of justice. I focused on my food and pretended they were talking about someone else.

An hour later, I was on the verge of calling in a Draconic air strike on the ranch, consequences be damned. Instead, I opted for a second helping of dessert, picking a slice of pecan pie guaranteed to put Neesy's waifish build in jeopardy.

As I sat back down, Vernon and Grace entered the room wearing sour expressions and their Sunday best. The woman with them wore a high-end business suit but looked nothing like a banker or a lawyer. The lunch crowd greeted her with a chorus of "Hello sister" and "Good to see you, sister." When she stopped to unbutton her jacket, the people at the table nearest to her hustled to move food and chairs to make room for her.

She put her briefcase in the chair and waved at the room. "Good afternoon, everyone. It's so nice to see friendly faces again. We had to go to Tulsa this morning to meet with the police about the...unpleasantness. And let me tell you, that was about as fun as being on the bottom of a two-story outhouse."

Her comment touched off a flurry of questions. She held her hands up as though warding them off. "Folks, folks, we can't answer too many questions yet. For one, we're not allowed to say anything about some specific topics since there is still an active investigation. I will say that we need everyone's prayers for strength and deliverance. Now, if all y'all'll give me a moment, I'm starving." She headed for the taco bar, with Vernon and Grace following behind her.

Wow. Triple Contraction. Welcome to Oklahoma...

I leaned over to Tuesday and whispered, "Who is she?" I was fairly confident I knew the answer, but Neesy wouldn't have a clue.

"That's Harper Wren, our pastor. She goes by Sister Harper. The older couple are that little girl's grandparents. You might want to talk to them if you can. I know Sister Harper is going to want to talk to you."

The way she said it set off alarms in my head. Something must have showed on my face. "Oh, don't worry about that. She talks to everyone who works here. She just wants to meet everyone. After all, this is her property."

"Her property? Doesn't this land belong to the church?"

"Yes, and the church belongs to her. She's the owner and majority shareholder of the non-profit organization governing the church. Don't worry, she has good accountants and better lawyers. It's all perfectly legal."

News of Harper's presence got around like wildfire; by the time she finished eating, the cafeteria was standing room only. Even the dog Aparna had been petting showed up. He nosed his way through the crowd and curled up under Harper's table. Nobody seemed to mind, or much notice, his presence.

When Harper finished eating, she stood up and clasped her hands together as she surveyed the room. I tried to be invisible, but she spotted me almost at once. We locked eyes for a lot longer than I was comfortable with before she moved on.

"I'll start by confirming the worst parts of the news," she said. "Phil Upton has confessed to going to Ramona, along with Gabe Holmgren and Nick Lauder, with the intent of assaulting, and, if possible, killing, Aparna's biological father. He told the police one of our associate pastors, I'm not going to say who, encouraged him to do this. The police are preparing a warrant for this person. I promised we would not interfere, and have asked our brother to surrender himself peacefully."

That hit like a bombshell. People erupted with protests and denials on all sides. Despite several people trying to talk at once, Rusty's voice sliced through the din, silencing the competition. "What are the charges?"

"What one would expect," Harper replied. "Beginning with murder in the first degree, assault, conspiracy, and possibly a hate crime in the case of Tyson Wainwright. He was gay, and Phil maintains they were told the Lord would approve of their actions because the Old Testament demands homosexuals be put to death."

An older man in a nice suit turned in his chair and glared at Vernon. "Did you have anything to do with this? I tried not to listen to the things you were saying about the girl's father, but this..."

"I had nothing to do with it," Vernon snapped. "We were at the damn airport when David was attacked! He must have caught the wrong plane, because we were there waiting half an hour before his flight arrived! He was a damn heathen liberal and I will never forgive him for leading Sharon into sin and degradation, but our granddaughter is the most precious thing in our lives right now. I would never do anything to endanger that! And we're damn well not giving her up, either!"

Harper raised her voice, cutting off the other man's response. "To that point....to that point, brothers and sisters, I need to ask everyone to exercise restraint and discretion when it comes to discussing this matter. Aparna knows her father is injured, but she's too young to be hearing all these details. I want everyone to be mindful of what they say around her and the other children. Now, I know this news is troubling to many. However, the law is the law, and we are subjects of it. This is already a difficult time. Please don't make it worse."

Agreement was slow and grudging, but she got it from almost everyone. Tuesday was one of the holdouts. She stood up and said, "I don't want to be the ram in the flock, Sister, but how can we allow one of our brethren to be put on trial for this? After all, Scripture *does* say homosexuality is an abomination punishable by death."

"So is wearing a poly-cotton blend shirt, which is what I'm going to put on as soon as I can. So was eating the bacon on my breakfast sandwich and the shrimp I put in my taco," Harper replied. "We're in the forgiveness business, Tuesday. We don't get to pronounce God's judgment on others, because we are all sinners."

"But we could at least make a stand! You could offer our brother sanctuary. We could have a blockade, or a human chain to keep the police out. A lot of people out there would flock to support us-"

"People with guns? An armed standoff? Taking up arms against the police? Is that what you really want?" Rather than glaring or looking outraged, Harper seemed amused. "If you think that's a course of action Jesus would approve of, you're reading from the wrong Bible."

Tuesday sat down, blushing dark scarlet. "I'm sorry, it's just..."

"It's just that the truth isn't always what we want it to be. I know. It would be easier if David Fraser really was a monster and a danger to his daughter. The fact is that he's just a normal, loving father trying to do what he thinks is best for his daughter. His injuries have changed the situation somewhat. If he passes away, Grace and Vernon become Aparna's closest living relatives. Given that, our legal team went to court this morning and secured an order allowing Aparna to stay here, with her grandparents, until Davis Fraser either dies or recovers."

Someone in the crowd asked, "How can we help?"

"Social media," Tuesday said. "Get the word out. We need word of mouth, press attention, donations-"

"Tuesday!" Harper shook her head, laughing. "I had no idea you were such a Crusader Rabbit at heart. Maybe I should move you into marketing and promotions. Seriously, though, while we do need all these things, the first thing I want everyone to do is nothing. The news story everyone is talking about is that three members of our church murdered one man and put another in the hospital as part of a custody dispute, and did so with the encouragement of an associate pastor. Our members must do nothing to make the situation worse."

"Then what can we do?"

"Pray. Pray for the Lord's wisdom and guidance in this trying time, and for all those hurt during these events."

Tuesday nodded. "Of course, Sister, but faith without works is dead. What about setting something up for people to make donations? Purely voluntary, of course."

Harper shook her head. "No, Tuesday. The church is providing legal services to Vernon and Grace because we believe Aparna should remain with her grandparents until her father's condition improves. We will be defending our brother pastor because I believe he is innocent. The church has the money to meet these needs without additional donations. I don't want anyone accusing us of exploiting Aparna's situation, or profiting from it. Do you understand?"

Tuesday sighed, but nodded. "Yes. I disagree, but...I'll, ah, rein myself in."

"Thank you. I do appreciate your ideas, but what's the sense of paying for a lawyer if you're not going to listen to their advice?" Harper waited for the chuckles to pass and looked me over again. "I know this situation is upsetting, but, if you don't mind, I'd like to change the subject. Tuesday, would you introduce the young lady sitting next to you? I'm quite certain we haven't met."

Great. Even the dog turned to look at me.

I stood up and waved. "Um, hi. I'm Neesy. If you can't tell by the bruises, I had kind of a rough morning. Taylor found me a room at the Spa, and...that's it, I guess. Nice to meet you all."

One of Harper's eyebrows arched up, but her smile didn't waver. "Welcome to Still Waters Ranch. It's fortunate Taylor was able to find room for you. What are your plans for the future?"

"I'm not certain yet. I don't think I know enough to make any solid plans." That, at least, was the truth. "Tuesday helped me file the paperwork for a background check so I can help in the day care. That's it, I guess. It's been kind of a busy day."

"It sounds like it. Being a minister, I do have to ask if you need medical treatment, and have you spoken with the police?"

"I thought being a minister meant you had to ask if I wanted to pray with you or something. Um, anyway, the paramedics looked me over and decided I didn't need to go to the ER, and yes, I talked to the cops. They said the description I provided wasn't enough for them to go on." I shrugged and tried for a self-deprecating grin. "You can't put out a warrant for 'a guy in a blue pickup'."

"Let's hope that justice catches up with that person regardless. And, being a minister, everyone knows I'm available for prayer whenever needed. That's why I don't ask." Harper gathered her belongings and waved to the room. "Well, I'd love to stay and chat, but I have a pile of things waiting for me in my office. I'll make a public announcement about everything that's going on before the end of the day. And Neesy..." She stepped around the table to take my hand. "...I hope we can chat tomorrow. Will you be coming to services on Sunday?"

Sunday services...most of the congregation in one tight group...oh, that would be very useful...

I matched Harper's smile with my own. "Absolutely. I wouldn't miss it for anything."

She gave my hands a comforting squeeze and stepped back. "Wonderful. I so look forward to seeing you there."

Likewise.

While she walked away, the dog emerged from under the table and sniffed my hand. Harper paused at the door, made kissing noises, and called out, "Oreo! Who wants a chewy-chew?" The dog nosed my hand once more and trotted after her.

Hmm. I suppose that if the dog likes her, she can't be all bad.

Chapter Twenty-Eight

The Lay of the Land

Rusty looked up from his computer screen, scowling. "Why would you need a map? You can see the sanctuary from every part of the property. Just walk toward it."

"Not from the inside," I said. "I'm sorry. I get lost easy, that's all. All these doors and hallways...I can't keep them all straight." Blessed Mother, it was hard not to bat my eyes. It wasn't my intention or desire to make Neesy an idiot, but for some reason it was ridiculously effective with some people.

In fact, it made me think back on all the end users I'd lumped in the 'too dumb to use a computer' category. A significant number had gotten me to do stuff that was out-of-scope or against policy just so I didn't have to deal with their incompetence any more. I wouldn't have believed it at the time, but it's possible I got played by some of those folks.

One of the ranch hands knocked on Rusty's door. "Need the keys for the Jimmy—oh, sorry, didn't see you were busy. I'll come back."

"Wait. I'm just finishing here." Rusty snagged a clipboard, flipped through the papers on it, and handed me a stapled bundle. "Here you go, Miss Avalon. There's a map in there and it's all yours now. Just...recycle the rest." He took a key ring from a row of cup hooks anchored to the side of a filing cabinet and tossed them to the ranch hand. "Fill it up when you're done."

"Sure thing." The ranch hand stepped back from the door and tipped his Stetson to me. "Nice to meet you, Miss Avalon, and may I say you look exceptionally pretty today."

I froze in my tracks, wide-eyed and staring. Catcalls I had expected to deal with, but flirting? I had no idea what to say. It didn't help that he was bloody good-looking. Tan, muscular, the perfect amount of stubble, and a damn charming smile on top of it. Just the kind of guy Neesy would go

185

for—and if I hadn't been a straight male all my life, I might have some idea of how to respond.

Since I had to do something, I took a deep breath and smiled back. "Pleased to meet you too, mister…"

"Roy. Just Roy." He tilted his head and cocked an eyebrow. Great. Now he looked both charming and roguish. "I got some errands to run, but I do hope to see you around this weekend, Miss Avalon. You take care now." He tossed the keys into the air, caught them without looking, and ran his finger down the brim of his hat before sauntering off.

"Neesy."

What? Why did I say that?

Roy turned around. "Beg pardon?"

Crap. "Ah…Neesy. My name. You can call me Neesy."

"Well, nice to learn your name, Miss Neesy, and I look forward to learning more." He walked away, this time with a good bit of swagger.

I found a restroom and hid in the farthest stall, burying my face in my hands. Today had already been an emotional crap storm; now I had to cope with someone hitting on me, too? And why didn't I just tell him I was a lesbian?

Because you're in the middle of a Christian church in Oklahoma.

Good point. Let's file that one under 'not really a good idea.'

Oh, by the way—your pee meter is in the red.

Great.

At least using the bathroom as a woman was getting easier. Or it would be, if Rose wasn't laughing her ass off over my encounter with Roy. I focused on her and thought, *Give me a break* as hard as I could.

You know, you could always give Aparna a sister, she replied. "Oh! Use your feminine wiles to convince him to help you rescue her!"

Yeah, yeah, yeah…Laugh it up, fuzzball.

I leaned back, resting the back of my head on the wall, and waited for the room to stop moving around. Talking to Rose like that took far more effort now. I told myself I should save it for emergencies. Myself promised to be good, but he lies.

Rose had made a good suggestion, though. Feminine wiles might not get me anywhere with Roy, but that command spell tattooed on my wrist might. However, first things first. I needed to see the sanctuary. Well, first thing after I pulled my pants up.

Despite Rusty's assurances the sanctuary was easy to find, I needed the map twice. The information on the papers stapled to it covered the church's active shooter response training plan. Not immediately useful, but worth looking over when I had time. The sanctuary was open and unoccupied. No lightning bolts struck me down, so I wandered in and looked around.

The architecture had a strong Japanese style, with timber supports, natural colors, and clean lines drawing the eye to the rough-hewn cross emerging from a formation of unworked granite. The pulpit was crafted of the same stone, simple and unobtrusive. Even the baptistry and the choir risers were concealed by front pieces that matched the wall behind them so that they blended in unless they were in use.

I picked a pew near the back and sat with my head lowered. Hopefully anyone seeing me would assume I was praying. Figuring out where to set the spell off would be easier if I knew what "the immediate area" meant. Several minutes later, my best estimate still had a ton of wiggle room. I'd just have to get as close to the middle of the crowd as I could and hope for the best.

My conscience picked that moment to act up again. *You're supposed to be the Lawful Good Hero, remember? Even if you're doing it for a good cause, a magical assault on a church full of innocent bystanders is still an evil act.*

I looked up at the cross, exhaling a hard puff of air. Prayer wasn't my thing, but it couldn't hurt to try, right? Especially since my plan involved committing a serious alignment violation.

I bowed my head and—for the first time in many years—prayed to the god of Abraham. "Hi there. I'm hoping you're listening, even though I'm not a believer anymore. My family still follows you. Especially my sister. I may not have the right, but I ask you to look out for them, and protect them from harm while the world sorts things out. And don't blame them for what I need to do here. I'll answer for my own actions, thanks."

"You know why I'm here, what I'm planning. I don't want to hurt any-one. I don't even want to go through with this plan if I don't have to. If you convince Vernon and Grace to turn Aparna over to child services, I'll call it off and sneak out of here. No one gets hurt. I'll even allow the Da-tonas to keep their visitation if they agree not to pull this sort of thing again. Back in Vegas, fighting that demon, I saw the blood on the spear bring dead people back to life. Changing someone's mind is a much smaller miracle."

I paused and racked my brain for ideas, but didn't have anything to add. "That's it, then. I hope we can work this out, but, either way, thanks for listening."

Just like that, I remembered what Nadia said the day of the Change: *Earth is an experiment in free will.* Following right behind that was a simple, obvious realization: *You can't have free will if a god tells you what to do.*

Well, shit.

I heard a brief clicking of claws on stone, followed by the touch of a cold, wet nose. Oreo snuffled my hand, probably looking for hidden pieces of burrito. When he didn't find anything, he shoved his head under my palm with an emphatic *brurf* noise, just to make sure I noticed him.

Obediently, I scruffed behind his ears. He closed his eyes, enjoying the moment. I chuckled and whispered,

He snorted. The scorn and derision were palpable.

I scowled back. "What's the matter, dog? Would you prefer some D.H. Lawrence? Something about birds dropping dead from a bough, maybe?"

Damn. I didn't know dogs could roll their eyes. At least with cats you go in expecting attitude.

Oreo shoved my leg with his nose. I got the hint and went back to showering him with affection. While petting his shoulder, I felt a hard ridge of skin under his fur. It had an even pattern to the rises and depressions along the sides—probably stitches, I guessed. I followed it with my fingertips, trying to keep my touch as light as possible. The scar turned out to be about six inches long, right across the ribs. A little exploring turned up quite a few more scars, all old, most of them appearing to have been closed surgically.

Dog fighting was a logical answer, but that didn't feel right. Maybe I was projecting a bit, but I couldn't see Oreo being as mellow as he was with that kind of background. Maybe a police dog or former military?

His collar didn't have any answers. A cute little bone-shaped tag said his shots were current and listed the church as his residence. No surprise there. Instead of a buckle, the collar had a metal clasp. I couldn't see any release for it, and had to stifle my urge to play around with it. Neesy could accept things without trying to figure them out.

One light blue spot a little smaller than my thumbnail hinted at the collar's original color. His name had been embossed with heavy block letters and was still mostly legible. Something had burned off most of the 'E,' leaving only the vertical line. The area next to the name held a partial impression of something rectangular, long since torn away.

There was something familiar about the style of the lettering. I'd seen something like it before. That much I was sure of, but I couldn't remember where. I traced the letters with my finger, trying to remember...

Panicked voices shattered the peace of the sanctuary and sent my train of thought off a cliff. Oreo's ears went back and he raced out of the room. I was tempted to stay where I was, but what if I missed a good diversion? I got up and followed the dog down the hall.

Outside the door for the church offices, four cops were escorting a well-dressed older man toward the door to the parking lot, and he was having none of it. "I didn't do anything!" he bellowed. "You've got the wrong person! You can't do this to me!"

One of the officers said, "Travis, it's a warrant. You're going to have to deal with it. Now quit fighting and walk like a man. I do not want to add resisting arrest to everything else."

Travis stopped and defiance changed to frightened tears. "Mike, what am I going to do? I'm innocent! I'd never do anything like this. My own son is gay! Mike, you know me. I'm not a murderer..."

Harper stepped into the hall. "Mike, could you give us a moment?"

Officer Mike grimaced, but nodded. "Of course. Not too long, though."

"Thank you. Travis, try to stay calm. I'm going to make some calls and see if I can get an attorney to meet you at the station in Tulsa. Is there anything you'd like me to tell Patricia for you?"

"Tell her I love her, and that I didn't do it," Travis replied.

"I will. Mike, please call me when you get to Tulsa and let me know where he's being held." Harper held out a business card, which Officer Mike tucked in his pocket.

"Sure thing. Thank you, Sister." Officer Mike took Travis by the arm and led him out to the waiting cruiser.

"Cut him loose, Harper." A middle-aged guy came out of the offices, stopping close enough to Harper for their shoulders to touch. He put his arm around Harper's shoulders and added, "The ministry can't-"

"Remove your hand, Preston, or I will," Harper said. Preston pulled back, holding his hands up and muttering an apology. Without raising her voice, Harper said, "*I* decide what the ministry can and cannot do. While I appreciate your input on the matter, it's not your concern. This is an issue for the *senior* leadership."

Preston's face darkened, his empty hands clenched into fists. For a long moment, I thought he might actually hit her. I moved forward, forgetting that I was now a literal 90-pound weakling. Lucky for me, Preston managed to swallow whatever level of anger he was feeling without doing anything stupid. He crossed the hall and went outside, letting the door slam shut behind him.

Unperturbed, Harper held her hands up and said, "Everyone, please go back to what you were doing. Brother Travis needs our support and our prayers right now. I have no doubt of his innocence and firmly believe that he will be vindicated. I'll be speaking to our legal team and getting them involved, so, please don't worry. We will take care of him. Thank you."

I turned to leave with the others until Oreo blocked my path, shoving me sideways. Harper caught my arm before my stumble turned into a fall.

"Careful there," she said. "Oreo is used to bossing the alpacas around. Two legs aren't as stable as four."

"Yeah, thanks. I've already fallen enough for one day." I stood up, but Harper kept hold of my arm, leaning in to look at the side of my face. I pulled back a little and asked, "Something wrong? Do I have a bug in my hair?"

"No, no. I was looking at the cut Taylor said you got this morning. It looks nearly healed. Even the bruises on your cheek have faded just since lunch. That's rather remarkable, wouldn't you say?"

These aren't the injuries you're looking for. Out loud, I said, "The ambulance guys said the cut wasn't as bad as it looked. It just bled a lot until I could get some pressure on it."

"You didn't even need stitches, I understand." Harper released my arm and brushed a wisp of hair away from my eye. "You know, rather than wait for tomorrow, perhaps we could have our conversation now? I'd also like to get some pictures of your injuries. As long as you don't mind, that is. It's nothing prurient, I promise. I'm seeing something extraordinary, and I want to document it."

In the back of my mind, a talking calamari was shouting, "It's a trap!" And I was pretty sure he was right. Still...Harper would be a much more useful person to mind-control, and this might be a chance to use the spell with no witnesses and no interference.

I nodded. "Fine, I guess. Just don't put any of these pictures on the Internet or anything."

Harper laughed. "Don't worry. I'll ask your permission before I show them to anyone."

Chapter Twenty-Nine

The Gifts of the Spirit

Her office was smaller than I expected. Aside from the mandatory desk and overstuffed bookshelves, she had a futon couch in front of a large window. It gave her a nice view of a rose garden surrounded by a low stone wall. Past that, open pasture sloped down to a small pond. Alpacas strutted and meandered through the grass, placidly ignoring anything they couldn't eat or spit at.

"Let me give us some privacy." Harper flicked a light switch on the wall behind her desk. Something at the top and bottom of the door clicked, and a heavy steel storm shutter rolled down over the window. "There. We should be quite secure."

I put my hand over the tattoo, fingertips almost touching it. I only had one shot at this spell. It had to cover everything I wanted from her and still be less than ten words. "Help me take Aparna into Bartlesville" seemed to cover it. I hoped.

I focused on the words, ready to trigger the spell, but something moved at the edge of my vision. Oreo. He was crouched down, ears back, staring at me and ready to leap if I made the wrong move.

Maybe he could sense the magic. Then again, maybe it was just me trying to be sneaky that alarmed him. It didn't really matter. My normal body could probably have fended him off long enough to bring Kindness out to play, but Neesy might as well be a Scooby Snack.

Instead of activating the tattoo, I held my hand out to him. "What are you looking at? You want to see me naked, too? I don't mind. You're probably the only guy who does..."

He snorted and looked away.

"Oh, fine, be that way." I crossed my arms. "I don't want to see you naked either, dog."

"You shouldn't think so negatively about yourself," Harper said. "And I only need your shirt off."

I hooked my thumbs in the neckband of my shirt, intending to pull it off the way I normally did in my own body. It worked the same way, but as I pulled it over my head, I felt... vulnerable. Exposed, and not just physically. Harper was smart, and, unlike me, had a lifetime of experience being a woman. If something was off with my pretense, she'd notice.

Well, Harper was a total stranger. Some nervousness would be normal. Maybe Neesy talked when she was nervous... I coughed and asked, "So, um, what was that Preston guy's problem? He looked really pissed when you told him to stop pawing you."

"I imagine he did." Harper grimaced but didn't stop taking pictures. "He and I started the church together. At the time, the only thing most people knew about me was that my mother had been a Vegas showgirl. It's hard to build a church with that hanging over your head. Preston was trying to establish a church as well. He had a presence and a name in the community, which I lacked. I thought he was twistier than a feed sack full of rattlers, but I needed him. For his part, he thought I would be nice eye candy to bring in younger members. And it worked fairly well. We were successful, but not as successful as he wanted us to be. Several years ago, he left to pastor for another church. At that time, he demanded I buy his interest out. I was more than happy to do so."

"Let me guess," I said. "He came crawling back, reeking of failure?"

"Let's just say it wasn't a good fit," Harper replied. "He asked for his old position as co-pastor back. At the time we needed a pastor for the senior men, so I offered it to him. He was grateful enough, but since then he's become more...demanding."

Harper lowered the camera and gave me a sad smile. "He took a chance on me way back when, so I took a chance on him. Shames me to say it, but he turned out to be as useful as tits on a bulldozer and twice as proud as Lucifer himself. He doesn't want an ordinary, successful church. He wants fame, a huge following, a television show..."

"Wealth," I said.

She nodded. "Wealth does seem to find its way into the list of heart's desires. I want the church to have success and prosperity too, but...not like that. Other things come first."

"Like what?"

"Like taking the rest of these pictures."

I took the hint and stayed quiet. Five minutes later, she stepped back and said, "All done. Thank you."

While I got my shirt back on, Harper downloaded the pictures to her computer. "Have a seat, Neesy. I think you'll find this interesting." She turned the monitor so I could see it, too.

Taylor must have sent Harper the pictures of me from this morning; she had matched the angles of her pictures to the evidence photos for a better comparison. Neither set of photos were great masterpieces, but

192

next to one another, they were clear and graphic proof of how fast I was healing.

After this many years of being with Rose, I'm used to healing a lot faster than everyone else. This was something different. More pronounced. And I had no idea what it was. Even if some of the magic Rose used to fix my concussion had bled over to the rest of me, her spell wouldn't still be in effect all these hours later.

"At the rate those bruises are vanishing, you'll be completely healed to-morrow morning. That's why I didn't want to wait." Harper took my hands. "It's possible you are one of the Changed and this is simply who you are now. It could also be something in your blood, something another person could benefit from through a transfusion. If so, it could be as much a curse for you as a blessing to others. My sincere hope is that the Lord has given you the gift of healing. Do you know what laying on hands means?"

"Is it like what Jesus did with the one dude's ear when it got cut off?" I was *not* going to mention D&D here...

"I think you mean Jesus healing Malchus after Simon Peter took a sword to him," she said. "Yes, pretty much like that. It's the ability to heal by touch. It's not widely known yet, but there are other people out there who the Holy Spirit has blessed with the ability to heal, and I think you may be one of them. I try not to cast my pride and desires on the Holy Spirit, but...it would be wonderful if you have that gift. You could do amaz-ing things. Think of all the people you could help."

I pulled back. "I'm picturing being crushed by a never-ending mob of people wanting me to fix them."

"Even Jesus had that problem," she said. "It didn't stop Him from teaching and ministering to the multitudes."

"Yeah, well, Jerusalem didn't have as many people as New York City does. Or, like...Rio, or Mumbai." I held my hands up, pushing the idea away. "I don't want anything like that."

Harper chuckled. "I totally understand. It's a terrifying idea. But I'd like you to think about it. If you have this gift, it could make a huge differ-ence in the lives of many, many people."

"It could also make the church rich," I replied. "Fame, a huge follow-ing, a television show..."

"Absolutely." Harper leaned back in her chair and spread her hands. "And there's nothing I can say that would convince you or anyone else that my desire is to help people, not to become rich. I won't ask you to trust me, but I will ask you to allow me to demonstrate my trustworthiness."

"What if I don't have this power?" I asked. "Sure, something is hap-pening to me, but I don't know what or how or why. Are you still going to be interested in me if it turns out to be something else doing it?"

"Of course. I want to see you become successful in life no matter what. We don't throw people out."

"I'm *really* glad to hear that. I was getting nervous." I rubbed my hands against my sides, trying to think of a subtle way to bring up Aparna. Nothing leapt to mind, so I went with something totally unsubtle. "Can I ask you something about the girl with the wings? Tuesday said some horrible things about her father, but you said he wasn't a monster. What's really going on there?"

The corner of Harper's mouth twitched. "It's a custody fight, and they are always ugly no matter who is involved. I'd stay out of it if I were you. The church is not involved with the custody fight, and we aren't going to be. The one thing I will say is that, despite what you may have heard, her father actually is a decent person. Aparna was not abused, or in any danger of abuse."

I nodded. "Well, okay then. She just looked so sad. I guess I kind of saw myself in her. I wanted to help."

"It's kind of you to offer, but honestly that girl is a closed book. She won't even talk to her grandparents. I think Oreo is the only one she's really bonded with since she came to live here."

I nodded out of reflex, preoccupied with thinking about how to get close to Aparna. Then Harper's comment sunk in. "She's living here? I thought she was just in day care."

"Her grandparents live at Covenant Center. She's staying with them. Did you try to have the tattoo on your back removed at some point?"

"No, why?"

Harper pulled up one of her photos. "It looks like whatever is healing you is also dissolving it."

She was right. The color was faded and some of the edges had chunks missing. It didn't seem to be vanishing as fast as the bruises were, but this was a problem. At least the spell tattoos on my arm still looked fine.

"Aw, man! That one really hurt, too." I shook my head. "I don't mind getting better fast, but I don't like it messing with my ink." *Especially considering what will happen to me when it vanishes...*

"Well, perhaps you can get another one someday." Harper took a large gold cross on a beaded necklace out of her purse, holding the top part of the cross and wrapping the necklace around her hand. "Would you mind if I ran a small experiment? I'd like to test the effectiveness of your touch in healing small injuries."

I shrugged. "Sure. I'm...not going anyplace. Just let me know when and where."

"No time like the present." She put her free hand flat on her desk, palm up, clenched the bottom arm of the cross between her teeth, and pulled. The bottom arm came free, revealing a thin, curved blade.

Harper brought the blade down fast and hard, leaving a thin red line across the heel of her palm. She winced, hissing, and dropped the necklace as she cradled her hand. The cross she'd been holding wasn't a cross; it was an ankh.

"Oh, shit!" I grabbed some tissues from the box on her desk and pressed them against her palm. "What did you do that for? I'm not approved for human testing yet."

She pulled her hand away from the tissues and said, "Try it. See if you can heal me."

I sighed, shaking my head. "Fine. What do you want me to do?"

"Touch my hand and command the wound be healed."

"Right, okay..." I put my fingers over the cut and said, "Heal!"

Harper snorted. "That's not what I was thinking of. It's a cut, not a show dog."

"Yeah, well, Oreo decided to ignore me, too." I took a breath to steady myself, focused, and said, "Be healed!"

No celestial light show, no music, nothing. When I lifted my hand up, the cut was still there. Apparently, I was not the Chosen One. I breathed a sigh of relief.

"No, no. You have to ask in Jesus' name. Like this..." Harper pressed her palm against the cut and said, "By the name and the power of our lord Jesus Christ, be healed." She held her hand out to me and said, "Alright, try it again."

"I don't think so." I pointed to her smooth, unmarred palm. Even the bloodstains had vanished.

"Merciful Lord!" Harper leaped backwards, knocking her chair into a bookshelf. She kept going until she hit the wall and stood there, shaking, holding her hand up in front of her. Hesitantly, she made a fist. When no blood appeared, she poked her palm with her finger several times. Still no response. She took a deep breath, closed her eyes, and gave herself a good slap. The cut insisted on staying healed. Harper slid down the wall until she was sitting on the floor, head buried in her hands.

Keeping my voice soft and steady, I asked, "Harper, are you alright?"

"Yes," she said. "This is...sort of funny, if you think about it. Ever hear the phrase, 'enough to make a preacher cuss'?"

I nodded. "Yes."

"I always wondered how much that would be. 'Enough' is hard to quantify." She looked up at me, chuckling and crying at the same time. "Not any more, though. I did it. I found out what 'enough' is."

"Haven't heard no cussing," I offered. "Maybe it's not that bad."

"The cussing is on the inside, Neesy. It's all on the inside. Mama was a Vegas showgirl, remember? I even out-cussed a piss-drunk master chief once. Trust me, I know cussing."

I chuckled. "Well, if it helps any, just think of what Preston is going to say when he finds out you can do miracles now."

Harper sputtered. She tried to say something, but the words got lost in her laughter. She tried once more, gave up, and rolled over onto her side, still laughing. After a moment, I lost it as well and joined her on the floor.

Not to be outdone, Oreo wedged himself between us and rolled over onto his back with his tongue hanging out.

Laughter alone triumphs.

Chapter Thirty

Plays Well with Others. Sort Of.

"I love that ankh, by the way. I spent a lot of time shopping for one at science fiction conventions, but I could never find one."

"Thanks. In ninth grade I was obsessed with vampires and David Bowie. I spent that year dressing in clothes from the 1940's and wearing more makeup than my mother did when she was on stage." Harper smiled and shook her head as she dropped the ankh back into her purse. "I thought I looked so cool, but now I look at pictures of myself and think I looked like a skinny, clinically depressed panda. Mama found the ankh for me at the Trove last year and gave it to me for my birthday."

"The Trove?"

"Her new favorite casino. The whole place is based on a computer game, and their player's club rewards are mostly things that only exist in the game. She auctions the stuff she gets off to people who actually play it. She makes some good money."

"Cool." I made a mental note to take Aparna to some of the kid-friendly shows in Vegas as soon as possible after we got her home.

Harper checked her hair and makeup in a compact mirror before opening the door. "I hate to rush off, but I need some time to think about all this." She opened the door an inch or so, paused, and closed it again. "You know, it's funny. It's not the crowds or the people wanting help that scares me. I can deal with all that. It's that something like this only happens for a reason. God wants me to do something with it, and I'm scared of doing the wrong thing. Does that make sense?"

I nodded. "Oh, yeah. Just don't do what I almost did when I thought I might be special."

"What was that?"

"Let my friend Harper talk me into doing something I really didn't want to do, because doing it would further her dreams."

"Ah..." Harper looked down and nodded. "Well, maybe your friend just got excited, and was looking at the big picture without seeing the details. Like, say, how it would affect you and your life. People have done that to me before. My mother, for one. Even before I was born."

I sat my skinny little rear on the edge of her desk. "How so?"

"I doubt you'd get it...then again, if you've been to a bunch of science fiction conventions, maybe you would." Harper pondered for a moment, then nodded. "Yeah, I'll tell you. See, Mama...well, she has never lacked for male companionship. The fellow who got her pregnant didn't want to be a husband and father, so he up and left. It didn't get her down, though. If one fish slips the line, you just bait up a bigger hook. Mama went out looking and found someone she thought might like the job. Well, her due date was getting close and she hadn't closed the deal yet, so she thought she'd give her babies names that would go with her prospective husband's name. She thought it might gentle him into the idea. So, I got named Harper and my brother got named Miner. And then, when she went to introduce her intended to his new family, she found out he already had one."

I winced. "Yikes. I'm sorry."

Harper waved it away. "Don't be. In all fairness, a blind man would have seen that coming. No, the worst part is the names she gave us. Not because of what they are, but because she picked them for the sake of someone else. The guy she wanted to marry? His last name was Hall."

"Oh, Blessed Mother... Harper Hall and Miner Hall?" I put my head in my hands. Then I realized what I'd said. Neesy didn't swear by the Goddess.

Thankfully, Harper didn't seem to notice my slip. "What can I say? Mama's a big Anne McCaffrey fan." Harper sighed. "I suppose we're lucky she didn't name us after the damn dragons."

"I'm glad you can laugh about it now, but those are still cruel names to give kids. Especially someplace like Las Vegas."

"She got hers back," Harper said. "When she married Arthur, her fourth husband, she became Mrs. Melody Singer."

That was worth another laugh. Before either of us could say anything else, Oreo scratched at the door and made a low *brurf* noise. Harper nodded and opened the door to let him out. We followed.

As she locked her office behind us, Harper said, "Neesy, Aparna and her grandparents are coming over to my house at seven for a dinner meeting with the church's attorneys. If you could play with Aparna and try to keep her entertained, I'd really appreciate it. Her English is pretty good and her grandparents are bringing some cartoon shows she likes, so I'm not throwing you totally to the wolves. Would you be interested in giving me a hand?"

More than you know. "I'd be honored. Thank you so much!"

"Don't thank me until after dinner. I'm making something called butter chicken, and I have no idea how it's supposed to taste."

"I do. Some of the kids at my last job were from an Indian family, and
their mom made dinner for us a few times. If you can get some fresh spinach and farmer's cheese, there's a side dish you can make...sack panner,
or something like that." I mispronounced *saag paneer* as badly as I could.
Neesy was not a linguist.

"That's it!" Harper clapped her hands. "I saw a recipe for that last
night and was going to make it for Aparna, but I couldn't remember what
it was called or what went into it. Bless you! I have to run to the store
really quick. See you tonight!" She hurried off, and I headed back to the
Spa. I needed to find something nice to wear.

Taylor and I had to dig through the program's supply of interview
clothes for a bit, but we found a coral orange and red broomstick skirt and
matching blouse I could wear. Unfortunately, they smelled like an ashtray.
I had a little over two hours, so I popped them in the washing machine for
a short bath with a lot of detergent.

Ofelia wasn't talking to me and no one else was in the shelter, so I
warmed up half a burrito and curled up in front of the television to eat and
catch up on the national news. The upcoming election was the main story,
of course, but only a few stories after that, they went to an update on the
reaction to Tyson's death. My own condition got a mention, too, but only
in passing.

Since Phil Upton, the surviving thug, had confessed to targeting Tyson
for being gay, a lot of people were demanding federal hate crimes charges
against him. Travis Dawes, the pastor I'd seen being arrested, was maintaining his innocence despite Phil Upton's claims. Someone had set up an
online petition asking that Grace and Vernon be charged as well.

The report showed a clip of Vernon walking out of a police station, saying, "I had nothing to do with this. Tyson was a good man, a good friend,
and I'm just sick to death over it."

The reporter added that the attack appeared to be related to an ongoing
international custody fight, and ended by saying, "The church at the center
of the controversy, the New Life Fellowship in Bartlesville, Oklahoma, has
not commented on these events. Authorities say the church leadership is
cooperating with the investigation. There are protests planned for tonight
in Tulsa and Oklahoma City. Police in both cities are appealing for calm."

Yet more reasons to get this wrapped up.

A woman carrying several canvas shopping bags on each arm kicked
the door open, bellowing "That dat-gum summbitch! I want to chain his
lying ass to the south end of a northbound semi and tell the driver to stick
to dirt roads!" She collapsed onto the floor and burst into tears.

Ofelia popped up with a handful of tissues and helped her to the
kitchen table. "Neesy, could you grab those bags? Fran, Neesy. Neesy,
Fran. Neesy arrived just this morning."

Fran blew her nose and gave me a feeble wave. "Ofelia, what am I going to do?"

I closed the shelter door and brought Fran's bags to the table. "What is it you need?"

Ofelia spared me a stern look. "I've got this, Neesy. Finish eating and clean up." She turned back to Fran and asked, "Whatever it is, we can find a way to deal with it. Tell me what happened."

"Elliot spent the money he promised me for Janey's birthday present on a dirt bike for that godless whore's brat. I can't ask for another advance at work and her birthday's tomorrow. What am I going to do?"

"What were you getting her?" I asked.

That got me another glare from Ofelia. "It's not your concern, Neesy."

Fran ignored her. "There's one of those build-your-own teddy bear places in Tulsa. Her father and I were supposed to meet there and split buying her one. There's this special thing they've got, one of those magic dream ponies. It's the one with all the colors in her wings."

"Spectrum Blaze?"

"Yeah, that one. She's Janey's favorite, and after the past few months, I wanted to give her something that would make her happy."

"It's just as well, Frannie. Those ponies are anything but Biblically sound," Ofelia said. "You could go over to the second chance store and get her something. I've seen some nice crosses there, and Janey doesn't have one of her own."

Fran started crying again. "Well, that's better than nothing, I guess. It's just...I already paid a deposit on the blessed doll, and if we cancel I'll lose most of it. That damn Elliot...I hope that slut gives him something that rots his tiny little pecker off!"

"How much do you need?" I asked.

Ofelia snarled, "Neesy, this is none of your business. Nobody asked for your opinion and nobody wants it. Why don't you go back to your room and stay there for a day or two?"

I pulled what was left of my hundred bucks out of my pocket and held four twenties out to Fran. "Will eighty bucks cover it?"

Fran reached for it, then pulled her hand back. "Oh, bless you, but...I can't..."

I pressed the money into her hand. "Take it. It's your daughter's birthday. Make her happy."

"Don't take it. You don't know where she got it." Ofelia pulled back, glaring. "Drug money, I bet. Or did you get beat up because that guy you met this morning didn't want to pay for your services?"

I looked at Ofelia and shook my head. "Your heart must be a really ugly place. Five bucks says Jesus doesn't live there anymore."

"Bitch!" Ofelia shoved Fran to the side and slapped me hard enough to knock me to the floor. She followed it with several kicks to my ribs. "Get up! Get up, now! I'm not finished with you by a long shot."

I rolled away from her and got to my feet. When I lifted my head, Fran gasped and scrambled for the door. Ofelia took a step back and whispered, "Get thee behind me, Satan..."

My blood was singing.

I smiled at Ofelia and took one step toward her. "Run," I whispered. "Run while you still have legs!"

She ran. Fran was right behind her.

I threw my head back, laughing until the battle-joy faded. Then I rinsed my face in the kitchen sink and put together an ice pack for my cheek. The last thing I wanted right now was a bruise shaped like Ofelia's hand.

Taylor and Rusty came down the stairs while I was picking up the stuff that had spilled out of Fran's shopping bags. Taylor looked around and asked, "Care to tell me what happened?"

"I fell down."

"That's not what the security video shows."

I moved the icepack so they could get a look. "I'm turning the other cheek. I don't want Ofelia to get fired or anything. I was trying to help Fran, that's all, and that's what I'd prefer to focus on."

Taylor held her hands up. "I appreciate your offer, but Ofelia already quit. I would have had to fire her regardless, because I won't tolerate that behavior. Do you want us to call the EMTs to make sure you're okay?"

"No. She just gave me a good smack, nothing serious." I looked at the stairway and asked, "Where's Fran? Is she alright?"

"Scared half to death, but not injured," Taylor said.

Rusty pointed up the stairs. "Since I'm not needed here, I'll let her know it's safe to come down." He took the stairs two at a time. Typical male show-off...

I set the ice pack on the table. "I'll be right back. Please tell Fran I need to talk to her." While Taylor was still nodding, I scampered back to my room and got another handful of twenties out of the safe.

When I got back to the kitchen, Fran was inspecting her purchases to make sure they hadn't been damaged. She looked up and said, "Glad to see you looking normal again. Damn, girl, I thought you were going to have her for dinner."

"I don't eat junk food." I looked at the goodies sitting on the table and held out the money. "I'd like to buy some of this from you. I have to watch another little girl who loves *Celestial Dream Ponies* over at Harper's house tonight, and I intend to be voted 'coolest baby sitter ever'."

Fran took the money, eyes wide. "Sure. Whatever you need. I...I can take Janey to pick out the toys she really wants now." She counted he money again and asked, "Are you sure you can afford all this?"

"More than sure," I said. "I want you to have a wonderful time and give her a fantastic birthday."

"We will, don't worry." Fran closed her eyes a moment, holding back tears, then sat up with an incredulous smile. "You know, there's enough here for us to go to Margaret's for supper! Janey loves it, and we haven't been in so long..."

"It sounds like just the thing." I picked up the brand-new Pony Princess Tea Party set and drew a circle around the picture of Mrs. Mulligatawny with my finger tip. "I'll need this, both coloring books, and the set of crayons. Do we have any gift bags and tissue paper around here?"

"I got wrapping paper with ponies on it in my room," Fran replied.

"That'll work just fine."

Was I resorting to bribery, emotional manipulation, and playing on a child's desires? Yes. I needed her to like me enough to listen to me. If I had to do the wrong thing for the right reason, then so be it.

Sometimes, wickedness alone triumphs.

Chapter Thirty-One

Custody Fight

I showed up at Harper's door at twenty till six. I have to admit, the skirt and blouse I'd scavenged from Taylor's office looked terrific and fit the cheerful, entertaining mood I wanted to project to Aparna.

The yard around the parsonage felt nothing like the open space between it and the church offices. When I stepped through the gate, the animal noises, voices, and the rumble of an old pickup making its way down the road all went quiet. I could hear insects, the rustling of the leaves, and the near silent wingbeats of swallows coming and going from their nest, high on a pole towering over Harper's roof.

A bright green mantis landed on my arm, poking at the fabric of my blouse and cocking its head to and fro, trying to decide if I was food or shelter. I scooped it up and set it on a glossy walnut leaf. "Stay out of trouble, buddy. A lot of humans don't know how much you do for us."

The mantis ambled off, heedless of my warning.

A squirrel cage taller than my normal form stood next to her door. Two pairs of eyes glared malevolently out at me, promising mayhem while still pleading for treats. They had plenty of food and water, so I ignored their outraged chitters.

Harper answered my knock and held the door for me. "I'm so glad you're here! My bedroom is just past the stairs, you can leave everything in there. I need you in the kitchen!"

The stairs were easy to find; a spiral staircase, done in steel and concrete, descending into the ground. The central axis rose to meet a steel I-beam in the ceiling, and the stairwell walls were made of cinderblocks. Probably reinforced with steel and filled with concrete; my mother's family had a tornado shelter in the basement built the same way.

I set the bags on her bed and hurried to the kitchen. No sooner had I walked in when Harper handed me a spoon. "Taste this!" she demanded.

It was pretty good, but... "A little thin. Do you have any plain yogurt or coconut milk?"

"No, used it all."

"Hmm...plain cashews or almonds?"

"Yes!" Harper pulled a large plastic tub out of her pantry. "Raw almonds. I use them in my squirrel chow."

"Put half a cup in the blender and grind it up, very fine." While she did that, I checked the *saag paneer*. Her spinach was only about half-done, so I covered it and let it keep going.

"How much of the almonds should I add?"

"Start with a tablespoon and see how that does. It shouldn't need much." I'd learned the ground almonds trick years ago, back when Sharon was alive and living with Manya. I brushed the memories away and focused. Getting choked up now would just complicate things.

A few minutes of stirring later, the sauce was perfect. With everything covered and on low heat, I finished setting the table while Harper warmed *naan* in the oven. Aparna and I would be sitting at a small table in the living room, where the latest pony movie was ready to roll. I couldn't have asked for a better setup.

Raucous chittering from the front porch announced our dinner guests. Harper gave me a hug and whispered, "Thank you!" before going to let everyone in. I made sure my hands were clean and dry, then stood to the side and waited to be introduced.

Amid the usual flurry of greetings, I heard a woman say, "Thank yoo so much for inviting us ovah, Haapah," and cringed. That was Paige Novella's voice. Oh, goody...

Pay her no attention. You don't know who she is.

"...and this is Neesy. I asked her to come over so Aparna has someone to play with while we talk about all this boring adult stuff. Neesy, I think you met Vernon and Grace at lunch. These other folks are our attorneys, Paige Novella and Rudy Turner."

"Pleased to meet you," I lied.

"And this is Miss Aparna." Harper stood to the side and gently urged Aparna forward. "Aparna, this is Miss Neesy. She has some games and movies for you tonight."

I got down on one knee and pressed my palms together. "Namaste. *Aap se milkar kushi hui.*" *I'm pleased to meet you.*

Aparna's face lit up. She returned the bow and said, "Namaste, Auntie-ji! *Aap-*" She looked up at Grace and all the happiness vanished from her face. "I has to speak English. Nice to meet you."

The look on her face was a knife in the guts. I held out my hand and said, "That's okay. I only know a few words some other children taught me. Why don't we get some dinner? I've got a present for you after we eat."

"Not hungry."

I held my hand out the way I'd seen Ember do. "I am. Take a sniff. What does it smell like?"

She took a small sniff. Her eyes widened, and she took a longer one. "*Murgh makhni!*" She all but ran into the kitchen.

"Great. Now she's going to be asking for that Indian crap all over again." Vernon snorted. "We only just got her liking spaghetti."

"Vernon Osgood Datona, that is the happiest that little girl has been in a week. Don't rock the boat if you ain't gonna' bail it out none." Grace folded her arms, glaring. Vernon backed down. Wise man.

Harper touched my shoulder. "Neesy, why don't you get her started while I mix up some drinks for everyone?"

I nodded. "Yes, Sister." *More than happy to comply.*

I got our plates together and started the movie. Aparna hadn't seen it yet and she was enthralled. I sat back and laughed with her. Mrs. Mulligatawny was still my favorite character, but I had to admit that, for a dewy-eyed pony, Spectrum Blaze could be a hardcore badass.

After clearing the dishes and having a bathroom break, I made Aparna wait with her eyes closed as I brought out the tea party set. I was hoping for shrieks of surprise, but when she saw the box, she stuck her face in the corner of the couch and said, "No. Take it 'way."

I moved it off the table and sat down next to her. "What's wrong?"

"Go 'way."

"It's okay. You can tell me if you don't like it."

She flailed an arm at me and shouted, "No! G'way!"

I laughed and switched to Hindi. "I can't do that, daughter-ji. Why are you sad?"

Aparna sat up, wiping her nose on her sleeve. "I gets in troubles if I won't speak English."

I got her a tissue. "Not with Mommy-ji, or Rasa-ji, or with Angel Mommy. And not with me. Now, why are you sad?"

She stared at me, unsure of what to say. I tried a different approach.

"I think I know. You had a tea set like this back in Mumbai, didn't you? And the night before you came here, you, and Mommy-ji, and Daddy-ji, and Angel Mommy, all had tea. And you all told Angel Mommy what you'd been doing. Remembering that is what made you sad. Am I right?"

Aparna nodded. "Uh-huh." She started crying and switched to Hindi. "I miss Mommy-ji! I don't like it here." Then it was like a dam breaking. Sobbing, she wrapped her arms around my neck and wailed, "Daddy-ji didn't come like he promised! He doesn't want me!"

Grace looked in on us, frowning. I smiled and gave her a thumbs-up, then pointed to Harper's room. She nodded and went back to the dining room while I carried Aparna out of earshot.

As soon as we were in the bedroom, I shut the door and said, "Aparna, sweetie, Daddy-ji didn't forget you. He got hurt by some bad people and went to the hospital. But he's fine, and it's time for you to come to

Colorado. When you get there, you can talk to Mommy-ji on the computer. How does that sound?"

Aparna shook her head. "Grampa said he wasn't coming."

I clenched my fists, then took a breath and relaxed them. "He did, did he?"

"Uh-huh."

I took Aparna's hands. "Your grandfather was wrong. *I* am your father, and I'm here now."

She stared at me, then giggled. "Nu-uh. Daddy-ji is a *boy!*"

Well, duh. I started laughing. Only then did the whole 'I am your father' thing click in my head. I laughed again, which got me another smile from Aparna.

"I might look like a girl now, but this is just pretend. Remember when Pinkette dressed in Moonbow's hat and coat, and everyone thought she was Moonbow? That's what I'm doing. I'm in disguise as a girl. But I am Daddy-ji, and I'm here to take you to Colorado."

She shook her head and looked away. Nope, there was no fooling her. I was a girl, and that was it.

I thought for a moment. "Alright, remember when we were on the plane here, and we were coloring? I colored Berrymint, and you told me what colors she needed to be. And you gave me a gold star for staying in the lines. Do you remember that?"

She nodded. I pressed on. "Remember me telling you about my friends who own the farm, where you could run and jump and glide all you want? Remember me telling you about the place with the really huge water slides, where you'd go so fast your wings would lift you out of the pool and I'd need a net to catch you?"

"Uh-huh. I'm going to fly away and *never* come back!"

I wagged my finger at her. "Uh-uh. No flying away, Bugbear. Mommy-ji is worried sick as it is. She'd cry all the time if you just flew away. And you know crying make her fur smell funny." I wrinkled up my face and added a *"Blegh!"*

Aparna giggled, but pulled her arms back. Her brow furrowed, her eyes narrowed, and her whole body went stiff as she concentrated. In Hindi, she said, "Are you really Daddy-ji?" As she did, she put every ounce of magic she had into her command spell and hurled it at me.

I smiled and let the magic work. "Yes, my jewel, I am. And I'm here to take you home to Colorado."

She threw her arms around my neck, tight enough to choke me. "Daddy-ji!"

I hugged her tight. "That's right, Bugbear. It's Daddy."

"Change back, Daddy-ji! I want you gimme shoulders ride!"

I let her go and said, "I will, sweetie, as soon as I find some boy clothes I can wear. This dress is too small for me. Now, let's be very quiet, and get your stuff so we can go."

"Okay!" She pulled me to the door and said, "Potty first."

Good plan.

Most of Aparna's things were still in her backpack. I was just as glad she didn't want to take the tea party set; it was way too big for sneaking around with. While she got the last of her stuff, I took a look out the window.

Outside, it was pure Oklahoma country night. Lightning bugs scattered across Harper's yard, placid and unconcerned. The moon was well-past full, so there were only a few patches of light between us and the gate. As soon as we got off the property, I could zap the first motorist we saw and get us into Bartlesville.

Damn, I had an actual plan.

I took Aparna's hand, holding my finger over my lips. The hardest part would be not setting off the squirrels. I eased the door open and stuffed two pieces of *naan* into the cage. The squirrels snagged them out of the air. Full mouths, no ruckus.

Then I heard Vernon say, "Aparna, we're having...what the shit do you think you're doing, missy?"

I turned and snapped, "Fulfilling Sharon's wishes!"

Vernon stopped in his tracks. "What? What wishes? How dare-"

"'I want my children to grow up singing *Rocky Mountain High*, not *Dixie!*' Remember that? How about, 'I don't care if you hate me for this. Just know I will always love you both.' Ring any bells?"

"Who told you that? Who have you been talking to?" His fists were clenched, white-knuckled, and his voice shook. "How did you get Sharon's letters? Who the hell are you?"

"I know those words because I helped her write them! As for who I am..." I smiled and patted Aparna's shoulder. "I'm Aparna's daddy. How you been, Vernon?"

"You can't be..." Vernon whispered. "This is some kind of sick joke. You can't be him!" Vernon took half a step forward.

I tried to pull Aparna out the door, but she slipped out of my grasp, planted her hands on her hips, and shouted back, "She *is* my daddy and I hope Mommy-ji *eats* you! Hmmph!"

"That's my girl!" I patted Aparna on the back. "You refused to follow Manya's directions when you arrived in Mumbai and it cost you, what, five hundred dollars? Grace, when Vernon demanded Manya send a driver to pick the two of you up at the train station, you told him that if you got raped and murdered, you'd take a sacred cow to bed instead of him. Remember that?"

Grace shook her head. "Miss Kitty heard all that. She could have told you all those things."

Vernon scowled. "That's it. Has to be. That damn cat-woman sent you in to steal our granddaughter!"

"Don't talk bad about Mommy-ji!" Aparna scowled back, glowering for all she was worth. "And stop being mean!"

"Inside voice, Aparna." I thought for a moment, and said, "Alright, I have something. Grace, when Sharon and I were about twelve or thirteen, you got mad because she was buying cosmetics behind your back. She was taking them and putting money in the till so the books balanced. You started searching her room but you couldn't find them, because I had them in my pockets. Vernon hauled Sharon outside for a spanking, and while he was out there, you saw a makeup brush in my back pocket. And you let me keep everything because I told you Sharon just wanted to be pretty like her mother."

I turned to Vernon. "Grace and Sharon went off to wash the makeup off her face, and you shoulder-checked me into the wall as you walked past. I had a makeup case tucked into the back of my pants and hitting the wall knocked it loose. You picked it up and I could tell you were going to spank Sharon again, so I said it was mine and I wanted Sharon to do my makeup because I liked dressing as a girl. Do you remember what you said?"

Vernon's eyes widened. "That's not possible."

"You said, 'If I made you put on a dress and go to the movies wearing lipstick and mascara, you'd wear the hell out of it just to show me up, wouldn't you?' Not only did you give me back the makeup case, you gave me five dollars so we could get popcorn at the movie theater. 'Don't tell Grace,' you said. Grace, you gave me another five bucks. You said I was a damn love-crazy fool, but I didn't cut and run on your daughter. Then you told me not to tell Vernon."

Grace whispered, "Oh, sweet Lord..."

Turner, the lawyer, snorted. "What a bunch of crap. I'm calling the police."

"Try it and I'll deck you," Vernon said. He looked back at me and added, "I must be nuts but...Christ Almighty, I believe you. How did you pull this off?"

"Great costume, isn't it? Rose helped me put it together." I put my fingers on the knockout tattoo. "I don't want to do this, but you took my daughter and sent a bunch of goons to kill me so you could keep her. I'm not going to let that happen."

Vernon held his hands up. "Stop! Wait...please. We were at the airport! We were at the gate half an hour before your plane landed, and you never got off it! We waited, we had you paged, we even checked with the flight crew! The stewardess said your seat was empty the whole flight. We tried to call you, and Rose, and your parents, and we got no answers. We finally decided to get something to eat and go home."

"That's when we learned you were in the hospital and Tyson was...was dead. On the blood of Jesus and my hope for eternal salvation, I had nothing to do with what happened to you." He got down on his knees, bowing his head. "I beg you...please, please, don't take our visitation away. I will agree to anything you want if you'll still let us see her."

Behind him, Grace got on her knees as well. "I swear to you too, we didn't do it. She's all we have left of Sharon! We would never, ever do anything to hurt her. Please..."

Harper stepped between me and Vernon. "I'm disappointed Neesy was an act. I genuinely liked her. If you possess any part of her decency, don't do this. If you want to leave, go ahead and go. I'd rather you stayed so we could work all this out. But either way, I will not let you harm these people."

"I'm not going to harm them, or anyone else. I use a sword for that." I held my hand up, thinking it over. If someone was using them as pawns, some of this made more sense. "Alright, Vernon. I can't say I believe you yet, but I don't disbelieve you, either. However, this isn't the time. We can work all this out once she's safe in Colorado. If you're telling the truth, then I won't hold you to account for what happened. I know you love Aparna. I saw that while we were in India. But someone organized that attack. Someone sent those punks to murder me and Tyson. Until they answer for it and I'm sure it won't happen again, Aparna stays with me. And we are leaving. Understood?"

Vernon nodded. "Anything we can do, anything we find out, we'll let you know first."

"Thank you." I pressed my fingers to the tattoo. "This won't harm you. It'll just knock you out for a little while. You should all sit or lay down."

Harper sat down on the couch. "I do wish you had come to me directly, David. I would have helped you from the first if you had just explained what was going on."

"Yeah. A lie is a very poor way to say 'hello.' Please give my apologies to everyone. I'll find a way to make amends. And again, I'm sorry."

Harper nodded, and I triggered the spell. Everyone but Aparna slumped over, asleep.

"Are they okay, Daddy-ji?"

"They're fine. They're just sleeping. Now let's get out of here." I gathered Aparna's belongings and we slipped out into the night.

The front gate was standing open but blocked by half a dozen pickups and at least that many cars and SUVs. People in camo and carrying rifles sprawled all over the place, caught in the spell's radius. Rusty, Preston, and a few others were stumbling around or down on all fours; they probably caught the edge of it. I stepped over the unconscious ones as fast as I could, but it was a proper mess.

A big guy got out of a pickup sitting out on the road and racked a shell into his shotgun. "What in Christ's name happened here?" He brought the shotgun to his shoulder and bellowed, "Tell me what's going on!"

I touched the command tattoo and pointed at him. "Your clothes! Give them to me!" Then I looked down at Aparna and added, "Honey, cover your eyes for a minute. I have to get undressed." She clapped her hands to her eyes and looked away while I stripped down. A few moments later, I was my old self again.

Mister Shotgun wore button-fly jeans. I took it as a sign to avoid putting on his shorts and went commando.

By the time I was dressed, the folks who had only been dazed by the spell were getting to their feet. Preston glanced around and saw me with Aparna. He grabbed Rusty's shoulder and shouted, "Someone is taking the girl!"

Time to be going. I tossed Mister Shotgun his wallet, lifted Aparna into his truck, and headed for Bartlesville. Behind us, the few who were awake rushed to move people out of the driveway and organize some pursuit.

This rescue would have been a lot easier if we could have teleported Aparna home. Since that wasn't an option, we'd have to use cunning. Rose sent me directions to a meeting place and reminded me to activate the *Don't Get Involved* tattoo. I couldn't see any lights behind us yet, but it was better not to take chances. Driving an unfamiliar car on a small, unlit, two-lane country road at night was risky enough as it was. One stray cow can ruin your whole day...

Something dashed across the road ahead of us. Probably just a rabbit. I slowed to the speed limit anyway. *You're almost done. Don't blow it now.*

Headlights appeared in the opposite lane, blowing past a few seconds later. Another old rattletrap pickup, this one flying a Confederate battle flag from a pole in the bed. *Well, Oklahoma is Good Ol' Boy central...*

In my mirror, the truck's brake lights flared, jerking back and forth in the darkness. Maybe he dropped his cigarette—or his beer—in his lap. I would have seen anything in the road when I passed that spot.

Oh, shit.

I hit the gas again, flicking on my high-beams and wishing my commandeered pickup had come equipped with the Interceptor's arsenal of pursuit deterrents—or even a tool belt with a pouch full of roofing nails. I felt around between the seats, hoping Mister Shotgun had stashed a pistol or pepper spray or something there. All I found was some old chimichanga wrappers.

A loud thump came from the rear of the truck and I saw something move in the mirror, illuminated for a moment by the glow from my tail lights. I yelled "Hang on!" in Hindi and yanked the wheel from side to side. The truck responded with a massive amount of oversteer, threatening to plunge off the road.

Something slammed against the rear window. The glass held, but it wouldn't for long. Aparna was staring, wide-eyed, too scared to talk. Holding the wheel as steady as I could, I felt along the bottom of the door and around the seat again. This time I felt a release lever and pressed it. The padded console between the seats popped open. What do you know?

Mister Shotgun had a pistol after all. I hit the brakes while twisting around to aim out the rear window.

The brake light on the roof of the cab lit up the empty truck bed. Nothing moved outside but the leaves. I dropped the gun on the seat, put the truck into reverse, and floored it.

Claws screeched on metal, right above my head.

I fired three rounds through the roof. The last resulted in a sharp yelp. I hit the brakes again, hard. Tires squealed, but nothing fell off the roof. Just to be safe, I pushed Aparna under the dashboard. "Stay down, honey. Don't say anything." Gun in hand, I listened.

I caught movement out of my left eye. By the time I turned, it was gone. At least the thing was off the roof.

Headlights appeared behind us. Several sets. No choice now. Holding the gun, I put the truck in gear. Then the left rear tire blew out.

Screw it. I shifted into four-wheel and put the pedal to the floor—just as the right rear went. The truck lurched forward, leaving a trail of sparks behind it.

The thing popped up in the passenger window. Glowing green eyes, massive teeth. I fired. It dodged to the side. I tried to follow it. It shoved itself through the shattered remains of the window.

Huge, black, canine features, fangs...

After all this, a fucking werewolf, too?

I fired at its chest. Blood spattered. It snarled and lunged. Not for the gun. It bit through my wrist.

I remember screaming. Then a tree came through the window.

The door flew open. I fell. Gravel scraped my face. I rolled onto my back, cradling my arm. I felt a rush of warmth between my shoulder blades as the healing spell discharged. Instantly, the pain faded to a manageable level and the stump scabbed over. Without the spell, I probably would have bled out in seconds.

The werewolf was bleeding, too. One front leg was injured. It crouched, growling, looking for an opening.

At least die well.

I got to my feet. Kindness came at my call, replenishing my strength and clarity. Holding her in my left hand, I called out, "That all you got?"

Those eyes. Bright green, hate-filled...he's going to rip my throat out.

Aparna pushed past the limp airbag and shattered branches filling the truck's cab. "No!" she shouted. "That's my daddy."

The werewolf looked back, turning to face her.

"Over here!" I kicked gravel at the thing. "It's me you want! Over here!"

It ignored me.

I stumbled toward it as best I could. "Turn around, damn you!" When it didn't react, I added, "Fine, I'll stab you in the back."

That got its attention. It turned and leaped, knocking me to the ground. Kindness bounced away. All I could see was teeth.

"No! Don't you hurt my daddy!" Aparna smacked it on the nose. "Bad Oreeon! No bite!"

Oreeon?

I tried to focus on the werewolf. Black, grey spots in the reflected glow of the headlights...It was Oreo. "Aparna, get back! Don't let him bite you!"

She threw herself on me. "Daddy, get up! You're not done rescuing me!"

Oreo stepped off my chest. He looked at Aparna, then at the rapidly approaching headlights.

"I know, honey. I'm sorry," I whispered. "Messed it up. First time I've...tried to save...a princess..."

The world was going dark. Oreo's head filled my vision. "Sorry for the cock-up, mate. I'll watch out for her."

Huh. I expected a German accent, not Australian. He must be part cattle dog...

Chapter Thirty-Two

Dragon at the Gate

Good news, everybody! I woke up on a hard, vinyl-covered exam bed surrounded by privacy curtains, in pain but alive. The bad news was I was handcuffed and shackled again. Twice in one week? I must be doing something right...

Bruises on my chest...oh, yeah. Airbag. The truck crashed. I hit a tree, hard. Probably gave me a head injury. Concussion-induced hallucinations would explain seeing a talking dog. I'll get better soon enough.

Where's Aparna?

I had a brief moment of blind panic, trying to sit up and yanking hard on the handcuffs restraining me...*what happened to my arm?!*

Oh. Right. Tree. Branches and limbs everywhere. Must have happened then.

The panic faded. Aparna had been walking and talking after the crash. Hopefully someone took her to a proper hospital. Thinking about any other outcomes...I shook my head hard to get the thought out of my mind.

Focus on right now. What's the situation?

I lifted my arm as best I could. The 'bandages' were basic gauze pads under a few turns of wrapping, all held in place by duct tape. Obviously not the work of someone who'd been to medical school.

No painkillers. No monitoring equipment, either. A hospital would have me on a pulse oximeter at the absolute minimum. No call button, no IV catheter, handcuffs, redneck first aid...Whoever brought me here—wherever 'here' is—did not have my best interests in mind.

They just don't want me to die yet.

Rose was...missing. I could feel her existence, but not her presence on Earth. Most likely she was back on her home world, probably organizing an all-out assault on whoever is holding me.

Well, my plan did go to shit, after all. Might as well try hers.

On the good side, the acceptance was still working. I was healing. Rose should be able to fix my arm, assuming she got here before more of me needed fixing. Wherever 'here' was...

No, wait...I said that already. Where am I?

It's not a hospital, but this room is set up for medical exams. The retirement center at Still Waters has a clinic. That would make sense. Rusty and his buddies were trying to come after me. Maybe they brought me back.

That would mean Aparna must be fine. If she was dead, they would have just killed me and let the cops sort it out. Yeah, let's go with that assumption. Otherwise I'll just have to slaughter them all.

I sat up as best I could and looked around. No sign of clothes, and the exam gown I had on was for a much smaller person. Well, that was one goal. Maybe I could find a set of scrubs or something. Getting jeans on one-handed might be tricky.

You're getting ahead of yourself. Handcuffs, remember?

Right. Kindness could slice through the handcuff chains in a heartbeat, given a good swing. That would be tricky under present conditions. Speaking of Kindness...

She answered my summons again—pointed straight up. All I had a grip on was the pommel. With nothing to support her weight, she fell to the side. I yanked my leg sideways, trying to avoid the toppling blade, and twisted on the pommel as hard as I could. The blade went through the body of the cuff on my ankle and the bed under it, missing the ankle itself by half an inch. One good pull and my ankle was free.

Damn. For a reckless combination of blind luck and stupidity, that worked really well. I'm going to tell people it was an actual plan.

Why does my sword have another evidence tag on it?

Never mind. I don't care why anymore.

With a better grip on the sword, I made short work of the cuffs on my other ankle and rolled off the bed. The handcuffs were secured to eyebolts screwed into the wood framing the mattress. Without leverage, I was stuck. Now, though...I wedged Kindness under the loop of the eyebolt, gripped the hilt with my right elbow, and lifted. Kindness sheared through the eyebolt like it was stale bread.

I also managed to lose the micro-gown I was wearing. The shoulder snaps popped and it fell right off.

Well, who hasn't wanted to do a naked barbarian costume?

I moved the privacy curtain out of the way with the tip of my sword. There were two other beds, both unoccupied. All the cabinets and drawers had neat labels on them. So did the linen closet.

There we go. Scrubs, Bottoms, XL. It took a bit to figure out how to get them on, but things got easier when I stopped standing on the leg I was trying to pull up. My discarded robe looked goofy wrapped around

Kindness, but at least it wouldn't immediately freak people out the way a naked blade would.

The door was locked.

Which is much less of a problem when the person who locked the door forgets the room has a dropped ceiling. Obviously, my captors had never seen *The Breakfast Club*. Getting out of a room with a drop ceiling is easy.

Well, easy when you have two hands. I shoved one of the exam beds against the wall, dumped out the contents of a small wooden bookcase, and wrangled the bookcase up onto the bed to serve as a stepladder.

Getting over the wall meant levering myself up on my elbows, grabbing one of the steel trusses supporting the roof, and flipping around so I didn't go face-first into the floor of the adjacent room. My arm was a mass of pain by the time I finished, but I finally dropped onto a desk in the office next door and hopped down to the floor.

Okay, I fell onto the desk, rolled onto the floor, and vomited all over a trash can full of fast food wrappers and diet soda cans. Yay concussions.

Unlike the room I'd just escaped from, this room had windows. Outside, a swarm of flashing red and blue lights pierced the night, lighting up the Still Waters sanctuary. Rusty hadn't been kidding; you really could see that thing from all over the property. From the looks of it, I was on the second floor of Covenant Center.

The road outside the compound was lined with police cars and other emergency equipment. The parking lot for the sanctuary, on the other hand, was close to half-full of non-police vehicles. An improvised barricade ran between the parking lot and the gate, providing cover for a row of figures in prone shooting positions.

What the bloody hell was going on? When did this turn into an armed standoff?

Tuesday had brought up the idea. Maybe she had friends in the domestic terrorism business. Then again, Preston and Rusty had seen me leave, and from the number of folks my spell knocked out, they may have been the ones organizing this party. Who knows? Maybe it was a group effort.

The 'ding' of an elevator sounded from out in the hall. I scampered to the door and peeked out the narrow, inset window.

Two guys in hunting camo escorted K out into the hall. Both guys had shotguns slung over their shoulders. I eased the door open a fraction of an inch after they passed.

"...the barrel is eight to ten ounces lighter than a standard AR-15. That might not sound like much, but she'll really feel it." K stopped in the hall, giving the guy she was talking to an impish grin. "On top of that, we use a longer gas system, which gives smoother cycling and a softer shot. It also has adjustable gas blocks for fine-tuning the whole system to her specific ammo and shooting style. If you're a hand-loader, that can make a big difference. The other feature she'll really appreciate is that the barrel and handguard are both removable for easier transportation and storage. No risk of accidents since it can't be fired, and it goes back together in about thirty seconds."

"Um, wow, nice." The guy sounded as lost as I was. "Does it come in pink?"

"The furniture does, yeah. If she wants them that way. What I'd recommend would be to buy her a box of ammo and wrap that. Then, when she opens it, you tell her the bullets are for her new gun and bring her down so we can fit it to her properly. That way you still get the birthday surprise and you don't buy her something she doesn't want."

The other guy nodded. "There are two things you should always let a woman pick out for herself, man: guns and lingerie."

I pulled the door open enough to hook the bottom corner with my foot. Standing that way while raising Kindness up to a usable position just about made me fall on my ass. Kicking the door open wouldn't work but using an elbow would. At this point, my arm couldn't hurt any worse.

Mr. Romantic was showing K and Mr. Advice a picture on his phone. Two steps and I slid Kindness under Mr. Romantic's chin, resting the edge against his throat. "Hello. My name is David Fraser. Someone at this church kidnapped my daughter..." I gave the blade a small twist. "Help me or die."

K and Mr. Advice froze. Mr. Romantic looked over his shoulder at me. "It that supposed to be a threat?"

"No, it was a glib witticism. In point of fact, I'd rather not kill you. I'd hate to ruin your lady's birthday."

Mr. Advice's eyes bugged out. "Is that thing real?"

"Quite real. This is a magical blade, forged by Dwarven weaponsmiths, bestowed on me by a dragon for deeds of valor and service, and bound to me by blood. Her name is Kindness...as in killing you with. But like I said, I don't want to kill anyone. All I want is to take my daughter and leave."

I'll give Mr. Romantic credit; he didn't back down. "I think you're bullshitting us. If you can lift it one-handed, no way that sword is real."

"I did say it was a *magic* sword."

K said, "David Fraser is supposed to be brain-dead."

"Quite correct, Miss K. All part of my cunning plan to slip in here undetected and rescue my daughter."

"How do you know who I am?"

"We met while you were sitting in front of the television assembling a rifle." I gave her a moment to put it together. "By the way, I never got a chance to thank you for the advice about getting burritos instead of doing the taco bar, or for putting my extras in the refrigerator."

K stepped backward. "No. That was...Neesy?"

"Yes, indeed," I said. "Sorry for the deception, but I wasn't going to just walk in here as myself. Not after someone tried to kill me. For what it's worth, I don't think either that Travis person or Harper had anything to do with it."

216

K looked at my chest, raising one eyebrow. "I recognize that skunk tattoo. What happened to the others?"

"Neesy's tattoos held different spells in them. I cast the others. This one is all that's left."

She took a ragged breath. "Alright. Promise not to hurt me, and I'll help you get your daughter back."

"Fair enough." I nodded toward the two guys. "Would you mind collecting their shotguns? Can't have one going off and waking the neighbors."

Mr. Advice surrendered his, holding it out to K by the shoulder strap. "Look, we came out tonight because of the monster. If it was my daughter, I'd want to get her and go, too. No argument."

"Thank you for understanding." I cocked my head at Mr. Romantic and asked, "How about you, friend?"

"I'm not your friend." He leapt to the side, spinning in a circle as he tried to get the shotgun up to his shoulder.

I pulled Kindness down, building speed to bring her up and around again for a downward slash. He blocked with the shotgun. Kindness sliced through the receiver without slowing down. The momentum was enough for me to bring the sword up and across, halting with the tip under Mr. Romantic's chin. As we stood there, two shells popped out of the ammo tube and clattered to the floor.

I cocked an eyebrow at him. "See? *Magic* sword. Any other questions?"

He dropped both halves of his shotgun and put his hands behind his head.

K looped the carry strap for her new shotgun across her body, then pulled four sets of handcuffs out of her purse. "Noses to the wall, hands on top of your heads." The guys grumbled, but complied.

"Do you normally carry handcuffs around in your purse?" I asked.

"No. Those were for you. Rusty wanted you extra-secure. Where do you want these two?"

I leaned my head toward the office I'd come out of. "They should be fine in there. Someone will find them in a few hours."

Once the guys were sitting down, K used the other two sets of handcuffs to secure them to one another and gagged them with mouse cables. Well, that's one thing you can't do with wireless computer accessories. We even turned on a small radio so they could listen to music while they waited.

With those two secured, K pulled a key out of her pocket and unlocked the exam room I'd woken up in. "Need to do a better job with your arm," she said. "You're leaking."

I nodded and sat down at one of the tables. "I don't want to sound ungrateful, but why are you helping me like this?"

"Because that little girl is miserable. Because Rusty's friends remind me of the guy who sent me here. Because I don't like assholes. Take your pick. You want a bullet to bite on? Got some spare 30-06 in my purse."

I shook my head and clenched a roll of gauze between my teeth.

Yeah. It hurt. The wound still had dirt and stuff in it, plus whatever was on the semi-clean snot-rag they'd used for a bandage. I tried not to look, but K didn't bat an eye. I finally asked, "How are you staying so calm? Did you have medical training or something?"

She didn't look up. "Don't talk. I'm pretending you're a deer."

I stayed quiet.

K washed the gunk out, applied antibiotic and did a proper dressing. As gentle as she tried to be, I still came close to passing out again. When she finished, I tried to stand up and help with the cleanup. She pushed me back into the chair. "Sit. Stay. You fall, I can't lift you."

"Yes, doctor." I sat back and let my healing ability do its thing. "Fill me in. Who are these friends of Rusty's, and what is going on?"

She chuckled and kept cleaning. "Well, you were brought in about two hours ago. As for what's been going on...I don't even know where to start."

"Start with Aparna. Where is she and is she okay?"

"Oh, she's fine, but I don't know where she is. She put up a fight when Tuesday hauled her off, though." She took a deep breath. "Sorry, I'm still a little rattled by all this. See, I think this started with the Friday night men's ministry group Preston and Rusty run. I don't know the details, but somehow Rusty found out the police were coming tonight with a court order to take your daughter. Remember that kid from Cuba who got taken from his mother's family by the feds and sent back to be with his dad?"

I nodded. "Yeah."

"Well, Rusty told the ministry group a raid like that was about to happen. Aparna's grandfather is one of the men in the group and I guess he's told them a lot about you and the custody fight. The ministry group decided to call in some friends and hold a protest. One person I talked to said it was supposed to be peaceful, but everyone who showed up was armed. I guess you took off with Aparna just as their friends were arriving and everyone lost their shit. Harper could have defused it, but she's missing. Rumor is you killed her."

"It's just a sleeping spell. It'll wear off in an hour or two."

"That's good. Well, a posse took off after you. That part I assume you know. After they brought you back, though...that's when more shit than you could pack into a fleet of dump trucks hit the fan. A dragon—a real, actual, very pissed-off *dragon* attacked the front gate. I know it sounds crazy, but I swear on a stack of Bibles. I saw it with my own eyes, and I am stone-cold sober."

That's my girl. Subtle as always. "I believe you. What happened then?"

"Ever heard the saying, 'when in doubt, empty the magazine?' That's what happened. Several dozen rednecks with deer rifles opened up on it and did exactly jack shit. It ignored everything. It just stood there, bullets bouncing off it right and left. I kept expecting it to incinerate everyone, but no. It just stood there, waiting for them to run out of ammo."

"Then Bo Breen pulled out his double rifle. It's an elephant gun, a Holland and Holland .700 Nitro Express. Next to it, a Browning .50 caliber is a deer rifle. He let go with that and *bam!* Right through the shoulder. Ol' Smauggie *drops*. The second shot just creased its neck and knocked some scales off, but when the thing got up, it was *mad*. It was pissed off before, but now...Jesus wept. Glowing red eyes, huge spikes erupted from every scale on its body, and it roared. I was fifty yards away and I could feel that roar shaking the ground. It was breathing out burning smoke and had liquid fire, like napalm or something, dripping out of its mouth. I thought we were all dead as fried chicken."

You would have been, but Aparna and I were inside. I grinned at her and said, "Looks like you survived."

K nodded. "Yeah. I don't know why, but it didn't roast us. It bellowed something, don't ask me what, and we all ran like rabbits. It only lasted a few seconds, but I have never been so frightened in my life. All I could think of was getting *away*. Then, just like that, everyone stopped running. The panic was gone. So was the dragon. Everyone else was cheering, thinking they had beaten it. Not me. That was when I get really scared."

She leaned close, lowering her voice. "It could have slaughtered us in a heartbeat. It didn't. It scared us off so it had time to get away, but it is coming back. I'm sure of it. It is coming back, it is probably bringing friends, and I do *not* want to be here when it does."

"Sound reasoning," I said. "So why aren't you halfway to Tulsa?"

"Because while I was packing, the cops showed up to take Aparna. Rusty's friends told them to shove it and everyone pulled their guns out again. The cops decided to pull back and set up a perimeter rather than start shooting. I went to leave, and Rusty wouldn't let me. Said he wanted everyone to stay inside as a show of unity." She snorted. "What a load of crap. We're human shields. The feds won't risk a bunch of seniors and battered women with kids getting hurt in the crossfire."

"Do you think Rusty has the same level of concern?"

K looked toward the ceiling and exhaled hard. "I...I don't know. I want to believe he does, but something about him scares me. See, at first, everyone thought you were just some random pervert out to kidnap a kid you could abuse. But when the posse brought you back, Aparna was hanging on to you for dear life, screaming 'Daddy' at the top of her lungs. Once Preston knew who you were, he had Rusty's boys move the seniors to the tornado shelters and ordered you locked up in here. I'm not sure why."

"So that no one would hear me screaming when they torture me," I said. "They only gave me enough care to keep me alive until they get whatever it is they want from me."

"Is it the dragon?" She snorted at my expression and added, "When I heard who you were, I knew why the dragon attacked. It came here because it knew you were hurt. That's why I offered to come up here and secure you better. I don't know or care what's going on with you and that dragon, but you two are connected somehow. So, for my own protection, I'm sticking with you like white on rice until we are out of here."

I smiled at her. "I guess we better find Aparna then."

Chapter Thirty-Three

Rescue, Party of Two

The master key Rusty had entrusted to K opened the 'left behind' store like a charm, and the clothes racks yielded a functional set of clothes that fit me fairly well, along with a camo-patterned rifle case for Kindness to hide in. The only thing I couldn't find was shoes that fit. Oh, well. I'd live.

While I was shopping, K grabbed a pair of disposable cameras and stuffed them in her bag. When I raised my eyebrow at her, she said, "Evidence photos."

I nodded. "Good plan."

I was trying to work out how to get the jeans on one-handed when K took the pants off my arm and said, "Alright, drop trou. I'll hold your arm while you step out of the scrubs."

"Um, I'm not wearing underwear."

She smiled. "I know. I'm sexually objectifying you for my own pleasure. Drop 'em."

"I'm also married."

"I'm not asking for a test drive. I just want to...you know...admire the lines."

I sighed. "Fine. Enjoy the view."

At least she didn't shout 'Woohoo!' or make any catcalls. She stuck to using the belt loops as much as possible, and I pretended not to notice her hand lingering on my left cheek for a few moments longer than it should have.

Once I was dressed, I said, "Thank you. I do appreciate the help."

K tossed her hair over her shoulder. "Thank you for reinforcing my commitment to heterosexuality. We should be leaving."

I hoisted the rifle case to my shoulder. "Agreed. If Tuesday took Aparna, what are the odds they're in the day care center?"

"That seems the logical spot, but they must know you would head there first, so it's probably a trap."

"Clearly I cannot choose the glass in front of me," I said.

"Don't," she said. "That movie gets my motor running, and I don't want to think of you that way. Let's give the day care a shot anyway. You never know."

Instinct screamed that we should hunker down and sprint from shadow to shadow as we crossed the open space between the buildings. Instinct was wrong. First rule of social engineering: act like you're supposed to be doing whatever it is. We walked, right out in the open.

The sanctuary lights were on, as were the ones in the church offices. Through the window, I could see a good number of people, all talking or texting on their phones. I sighed and shook my head.

"What?"

"It looks like Rusty has everyone who can spell 'standoff' hitting social media to spread the word."

K snorted. "That's Ofelia's idea. She wants this to go viral so it gets more media attention."

"If it weren't the middle of the night that could be useful." I glanced at the swarm of emergency vehicles out on the road. "I wonder what Rusty would do if all the seniors grouped up and marched out the gate."

"Thinking of a diversion?"

"No. An insurrection."

K paused for a moment. "Really." Even in the darkness, I could see her eyebrows going up.

"I don't see many seniors and elder members of the church liking the idea of an armed standoff in their front yard. They live here; the gun-toting yahoos don't. They'd have the gravitas to shame this lot into giving up and going home."

"'Gravitas'? You actually talk that way?"

"I use the Oxford comma as well."

"God, you know how to turn me on. Stop doing that."

Even with all the crap going on, I have to admit, I was enjoying bantering with her. More conversation would have to wait, however. We'd reached the tree Neesy had been sitting under.

The lights in the daycare were out, except in Tuesday's office. From the flickering glow in the main room, I guessed someone was watching television with the lights off.

"How do you plan to get in there?" K asked. "My ID won't work on the door."

I shrugged. "We knock." I tried to sound confident, but I really wished I had borrowed the Movable Hole from Nadia. Walking through walls is a lot easier when there's a nice big opening in exactly the right spot. Since magic wasn't an option, K badged us into the building. Mundane, but it worked.

K had to knock twice before Tuesday opened the door. As soon as she did, I bulled through, pushing Tuesday back and clamping my hand over her mouth. K followed on my heels, shutting and locking the door behind us.

"Hello," I said. "My name is David Fraser. You took my daughter…" I waited a few heartbeats and added, "It's time for her to come home now."

When I took my hand away, Tuesday said, "She isn't here, and I don't know where she is."

"Who took her?"

Tuesday's mouth twisted into an ugly sneer. "After what you did to Harper, I'm not telling you anything."

"All I did to Harper was make her go to sleep for a while. If she's been hurt, I didn't do it. What about Grace and Vernon? Where are they?"

"Don't play innocent. You butchered them to get your hands on that little girl. You might as well kill me, too. I'm not going to tell you anything!"

I stared at her. "Butchered? Tuesday, what happened? Tell me what happened!"

She shook a bit, trying to keep her war face on, but it crumbled. She sank to the floor, sobbing. "You shot them. All of them. You lined them up and shot them in the back of the head. You murdered them!"

I knelt next to her. "I don't know what you were told, but I swear to you by everything I hold sacred, I didn't hurt them. If someone did kill them, I want to find out who it was and make them pay."

"You did it. You're a monster!" Whatever else was going on, the pain in her voice was real.

"Who told you I was responsible? Was it Rusty?" If he was trying to set me up as his patsy, he and Kindness were going to have a short, sharp conversation…

"No. Yes." She shook her head, violently, as though trying to free herself from an iron grip. "I don't…it's…I just *know!*"

"Was it the person who took Aparna from you?"

Her face blanked for a moment. "No. It was…no. I don't…no one. No one said it."

K nudged me with her elbow. "What does that mean? What's wrong with her?"

"I'm not sure. I really wish Rose was here." I ran my fingers through my hair, trying to recall anything Rose, Nadia, or Eric might have mentioned that might apply here and came up empty.

I might not have them to call on, but I had the Doctor. Something he had said about reconstructing a person by the hole they left behind… "Tuesday, did someone from outside the church tell you I killed Harper and the others?"

"No."

"Was it someone who belongs to the church?"

"I…I don't know." She frowned and furrowed her brows. "I can't remember anything about it. Why can't I remember? It was…Aparna fell asleep watching a movie. I went into my office and came back out for something. Then I was in my office, and you were knocking."

I sat back. "Tuesday, I think someone used a spell on you, and I might even know which one. If I'm right, somebody hit you with a spell called *Retcon*. It erases and rewrites memories. But I don't think the person who used it on you knows how it works or how to use it correctly. Now, as best as you can remember, had you heard about Harper and the others before Aparna fell asleep?"

"No. I'm sure of that." For the first time, she looked at me with something other than loathing. "It couldn't be a spell. Magic doesn't work on Christians."

"Yes it can, actually. There are some spells that don't, but most do. I know for a fact that a necromancer can't animate the body of someone who was a devout Christian, for example. On the other hand, *Lightning Bolt* doesn't care what religion you are."

Tuesday looked away. "You're just trying to deceive me. You're a godless pagan and a liar. You don't even believe in Jesus and I will listen to nothing you say."

I laughed. "Pagan, yes, but godless, no." She didn't look at me, so I placed my hand lightly on hers. "Tuesday, I don't like talking about this, but I've seen the power of Jesus' blood firsthand. And I mean that quite literally. Do you remember the Gospel's account of a Roman soldier stabbing Jesus with his spear during the Crucifixion?"

She nodded. "Of course."

"I've held that spear. Myself, personally, two years ago. The blood that was dried on it became liquid again. I dipped my fingers in it, and used it to bring close to a dozen people back to life. When I was done, the spear zipped straight up and out of sight. I don't have any powers of healing, Tuesday. If I did, I'd have grown my hand back already. But the blood of Christ does, and I was allowed to use it."

Tuesday stiffened and turned back around. "You're mocking me."

"No." I shrugged. "I don't have any proof, of course. And I admit, I'm a pretty unworthy vessel for a miracle like that. So, I won't blame you if you don't believe me. But it is the truth. You'll just have to...have faith."

She shook her head. "I don't think so. In fact, I don't believe any of that ever happened."

"Why not?"

"You say you brought people back from the dead using the actual blood of Jesus. If that were true, if you actually had seen the power of His blood with your own eyes, there's no way you could stay a Pagan. Only an absolute fool would do something like that, and you are not that much of a fool. So, no, I don't buy it."

I held my hand out to her. "Take my hand, and pray for God to reveal the truth to you. I think you'll be surprised."

224

Tuesday sat for a long moment, eyes narrow and heavy with judgment. Finally, she took my hand between hers and bowed her head. A moment later, she looked up, eyes radiant and full of joy. "I believe you," she said. "God has made you a weapon against the false prophet who seeks to defile this place, and I will stand with you in the Lord's name."

"Ah, okay..." I cocked my head a bit. "I'd be glad for your help, but why the change of heart?"

"God revealed His will to me," she said. "All my life I've thought I was hearing God's voice whispering to me, but it was just my own thoughts and desires. God's voice is...glorious. Resounding beyond measure...I don't even know the words to describe it."

K sank to the floor as well. "Um, Tuesday, are you okay? You're sounding kinda scary here..."

Tuesday smiled. "I'm better than okay, Harriet. That's your name—your real name—isn't it? Harriet Catherine Tribble, from Norman, Oklahoma."

K turned pale as a sheet. "No. No one knows that name."

"God does."

"Then God should know how much I hated it." K looked down, twisting the hem of her shirt in her fists. "I will never forgive my parents for doing that to me."

"Why?" Tuesday looked blank. "What's wrong with it?"

"Seriously? You don't see what the other kids would do with that?" I didn't wait for Tuesday to answer. "Hairy Tribble. How do you miss that?"

Tuesday shrugged, shaking her head. "What does 'tribble' mean? Is it ghetto slang or something?"

"Let's just drop it!" K exclaimed. She took a ragged breath, blinking back tears. "Tuesday, I don't care how or why you learned that name, but I don't ever want to hear it again. For any reason."

"I only know it for one reason. God revealed it to me so that I could say 'Shibboleth' unto you. Which I've done. I won't bring it up again." Tuesday turned to me. "God gave me a message for you, too. A battle is coming; go and prepare for it. The weapons you need will be given unto you, if you but seek them out."

"Oh, great..." I rolled my eyes. "The last time I heard something like that, Kirk had to take out a giant lizard using an improvised cannon. I really hope that's not what your lord and savior has in mind."

K laughed and punched me in my good shoulder. "At least that's something I could help you with," she said. "The high school I went to had a civil war cannon we'd fire when the football team got a touchdown. It was my first piece of heavy artillery."

"Let's hope it doesn't come to that." I turned back to Tuesday. "As much as I appreciate getting a personal message from the Lord God of Israel, did He happen to mention where His fan club is hiding my daughter?"

"I'm sorry, but no." Tuesday raised her hands in surrender. "You can't be told the path. You have to walk it."

"I knew you were going to say that." I looked up at the ceiling. "That's fine, oh you who are called 'I Am.' I've got this. All I need you to do is stay out of my way."

Tuesday's jaw dropped. "What? Ooooh! You..." She gave my hand a short, crisp smack. "That's for blasphemy. You are a vessel of God in this. You should act like one."

"So was Genghis Khan. As he put it, if the people he conquered hadn't done such great wickedness, God would not have appointed him to be their punishment." I chuckled. "In this, he and I are in one accord."

"Be that as it may, righteous thought and action are always appropriate. Now, it's time for me to go." She got to her feet, brushing off her pants.

K and I got up as well. I had to push myself up using a table, but I did it on my own. The movements triggered a rush of pain from my stump. I closed my eyes and sagged against the wall, trying to breathe until it passed.

"What do you mean, 'go'?" K spread her arms, gesturing at the rest of the compound. "We are locked in here by a bunch of guys who think they can hold off tanks, Predator drones and attack helicopters with bolt-action 30-06s and pickle buckets full of hand-loaded ammo."

Tuesday nodded. "And when I walk out there, everyone's attention will be on me. That will give you a chance to keep looking for your daughter." She hugged K, then took her hands. "You can stop running. Make this your home. Everything you've been looking for is right here, waiting for you to accept it."

K pulled away at first, but after a moment she hugged Tuesday back. "As much as I want to believe that, the fact you even know these things makes it sound really scary and creepy. No offense."

"None taken. Now, go with God." She gathered her purse and slipped out the door, pretending to lock it behind her.

"Why don't you believe in Jesus?" K asked.

"I do. It's Hell I don't believe in."

"What does that mean?"

I sighed. "I refuse to believe that an entity capable of creating something as magnificent as our universe would be so insecure as to demand adoration on pain of eternal torture. Nor can I believe that out of all the millions of galaxies and billions of stars, we alone have the absolute truth of what lies beyond death. I believe in a God that is more loving, more forgiving, and more wonderful than the human mind can conceive, and I believe that God accepts everyone without reservation."

"Um, okay. Thanks." She shook her head. "We should..."

"Yeah."

226

There was an emergency evacuation map of the grounds hung on the wall near the door. I looked it over, trying to remember which areas were which. "Where else would they keep her? If I were trying to hide a little girl with big wings, I'd want someplace safe, out of sight, reasonably roomy, and hard to get in to..."

We both pondered the map for several seconds. I was beginning to think it was hopeless when K burst out laughing. She turned away, holding her sides.

At that moment, something clicked in my head. I looked at the map again, and it was my turn to start laughing.

K's laughter slowed and she shook her head. "I can get in there, but there's no way they're going to let you into the Spa now. They'll see you on the monitors and deadlock the door. You can't even sneak in."

"I won't have to," I said. "They're going to let me in the front door and be glad to see me. In fact, they're going to call me and insist I come down immediately."

Her eyebrows went up. "How do you figure that?"

I smiled. "Because I'm the IT support guy."

Chapter Thirty-Four

Helpdesk, This is David

"Are you sure you know what you're doing?"

"Absolutely." Once again, Rusty's master key worked its magic, this time allowing us into the network closet nearest to Taylor's office. My assessment of Rusty's infrastructure management style had been correct; every bank of ports on the router was labeled, all the cables were bundled and secured with Velcro ties, and he had a map on the wall with this closet's service zone marked out. His telephony was just as organized, right down to a map with phone and data ports marked and a hard copy list of names, ports, and phone numbers. He even had his circuit testers, cabling gear, lineman's buttset tool, and punchdown tool hanging on a pegboard next to the distribution frame.

Goddess bless anal-retentive control freaks.

K looked around, totally lost. "My god, this looks like some kind of wizard's laboratory. If the wizard was really tidy, I mean. How do you know where all these wires and stuff go?"

I laughed. "This is nothing. There are only ten phones and thirty network ports in this zone. I did desktop support for an aerospace company in Boulder after high school. By the time I got my degree I was the team's network lead. This is like...I don't know, someone asking you to service a BB gun."

That got a smirk. "I'll take that as a compliment. What's the plan?"

"Who is on duty at the Spa tonight?"

"Bethany. She's cool."

"Good. That makes this easier." I looked through the list of phone numbers until I found the one I was looking for. I clipped the buttset into the Spa's telephone line and set it to ring when a call was made. Then I unplugged the cables from the Spa's network ports.

"And four...three...two..."

Right on cue, the buttset rang. I waited for the third ring, then clicked in. "Um, yeah. Hi! I mean, Mr. Gates' office, this is Steve, may I help you?"

The woman on the other end hesitated. "Hi, I need to talk to Rusty."

"I'm sorry, he's out dealing with all the craziness out front. I volunteered to watch his phone. Can I help you with anything?"

"How do I know that's true?"

I chuckled. "Well, I don't want to sound rude or anything, but you did call his number, right?"

She sighed, and her voice warmed up. "Good point. Well, I'm Bethany, the counselor on duty in the Spa. All of our security cameras are out. And, I don't know if this is related, but the Internet crashed. Can you reboot it?"

"The Spa? Oh! The, um, the shelter, right? Sure, I can have a look. The network is still working normally here, so it may be just your router. Would anyone there be upset if I came down to check the circuits in your area?"

"Um...hmm..." Bethany didn't sound happy with that idea. "I don't know..."

"I understand. I know I sounded a little scattered, earlier, but really, I know what I'm doing. I'm the network team lead at St. Francis hospital in Tulsa."

"Oh," she said. "How do you know Rusty?"

"I did a side contract a while back, helping him replace some cable over at the retirement home. He invited me to come to the men's ministry group sometime, and I finally had a Friday off. So, here I am."

The line was silent for a long moment. "Well, you're right, I did call you. Do you know where we are?"

"Not really. Um, wait a moment." I held the buttset out toward K. "Do you know where the shelter, um, the Spa is?"

She took the handset. "It's K. I'll bring him down. Because Rusty gave me his keys and asked me to show Steve around if anyone called. See you in a minute."

I bid Bethany goodbye and disconnected both the buttset and the Spa's phone line. Rusty could fix it later. We turned out the lights and left.

"You're pretty good at this," K said. "What do you actually do for a living?"

"You should see what I can do with proper tools," I said. "And to answer your question, I run a game company. I used to own it, but Avalanche bought us out a while back. It was a good decision for everyone."

"And you really are rich?"

I paused and glanced around the empty hall. "Well, that depends on what your basis of comparison is. Rose and I are 'never have to ask about prices' rich. Manya, Aparna's birth mother, is *Beverly Hillbillies* rich. My office manager's family is somewhere between Daddy Warbucks and Scrooge McDuck rich." I gave her a grin. "Why, need a loan?"

She snorted, shaking her head. "Never mind. Let's just go get your kid."

"No, wait," I held up my hand—well, I tried to—and said, "I'm sorry. I gave you a flippant answer and I shouldn't have. The truth is that I have more money than I will ever need. And I don't mind helping people with it. Now, you asked how much money I have for a reason. I'd like to know what that reason is. Did you need money for something?"

"Everyone needs money. I'm no different. That's all."

"Money does make things easier," I agreed. "But money isn't a desire. It's a means to obtain a desire. So, please, what is it you want?"

"You can't buy it for me, so it doesn't matter."

"The most precious things in life are purchased not with coin, but effort, time, blood, or love." I swung the gun case off my back and opened it enough for Kindness' hilt to show. "You're willing to pay those prices to help me. That's a debt I want to repay. I may not be able to help you, but if I can, I will. And I'm willing to swear that oath on this blade if I have to."

K stared at me, then shook her head. "You play too much D&D."

"Oh, please. I'm carrying a magic sword and looking for a cleric to heal my arm so I can continue my quest to rescue a winged princess. How much more D&D can I get?"

"I don't want to talk about it. You'll laugh."

"Possibly," I admitted. "I can't promise not to. But I'll make you a deal. You tell me what it is you really want, deep down inside, and when the time is right, I'll tell you about the Dragon."

"Not enough," she said. "I want to meet him. Socially. Like for tea. And I want you to promise to protect me. If I'm going to meet a dragon, I want to survive it."

"Well, I can at least promise that. You are in no danger from that Dragon. You might even score a ride."

"Do not bullshit me," K snapped. "Just don't. I have a shotgun and-"

"Shhh." When she stopped speaking, I took my finger off my lips, leaned in close, and whispered, "It's not bullshit. The promise is real. It's the Dragon's decision, but I know her pretty well. Want to know how?"

K's breath caught. Her nod was almost a tremor.

"She's my wife."

"What?!" K stepped back, eyes wide. "Your wife turned into a *Dragon*?"

"No, she was born a Dragon. Well, hatched. The human woman people see me with is a disguise. Same spell she used to turn me into Neesy."

"Dragons have been here all this time? Just...hiding? Pretending to be a myth?"

I hesitated a moment. "Yes and no. This world never had Dragons of its own, but Rose and the others aren't from here. They're from another plane of existence, but they've been coming here for a long time. Speaking of which..."

A quick glance up and down the hall confirmed we were still alone. I beckoned her closer and lowered my voice. "I'm pretty sure your friend with the BFG hurt her, just like you thought. You're also right that she'll be coming back. And when she does come back, she's going to bring along her family, all her friends, and every mother-loving warm body she can find. If I'm not able to walk out of here with Aparna by then, they will tear this place and everyone in it apart in order to find us."

K shook her head. "You're exaggerating."

"I wish I was, but Rose already proposed doing just that. I talked her out of it. Now that she's been injured, this is more than a case of her pet human getting into a squabble with some other short-life. Now one of the shaved monkeys managed to hurt a Dragon, and in her true form, no less. As a rule, male Dragons really don't like Humans. There's no shortage of males who would love to soak their claws in man-blood, and this is the perfect excuse."

"And you're okay with that?"

I shook my head. "No! Absolutely not! I want to find Aparna and go home. I'm not trying to scare you, just to impress on you that Rose has a lot of resources to call on. You've already helped me immensely, and when this is over, that means you will have her gratitude. Anything you want in this world is a lot more achievable with a Dragon backing you up. Trust me."

"Alright. Just...don't laugh." K pulled away, wrapping her arms tight around her chest. Almost inaudibly, she muttered, "I want the Man in Black."

I blinked. "Johnny Cash? Oh! Right. You want someone like Wesley?"

"No! Idiot..." She punched me in the shoulder. "Wesley is just a good-looking farm boy. And he's in love with someone else. No. I want a Dread Pirate. Strong, dark, mysterious, intense, and unstoppable. A gentleman and a scholar who's really good with a sword. He doesn't have to be rich, but he should have prospects."

"Ah. I see what you mean. Yeah, big difference." I gave her a sympathetic smile. "Kind of a rare breed, these days."

"Tell me about it." K waved the thought away. "I don't see your, uh, wife, being able to do much for me in that area."

"You're right about that. However, someone else I know can. Have you ever heard of Llewellyn Industries?"

She nodded. "Yeah. They manufacture a top-of-the-line biometric trigger lock system for pistols and long guns. Costs a bundle, but any firearm using it only operates if it validates the user's palm print."

"Cool. Does it blow up if the wrong person grabs hold of it?"

"No. Now, why did you ask? Focus, dude."

"I'm getting to that," I said. "If you are looking for dark, mysterious, and good with a sword, you need to talk to the Llewellyns. The family, I mean. Go to their web site, get the main office number in Vancouver, and call the front desk. Are you the oldest girl in your family?"

"I'm the only girl."

"Perfect. Introduce yourself as 'Firstdaughter' and your legal name. Then ask to speak to Seconddaughter Josephine Llewellyn. When she comes on—and she will—tell her I told you to call."

K's eyebrow went up. "What happens then?"

"I'm not sure on that part. You might get whisked off to Canada for an expensive dinner and a carefully rehearsed speech." I chuckled to myself. "They will probably offer you a job, but either way that turns out, you should tell Josephine about your Dread Pirate search. I'm quite sure she will be able to help you in that regard."

"Seriously? You aren't just jerking me around?"

"Very serious. They...well, I can't say too much, but they have what you are looking for."

"Guys with swords?" She didn't sound convinced. "Dark, mysterious, intense guys with serious sword skills are just lounging around western Canada waiting for gun-crazed American chicks to pop out from behind a moose and want to go get dinner?"

"Yes."

Something flitted across her face and she turned away for a long moment. "Sorry," she said. "It's just...I've been lonely for a long time."

"You don't have to be lonely anymore."

"Look, I...I'll think about it." She rubbed the back of her hand across her eyes. "Let's...we should be getting your daughter. We can talk about this stuff later."

She started walking. I followed.

Everything in Taylor's office looked a lot smaller to me than it had to Neesy; not surprising, I suppose. A stack of papers, all photocopied pages from a *Celestial Dream Ponies* coloring book, lay scattered on the floor behind one of the desks. I reached for them, then pulled my hand back. Screw it. I can buy her new coloring books.

K opened the stairway door. "Ready?"

I took a deep breath and puffed it out, hard. "Yeah. Let's go." Holding on to the rail for balance, I followed K down the stairs.

The woman waiting at the bottom stood no taller than Neesy had, and was as dark as Neesy had been pale. "Are you Steve? The computer guy?"

"Pretty much," I said. As I did, something caught my eye and I knelt next to the door frame. There was a small, partially bent, sky-blue feather on the floor. I picked it up and stepped into the Spa, twirling the feather between my fingers. "Did someone buy a new parrot today?"

"Not that I..." Her voice trailed off and her eyes widened for a moment. "No. It must be from a craft kit one of the kids was using. Anyway, I'm Bethany. We talked earlier. The computer is right over here." She pointed toward her desk.

"I hate to tell you this, Bethany, but I lied to you when we spoke earlier. My name is David Fraser, and I'm pretty sure this feather came from one of my daughter's wings." I slipped the feather into a pocket. "She's either here, or someone who was in contact with her is. Either way, I want to see the person who dropped that feather. Now."

"I don't know what you're talking abo-"

That sentence ended in a small shriek as I stepped into arm's reach and summoned Kindness. I rested the blade over my shoulder and said, very calmly, "I don't think you heard me. I'm Aparna's father, and it's time for her to come home. I've already sacrificed my hand to get her back. Don't get yourself or anyone else hurt trying to stop me."

She swallowed hard. "Y...you're just saying that to try to scare me. If you were going to hurt me, you'd just do it."

"Don't confuse my having a moral code with weakness." I started toward the apartments. "K, please bring Bethany back here too."

She nodded and waved Bethany down the hall in front of here. "Just give him his daughter," she said. "I don't want anyone else getting hurt. Rusty and Preston have screwed everything up enough already."

Bethany rolled her eyes and said, "Lord knows that's true enough."

"Let's start with Neesy's room," I said. "K, there's a pile of money in the safe you're welcome to take. Use it however you wish."

"I'll order pizza for the other ladies when all this is over," K replied. She nudged Bethany. "Master key. Open it."

Bethany shook her head. "I won't. No matter what you do to me. This is God's will, and I shall not transgress it."

"Fine." K patted her down and pulled the keys out of Bethany's pocket. "This is disappointing. I told David you were cool, and you went and made me a liar. I hope whatever they're giving you is adequate consolation when you're explaining to a judge why you took part in a kidnapping. Now sit down, hands on your head."

While Bethany complied, I leaned Kindness against the doorframe and took the keys. If Aparna was in here, I didn't want her first sight of me to be holding a sword. If it was a trap...well, Kindness was never far from my hand. I unlocked the door, pushed into the room—and froze in my tracks.

Harper was in the middle of the room, beaten bloody, gagged, and tied to a wheelchair. She slumped to the side, half-conscious, supported only by the ropes around her torso.

"What the hell?" I grabbed Bethany's arm and hauled her to her feet. "Is this the will of Jesus, too?"

"Yes," she said. "Harper is a wonderful minister, but she's lost her way and been enslaved by greed. That's why Preston wants her to give the church elders control of the land. The property should belong to the congregation, not one person. The sooner Harper is delivered from her demons of self-interest and signs the property over to the congregation for stewardship, the sooner all this will end."

"Wrong. This ends now." I stepped behind Harper, and Kindness cut through the ropes as though they were smoke.

Once they were loose, K pushed me to the side so she could get Harper free. I stayed nearby, sick to my stomach. Even though I know this was Preston's doing, I couldn't help feeling responsible. Unfortunately, we were so concerned about Harper, we forgot about Bethany. Then we heard the *click-clack* of a pistol round being chambered.

Glocks seem a lot bigger when you're downrange from one. I leaned closer to K and said, "I thought you frisked her."

K grimaced. "Looks like I missed a spot."

"I guess." I turned back to Bethany and asked, "Where were you hiding that?"

"Bra holster." She gave K a sympathetic smile and added, "Don't feel bad, sweet cheeks. I could hide an M-60 and a couple cans of ammo in there, and we aren't friendly enough for you to find everything." Her voice sharpened. "Now get away from her. Put the weapons on the floor and your hands on your heads."

I stepped in front of K and Harper. "No."

"Don't think I won't shoot you, hero. Toss the sword and get on your knees," Bethany ordered. "Do it, or I'll drop you where you stand."

I glanced down at the Glock and smirked. "Good thing for me the safety is on."

Which was bullshit. The safety on a Glock is on the trigger. Bethany had to know that. She looked anyway, turning the gun to the side and taking her eyes off us for a brief moment.

I charged.

Bethany looked back up, eyes wide with panic, and squeezed the trigger as fast as she could, right up until I drove Kindness through her heart. The force of my charge knocked the gun out of her hand, shoving her back. Kindness pinned her to the wall like a butterfly. I stayed there a moment, until her face went slack and the light left her eyes. I'd killed her; the least I could do was honor her passing. Once she was gone, I pulled the sword free and turned around.

K was on the floor, eyes wide, blood staining her shirt and the side of her face.

Chapter Thirty-Five

They Have Us Surrounded,
the Poor Bastards

The gunshots woke everyone in the Spa. Fran and Sara popped out of their rooms, gasping and screaming at the carnage. I pulled my shirt off and pressed it to K's wounds. One bullet hit under her right breast, the other in her stomach. A third took part of her ear and creased her skull.

"Get away from her!" Fran screamed. She pushed her daughter back and advanced on me, waving a baseball bat.

"I'm trying to save her life, Fran. Get the first aid kit!"

Fran wavered. "I...I don't believe you. Get away from her, now!"

I half-turned and raised my stump so she could see it. "Damn it, Fran, I didn't do this, Bethany did! I can't help her one-handed. Now get the damn first aid kit!"

Sara grabbed Janey's hand. "Come with me, honey, your mama's gonna' be busy. Frannie, help him. We can shoot him later."

"Well, shit fire anyway." Fran handed Sara the bat and ran for the front room. She was back in seconds, putting a pillow under K's head and pressing a gauze pad to her head wound. "So what happened to Bethany?"

"I killed her. I was just too damn slow about it." I got to my feet. "Keep pressure on her, I'm going to check Harper."

"Harper?" Fran got halfway to her feet, then knelt down again. "Harper's here? What's wrong with her?"

"Someone beat the crap out of her. K and I were trying to get her loose when Bethany pulled the gun on us. That's why I killed her."

Harper was on the floor, blood soaking the thigh of her jeans. "So this is what you really look like, eh?" She held her hand out. "Help me up."

I lifted her to her feet and got my arm under her shoulder. "Can you heal yourself?"

"Don't worry about that. Take me to K."

I didn't argue.

"Oh, lord..." Fran winced and looked away. "Who did this to you?"

"Rusty and Ofelia," Harper said. "Maybe someone else, I don't know. I was unconscious for most of it." Harper knelt, pressed her fingertips to K's chest, and bowed her head. "Lord, I humble myself before You, and beg You to bestow Your gift of healing on Kaitlyn. Make her whole and healthy again. In Christ's name we pray, amen."

K's wounds vanished. Gasping, she sat bolt upright, wide-eyed, and scrambled backward until she hit the wall. She sat there, quivering and repeating "Ohgodohgodohgod..." Something made a metallic clicking noise and she froze. Gingerly, she reached under her shirt and came out holding two bullets. She stared at them and whispered, "Inconceivable."

I chuckled. "Be glad you were only mostly dead."

Fran gasped. "How...Sister, how did you do that?"

Harper shrugged. "God granted me the gift of healing, Fran. I have no idea why, but there it is."

"Incredible..." Fran looked at K and started snickering.

"What's so funny?" Harper asked.

"Preston. He wants you gone so bad, but he has no idea of what you can do." Fran started laughing. "When he finds out, he's gonna' crap bricks."

Harper laughed, too, until she saw Bethany's body. "What happened?" she asked.

"She's the one who shot me," K said. "Dibs on going through her pockets for loose change."

"She shot you, too," I told Harper. "She also knew you were in there. I'm sorry, but she was one of the bad guys."

"Then it's a good thing Christianity is a religion of forgiveness and mercy." Harper knelt next to Bethany and took her hand.

As soon as she did, she convulsed, shrieking, and hurled herself away from Bethany's body. Harper hit the wall, knocking herself and two framed pictures to the floor. She kept going scrambling backward until she was stuck in the corner. Unable to retreat further, she doubled over, hands in front of her eyes, sobbing.

K scampered over to Harper and crouched down, reaching for her shoulder. "Are you-"

"Don't touch me!" Harper shrieked. She pulled back, holding her hands over her face as though warding off an assault.

K backed off. "No problem, Harper. No one is going to touch you until you say it's okay." She sat down and added, "When you're ready, can you tell us what happened? We're all a little scared for you right now."

Harper looked up, wiping tears away. "Bethany...won't be rejoining us. She was judged and...found to be a goat."

"Matthew 25?" I asked.

Harper nodded. "She sold her hopes of eternal life for empty promises of wealth and fame."

"Harper, it's not your fault," Fran said. She took the comforter off the bed and covered Bethany with it. "It's not for us to question God's will."

"God's will?" Harper whispered. "I wish it was. I can accept that God knows best for us all. But it's not God's will this time. It's mine. I could do it, Fran. I could bring her back. All I have to do is command it. God gave me the power to raise the dead, but it's *my decision*. And...because it *is* my decision, I have to—*have to!*—see the person the way God sees them. All the flaws, petty thoughts, and personal failings. Their dream, desires, and needs, all at once. It...it's horrible."

Fran turned pale. "Jesus wept..."

That got a chuckle out of Harper. "Yes, exactly. I was just wondering if Jesus had wept after seeing Lazarus the same way." She grabbed a tissue and blew her nose. "I think I'll stick to healing people. Bringing back the dead is too much power for a mere human to have."

I sat down on the bed. "I'm sorry, Harper. It may sound cruel and selfish, but I don't regret killing her. Even knowing it would put you through this, I'd do it again. If that makes me a bad person in your eyes, well...I can live with that. You and K are alive, and that's what matters."

Harper's eyebrows shot up. "Wait...wait...you're worried about what I think of you? You *killed* Bethany! How can you not be haunted by that?"

"Because I stopped feeling guilty for killing people a few years ago."

She sagged back against the wall. "Oh, my lord...you're serious, aren't you?"

"Yes." I glanced at K and Fran. K seemed fascinated, while Fran was visibly horrified. "If it helps any, almost all of the people in my ledger were armed and far from innocent. Most of them were trying to kill me or someone I care about." I ran my hand through my hair and sighed. "I got tired of feeling bad about killing them."

Harper wiped her eyes and stood up. "No more killing," she said. "I need your help to get control of this situation, and you need my help getting your daughter back. We can work together and fix all this, but no one else dies. I won't have it."

"No deal," I said. "I don't like hurting people, but I won't stand by and allow others to come to harm if I have the power to stop it. I stood aside once before, and Aparna's mother was murdered. Never again."

Her eyes hardened. "No killing. It's not for you to judge."

"Bullshit. You own a gun store. Hell, you're an arms *manufacturer*. If it's okay for your customers to use lethal force, you have no grounds to say I can't. I just use a sword instead of a gun."

Southern women have their own version of battle-joy. It's called 'givin' 'em what-fer.' From the light in Harper's eyes, she was full up on it and looking to unload some wrath on my ass. She balled up her fists and shouted, "Well, maybe I need to rethink that part of my asset allocation!"

I blinked and nodded. "Um, yeah, maybe so."

"Fine!" she yelled. "I'll just do that! Thank you for pointing out my moral inconsistency!"

"Glad to be of service!" I bellowed.

We glared at each other for a long few seconds, then both started laughing.

After it passed, I said, "Harper, I won't hurt anyone unnecessarily, or hurt them any more than I have to, or kill unless there's no other option, but I'm not ruling anything out. I respect you, but I will not let my hands be tied."

"And I can't know another person that way," she said. "I can't. God should just take this blessing from me now, because I'm never going to use it."

"Harper, with all due respect, we'll have plenty of time to worry about that later." K took Harper's arm and pointed toward the bed. "Now, why don't you lay down and let us look at your leg?"

Harper held a bullet up between her thumb and forefinger. "I already took care of it. Speaking of your hands being tied, David, how did you manage to lose one?"

"Stole a truck and crashed into a tree during my great escape. I heal insanely fast—you saw that with Neesy—so I'm not nearly as messed up as I should be." I looked down at the bandage-covered stump and sighed. "Although I am hoping Rose can fix this when she gets back."

"Will you let me try to heal you?" Harper held her hands up. "At least I know I can do that."

"Absolutely," I said. What do you need me to do?"

"Nothing. We just need to take this bandage-" She jerked her hand away from my arm and sat down, frowning. "Alright then, I guess not."

"Problem?"

Harper nodded. "I'm sorry, but it's not God's will that you be healed at this time. Rusty and Preston know you're missing a hand. If you show up with it fixed, they'll know someone you've encountered is able to perform miracles. They'll want to find that person. Right now, they want me alive so I can sign over the property. If they find out I can heal, they'll kill me in a heartbeat."

I thought about it and nodded. "I can't fault your logic. Did you get any advice on what to do instead?"

Harper nodded. "Keep looking for Aparna. I'm not sure where to look next, though."

Fran said, "Try the church offices next. Ofelia said something about your daughter talking to the police when she came to get her."

That got my attention. "When was this?"

Fran grimaced. "About...eleven, I think. I was surprised to see Ofelia, but Rusty was with her, so I thought it was okay. Rusty just scooped your little girl up and she kept right on sleeping. I asked if they were going to return her to her parents, and Ofelia said it would all be over soon."

238

"Proof of life," K said.

"Probably Manya and her lawyers," I replied. "Thanks, Fran. That helps a lot."

"Good luck getting your little girl back," Fran said. "I'm going to get Joanie and call it a night. See you all in the funny papers."

"I need to talk to the residents over at Covenant Center," Harper said. "All of them have money invested in the Center from buying their apartments. Collectively, they're the other major stakeholders in the church. They stand to lose as much from Preston's plans as I do. I think I can count on their support."

"They're down in the tornado shelters," K called from her room. "Rusty moved them down there for their safety, or so he claimed."

"How odd that he'd think the people he invited here would be a threat to the residents," Harper muttered. "Well, David, good luck. If you get a chance, tell the authorities what Preston is doing. Oh, and tell him he's fired."

"Will do." I looked around, but Kindness was missing. "Alright, who grabbed my sword?"

"I did." K emerged from her room holding Kindness. "I hope you don't mind me cleaning it. You don't want to leave...stuff...on the blade."

"No, thank you." I tucked the sword back into the gun bag. "Cleaning her one-handed would be tricky. What did you use, anyway?"

"Gun oil, what else?" My reaction must have showed; K rolled her eyes and snorted at me. "Oh, please, any sword that can cut a shotgun in half isn't going to wilt if it gets a little modern technology on it. *Especially* a Dwarf-forged blade won from the hoard of a dragon."

I managed a smile. "How can I argue with that?"

"You don't. Now, let me see your hands. I have something for you."

"What, one sequined glove?" Nevertheless, I held my arms out for her.

"No, two armored ones."

She wasn't kidding. They were tactical black, with chain mail lining the palm and inner wrist. The outer side had rigid plates along the forearm and the back of the hand. Buckles above the elbow and around the wrist held them in place.

I gaped at them and asked, "What the hell are these?"

"Riot gloves."

"What do you use them for?"

"Going to riots, duh." She rolled back my shirt sleeves and worked the left one on. "One of my asshole ex-boyfriends left them behind when he dumped me. They're loose on me, but fun when I go clubbing."

"I bet."

For my stump, she padded the glove with two of Neesy's shirts and some spare socks. Once they were buckled on and hidden under my shirt sleeves, I looked normal. She topped the whole thing off with a sling and a bit of athletic bandage. "There. Tell people you sprained your wrist. If things go south, the plates on these are Lexan. They won't stop a bullet, but knives, chains, and dog bites shouldn't be an issue."

"Much appreciated. Are you coming with me or with Harper?"

"With Harper. I'll back up what she tells the residents. However, if any dragons show up in the meantime, you be sure to tell them not to eat us."

Harper looked alarmed at that. "Dragons? Please say you're kidding."

"Wish I was." K glanced at me out of the corner of her eye. "Just one so far. Bo Breen hurt her and she took off, but she'll be back."

"How do you know this one was female? Lipstick?"

I said, "We know because I'm married to her. She's...ah...not local. I know she's alive and back on her home world. And K is right. She's coming back, and she's bringing friends."

Harper buried her face in her hands, shaking her head. "Oh, Christ, be merciful..." Without looking up, she asked, "What do we do if they attack?"

"Um, let me think..." I honestly had no clue what to tell her. It's not like I knew Draconic...

You don't need to know Draconic. You know Dragons.

Yes, I do. "Get a big white sheet or a tablecloth and as much coinage and jewelry as you can find. Lay the sheet on the ground with the loot in the center and have everyone with you kneel, hands out to your sides, heads bowed. That'll get someone's attention. Say 'Mighty one, we ask your protection according to the design of the Caretakers.' Then ask to speak to Rose or her mother, Arwydd."

Harper raised her eyebrows. "Are you sure that will work? I'm not sure I like kneeling to anyone."

"Think of it as a police officer making sure you're not a threat. You aren't pledging fealty or anything, you're demonstrating that you're un-armed and cooperative."

"Is that what we're actually doing?"

I laughed. "Oh, hell no. But appealing to greed and ego go a long way with Dragons. To them, you're just showing proper respect, which is in short supply these days. Dragons used to teach and protect Humans on Rose's world. You're asking that protection for yourself, that's all. It's al-most unknown these days. That's why it will attract their attention."

"Alright then. I'll hope it doesn't come to that, but we'll be ready, just in case." Harper put her hand on my shoulder and smiled. "God bless you and keep you, David."

I returned the gesture. "Merry meet, merry part, and merry meet again. Blessed be, Harper." I turned to K. "And you. Have fun storming the castle."

K thumped me on the shoulder. "I told you not to do that," she mut-tered. She grabbed her purse and headed for the stairs. Harper and I fol-lowed.

Now, if I only had a wheelbarrow and a Holocaust Cloak...

Or at least some shoes.

Chapter Thirty-Six

Rescue, Take Two

The first light of dawn was tinting the eastern sky as I made my way to the church offices. A hazy layer of fog hugged the ground, wrapping around dozens of tents, pop-up campers, and pickups lined up on the grass beyond the office parking lot.

Even at Oh-God-Thirty, people were up and around outside. Three propane grills and one of those gas-powered rigs for deep-frying turkeys were lit and warming up, ready to pump out breakfast for the camp. From the aroma wafting over to me, the turkey fryer was boiling water for coffee.

It smelled fantastic. Goddess knows I could use a cup right now. It also meant the camp would be waking up soon. Time to move my ass.

One guy was in the hall outside the church office. I nodded at him and said, "Folks are getting some coffee and breakfast together outside. I can cover for you if you want to grab some and hit the head."

"Thanks, man. My teeth are floating." He handed me a radio. "The traffic was keeping the kid awake. If the front line needs anything, just turn it down before you go in or that fat bitch will rag your nuts off."

I snorted. "Like anyone needs that crap this early in the morning."

"No shit." He headed off, walking fast enough for me to think his bladder had been complaining for a while. I waited until I heard the bathroom door, then killed the radio volume and opened the door.

The only light was what leaked in around the blinds; everything else was off. Someone was sleeping on the little loveseat by the door—I think it was Rusty—and I heard snoring coming from one of the side offices, even with the door closed. I tiptoed past both of them.

Someone had unlocked Harper's office with a sledgehammer. The doorknob was missing entirely. All of her files were piled on her desk or sorted into one of four large bins.

Well, what do you know? Somebody's been sleeping in Harper's bed, and she's still there! It was my good buddy Ofelia, crashed out on the unfolded futon. She had a big, well-worn sledge hammer on one side of her, and Aparna on the other.

After all this crap—the violence, the pain, the betrayals—all I could do at first was look at her. My perfect, beloved angel of a child, sleeping with her head back, mouth open, and drooling on her pillow.

She'd gone to sleep on her side, allowing her wings to hang over the side of the bed. Lifting her one-handed wasn't going to be easy.

A shadow wrapped around her feet moved. I'd thought it was a blanket; it turned out to be Oreo. The last thing I needed was for him to start barking. I skritched him behind his ears and whispered, "Shhh, boy, go back to sleep. Good dog…"

His ears went up and he made a soft snorting noise, but he stayed quiet.

Carrying Aparna was going to be tricky, even without the gun bag moving around on my back. That aside, I didn't want one of the cops seeing it and thinking I was a threat. I stashed the gun bag under the futon frame and pushed it back as far as I could. Kindness would come if I needed her. As an afterthought, I snagged the sledgehammer and tucked it under the futon as well.

"Psst."

I looked around the room. There was no one here and awake but me and the dog. No one visible, anyway. These days, there was no way to rule out an invisibility spell. In a D&D game, I'd start throwing flour or chalk dust around to see if it settled on anything. Since I didn't have either, I put my back to the wall and looked around for visual anomalies.

"No, you idiot. Over here."

It was coming from the foot of the bed, but I still didn't see anything except…the dog.

Oreo waved me over, glanced at Ofelia, and waved harder. "Come here! Quietly!"

Well, I already know a talking cat; if I could find a loquacious ferret and a gregarious otter, maybe I could finally run that *Bunnies & Burrows* game I'd been thinking about. I dropped to one knee and hissed, "What?"

"Do yourself a favor, mate. Kill this one, now, while she's sleeping." He waved one paw at Ofelia.

"I don't want to kill anyone," I whispered. "Especially not an unarmed, defenseless woman!"

"Look, you sackless greebo, giving you that advice was important enough for me to break cover. How often do you think I expose myself like this?" He glanced out the office door. "If you care for your daughter at all, kill this slag while you can."

"Sorry, but I don't work that way," I said. "If I ever do kill her, she'll be awake, she'll be facing me, and she'll be armed. Now, do you have anything useful to add?"

"Not if you aren't going to listen. Grab your girl and let's fang it!"

Sure, arguing with a talking dog was unusual even for my life, but, as I said, there was precedent. I got my left arm behind Aparna's back and my stump under her knees, leaned over so I could press her to my chest, and lifted with my back. Bugger health and safety.

It worked. She slumped against me, head on my shoulder, and kept right on drooling.

During our stay in India, Manya taught me how pressure between Aparna's shoulder blades made her wings pull in close to her body. It was a good trick for getting her through narrow doors or in and out of a car. Once her wings were pulled in, I snagged a Still Waters windbreaker off a coat rack and draped it over her shoulders.

Now it was just a quick run across the parking lot.

Out in the hall, I headed for the nearest exit. Oreo shook his head and said, "This way, greebo. Service door back of the baptistry."

"Good plan." I fell in next to him, walking fast. "Why are you doing this?"

"Well, I did bite your hand off. Trying to make up for it."

"Right...so that wasn't a trauma-induced hallucination. Can I at least say, 'bad dog, Oreo'?"

"Try it and I'll bite off your dangly bits. And since we're chatting, it's Orion, not Oreo. Some of the letters got worn off my collar."

Orion...something ticked the edge of memory with that, but...never mind, I'd worry about it later.

The sanctuary was closed. Orion grabbed a door handle with one paw and swung it open. "Straight on, behind the choir risers on the right."

"Gotcha. So, were you human before the Change, or a dog, or what? No offense, just curious."

He flicked an ear at me. "Me? I'm just a poor sinner, unburdened by purpose and searching for absolution."

"Sorry to hear that." He didn't want to talk. That was fair. I had to shift Aparna around to avoid falling down the stairs. While I was negotiating them, Orion ran ahead to the door and stood there, ears up and head cocked to the side.

"Three people walking by, about twenty feet away," he whispered. "Have you seen Harper?"

I nodded. "She's gone to the tornado shelters to get the Covenant Center residents to back her for control of the property. She was fine, last I saw her."

"Good. Once you're out of here, I have to go find her."

"You her bodyguard or something?"

He managed to shrug somehow. "I have my reasons. Let's just say it keeps me busy. Get ready."

"Ready and waiting."

Orion listened at the door again and nodded. "I'll go first. Give me thirty seconds and I'll distract as many as I-" He looked toward the entrance to the sanctuary. "Company! Go!"

I hooked my stump under Aparna's rear and pushed the door open. Instantly, a loud buzzing filled the sanctuary.

"Bugger!" Orion took off at a run. I slipped out and pushed the door closed, then started walking as fast as I could toward the police line.

At least, where I thought the police line was. The ground fog was still heavy, and in the predawn gloom, I had nothing to go on but the brief glimpse I'd gotten when Taylor brought me here. I could see roughly where Rusty's folks were positioned, so I veered away, hoping the fog would keep them from spotting me.

Over by Harper's cottage, Orion went into full meltdown—barking, snarling, and running back and forth. His plan worked. I heard running feet and a lot of cursing headed toward the barking.

I reached the parking lot and skirted it, moving into the grass until I could barely make out the edge of the blacktop through the fog. The grass was up almost to my knees, but it was easier on my feet than the parking lot had been. Worst-case scenario, I could live with a few chiggers.

A wall of brush came into view and I turned to move along it. The blacktop was nowhere in sight. Hopefully that meant I had passed the far edge and was next to the fence. Almost clear...

My foot came down on metal. With a crack like a giant mousetrap, something slammed into either side of my ankle. I twisted as I fell, landing on my shoulder rather than on top of Aparna. I cried out once, then stuffed a knuckle in my mouth to stifle any noises.

Any movement or shift to my ankle was agonizing. I rolled over and saw a blood-covered leg trap around my foot. Damn it, Taylor had even taken the time to warn me about this patch of grass! If I'd had boots or even decent shoes, it would have hurt but not much more than that. As it was, I was pretty sure something in my ankle was broken.

Over on the front line, cowbells were clanging. Triggering the trap had set off some kind of alarm. Frakking redneck ingenuity... I pushed myself up to my knees just as the first of Rusty's friends ran up and aimed a rifle at me.

I held my hand up. "Stop, please! I'm not a cop! I just want to get my daughter out of here before anyone gets crazy. Please! Her mother is dead, I'm all she has. Help me get her to the police and I can prove I'm her father!"

Ofelia appeared out of the fog. "So, you're David Fraser," she said. "I've heard so much about you." She scooped up Aparna and stepped back, pointing something at me.

The Taser prongs lodged in my right shoulder and she poured on the voltage until my thrashing knocked one of them loose. By this time, at least half a dozen more of Rusty's friends had arrived.

Ofelia said, "You boys have ten minutes. Don't do anything permanent. Bring him to the sanctuary when you're finished." She walked off, and Rusty's friends moved in.

Two of them hauled me to my feet and held me while another released my foot from the leg trap. They kept on holding me as the other guys took turns punching me like a heavy bag. Thankfully, I passed out somewhere around the third guy.

I woke up with Ofelia dumping a bucket of water over my head. It left me coughing and gasping, at least until I started gagging. She grabbed my hair and yanked my head sideways so I didn't drown in my own vomit.

As soon as I could talk, I asked, "Where's Aparna?"

"Safe and waiting to be reunited with her grandparents...when the time is right."

"Give her to me and I promise, I will let you live. In fact, I'm feeling so generous, I'll even spare Preston and Rusty."

She sat back and chuckled. "I am imm-*pressed*, I tell you. You are a tough sumbitch, I'll give you that. Knew you would be. Grace talked about how you got rid of that animal who murdered Sharon. Rolling your own car at highway speeds! That takes guts. But walking away from it? That's just plain cussedness." She paused to wipe the vomit off the side of my face. "I really should have sent more boys to kill you."

"Rookie mistake. Should have killed me when I was unconscious."

"I thought about it," she said. "You're just too valuable an asset to waste. I did wonder if you would have killed me, were our situations reversed."

"I already spared your life once," I replied. "I could have killed you while you were asleep in Harper's office. And I had good reason to do it. You kidnapped my daughter. You tried to kill me. You did kill Tyson. That's more than enough to justify ending you. But I didn't. Next time, I won't be so forgiving."

She laughed. "My goodness, that's a terribly bloodthirsty attitude for a tree-hugging hippie. I thought you Pagans were afraid of getting bad karma."

I snorted. "Bad karma? I've saved the world two and a half times so far. Anything short of building my own Death Star and I'm good."

"Oh, really?" The derision in her voice was palpable. "Video games don't count, I'm afraid."

"I wasn't talking about video games," I said. "You might remember hearing about a bunch of UFO cultists in Las Vegas staging a mass suicide a year or so back. That was a cover story for what really happened. Want to know the truth?"

"Oh, heavens, yes. Enlighten me."

"A demoness from another world tried to establish herself here on Earth and ascend to become a minor goddess. I was able to kill her because the God of Abraham led me to the spear that pierced the side of

Jesus, and allowed me to use it." I grinned. "He wanted her dead, too, and anointed me to carry it out."

"Only the prayers of one saved by the blood of Jesus can destroy a demon."

"A spear covered in the *actual* blood of Jesus does a good job, too. After I killed her, I used the blood to bring some innocent victims back from the dead." I shrugged as best I could. "Like you said, I'm Pagan. And yet, I was allowed to use one of the holiest artifacts of the Christian faith. You might want to keep that in mind when you contemplate your next move."

"That's a lie...a lie from the pit of Hell!"

This time I laughed. "Oh, ye of little faith."

She snarled and stormed away, slamming the door closed behind her. I kept laughing.

Unfortunately, I wasn't doing nearly as well as I wanted her to believe. My head, ankle, and chest hurt almost as much as the stump of my wrist. I was sick to my stomach, trussed up like a Thanksgiving turkey, and stuffed in a janitorial closet. Worst of all, I still couldn't feel Rose's presence on Earth.

As before, getting free was the first priority. I pulled against the ropes with all I had, but they didn't budge. My captors had done a much better job of securing me this time. Since getting free wasn't an option at the moment, I decided to relax and let my enhanced healing do its thing. Maybe it had a high gear when body parts were missing.

Hey, one can hope.

Chapter Thirty-Seven

Preston's Gambit

Damn, bare concrete gets miserable fast. The one good point was that the cold had numbed the pain in my ankle. Or maybe my broken bones had mended already. I had no way to tell, really.

I'd managed to doze off somehow, until the sound of footsteps and voices woke me up. It wasn't much warning, but it was enough for me to shake my head and take a long, deep breath. When the door swung open, I said, "Hi, folks! Sorry I couldn't get the door. I'm all tied up at the moment."

Rusty scowled at me. "Don't be a smart ass."

I grinned and said, "Better than being a dumb ass. So, how's the siege going? Feds overrun the front gate yet? You know, I have this terrific recipe for dealing with tear gas..."

His reply was to jam the business end of a cattle prod against my ribs and let me have it. And he kept letting me have it.

I couldn't avoid it, or try to get away, or strike back. I couldn't even focus enough to remember my sword's name, much less summon her. All I could do was scream.

Finally, mercifully, he stopped, leaving me gasping and barely conscious. "That was three minutes, Buckwheat. Get mouthy with me again and we'll go for ten. Got it?"

I wanted to agree, to beg for mercy, to give in and do whatever he wanted. By myself, I probably would have. Rose wouldn't let me. Whatever part of her that was still in me refused to let me submit. Instead, I winced and said, "Oh, dude, you're sporting wood—in a *church*! Inappropriate..."

No warning at all. He punched me in the nose. Again. No aim, no fitness, just furious pounding. He landed...eight...maybe nine punches, all to the face. I lost track.

He grabbed my hair, yanked my head to the side, and hissed, "Got something else to say, freak?"

Getting that close was a mistake. I spit blood in his face. He replied with a kick to my chest and more punches. Again, there was no finesse to it. He was just swinging fast and wild, almost frenzied.

Soon enough I couldn't breathe. Not long after that I passed out.

Some unknown time later, another splash of water brought me around. Every breath hurt, even though I could only take shallow breaths to begin with. The inside of my mouth tasted like a cotton ball soaked in blood and turpentine. On top of that, several of my teeth were missing or broken.

Preston set the bucket down. "Merciful Christ, Rusty! I said you could punch him once or twice! This is...what in God's green Earth is wrong with you?"

I coughed, spit something out, and said, "*Bzzz*! What is impotence-induced sub-psychotic rage?"

Rusty's fist rocked my head backward. I tasted fresh blood. He either split my lip or cut the inside of my cheek on broken teeth. "How was that, funny boy? Want to make some more jokes? Go ahead. Please. I'd love to get Saudi Arabian on you, punk. We'll start with caning your feet until you can't blessed walk!"

"You'll do no such thing, Rusty. I'll not have the church defiled with some Muslim nonsense." Preston flicked the light on and I finally got a good look at both of them.

Rusty looked totally different from the calm, professional guy I'd seen earlier. Now he was twitching, growling under his breath, and glowering at me. Preston, on the other hand, had changed into a new suit (and a nice one at that), shaved, and was even wearing a respectable, high-end cologne. In moderation! I nodded to him and said, "Morning. So, you're the brains of this outfit?"

"Oh, no. Not at all," Preston replied. "God is, Mister Fraser. May I call you David?"

"Sure, Preston, go for it."

"Thank you. I have to say, I'm impressed with how much you seem to know about our little church. I'm even more impressed with your remarkable return from the brink of death. I'd love to know how you fooled the police and the doctors so easily."

I waved the question away. "Just good planning and preparation, that's all."

"Yes, well, I suppose I could say the same. I was worried you might cause us some problems, but so far you haven't really presented a challenge. If it were up to me, I'd be fine letting you go. My associates, however, aren't keen on that idea."

"It's okay, really," I said. "Rusty can learn to live with disappointment. The rest of you simply get to live. Like the bumper sticker says, choose life."

248

"Amazing. You look like week-old roadkill, you have to know you're going to die here, and yet you still manage to make jokes."

I shook my head, and immediately regretted it. A wave of nausea hit, and I spit blood and bile. When I finished, I rasped, "I wasn't joking. Or making threats. You only have a few hours at most before my backup arrives. Bring Aparna to me, let us leave in peace, and no one gets hurt."

He chuckled. "Your backup? And what backup would that be? The police and several Federal agencies are already here. Who else are you waiting for?"

"The Dragon that stopped by last night. We're on really good terms. Out of respect for the sanctity of life, I have to tell you she is coming back, and she will be bringing friends. End this, now, and I swear by those things my faith swears by, you, Rusty, and Ofelia all get to live."

Preston laughed. "How very magnanimous of you. No matter. Rest assured, we are taking steps to deal with your scaly friend. Permanently."

"Really." I tried raising my eyebrows, but I couldn't tell if they responded. "I feel obligated to warn you, craigslist is no place to find competent dragon slayers."

He blinked at me. "Is that supposed to be a joke? Or is it something from the Internet?"

"Good grief, Preston. How do you expect to become a famous television preacher if you don't understand social media?" Laughing hurt enough to knock the wind out of me. Rusty may have broken some ribs. "You look the part, but you just are not meme material."

"Enough talk," Rusty growled. "Let me finish him! He's a miserable, scum-sucking murderer, and he needs to pay!" He advanced on me, fists clenched.

"Hate to burst your little bubble of crazy, Rusty, but I don't know what you are talking about." A hard knot of suspicion crystallized in my chest. I sat up as best I could and asked Preston, "Have you done something to Harper or the others who were at her house?"

He looked blank for a moment, then furrowed his brow. "Perish the thought! Harper is a dear, precious friend, and I wouldn't dream of harming a hair on her head. You're going to do it."

I lunged against the ropes as hard as I could, trying to summon any scraps of magic I could grab hold of to aid me. Useless. The ropes held.

Preston scowled. "You needn't bother fighting it," he said. "You can't win. We have your sword, and when we're finished talking, you're going to use it to kill Harper and Grace. Then Vernon is going to shoot you dead. Losing Grace in such a terrible massacre will generate enormous sympathy for him. He'll have no problems keeping that little girl, and we will take good care of both of them."

"So what's it all about? What the hell do you gain by doing this?"

He looked surprised at that. "Why, fame, you silly boy. Wealth. Power. All the things everyone wants. And I'll gain it all through preaching the Gospel and improving the lives of others. It's going to be glorious."

I snorted. "Bullshit. You're not gaining all that by preaching. This is murder. Even if you do have some way of compelling me to do the act itself, that won't matter. You'll still be the one who willed it to happen. The sin will be on your soul, not mine."

He shrugged. "Yes, I suppose it will be, but it's all under the Blood. This will open so many hearts to the Lord in years to come. You should be proud. You're going to help give rise to something marvelous. I know you're worried about you daughter, but you needn't be. I'm going to make sure she's well taken care of. After all, how many churches have their own resident angel?"

"Keep talking," I said. "All you're doing is giving me more reasons to kill you."

"No, all I'm doing is following God's will."

"Yeah, right. You know, the bad part about being a raging Islamophobe is that you miss out on some wonderful teachings. Like the one that says, 'Beware the supplication of the oppressed, even if he is an unbeliever, for there is no barrier between it and Allah.' And right now, I'm feeling pretty damn oppressed."

"The only thing oppressing you is your own sin." He cleared his throat. "David, I want you to stay quiet and listen to me. It's not me you're angry at," he replied. His voice deepened, becoming richer, more stentorian. "You are angry at Harper. Remember that. Harper is going to take your daughter away from you. You need to stop her. Grace and those lawyers are in on it. Remember that. You need to kill them. Leave Vernon alive. Remember, all the others must die. Take your sword and kill them."

His words kept buzzing around in my head, getting louder and louder. I focused on the truth...blame Preston. Blame Preston. Blame...Preston. Blame...

Harper

Of course it was Harper. She's in charge of this place. Sharon never trusted her parents; why should you? They're the threat. Protect Aparna.

Remove the threat.

Preston leaned over me. "You can respond normally now. How do you feel, David?"

I glanced around. "How I feel doesn't matter. Preston, I know Harper is a friend of yours, but she has my daughter. I need to get her back. Please, you have to help me."

He nodded. "I want to help you, but I can't. I'm afraid of what Harper will do to me if she finds out I helped you. You don't know how dangerous she is. I'm sorry." He turned to walk out the door.

250

"Wait!" Panic swelled, tightening my chest. I lunged against the ropes, fingers clawing at the air. "Don't walk away! Preston!"

He kept walking.

"Preston! She can't hurt you if she's dead!"

He stopped. "Dead? What are you saying, David?"

"I'll kill her for you!" I had to get through to him, to make him *see.* "Preston, you're her partner. With her gone, all of this will be yours. Think about it! Look at what she's built—how much more you could build. All you have to do is let me go and I'll take care of the rest!"

"Hmm...well...I might be able to accommodate you. Just sit there and let us talk." Preston rubbed his chin and glanced at Rusty. "What do you think?"

Rusty scowled. "Was I that pathetic?"

The question brought a smile to Preston's lips. He clapped Rusty on the shoulder and gave him a companionable shake. "You were worse."

"Mmm. Maybe." Rusty stared at me a long moment. "Make sure he kills Miss K along with the others."

"I thought you liked her?"

"Oh, I do. But she's heard too much, from us and from him. I don't want to risk her saying anything to the wrong person at the wrong time."

"That's probably prudent." Preston took a deep breath, closing his eyes for a moment. "I hope that's all you want to add. It's taking more effort than usual for me to condition him."

"I still owe him a few punches for the damage he did in the closet."

"You already did enough." Preston sighed and checked his watch. "You know, I wish we had cameras in the shelters. It's a shame we have to miss the show. Is everything set up for our frantic call to the police?"

Rusty nodded. "Yes, for the third time, we're ready. Just to be safe, I want to make sure the outside security cameras are rolling. Give me ten minutes." He left the room, leaving me alone with Preston.

"David, it's time for you to be quiet and listen to me again." His voice changed again. Now I could hear whispered echoes, both before and after he spoke. "You remember that K can't be trusted. K is in with Harper. She wants to keep your daughter from you. Remember that. You can't allow that. She must be eliminated. When you see her, you will remember your rage. You will remember that she came between you and Aparna. You will remember vowing to kill her. You *will* kill her."

He paused, holding a handkerchief to the blood leaking from his nose. His eyes look different...they had a distinct silver sheen to them.

"Lord, I hear you. I understand." The handkerchief muffled Preston's voice a bit. "You told me not to overuse this blessing, and here I am defying You. Forgive my pride, Lord. Forgive my pride."

He tipped his head back and sat, unmoving, eyes closed, for several minutes. When he looked at me again, the bleeding had stopped, but his eyes still weren't normal. If anything, the silver sheen was more pronounced. He looked like Gary Lockwood's character in the second *Star Trek* pilot—the guy who thought he was a god.

What did Rose call it? Spell-lashed? I should tell him what Rose said. He can't help me if he melts his brain.

But he said to be quiet.

So, I was quiet.

Preston looked at the blood on his hands and handkerchief, shaking his head. "Excuse me for a moment, will you. I need to go get cleaned up." He patted me on the cheek. "Don't run off, now."

I didn't even try to get loose while he was gone.

When he came back, his irises were solid silver. "Well, I guess I'm just going to have to tell people I was touched by the Lord. Now, let's go for a quiet walk."

It took just moments for him to untie me and help me to my feet. I stood, swaying for a moment until I got my balance back. I was limping, but I could walk. Preston put his hand on my arm and led me into the sanctuary.

Ofelia was sitting on the front pew. She got up and put her arms around Preston, followed by a full-contact kiss.

He spun her around and ran his hands inside her blouse, caressing her breasts. Ofelia responded by rubbing the front of his pants. "How long before he reacts?" Ofelia asked.

"Long enough," Preston murmured. "Did you lock the doors?"

"Oh, yes," she purred. "How can I be a helpmeet unto you?"

Yeah. It went downhill from there.

Once they were presentable again, Preston clapped me on the shoulder and said, "As much as Ofelia enjoyed having an audience, I'm afraid I can't have any witnesses. So, you don't remember any of what she and I just did. You know nothing of our relationship. You and I have never spoken. Your reasons for killing Harper are all your own. If you survive and are captured by the authorities, you will confess and say you acted alone. Now, remember your rage, take your sword, and carry out your mission. Think of nothing else until Harper is dead."

Everything, even the pain in my jaw and ankle, faded under the sudden rush of overwhelming anger. I had to kill Harper, and to do that, I needed Kindness. I held out my hand and called.

The sword didn't respond.

I called again, harder. Still no response. I looked at Preston and said, "Something's wrong. I need to find Kindness."

"Quite alright, my boy." Preston looked over his shoulder at Ofelia and asked, "Beloved, where did you hide David's sword? He has business to attend to."

Ofelia fetched the gun bag from under one of the pews. "You sure about this? Handing him that giant dat-gum sword seems a mite risky."

"David knows what he needs to do. Don't you, David?" He passed the bag to me and I nodded as I slung it over my shoulder.

"Now, beloved, be a dear and show David to shelter two? I don't want him getting lost. I'd do it myself, but Rusty and I have an armed standoff to defuse. You should come join us after you get David on his way. No sense risking becoming collateral damage."

"Of course, Brother Preston."

While Ofelia unlocked the sanctuary doors, Preston folded his hands together and said, "Remember what the Lord has commanded: 'So it shall be a reproach and a taunt, an instruction and an astonishment unto the nations that are round about thee, when I shall execute judgments in thee in anger and in fury and in furious rebukes.' Go, my son. Deliver this teaching to Harper and the poor, lost sheep she has led astray."

Ofelia held the door open for me. I stepped through and followed her down the hall.

Chapter Thirty-Eight

Reunions

Outside, the air was sweet and the morning sky blazed with light. This part of living in Oklahoma I loved. Especially out here, away from the cities. Everything smelled of good, clean earth and growing things. I took a breath and, for a moment, the rage Preston had created in me faded. So did my conviction Preston was the one to believe around here. I grabbed at that realization, trying to hold on to it.

The next moment, the rage was back, just as strong as ever. I shook off the doubts and kept walking.

The entrances to the tornado shelters were squat, blocky huts of reinforced concrete, fronted with steel security doors. Ofelia pointed me toward the correct one and ran back to the church offices. I kept walking.

The door wasn't even locked. What was the point of retreating to a safe haven if you were going to leave the door open?

It didn't matter. I brushed the thought aside and made my way down the stairs. I could hear people singing *That Old Rugged Cross*. Who sang hymns while planning kidnapping and murder?

It didn't matter. I could hear Harper's laugh coming from somewhere near the door. No one even noticed when I cracked the door open.

Kindness slipped soundlessly out of the gun bag, but her balance was off. She twisted and lurched in my grip, threatening to slip from my fingers. I rested the blade's tip on the floor and got a better grip. This time the blade didn't move.

Shock and awe are overused words, but that was the effect I wanted. Kill Harper first, as fast as possible, and hope the carnage shocked the onlookers into immobility. Then deal with the rest. Cunning plan firmly in mind, I shoved the door open and stalked inside.

Harper was sitting with her back to the door, singing along with the gathered residents. Good. She was defenseless. I charged, bringing Kindness up for a killing thrust.

At the last moment, Kindness twisted in my hand. Instead of going through Harper's heart, the sword lodged just below her right collarbone. She screamed, arching her back and grabbing at the wound. I pulled the sword free, setting my feet for a second thrust.

A metal cane slashed down on my wrist, knocking Kindness out of my hand. Another blow cracked across the back of my skull.

I grabbed the nearest figure by the shirt collar and hurled whoever it was behind me. Shouts and curses told me I'd hit someone. I got my hand around her throat...

Hands grabbed me, pulling me away from Harper. I punched, kicked, and flailed about, heedless of who I was pummeling. Another cane hooked around my ankle, yanking my foot out from under me and pitching me to the side.

I fell against someone in a Bermuda shirt and hung on to keep from falling. Once I had my balance again, I repaid my savior by headbutting him.

K shoved herself between two retirees, shouting "Get clear! Everyone, clear!"

Most of the hands gripping me fell away. I shook off the rest and looked up at K, snarling. "You should have run when you had the chance!"

She crooked her finger, beckoning me to her. "Come on, big boy! Come and get me!"

Rage won out over common sense. I charged at her.

K lunged forward and punched me in the stomach. A massive jolt of electricity ripped through me, knocking me to the floor. I pushed myself up for a moment. She tapped me on the shoulder, sending another lightning bolt ripping through me.

I rolled away, but not far enough. She hit me one more time. It wasn't as strong as the first two, but it was enough. All I could do was gasp for air as Harper approached.

She knelt next to me, shaking her head. I tried again to summon Kindness, and again the sword ignored me. Her hilt was only five feet away, but it might as well have been on Mars.

Harper touched my head. "Lord, foul magic has clouded this man's mind. His free will is a blessing from You, and we beseech You to set him free again. We ask this in the blessed name of Jesus, amen."

Preston's spell shattered. The rage and false memories vanished, snuffed out like a candle flame. I looked around and asked, "Did I hurt anyone?"

"Yes and no," Harper said. "We need to talk, but first, I think everyone will feel better if we make sure you can't hurt anyone else. Do you mind?"

"Not at all." I held my arms out in front of me. "Do what you need to do."

I wound up with close to a dozen belts securing my arms and several men's ties knotted around my ankles. Eight senior men lined up behind me. Judging by their expressions, they were ready to practice more Cane Fu on my ass if I moved wrong.

On the good side, the rage was gone. I remembered it, but nothing else.

Vernon knelt down next to me. "Missing a hand, already had the crap kicked out of you a few times today, and it still took a hell of a pounding to bring you down. I might not like you, son, but you're a tough SOB, I'll give you that much."

"I...have a few advantages. Problem is, my mind is just as vulnerable as anyone else's."

"Don't worry, you didn't do any permanent damage." He waved at the guys circled around me. "Now, are you still feeling murderous? The boys would be glad to bang some sense into you if it would help."

"I don't know, and that's the truth. Better keep me restrained just in case. Can you help me into a chair?"

"Certainly can."

It actually took Vernon and three other guys to get me up and into a chair. Once I was settled, I nodded at the door and said, "You should probably bar that door. I may not be the last person sent to kill Harper. And if there's a security camera down here, disable it."

"Who used the mind-control spell on you?" Harper took a seat just out of lunging range. She was pale and had safety pins holding her blood-stained shirt together, but the wound was gone. "I'm pretty sure I know, but I want to hear it."

"Preston. He didn't so much mind control me as mess with my memories. From what I could tell, it's similar to a spell a friend of mine uses called *Retcon*. He told me what he wanted me to remember and my memory adjusted. He knew enough about how his powers work to produce specific results and to wipe himself from my memory. My guess is he's been practicing for a while."

"That...would explain a number of things," Harper said. "How did you get captured?"

"I was doing pretty well. I had Aparna and we were almost to the front gate. I was walking on the grass, trying to hide from Rusty's friends, and I stepped on one of those leg traps. I thought it broke my ankle."

"It did," Harper said. "I took care of it when I fixed your concussion. I also fixed some nasty electrical burns."

"Some of that was Ofelia, some was Rusty. I know he beat the snot out of me while I was tied up. I just don't know why he was so vicious about it."

K raised her hand. "A few of the burns were me. Sorry for zapping you. I meant to do that, though."

"No problem," I said. "What in blazes did you use, anyway?"

"The disposable cameras I took from the shop and couple of paper clips. Didn't think they'd work terribly well, but I'm glad I was wrong."

I had to laugh. "Man, the Llewellyns are going to like you."

256

Harper smiled at that, but the smile vanished as she leaned forward. "I hate to be a wet blanket here, but I have to ask if you learned anything about what in God's green Earth Preston is trying to accomplish."

"Oh, yes." I sighed, shaking my head. "Preston and Ofelia want you dead so they can take over the church. K, they want you dead, too. Apparently, you know too much."

K snorted. "And here I thought everybody liked me."

Harper said, "Why send you to kill me? They have plenty of guns, why not just shoot me in the head?"

"Because if I did it, they'd have a dead suspect who had motive, method, and opportunity. They'd be off the hook. Preston's plan was for me to kill you and Grace. He's already conditioned Vernon to shoot me when Grace dies. Vernon is supposed to come out the hero and get a huge flood of sympathy. Since Manya has no blood relationship to Aparna and my parents will be stigmatized by my murderous rampage, Vernon will also get to keep custody of Aparna."

Grace shot out of her seat. "That's it. I'm gonna' shove my fist up his ass, grab his lying tongue, and snap him inside-out like an old sock."

"I might just join you," Harper muttered. She cleared her throat and took a deep breath. "Let me see if I can guess the rest. Preston weeps and rends his clothes on national television, lamenting my death and promising to see our vision for the church realized. He takes over and turns this tragedy into a blessing from God, incidentally becoming obscenely wealthy in the process. Did I miss anything?"

"I think that covers it."

Harper buried her face in her hands a moment, then looked up, wide-eyed. "Vernon, I have to ask you to do something for me."

"Anything, sister."

"I need you to put your hands on your head. Gunny, will you please search Vernon for weapons?"

"God have mercy," Vernon whispered. He turned around and did as Harper asked. His hands shook, but he held still while a man with a high-and-tight military-issue buzz cut and a perpetual scowl patted him down.

"Jackpot." Gunny pulled a Walther PPK from the back of Vernon's shorts. He set it aside and kept looking. I was glad he did; a moment later he came up with a .38 revolver in an ankle holster.

Harper said, "Vernon, are these your guns?"

"No," Gunny interjected. "They belonged to Jenny Harris, Lord bless her. She asked me to take her to the range with them after Lou passed away. I thought her daughter took them when they cleaned out her apartment."

"Like Gunny said, those aren't mine." Vernon sat down and took Grace's hands. "I got a Ruger Blackhawk, but it's locked in Rusty's gun safe. I've never seen those before. I didn't even know I was carrying them."

"I believe you," Harper said. "I think you've confirmed what David said. Preston can make us believe anything he wants. Christ's power can disrupt that bondage, but there's no reason to think I'd be immune to it."

"True." I thought for a moment. "He may be burning himself out, though. He pushed himself hard controlling me. It seemed to exhaust him, and his eyes turned solid silver."

"Like in that *Star Trek* episode?"

"Pretty much."

Harper nodded, then asked, "So, what does that mean?"

"As I understand it, he may be drawing on his own life energy to power his magic. I've done it myself. The last time, Rose implied I could burn out part of my brain if I kept it up. I don't actually know anything beyond that."

"Hmm." Harper nodded. "Maybe we'll get lucky and he'll blow a fuse or something. I'm not going to count on it, though. That still leaves the question of what to do."

I sighed and leaned back in the chair. "Well, all of my ideas have blown up in my face, so I'm open to suggestions."

Gunny said, "Sister Harper, I don't understand most of what you two have been talking about, but I do understand that Preston wants you dead. Anything you need, up to and including hospitalizing that rat bastard, I am at your disposal."

Harper said, "Thank you, Gunny, but I think a non-violent solution would be best."

"Of course, sister, but we can't just roll over and let them do this." He punctuated his comments by pounding his fist against his open palm.

I said, "Whatever we do, we need to do it soon. Preston has to know I failed by now. He's going to be working on a backup plan. We need to move before he puts it in place."

Harper stood up. "Agreed. And the first thing we're going to do is fix you. Anyone have their phone with them?"

A dozen people raised their hands. One of the women said, "We still don't have any signal, sister, and Rusty obviously isn't going to fix that."

"I know. But a hundred yards from here, it's a different story. Get your phones out. I want video of this." Harper nodded to the guys surrounding me. "Get him loose. I'll also need the bandage off his arm."

Despite their grumbled reservations, the guys complied. K cut the bandages off my arm, then stepped back with a loud, "Holy crap!"

Gleaming white spikes of bone poked out of the stump, with tendrils of pinkish-white tissue clinging to them. A haze of something—capillaries, maybe?—covered the exposed flesh of the stump.

Regeneration is damn creepy. And a bit gross.

"Well, that's...interesting." Harper pulled her chair closer to me and took my forearm between her hands. "I'd love to see how that progresses, but we don't have time for it. I hope you have no objection?"

258

"None whatsoever. My cover is blown anyway."

"Thank you. Alright, everyone. Lights, camera, action!" Harper waited for the cameras, then bowed her head.

"Lord, I thank You for this gift and pray that I may ever use it to Your purpose and glory. Now I must ask more than I have ever before. I pray you bless this man, heal him, make him whole again. In Christ's name we pray, amen."

And my hand was back.

More than that, I was clear-headed, pumped up, and hard of purpose. I nodded to Harper and said, "Thank you. I'm in your debt for this."

"And that debt can be paid in lives," Harper replied. "Nobody dies to-day. I want your solemn oath, David."

Gunny snorted. "What's a Godless heathen like him going to swear on? The nearest tree?"

"This," I said. I held out my hand, and Kindness leaped across the room. I saluted Harper with the blade, then ran my left palm along the edge. "I swear on my blade and the blood that binds it to me, when facing Preston, I will harm none except to prevent greater harm, and will kill only to preserve life, until your words or your death release me."

Harper blinked. "I...would have been satisfied with 'I promise'."

"What can I say? The old gods love drama and spectacle." I looked around the room. "I want to check in with my friends before we do this. Does anyone have a phone that works?"

Chapter Thirty-Nine

Harper's Army

One woman in the back of the room raised her hand. "I've got one bar, mostly. I tried to call my daughter earlier, but the connection kept dropping."

Kindness's scabbard had appeared when I called her to my hand. I sheathed the sword and set her on a chair. "That's enough to work with. Do you mind if I make a call? I'll pay you for the long-distance charges."

She smirked as she handed the phone to me. "Sonny, just because I live like a church mouse don't mean I'm poor as one. Make your call."

"Thank you, ma'am. Much appreciated." I moved a half-finished jigsaw puzzle to the side and climbed up on one of the tables, holding the phone above me. Three dots. I turned on the speaker and dialed.

"Nadia's phone, this is Geneva. May I take a message?"

I let out the breath I hadn't realized I'd been holding. "Geneva, this is David Fraser. I'm on the speaker so I can get signal, so this is a public conversation. I need to find out how Rose is doing, and I was hoping Nadia would ask Eric to find out for me. Is that something you can help me do?"

"Of course." Geneva managed to sound like she'd been expecting me to call. "Just to be safe, though, I have to ask if you are intending to use her to get help from Aerin or Angus."

I bit back my first answer and went with, "No, but since you mentioned it, are they available?"

"No. Angus is meeting with a client and Aerin is responding to a Ferrari vs. woolly mammoth accident on Highway 1 up by Vandenberg. She pulled flight crew duty today, so you *really* don't want to interrupt her. The flight crew gets all the good trauma calls."

"Well, with Aerin along, I'm sure the folks in the Ferrari will be fine."

"Oh, no, the driver's pretty much a drippy bag of chunky salsa. Aerin's crew is trying to save the mammoth. Those things are damn rare, obviously, and the National Zoo wants it for their new breeding program."

Honestly, I didn't have any idea how I should respond. Time to punt. "Well, don't worry, I really am just trying to reach Nadia."

"Thank you for understanding. To begin with, please convince me the people with you are trustworthy and you are not under duress."

"Dark Elves look great in a hot tub."

"We look great all the time. What is the level of urgency?"

"Someone has my daughter."

"Thank you. Eric received a summons home two hours ago. Nadia is with him. She left a message spell running in case someone needed to reach her, but it's limited to one use and is a bit tricky to trigger. Are you ready to begin?"

I nodded, even though she couldn't see it. "Yes."

"This is going to sound like a demented game of Twister, but you have to follow these directions precisely. The instructions begin now. Put the pinky of your right hand in your right nostril and your right thumb in your right ear canal."

I switched hands with the phone and complied. "Done."

"Hook your right ankle behind your left knee."

"Done."

"This is the final step. Say nothing until the instructions are complete. You will need to recite the most famous three-word command ever given to an alien robot in a classic science-fiction movie. You will then feel like you are in a giant wind tunnel. It lasts about three seconds, and you can say one word. I know it's not much, but the message has a long way to travel. This completes the instructions."

One word? I opened my mouth to ask a question, then thought better of it. That might result in miscasting the spell. For several long seconds, it seemed impossible to do this in one word. Then I thought of a dozen that would sort of work, but not well.

'Help' and 'Attack' were out. The thought of hundreds of casualties didn't sit well. I didn't want to see anyone, even Rusty's buddies, getting hurt.

Then again...

There's an old proverb among Dragons that states, 'Power needs no translation.' Everyone understands it—even a bunch of shaved monkeys with deer rifles.

So let's make sure they get the message.

I smiled and said, *"Klaatu barada nikto!"*

A small cyclone erupted in the air, creating a tunnel of wind and sheet lightning. I could see someone looking back at me from the far end. It was too far to see their face, but I recognized Nadia's bright magenta hair. I waved and shouted, "Havoc!"

The word echoed and re-echoed through the tunnel. Nadia gave me a thumbs-up, and the tunnel vanished.

"That sounded as though you were successful, David. Is there anything else I can do to assist you?"

I untangled myself and got both feet firmly on the table. "Just one more thing. There's a young lady here who is looking for a Dread Pirate to call her own. You know-tall, dark, mysterious, good with a sword. I thought Auntie Josephine would be able to help her out. Would you ask-"

"Leave it to me. I am a magnificent yenta. What is the young lady's name?"

I looked at K and nodded, pointing to the phone. She came over to the table and called out, "I, uh, I go by K. The letter K. Just that. I don't use my birth name any more."

"Neither do I. What does the 'K' stand for?"

"Kaitlyn."

"Pleased to meet you, K. My name is Geneva Rolling Thunder. I only have one question for you. What couple, real or fictional, do you most want your ideal relationship to be like?"

K blushed but answered. "Burt and Heather Gummer from *Tremors,* crossed with Gomez and Morticia Addams."

"That sounds wonderful." Geneva collected K's cell phone number, then added, "I should have something for you in a few hours. David, good luck. Fight well and earn victory."

"Thank you. I'll take all the good wishes I can get." I ended the call and hopped off the table.

Harper did not look happy. "You could only send one word, and you picked 'havoc'? As in, 'let slip the dogs of war'? You do know what Shakespeare was calling for in that little speech, don't you?"

I nodded. "Yes. Rose and I had discussed this before. It will tell her I'm admitting she was right, and that she should go with her original plan."

"And what was her original plan?"

"Fire isn't the only thing Dragons can breathe. One of the other options is Happy Gas. It causes euphoria and mild hallucinations for about half an hour. A handful of Dragons could make every living thing on or around the property high as a kite."

"Well, that's not bad...I guess." Harper didn't sound convinced. "What about the people who actually took your daughter? Is she going to let them get stoned and sleep it off? Or does she have something else in mind for them?"

"I have something in mind for them," I said. "And before you ask, 'What they are, yet I know not: but they shall be the terrors of the earth'."

A rush of wind cut off Harper's reply. The cyclone message tunnel reopened, strong enough to knock over the table I'd been standing on and blow two shelves of books off the wall. A heavy leather pouch flew out of the middle of the maelstrom. I caught it out of reflex, then dropped it. The whole thing was searing hot, scorched black and smoking in places. By the time I looked up again, the tunnel had vanished.

K snapped the pliers on a multitool open and passed it to me. "I really hope that's not just a picture of your wife's boobs."

"Nah, that she'd make a production of." I picked the bag up and waved it around, blowing on it until I could touch the thongs tying it closed. At least the searing heat had burned through the thong enough for me to snap the knots with minimal effort.

A slave bracelet connected by a chain to a dragon-winged collar slithered out of the bag. It was the same type of instant-armor item Eric had given Nadia. The kind only Dragonbound could wear.

The other item in the pouch was a folded piece of slightly scorched parchment. I set the bracelet aside and opened the parchment.

I'm fine. We'll be there soon. The Lairkeeper's Array was created by my grandmother. It hasn't been used since her time. Bear it well, until I see you again.
> *Rose*

Even through the reek of smoke and burnt leather, the note smelled like her. I inhaled, savoring the scent. For a moment, our minds brushed together...

I gasped, clutching at my head, stunned by what I'd seen through Rose's eyes.

Dragons. Row upon row, standing at attention in armor that glowed like molten gold. Above them, two five-by-five formations practiced ground attack drills. When the front ranks exhausted their breath weapons, they climbed and braked, allowing the following flights to pass beneath them and giving the new leading ranks a clear field of fire. The exhausted Dragons settled in to the rear rank, moving up while their weapons recharged.

They could sustain this attack for hours if needed, laying down strips of fire that extended for miles. They could also carpet a confined area, triggering a Dresden-like firestorm that could rage for days.

A rush of abject horror washed over me, breaking my connection to Rose's mind. The acceptance was still there, though, and she flooded it with calm feelings.

Fine, I'd trust that she wasn't planning on mass murder. I shook my head and managed a weak smile. "Sorry. I'm...just missing my wife. Got a little emotional reading this note."

"Glad to see romance isn't dead." K picked up the bracelet. "So, what's this? Bondage equipment for Harry Potter fans?"

"Oh, great, thanks for the image."

"This is never going to fit you." K slipped her hand into the bracelet. It contracted as soon as she got it on, then slithered off her hand.

"I've seen one of these before. I don't think we'll have any problems." As soon as I picked it up, the bracelet and collar popped open. The claw tips fit my fingers perfectly. I closed the bracelet around my wrist and locked the collar into place.

The collar sent an electric pulse zinging through me and into the brace-let. Just as Nadia's had done when she first donned it, the assembly en-veloped me in armor.

Nadia's armor was an Elven mix of chain, plate, and scale. Mine was half-plate over chain. The armor looked familiar, and it took a moment to place it—it looked identical to the *Valkyrja* armor Tony Doyle was wearing the last time I saw him. The only difference was the color. His had been gold and scarlet, this was matte black.

I clenched my fists, curling my arms up as though lifting weights. The armor was liquid smooth, no tension or binding inhibiting my movements. Drawing Kindness shouldn't be an issue, so I picked her up, intending to sheathe her across my back.

Another jolt went through me, rattling my teeth. Without thought or intent, my right hand snatched the blade from the scabbard. Tiny, shadow-clad chains emerged from the armor and wrapped around the sword's hilt, integrating the sword and the armor into a single unit.

No. More than that. Kindness and the armor recognized each other and... rejoiced. They weren't just a matched set; they were long-separated lovers. And now they were reunited.

They were a part of Rose and me now, woven into the acceptance itself. Dragon magic gave them power, while Human valor gave them purpose. Only Dragonbound could use either—and they *wanted* to be used.

I dropped into *seiza*, bowed, and began one of the *iaijitsu katas* I'd learned years ago at the Japan House. The forms flowed together with a speed and precision I'd never achieved before.

When I finished the *kata*, Kindness refused to stop. This time, the *kata* was from the Reversed Hand school of *kenjitsu*. I'd never mastered this one; hell, I barely remembered it. But Kindness knew it well, and she guided me through it with flawless grace.

As I moved, the armor changed again. Color, this time. The chain glis-tened silver now, while the plate overlaying it was the same metallic purple as Rose's scales.

Kindness changed as well. Draconic symbols made of purple fire glowed along the length of the blade, moving and changing endlessly. And she was singing.

It was soft and distant, but it was there, right at the edge of my hearing. There were no words—at least, no human words—but I knew the meaning. She was singing of duty, of joy, of bloodshed, and of love.

Despite all that was happening, I had to take a moment for sheer geeky excitement. Growing up, I'd devoured Moorecock's *Elric* stories. Now, I had a runesword of my own.

Hopefully, our relationship would turn out better than Elric and Stormbringer's did.

I sheathed Kindness and turned to Harper. As I did, the visor on my helm snapped up, then the entire helm folded back into the armor. A moment later, both the armor and Kindness vanished, becoming a silver wristcuff engraved with tiny, intricate knotwork.

They would be back if I needed them.

Harper took my hand, turning it so she could look at the wristcuff. "That's amazing," she said. "Do you know Ephesians 6:11?"

"That's the one about putting on the whole armor of God, right? I may not be a believer any more, but I remember that one from Sunday School."

"You should. That one's easy." Harper looked up and clenched her hands over her heart. "I know it's talking about spiritual preparedness, not actual armor, but after seeing your...whatever that is..." She paused to blink several times and wipe a tear off her cheek. "...I *really* would not mind putting on a full set of the *bullet-proof* armor of God."

"Then I'll walk in front of you," I said. "Soaking up bullets is what meat shields do."

Gunny stepped forward. "I'll walk in front of you too, sister." He donned a baseball cap emblazoned with the words 'Purple Heart' over the Marine Corps emblem. "I doubt any of these punk kids have the stones to try anything, anyway."

Grace moved next to Harper as well, pulling her phone out of her purse. "Come on, folks! Cameras on! Film the whole thing! That's why your grandkids bought you these things, right? Well, time for some live-streaming content!"

One fellow with a walker snorted. "Live-streaming? Isn't that what I take those damn pills for?" Nevertheless, he pulled a brand-new phone out of his pocket as well.

Grace flitted around for a few moments, answering questions and helping people get set up. I was impressed, to be honest. I snagged her and asked, "How did you learn so much about smartphones?"

She grinned. "Well, young man, you're not the only one who knows about Wired and C-Net and WikiHow. There is no way I'm going to let my granddaughter know more than me about this stuff. With all this sexting and Internet predators, 'be prepared' isn't just for Boy Scouts anymore."

That was...totally understandable. I nodded and said, "I'm with you there."

She chuckled and patted my hand before rushing off to help someone else. I watched her for a moment and realized I was smiling. For the first time since all this started, I felt good—authentically *good*—about Grace and Vernon being part of Aparna's life.

Blessed Mother...did I just show mature adult behavior and parenting skills?

The other half of me smirked and nodded. *Yep. You just acted like a father. Might as well pick out a new recliner and learn to Dad Dance.*

Loud barks echoed off the walls, and harsh, insistent scratching noises came from the front door. It startled me more than I want to admit, but it also saved me from more embarrassing internal dialog.

Harper got out of her chair. "It's Oreo. Someone let him in." Even though she sounded confident, she stayed off to the side so she couldn't be seen when the door opened.

Orion dived inside, turned around, and threw his weight against the inside of the door, bellowing "Shut it, shut it!"

The guys at the door didn't ask questions; they just threw themselves into it and held the door until someone could wedge a steel chair under the doorknob.

"Right, thanks mates." Orion looked around the room for me. "Oy, greebo, whatever shite you're gonna' pull out'a yer arse to fix this Charlie Foxtrot, y'need to shift it, now. Preston's makin' as much sense as sitting on the bottom floor of a two-story outhouse, but the crowd is eating it up."

"What?" Harper stared, open-mouthed. "Since when have you been able to talk?"

Orion cocked his head to the side. "Since always, darlin'. Sorry for snowin' you, Harper, but I had good reason. We can talk later if y' want."

"I think I do," Harper muttered. "Is there anything else I need to know?"

"Yeah. The name's Orion, not Oreo. Collar's a good bit worn, so I don't blame you for getting it wrong."

"Would you like a new one?"

"Bugger me, no. It's all I have left of home."

"I don't mean to be rude, but we do have some business to attend to." I grabbed the handle for the front door and pulled it open. "Let's end this."

Harper held up her hand. "I just have one question first." She looked at Orion and asked, "Can any of the other animals living here talk? If I go out to the barn, am I going to find the alpacas...I don't know...arguing philosophy, maybe, or having a poetry slam?"

Orion nodded. "Yeah, but they only talk philosophy on special occasions. Like that 'Harvest Hayride' thing last year."

"Really?" Harper's eyebrows went up. "What was so special about the hayride?"

Orion smiled, tongue lolling out the side of his mouth. "Because it gave them a chance to put Descartes before the horses."

Harper buried her face in her hands. "I had to ask."

Chapter Forty

Power in the Blood

We assembled around Harper, phones out and rolling video. Now that we were above ground, everyone had a good signal, and they were spreading the word.

We didn't have far to walk. On our right, the assorted militia types were gathered on the lawn between us and the parking lot, out of sight of the police. On our left, Preston was standing with his arms upraised, speaking in urgent, measured tones. Ofelia and Rusty flanked him on either side.

The militia had our little band outnumbered, but looking at them, I had to wonder if that was going to be a problem. Even from a distance, they didn't look right.

They weren't moving, just staring straight ahead as Preston held forth. Thankfully, whatever magic he was using kept them from responding and warning him we were there.

His voice sounded the way it had when he used his spell on me—measured, resonant, and powerful. "I want you all to remember we assembled here intent on non-violence. Remember that we have done nothing despite repeated provocations. Remember that those who want to destroy us have already killed our beloved sister in Christ, Harper Wren..."

"Sorry to disappoint you, Preston, but I'm very much alive."

Rusty and Ofelia whipped around to stare at her, but Preston remained unmoved. The mesmerized crowd didn't react at all.

Harper pushed Gunny and me to the side. "Preston, you're fired! You too, Rusty. Ofelia, you're twice as fired as you were last night. Turn in your keys and badges. Your final paychecks will be held until you do. As for the rest of you, this is private property and I am the owner. You all have one hour to break down your campsites and leave. If you are still here after that, you will be arrested for trespassing. Any questions?"

"It shouldn't be your personal property in the first place," Ofelia said. "It should belong to the congregation!"

"When you've built your own church up out of nothing, you can make that decision. Until then…" She paused for a moment, then snarled, teeth bared and eyes flashing. "…get the fuck off my land!"

For a long moment, no one moved. Everyone was staring at Harper.

Preston finally turned to face her. His cheeks and lips were sunken, drawn tight and parchment-thin against the bone. Wisps of turbulent silver fire drifted from his mouth and finger-tips. "That's no language for a lady," he hissed.

Ofelia's eyes widened. She reached for Preston's hand, then drew back. "Oh, my love…what's happening to you?"

"He's using too much of his life energy," I called out. "Preston, just stand down. I know someone who may be able to help you, but you can't use any more magic! You have someone who loves you, who wants to spend her life with you. Don't throw that away."

Ofelia glared at me but took Preston's hand. "He's right, Preston. It's over. Let him help you, and we can go build a ministry of our own. Together. Just you and me."

Preston took her other hand. "Build a ministry? Together? Is…is that what you want?"

Ofelia nodded, trying to smile. "Anything to be with you. We don't need a big church. We…we can travel around. Do tent revivals. Doesn't that sound good? Spending our days preaching and singing the Lord's praises. Together."

"Singing…together." Preston sank to his knees, wrapping his arms around Ofelia's waist. "Will you sing with me?"

Ofelia stroked his hair. "Of course. Anything you want."

"Just sing with me." Holding tight to her, he began rocking back and forth, singing. His voice was rough and off-key, but earnest nonetheless.

> *"Would you be free from the burden of sin?*
> *There's power in the blood, power in the blood"*

Ofelia joined him, her voice clear and firm.

> *"Would you o'er evil a victory win?*
> *There's wonderful power in the blood!"*

Preston took Ofelia's hands between his own. She smiled at him as she sang—and trickles of blood ran out of her ears, nose, and eyes.

> *"There is power, power, wonder-working power*
> *In the blood of the Lamb…"*

Ofelia went from singing to shrieking as she noticed the flow of blood down her arms and chest. She tried to pull away, but Preston's grip was like iron.

I didn't need to see any more to know where this was going. I charged, shouting, "Ofelia, run!"

Preston waved his hand, and a bolt of silver fire blew a crater in the ground in front of me. The blast sent me sprawling. When I stopped rolling, I shook my head and clambered back to my feet.

Preston put his hands on either side of Ofelia's face. She shivered, trying to pull away, but couldn't get loose. He smiled and kept singing,

> *"There is power, power, wonder-working power*
> *In the precious blood of the Lamb!"*

Ofelia managed one final scream. The skin on her arms and hands ruptured, releasing coils of robin's-egg-blue...something. It was thick, like old syrup or half-set gelatin, and Preston absorbed it in a heartbeat.

Ofelia stood for a moment, staring straight ahead, eyes wide and mouth frozen open in a shriek of terror and pain. Preston opened his hands, and Ofelia collapsed into a heap of clothes filled with fine, gritty black ash.

"Bastard!" Rusty threw himself at Preston and landed a ferocious haymaker right in the family jewels. For a moment, Preston just stood there openmouthed, eyes wide and staring. Then he clawed Rusty open from crotch to sternum.

I backed up, looking over my shoulder at Harper. "Run," I said. "Get these people out of here."

"I'm not leaving," she replied. "I won't let him-"

"Harper! That's not Preston anymore!" I pointed at the ash-filled pile of clothes that used to be Ofelia. "I've seen something like this before. He's using people's life energy as fuel. Now, get out of here!"

"What about you? You're in just as much danger as I am."

I nodded. "I know. But I'm a Hero. Dying so others can live is in the job description."

Rusty's screams cut off Harper's response. Preston held him by the neck, a foot off the ground. Just as he had done to Ofelia, Preston was pulling coils of blue energy out of Rusty and absorbing them. In seconds, Rusty also dissolved into empty clothes and gritty black ash.

Preston licked bits of Ofelia and Rusty off his hand and shivered. "Whooo-eee! Now that's a plate of barbecue."

Gunny unleashed a stream of profanity and pulled a pistol from the back of his pants. Faster than I would have believed possible, he emptied the magazine, popped in a full one, and went through it as well. Thirty rounds in a little over twenty seconds.

His aim was good, too; he hit Preston center mass two dozen times—and did nothing. Preston looked startled at first, but by the time the second magazine was empty he was laughing.

"Well, ain't that a giant bag of dick tips..." Gunny popped his last magazine in and holstered his pistol. "Anyone else got any bright ideas?"

Preston smirked and flicked his fingers as though shooing flies away. "Go away. Run! I don't need your scraps of life when I have the abundance God has set before me." He turned back to face the crowd of mesmerized rednecks. "Lord, bless this thy bounty to the nourishment of our bodies..."

Harper stepped forward, bowing her head. "Lord, hear my prayer in this, our hour of need. As the centurion in Capernaum believed in the authority of Jesus' name and word, so do we believe. These people are afflicted by an unholy power, and we plead for their deliverance!"

Preston whipped around. "Stop that!"

I stepped in front of Harper. "Keep going! If he's angry, it's working."

Harper dropped to her knees. "Lord, let not their tongues and minds be stilled! Return them to health and clear their minds of this evil magic! In the name of Christ Jesus our Lord, amen!"

She threw her head back and her arms wide. In the same moment, all the rednecks staggered to the side or dropped, holding their heads. Harper swayed a moment, then fell backward.

"Harlot!" Preston pointed at Harper's unmoving form, his hand wreathed in silver fire. He had her, dead-bang, and he knew it. As tight and desiccated as his skin was, he still managed a gleeful smile...

...which vanished when the bolt hit my shield and bounced off, blowing a hole in the turf twenty feet away.

It was a moment before I realized the armor had activated itself. More than that, it had given me a large *hoplon*-style shield and moved me in front of Harper without me intentionally doing anything.

Cool! Jedi armor!

Kindness had changed, too. Instead of being a hefty two-handed sword, she was one of the katana-like Drow swords Angus used. She had the curve of a katana, but with a saber's tip. The spine extended halfway down the blade; from there to the tip, the back was as sharp as the front.

I gave her a flourish to get used to the balance, and resisted the urge to smack the flat of the blade against the shield. It was an old sword-and-board habit from my stick-jock days in the Society. Kindness was not rattan.

Preston sneered. "A sword? Really? Didn't you notice that I'm bullet-proof, you musclebound ignoramus?"

"We'll see about that," shouted one of the rednecks. "Smoke that...thing!"

I rushed back to Harper's side and dropped to one knee, holding the shield in front of us. As soon as I did, the shield changed to a Roman *scutum* with a thick mail curtain trailing from the bottom edge—coverage against stray rounds, I guessed.

Once again, the redneck militia went with throwing all the lead they could, as fast as they could. I swear the cacophony of gun shots must have been heard in Tulsa. When it ended, I counted to five before peering around the shield.

Preston was still standing.

He made a grand show of brushing himself off, grinning from ear to ear. When he finished, he chuckled, and silver fire blossomed in his hands.

"Laugh this off, asshole." A heavyset man with an NRA cap put a high-caliber double-barreled rifle to his shoulder. Even with his mass, he was leaning forward and bracing himself with his back foot. It had to be Bo Breen and his infamous double rifle. I ducked again.

The report was a thunderclap that put all the previous gunshots to shame. Preston flew into view on my left, greenish-black blood streaking his crisp white shirt. He bounced once and rolled to his feet with a snarl, eyes now solid, burning red.

He unleashed a massive bolt of silver fire. It left a hole the size of a soccer ball clean through Bo Breen's chest and killed three more guys standing behind him.

That was all it took; the rednecks took off running. Hopefully the residents were running, too.

Preston didn't chase them. He was focused on Bo Breen's corpse, so much so he didn't even look at me until I shield-bashed him across the face.

He staggered away, holding his nose. "You can't do that to me," he howled. "I'm invincible!"

I laughed and gave him the only response possible. "You're a loony."

"How dare you free them from the ecstasy of the Lord?" Preston threw another bolt of silver fire at me, and again the shield sent it ricocheting into the ground. He brushed dirt off his suit and hissed, "I'm going to kill you with my bare hands!"

The shield vanished as I changed to *waki-gamae* stance. All Preston could see of Kindness was her hilt; I felt her balance change as the blade lengthened from a *katana* to a *tachi*.

Preston's eyes grew brighter. "What was that? I smell power—incredible power! What do you have?" He crept closer, sniffing the air until he focused on me. "The armor...the sword...they *reek* of power!"

He stalked closer, silver fire dancing along his arms. "I'm so hungry...you don't deserve so much power. You'd just squander it. Give it to me." His voice hardened. "I must have those items! Give them to me or die!"

I laughed, shaking my head. "*Molon labe.*"

His snarl vanished. "What?"

"Oh, good grief... Didn't you take history in school? Leonidas at the battle of Thermopylae?"

"Pagan sodomites have nothing to teach me," he sneered.

"Oh, so you're already an expert on Pagan sodomy, then? Fair enough. It means, 'come and take them,' bitch."

Preston howled and brought his hands together, unleashing a massive bolt right at me.

The shield reappeared and deflected most of it, but it still knocked me flying. I hit the ground hard, and Kindness bounced out of my hand.

"Now, boy, just lie still so I can kill you." He stopped a good twenty feet away from me, letting the silver fire play between his fingers. "Didn't anyone ever tell you swords don't work at a distance?"

I grinned at him. "Wanna' bet?"

Kindness leaped to my hand, changing into a big two-hander again. This time she had *three* blades.

I aimed her at Preston and triggered the two side blades. With a loud *whoosh* and trails of smoke, the rocket-blades shot across the space between us, striking Preston's chest and abdomen. They tore through him, ripping away chunks the size of grapefruit and knocking him a good fifteen feet.

Goddess bless cheesy '80s sword and sorcery movies!

Since the best time to kill a dangerous enemy is when they're pretty much helpless, I charged.

Right into a bolt of silver fire. It clipped my shoulder, knocking me off my stride and spoiling my thrust. Momentum carried me past him. I skidded to a stop and dropped back a step to regain firm footing.

Preston rolled up on one elbow, hurling his silver fire again. His aim was off, and the tree Neesy sat under so long ago exploded into toothpicks.

"Lord...bless it!" Preston pointed at the wreckage. "That tree was here when the first land claim was filed!"

"Then you should apologize to its spirit." Two fast steps and Kindness sliced through Preston's shoulder. "I'll be happy to make introduction."

He threw himself back, tossing a wild burst of fire at me without aiming.

I ducked behind the shield again. Too slow this time. The bolt hit high on my sword arm, tearing through the mail and the muscle beneath.

The acceptance kept the pain to a minimum and flooded my system with adrenaline and endorphins. I fell back and circled to the left, keeping the shield in front of me.

Preston scrambled away, trying to turn with me as he did. When that failed, he hurled silver fire into the ground at my feet. Dirt fountained up, bouncing off my shield.

With the shield blocking his view, I tested my arm, moving Kindness through two quick cuts as though carving an 'X' into something. Everything still worked.

My foot came down on a dirt clod. I took a half-step to the side and kicked. Preston knocked the flying dirt away. While he was distracted, Kindness took off his left arm.

He howled, blasting me in the center of the chest. The armor held, but the impact knocked me backward. I landed on my ass and kept rolling, bouncing to my feet just in time to deflect another bolt into the ground. More dirt rained down on me.

He took his time aiming the next one. I managed to block it, but the force of it knocked me to one knee. I got back to my feet just in time for him to hit me again.

This time simple bolts of fire weren't enough. He poured everything he had into the assault, bathing the shield in a continuous stream of silver fire. It wasn't as powerful as the bolts had been, but it was unrelenting. All I could do was brace myself against the pressure and hang on.

Tendrils of lightning lashed out from the stream of flame, scoring deep gouges in the earth. Another raked across the daycare fence, tearing it in half.

Under our feet, the grass crumbled into gritty black ash. So did the remains of Neesy's tree. The destruction spread out around us until every plant within twenty yards was dead.

The pressure faded and vanished. I risked a look around the shield.

Preston was slumped over, skin tight and drawn as a drumhead. The silver fire that had wreathed his hands was little more than a haze, like smoke drifting from a crushed cigarette butt.

He looked up, blood oozing from around his eyes. "I don't understand. I was anointed by God to wield His holy might. I should have crushed you as Moses crushed Pharaoh's magicians."

"Magic sword, magic armor. And what you were using wasn't God's holy might. You're not anointed. You're just one of the Changed. You gained the ability to do a simple memory spell. What you didn't get was the knowledge of how to power it without consuming your life energy. I even warned you that you should stop. You didn't listen."

I raised Kindness to *chudan-no-kamae*. "*Sayonara*, Preston. Rejoice in the knowledge that your plan succeeded. You've guaranteed Still Waters will get national exposure. Fame. Interviews. Network talk shows. Everything you wanted is going to happen now...for Harper."

His shoulders sagged and he bowed his head. "No..." he whispered.

"Yes. That's not all. Harper has the gift of healing. People are going to flock to her. She's going to need a much bigger church before long. If you hadn't been such a dick, you could have been part of it."

Preston moaned and ripped his shirt open, revealing a withered body that was leaking blood thick as molasses. "Enough!" he howled. "Stop talking!"

"Want to know the real pisser of it all? If you hadn't tried to kill me, I never would have come here. All you had to do was let me take Aparna back to Colorado and you could have had it all. Harper would have discovered her gift sooner or later, and you would have become associate pastor of one of the few churches to have a leader who can perform miracles of healing. But, no. You threw it all away and went with kidnapping and murder. Big mistake. Just thought you should know."

Preston looked up, tears of oily black sludge creeping down his cheeks. "Lord," he cried. "All my life I have served You. How can You turn away from me now? How have I displeased You?" His voice dropped to a whisper. "Why hast Thou forgotten me?"

Kindness returned to her normal form, runes blazing along the blade. I edged closer to Preston, treading as softly as I could. Maybe it was too loud; his head whipped around and he looked up at me—just as I brought the sword down.

Preston's head bounced once and rolled to a stop amid the ash and dust—his face frozen forever in open-mouthed, wide-eyed disbelief.

Chapter Forty-One

Aparna

Preston's body and head dissolved into acrid pools of black ooze. Then, even the ooze died, dissolving like dew in the morning sun.

Behind me, Harper sat up, holding her head. She looked at the destruction around us and at the vanishing pool of slime that used to Preston. "You broke your word," she said.

"Preston was already dead. All I did was kill the thing that took his place." I helped her to her feet. "Killing monsters is another big part of the whole Hero gig. It's what we do."

"I guess it is at that." She looked around again. "What now?"

Preston's shoes, belt, and suit jacket were still mostly intact. There was a silk handkerchief in his jacket pocket; I snagged it and wiped the streaks of tar-like blood off Kindness's blade. "As soon as I get this gunk off my sword, I'm going to look for Aparna."

The retirees were gathering around Harper again, looking to her for leadership. She pointed toward the nearest door into the church. "We need to secure the church offices. Chances are that's where Aparna will be."

"Hold up a sec," called Gunny. He jogged over to Rusty and Ofelia's remains and went through their pockets. I did the same with Preston's clothes. His phone had multiple bullet holes in it, but his keys and wallet were undamaged. I turned them over to Harper.

Gunny returned with Rusty's keys, ID card, and phone, along with Ofelia's purse. Harper looked at the dust and ash clinging to them and shuddered. "Do you mind hanging on to those for a bit, Gunny? I don't want to touch them right now."

"I understand, sister." Gunny dropped Rusty's stuff into Ofelia's purse and slung it over his shoulder.

Before Harper could enter the building, I stepped up and blocked her. "Let me go first. I'm the one wearing armor."

"You go second, greebo." Orion pushed me out of the way and paused by the doggie door. "No one wastes ammo on a dog. Give me ten seconds before you come in." He nosed his way inside without waiting for me to agree.

"Lor-dee, I sure hope farm animals don't start talking," one of the retirees said. "I like bacon way too much."

Loud snarls filled the air, followed by screams and gunshots. I yanked the door open and charged in.

Desks from the office had been hauled into the hallway and tipped over to form a barricade. Bullet holes and a spatter of blood marred the surfaces of the desks. The blood concerned me for a moment, until I spotted a severed arm on the floor next to the desks.

"Orion? You still with us?"

The dog poked his head around the bottom desk. "Yeah. Not for lack of trying, though."

Three bodies were sprawled behind the barricade. Two had their throats torn open. The third had been beheaded completely.

Orion had a bullet graze on his shoulder and a through-and-through to his back right leg. He looked back at me for a moment and returned his attention to the office door.

"What do you think?" I whispered.

"At least two in there. I can hear a man on the phone and a woman praying." He shook himself and stretched. "The door's not locked, but the folks inside have guns. I can smell them."

"No problem. I'll crouch down in front of the door and yank it open. If nothing blows up in our faces, you jump on my back and launch yourself into the room. And try not to kill anyone. We are looking for my daughter."

"Right, right...always something." Nevertheless, he got into position. "Ready to roll, mate."

I changed the shield back to the *hoplon* and knelt, hand on the door. Behind me, Orion whispered, "Ready...steady...go!"

His paws hit my back as I opened the door. The praying woman froze, dropping her shotgun. Orion plowed into her full-force, knocking her out of the office chair she'd been sitting in.

The guy on the phone dropped it and reached for his belt holster. I shield-rushed him, slamming him into the wall. He kept clawing at the butt of his pistol, so I banged the shield on his head a few times. He finally fell over.

The woman abandoned the shotgun, pulling a small revolver out of an ankle holster. She fired at me without aiming. The round glanced off my helm, burying itself in the wall.

Orion leaped again, catching the gun in his teeth. He bit down. The gun shattered, sending fragments everywhere. With her disarmed, I poked my head into Harper's office.

Her desk drawers and filing cabinets hung open, contents strewn about the room. Her books were laying open and askew in a corner—probably thrown there after being searched.

I hit Preston's office next. Everything was in order—in fact, it was immaculate. I made sure Aparna wasn't under his desk and went back out.

The woman was trying to rouse the guy I'd shield-bashed. I said, "Cooperate and he gets medical attention. Who are you?"

"I'm...Jill Ferguson. I don't know anything! I'm...one of the residents in the women's shelter."

"Bullshit. I've met all the women staying at the Spa."

"She's Preston's secretary," Orion said.

The woman's eyes bugged out. "Oh, blessed Lord..."

"Save it," I snapped. "Worry about me, not the talking dog. Now, where is my daughter? Where is Aparna? Either Preston or Ofelia would have made sure she was somewhere safe, because he needed her for his big scheme. Start talking."

She looked frightened for a moment, then shook her head. "I don't know what you're talking about."

"Lady, I just cut Preston's head off for jerking me around. Don't piss me off."

"Okay, okay!" She licked her lips. "She...ah, she's...at Harper's house."

Orion's lips curled back. "She's lying."

"Congratulations," I said. "You just won a free trip to the hospital." I stood up and drew Kindness. "It's against my religion to harm women, but you're party to kidnapping my daughter. You forfeit all protections."

"Wait!" Jill looked at the sword and fumbled in her pocket for a set of keys. "Downstairs! She's...she's downstairs, in the old tornado shelter."

"Orion?"

The dog nodded. "She's telling the truth. At least, she thinks she is."

"Good enough for me. Do you know how to get there?"

"Yeah. Let me grab Harper first." Orion headed out the door, leaving Jill and I alone.

"You...didn't really kill Preston, right?" Jill clutched at her small cross pendant. "You were just trying to scare me, right?"

I shook my head. "Preston died before I laid a finger on him. He was consumed by his thirst for magic, and it destroyed his humanity. I killed the thing he turned into. He had already killed Rusty and Ofelia, and he wasn't going to stop. So I stopped him."

She looked away. "You're lying. Preston would never hurt any of us. We're on his side."

I laughed. "Tell that to what's left of Ofelia and Rusty. He devoured their life force and reduced them to dust. If Preston would do that to someone he was schtupping, what makes you think he'd spare you?"

Jill turned dark red and her hands clenched into fists. "No. He would never...that's not true!"

"Which isn't true? That he killed them, or was boinking Ofelia?"

She turned away with a muffled sob. Only then did the lights come on.

I handed her a box of tissues off the desk next to me. "I didn't know you and he were together. I'm sorry."

"For what?"

"For breaking it to you that way. There's no good way to find out something like that, but this was a bad way. I'm sorry for hurting you. And, as strange as it might sound, I'm sorry for your loss."

"Go to Hell! You boasted about killing him!"

"I boasted about killing the monster he became. You're entitled to mourn the man."

Orion trotted back in, followed by Harper, K, and Gunny. Harper looked around and sighed. "Well, on the good side, this gives me an excuse to repaint the walls in here. Jill, are you alright?"

"No," Jill whispered. "I'm really not."

"She's distraught over Preston's death," I offered.

Harper nodded. "I thought you might be, and I'm so sorry about all of this. I know you loved him." She chuckled at Jill's expression. "It's a small office, Jill, and I have eyes. If it's any consolation, I was glad for you. I thought you two would do very well together."

"I guess we were both wrong," Jill said. "I'm sorry, Harper. Sorry about everything."

"It's fine, Jill. As I told David, we're in the business of forgiving people. And I forgive you. For everything."

"Thank you. I needed to hear that." Jill wiped her eyes and nose with the back of her hand, then picked up her purse. "Where are those tissues..."

Her hand clenched on something. She didn't try to remove it from the purse; she brought her hand up and aimed at Harper.

I lunged, grabbing her wrist and pushing down. She yanked her hand back. I held on. She got off two shots before I punched her. Both rounds hit my upper thigh.

She dropped the revolver and grabbed her nose, howling in pain. My left leg buckled and I hit the floor.

Jill dived after the revolver. K tackled her. Jill went for scratching and pulling hair. K grabbed the front of Jill's shirt and yanked her forward, slamming her palm into Jill's sternum. Jill convulsed in agony, screaming and writhing on the floor.

My jaw dropped. "Bloody hell...was that your improvised Taser again?"

K nodded as she emptied the rounds out of the revolver. "Yeah. I'll show Aparna how to build one when she's older. Should make kindergarten interesting. Tacks on the teacher's chair are old hat."

While Gunny got Jill and the unconscious guy secured, Harper cut my pants open and prayed over the wounds. A moment later, my leg was healed.

Jill's eyes bugged out. "What was...how did you do that?"

"With the name and grace of the Lord," Harper replied. "Now, let me look at you." She rested her hand on Jill's shoulder for a moment. "Minor burns and a broken nose. You could have seriously hurt her, David."

"Pain is nature's way of telling you to make better decisions."

Harper rolled her eyes, but didn't say anything. A moment of silent prayer later, Jill's nose popped back into line and the burns on her chest vanished.

Jill gave her nose a tentative touch. When it didn't hurt, she wiggled it a bit harder. Her hand dropped. "You healed me? After I tried to kill you? I... I don't understand."

"I told you. We're in the forgiveness business. Now, who is downstairs with David's daughter?"

"Paige. Preston told her to keep the girl safe."

"Why am I not surprised..." I said. I picked up Jill's keys and nodded to Harper. "Since you have a standoff to defuse, I'll get out of your way."

"Don't hurt anyone, David." Harper wagged her finger at me. "Use your words."

"Yes, Sister Harper."

"No worries," Orion said. "I'll keep the greebo here out of trouble."

"Says the dog that killed three men out in the hall," Harper replied.

"Three *armed* men. Who would have shot you on sight and felt good doing it," Orion retorted.

I signaled for a time-out. "You two can argue later. Harper, Orion's leg was hit. Can you do something for him?"

"Save it. I'm fine. Let's go get your daughter, greebo." Orion left the room without looking back. I shrugged at Harper and followed the dog.

The tornado shelter sign was easy to find. I stood behind the door when I opened it, half expecting a shotgun to go off.

The dog snorted at me. "Paranoid much?"

"Just a reasonable degree of caution, fuzzybutt. Some of these folks are bat-shit crazy."

"Too right there, mate." The dog started down the spiral staircase without waiting for an answer.

We were halfway down the stairs when we heard the gunshot.

I didn't need the key. Kindness sliced through door and lock as though they were smoke, and I charged into the room.

Paige was crawling backward, holding a pistol in one shaking hand, eyes wide and mouth open in a soundless scream.

Sharon was standing over her.

She was wearing the same ripped jeans and white tank top she'd died in. For a moment, she looked like her last picture had come to life. Aparna had been right. Her wings and Sharon's did look alike.

Paige shook her head, firing round after round into Sharon's chest. They went right through her, burying themselves in the wall.

Sharon's wings erupted into flame. Her tank top changed, becoming torn and blood-soaked. The injuries that killed her appeared as well, looking as if they'd just been inflicted. The slash across her throat and the stab wounds on her face were still bleeding.

Paige shook her head again. She pulled the pistol to her, under her jaw, and pulled the trigger one final time.

I stepped forward, reaching out one hand. "Sharon..."

The wounds and the blood vanished, but the flaming wings remained. Sharon blew me a kiss and whispered, "Take care of our little girl, Bigwig."

"Sharon!" I lunged for her, but my had closed on empty air. She was gone.

"What the bloody hell are you on about, greebo? Who's Sharon?" Orion looked me over and his ears went back. "Christ on a pogo stick... You look like you've seen a ghost."

"Not a ghost," I said. "An angel."

Orion looked at Paige's body, then back to me. "What kind of angel would scare someone into blowing their own brains out?"

"The avenging kind." As I said it, an icy fist grabbed my heart. "Those shots should have brought Aparna running."

"Check the store room." Orion led me to a closed door next to the bathroom. I eased the door open and looked inside.

Aparna was sprawled on a stack of yoga mats, sound asleep. I knelt down and shook her shoulder. "Hey, little girl. Time to wake up." When she didn't move, I shook her harder. "Aparna! Come on, wake up."

"Easy, mate." Orion sniffed at Aparna's face. "Smells like that slag gave your girl a drop of the pure. Time-honored way of getting kids to sleep."

"I'm familiar with it." I went back to shaking and prodding Aparna awake. When she finally opened her eyes, I smiled and said, "Good morning, sweetie."

"Daddy-ji!" Aparna wrapped her arms around my neck in an octopus-like stranglehold of a hug. I hugged her as tightly as I dared, reveling in the reality of her.

I had my daughter back.

She loosened her grip before I passed out and scowled at me. "Daddy-ji, you're late! Hit's furry rude!"

It took a lot to choke back a laugh. "I... I know, sweetie. I'm sorry. Hey, I heard there's a place in Tulsa where we can build a really fluffy Spectrum Blaze plush doll. Does that sound fun?"

"Uh-huh!" She looked at my armor and banged her fist on it. "What's this?"

"It's called armor, honey. I'll change clothes before we go shopping." I let her go and said, "Why don't you go say hi to Orion while I get your stuff."

Off she toddled, entranced by warm fuzzy dogness. While she was distracted, I went back to the main room and tossed a blanket over Paige's body.

Her laptop was on the table next to her purse. She'd been writing a diary entry when she got...interrupted. Most of it was a rant about how badly Preston was screwing everything up. I scrolled back a few pages and discovered she'd been schtupping him, too. Go Preston.

On a hunch, I did a search on Aparna's name, and struck gold.

As part of the discovery process for our custody hearing in India, she'd gotten Aparna's medical records. One of the doctors had noted Aparna's developing ability to command people.

Under that information, Paige had written, "This child can make people do what she wants, and Preston can change their memories. Together, we could get anything we want in this world. Convincing Harper to sign Still Waters over to us is the first step."

She was the mastermind. Not Preston. All of this had been her idea.

For a brief, burning moment, I could have killed her a thousand times over, and it still wouldn't have been enough.

I disabled the password on the laptop and collected Aparna. With the dog leading the way, we went back upstairs.

Harper was in her office, talking to several uniformed officers and two guys in government-issue suits. I handed her Paige's stuff and said, "You need a new door for the tornado shelter. And a new lawyer. I'll pay for the door. Just send me the receipt. Oh, and I'd like all the stuff in Neesy's room to go to the Steps program. Except the jacket. K can have it if it fits her."

One of the suits said, "You must be David Fraser. Please have a seat, sir. We have some questions-"

"You don't need to ask me anything," I said. "Harper and I are the victims here."

"You and Harper are the victims here," they echoed.

The response caught me flat-footed. Maybe Preston had created the anti-magic shield on the property. If so, maybe it vanished when he died. Didn't really matter, I suppose. Whatever the reason, I had my mojo back!

I drew energy up from the earth until I couldn't hold any more and focused it into the imperative form. "You're satisfied that Ofelia, Rusty, and several others were murdered by Preston. You're satisfied I killed Preston in self-defense. All your findings will support these conclusions."

They echoed their instructions perfectly.

"You'll accept as possible any credible evidence or testimony involving Preston using magic or becoming some kind of monster. You will investigate that evidence or testimony as you would any other."

"David, whatever you are doing, stop it." Harper folded her arms and set her jaw. "Stop it, or I will undo whatever spell you're using."

I nodded but held up one finger. "You don't need Aparna or I to stay here any further. My daughter and I are free to go."

One of the Feds nodded. "Thank you for your cooperation. You and your daughter are free to go."

I shook his hand. "No problem at all, agent. You and your team have my thanks for all your hard work resolving this situation."

He passed me his card. "Our pleasure, sir. You and your daughter have a safe trip back to Colorado."

Harper rolled her eyes but didn't say anything.

Outside, Vernon and Grace were waiting with their car and Aparna's luggage. While Aparna and Grace were saying their goodbyes, Vernon took me to the side.

"Who was down there? Who took her?"

"Paige Novella. Although, she's a little short for a novella now."

His brow furrowed. "What? Paige? What's her part in all this?"

I shrugged. "I decided answers really weren't that important. I turned her laptop over to the authorities. They'll figure it all out."

"I guess." He sighed and added, "What say we drive you to Tulsa? Or is Rose coming to meet you?"

Right on cue, resounding thunderclaps shook the ground, and a massive bank of storm clouds erupted to the south. In seconds, they filled a quarter of the sky, stopping just short of covering the sun.

I pointed up. "Here she comes."

Almost hidden by the glare of the sun, a long, sleek, purple form burst out of the storm clouds and streaked down toward us, a misty, rainbow-colored haze billowing from her wings.

Behind her, the clouds opened, and the sky was full of Dragons.

Chapter Forty-Two

Enter the Dragons

Rose told me once that her people had professional warriors, but no standing army. In times of war, Dragons called up a militia. Neighbors and family members served side-by-side, organized into flights of five Dragons each. Five flights made up a wing, five wings made a claw. And at that moment, *two* full claws were screaming down on us from out of the sun.

The mist coming off their wings meant they were using velocity spells, the Draconic answer to nitrous oxide. A skydiving Dragon is able to pass a stooping peregrine on wing power alone. These spells pushed them well past that.

Just when I was sure they were going to plow into the ground, they pulled out of the dive and shot toward us just above the treetops, still clocking well over a hundred miles an hour.

A single, gigantic male with dark red scales and silver armor lead the assault. One claw formed up in a right echelon from him, like stealth fighters following a B-52. Before anyone could react, they covered the police, rednecks, press, and onlookers with euphoria gas. By the time they circled back to land, every human in the area was high as a kite.

The second claw peeled off, following Rose. Four of the wings split up and spread out to cover the surrounding area. The fifth wing landed, securing the buildings by yanking the doors open and flooding the halls with happy gas.

Rose slowed to a halt, hovering over the roof of the sanctuary. She raised a claw, surrounding the steeple with a golden aura. At the same time, trumpets sounded and music filled the air,

> *"...in every soldier's heart in all the Infantry,*
> *Shines the name, shines the name of Rodger Young!"*

Oh, yeah. That was indeed suitably geeky. I smiled at Aparna and asked, "What do you think? That's what Rose really looks like."

"I loves purple! Can she teaches me to fly?" Aparna didn't wait for an answer. She shouted, "Rasa-ji! Rasa-ji!" and took off for the sanctuary—head up, eyes bright, and on the bounce.

Rose dropped to the ground, shifted to Human, and held her arms out. Aparna leaped the last ten feet, flapping hard to stay airborne. Rose caught her, whirled her around, and tossed her into the air. Fifteen feet into the air...

On the way up, Aparna's wings pulled in tight to her body. Then they flared out, slowing her by at least half. Rose caught her and exclaimed, "That was great! You did so well!"

"Throws me again, Rasa-ji! Throws me again!"

"Alright, one more time. See if you can fly to Daddy on your way down!"

This time Rose put some extra welly into it, getting Aparna close to twenty-five feet up. Her wings spread out again, and her body stiffened into the typical 'flying superhero' pose. She didn't fall, either; she glided nearly forty feet.

Just before landing, the stiffness left Aparna's legs and she touched down at a run, stumbling and careening into my arms. My heart was in my throat, but Aparna and Rose were downright giddy.

Once the shrieking and giggling died down, Rose said, "Her wings aren't ready for flight yet, but she's getting close. She needs to exercise them and do more short glides. Just be warned, she's going to fall, and crash, and get hurt, but she has to go through it."

"Yeah. Not right now, though. Vernon and Grace have offered to drive us in to Tulsa so we can do some shopping. We also need plane tickets, a hotel, and I'll probably need to have a chat with the police."

"Nadia and Eric already took care of the hospital. The records show you woke up and checked out against medical advice. As for the police..." She nodded toward the front gate. "...I don't think they're going to be a problem."

The huge male Dragon I'd seen earlier landed some distance away and walked over to us. As a Dragon, Rose has fairly long legs and tends to walk like a cheetah. This guy moved like a stalking tiger, ready to spring in any direction or erupt into swift and blinding violence in the blink of an eye.

Up close, his scales were scored and pitted with countless scars. His armor had a silver-white sheen, but wasn't metal, and I didn't need to see the glow to be sure it was enchanted.

One plate covered his head, from the end of his snout to the tips of his earfins. His eyes burned like coal embers behind the armor, and his gaze was fixed on me.

He halted twenty feet away, which sounds like a lot. Except, this guy was bigger than Rose's mother. He loomed over us like the prow of a

284

battleship. When he walked, his claw prints sank eight inches into the ground.

He said something in Draconic. Rose bowed and leaned over to me. "David, this is General Lunus, Commander of Flame and Talon, Destroyer of Men, Defender of What Is Ours, and Guardian of the Ancient Ways. He's also the leader of our largest political faction. I'll translate what he says. You may speak to him directly, he'll understand you."

I bowed, waving at everyone in the area to do likewise. "My deepest gratitude to you, mighty one, for aiding my family in this time of need. I am in your debt."

He replied again in Draconic. Rose said, "He likes your manners, and wants to know where the guy who shot me is."

I pointed to Bo Breen's corpse, now hidden under a tarp. "Here, General. He died well, fighting and wounding the monster I killed."

"Where are those who wronged you?"

"One died on my blade, mighty one, the other by her own hand. I hope it doesn't offend you that they're already dead."

General Lunus grimaced (or maybe it was a chuckle; I couldn't tell) and made one final comment to Rose. She bowed, and he leaped into the sky. The downdraft from his wings sent ash, debris, and people scattering in all directions.

I got up, brushing myself off. "Something tells me he doesn't like Humans much."

"He likes Humans fine, as long as they know their place. The fact that you've taken up the Lairkeeper's Array pleased him. Killing those who wronged you pleased him even more. In fact, the last thing he said was that you were...acceptable."

"Acceptable?"

"From him, 'acceptable' is practically glowing praise."

"In that case, I'm duly honored." I pulled her close for a kiss, which she was eager to return.

After a wonderfully long moment, I asked, "So, Dragons have political divisions?"

She nodded. "Mother and I follow Helian's teachings. She's an accomplished scholar and philosopher who believes we should serve as teachers, guiding and inspiring Humans. General Lunus and his followers believe Humans need to be managed. Assertively. Not slaughtered, of course, but kept in line."

"Ah. So, you both want to control the Humans. You just differ on how."

"Exactly. It's like in that book with the talking horses and the tiny people. The ones fighting over eating eggs."

"*Gulliver's Travels?* The Big Endians and the Little Endians?"

She grinned. "That's it. The ones who fought six wars and never discovered omelets."

My stomach rumbled in reply. "I vote we get breakfast. What do you think of going to Miami for a genuine tender-*lion* sandwich?"

"I'd rather have a burrito or something. Lion is too gamey for breakfast, no matter how tender it is."

That's my girl. "Alright, we'll find something else. How is the assault and subjugation going?"

Rose looked at her watch. "Nadia's team should be almost finished hitting everyone with *Retcon.* Officially, the police came in, the militia surrendered, and the cops promised not to charge the militia members if they just left."

"I like that idea. What say we leave, too? Before they regain their senses?"

"We could. They'll be out of it for ten more minutes or so, then be really happy for an hour or two. If there's anyone you haven't settled accounts with or any bodies you need to dispose of, now's the time."

Crap. "Now that you mention it..."

"Oh, smoke and ash." Rose crossed her arms. "How many times have I told you not to leave dead bodies lying around?"

"I know, I know. Anyway, it's just two, and they're out of the way. I doubt anyone's found them yet. I told the feds to conclude Preston killed them."

"Did you use your sword?"

"On one of them."

"They'll match the wound to the other idiots you killed. Show me."

The humans in the building would be waking up soon, so we only had a few minutes to retrieve Paige's body. I carried her up the stairs while Rose cleaned up the bloodstains. She cleaned the Spa as well, then we took Page and Bethany to Rose's world.

We appeared in a meadow filled with copper-leafed, dark purple flowers. High mountain peaks, shrouded in clouds, surrounded the valley. Rose dug two graves while I fashioned crosses to mark them.

It was twilight when we arrived. By the time we finished, it was full night. Two of the moons were up, and the sky glittered with stars.

So did the meadow and the sides of the surrounding mountains. The flowers had opened, and the heart of each blossom glowed and sparkled in the night.

I took Rose's hand. "Are those midnight sun roses?"

"Yes." She snuggled under my arm. "This is where I was conceived. It's where Mother learned what she would name me. My grandmother came here to enter the Final Dreaming, just as her mother did, and her mother before her. All the years of their lives became stone, and brought forth the mountains around us."

"It's beautiful." I looked down at the graves. "I'm sorry, ladies. I hope this place is okay with you. *Requiescat in pace.*"

Rose placed several of the glowing flowers on each grave and said, "I know these are not your lands, but my family is here, all around us. They will welcome you and keep you safe. Fly free, always."

We stood a moment in silence, then Rose took us home.

Back on Earth, five minutes had passed. Outside, the skies over the compound were full of departing Dragons. On the ground, Nadia was introducing everyone to Eric. The Covenant Center residents were maintaining a cautious distance from him, but Aparna was enthralled. She'd charged right up to him, dragging Grace and Vernon with her.

Harper walked out of the building, Orion loping at her side. She dropped her voice to a whisper and said, "David, I'm sorry to tell you this, but...I don't have a choice. You killed Bethany and Paige. I...I can't...I'm sorry, but I can't resurrect them! I can't face knowing either of them that way! I know it's weak and cowardly..."

"No, Harper, wai-"

"Please let me finish. I owe you more than I can say for stopping Preston, and I hate myself for doing this, but after seeing what you did to those men, I can't let you just walk away. I know you just got your daughter back, but I'm asking you to turn yourself in. And...and if you don't, I will."

I held my hand up. "Paige killed herself, Harper. Not that it matters. They've already been laid to rest. Rose and I took them to Rose's world. We gave them both proper burials in a place sacred to Rose's family." I gave her a description of the meadow and added, "I'm sorry, but there's no evidence left to find. Even if you did turn me in..."

"They'd never be able to prove anything. Yeah." Harper shook her head and ran her fingers through her hair. "God forgive me, but...I think I'm going to let everyone assume Preston killed them the way he did Ofelia and Rusty. Lord, I have some praying to do."

Orion said, "Don't bash yourself up, Harper. Dogs always know good folks from bad. Trust me, you're a fair dinkum sheila-"

"Seriously? A hundred years later and you still insist on using that stupid Australian accent? God above... You're lucky a real Aussie doesn't kick your ass until you're wearing your butthole for a collar." Thirteen walked out of the shadow under Vernon's car, hopped up on the hood, and snapped to attention, saluting by holding his paw between eye and ear. "*Semper Vigilo.* It's good to see you again, Captain. It's been too long."

Orion sat down, staring. "Fookin' hell..."

That's when everything clicked into place. I'd been so distracted, I'd never realized I'd seen Orion's picture before. It was hanging on the wall of Thirteen's office.

Orion returned the salute. "*Semper Vigilio*, Dustybutt, and for the record ladies love this accent. Now where the bloody syphilitic hell have you been?!"

Thirteen shrugged and dropped to the ground. With a flick of his paw, he produced a dried catnip stem and stuck it between his teeth. "Oh, here and there," he said. "Miss me?"

"Thought I did," Orion replied, now sounding decidedly Bostonian.

"Turned out it was just a splinter in my ass."

The two of them stared at each other for a moment, stone-faced. Then they embraced, clapping each other on the shoulder and laughing.

Thirteen broke the embrace first and waved in my general direction. "I had a feeling you and this lunk would be drawn together, and I was right. You're a sucker for hard-luck cases and David here is a goldmine of need."

"So I've noticed." Orion chuckled for a moment, then his ears went back. "What happened? Afterward, I mean. Has anyone...checked in?"

Thirteen sighed and took his hat off. "No, sir. All but three biotraces returned finality in the initial exchange. Navarro lingered five hours before finality. I don't think he was...aware...of his situation. But you and Caravan, your biotraces just stopped. Not finality, just...nothing. It sounds odd, but that gave me hope you two might still be alive somewhere. I tried to find you for ten years, but I had no idea where to look."

Orion nodded. "Caravan had arranged to meet a... family friend for lunch. I went out sightseeing-"

"There's no need to be coy. I figured you guys out a while ago." I looked around and added, "They were spies. Not on our Earth, though. They're from a different Earth."

"Of course," Harper muttered. "Where else would they be from?"

"Fine," Orion growled. "Caravan went to her contact's dead-drop. I was on overwatch. She'd just found the spot when we saw missiles launching from Santacruz Air Base. We tried to take cover, but there was nowhere to run."

Thirteen closed his eyes. "But there was."

Orion nodded. "We linked up. I tore a manhole cover open and dropped down in it. Then the sky lit up from the first detonation over Malabar Hill. Caravan was out in the open. She caught a lethal dose right there. She dropped in, too, but it was too late. We were dead. I knew it. Caravan grabbed me and whispered, "Bast forgive me." Then we were here."

"Why didn't you come back?"

"Caravan had absorbed too much radiation. She said you'd survive and come for us. She died the next night." He shook himself, looking at the ruin Preston had made of the grounds. "I buried her and planted a tree on her grave. And I stayed here, tending it."

"The Native tribes in the area thought I was a spirit, tied to the tree. They...I fought alongside them against the Europeans. And watched them get decimated. Then settlers arrived, looking to homestead the land. I ran half a dozen idiots off before a good family arrived. I spoke to them and told them to leave the tree alone. It was the first time in a century I'd spoken out loud. I worked with them. Protected their flocks. When Esther died, Harper moved in. I liked what she was doing, so I stayed with her."

Harper knelt next to Orion. "You've been here over two hundred years? How is that possible?"

288

Thirteen snorted. "We were immensely expensive intelligence assets. The government wanted their money's worth, so they gave us all cutting-edge life extension treatments. You're lucky what they did to us isn't hereditary, or I'd have you up to your asses in immortal cats with thumbs. That would screw you all up for damn sure."

Harper shuddered. "I see what you mean." She looked back at Orion and scuffed him behind the ears. "So you're the legendary 'ghost dog' I used to hear stories about. People said you could outrun a car. And that one time, after a tornado blew a tree onto the doors of a root cellar, you bit the tree in half and saved six people."

"What a bunch of crap. I only bit the limbs off until it was light enough to drag off the door."

"Only, eh?" Harper smiled. "Well, very soon I'm going to need someone by my side who has a nose for people. I'd like you to take the job."

"That could be interesting." Orion scratched behind one ear, looking thoughtful. "Give me a day or two to think it over. Besides, I want to go home for a while."

Harper nodded. "I understand. Just don't take too long."

Aparna tugged at my hand and asked, "Daddy-ji, can we gets Spectrum Blaze most soon?"

I scooped her up. "Yes, Bugbear. Most maximum soon."

After a chorus of farewells, we piled into Grace and Vernon's SUV and headed out, Aparna shouting "*Nahin! Chalay jo!*" at the reporters in our path. The ones who resisted her command spell yielded to steel and horsepower.

Once we were out on open road, Grace said, "David, you got enough room back there? We can pull over and you can sit in front. Has to be a lot more comfortable."

"I'm fine, Grace. Thanks for asking."

And I was. I put my arm over Aparna's seat so I could take Rose's hand, leaned back, and listed to my little girl read a heroic tale about three little wolves beset by a very antagonistic pig.

Love alone triumphs.

Chapter Forty-Three

Home and Family

"Daddy-ji! You's holding the camera like a monkey with a itchy butt. Holds it right this time!"

"You let Daddy-ji worry about the camera, Little Miss Albatross. You worry about keeping your wings straight." Rose sounded stern, but she was smiling.

"Hy wills!" Aparna raced back up the hill, extended her wings as much as she could, and waited.

This time I remembered the picture stabilization, made sure the camera was on video, and verified it was actually recording before announcing—again—that this was Aparna in flight training. Lesson One: Fundamentals of Gliding.

Right as I finished the intro, Aparna launched into motion. She sprinted down the hill, charged up the ramp Wiley had built for her, and flung herself into the air.

This time her wings were as straight as Rose could have asked for. Her back and legs stiffened, staying aligned with her torso to reduce drag as she sailed toward the barn.

Aparna was doing so well, her glide path wasn't going to end with her touching down at the bottom of the hill. She was going to hit the side of the barn.

She saw it too. She shifted her weight, using her legs as a stabilizer, and turned to the right at the last moment. I could swear the tips of her feathers swept cobwebs off the side of the barn.

The turn gave her more room, but now she was sailing toward the fence around the alpaca pasture. Hitting the fence would be painful, but landing in the pasture would be worse. A 400-pound llama could do a lot of damage.

Beside me, Rose bellowed, "Flap! Flap hard! Get some altitude and come around again!"

Flap she did. We could hear her grunting with every down beat, but she did it. She gained another twenty feet or so, turned back toward us, and glided in for a landing, giggling and shouting "Didja seeme didja seeme?" all the way to the ground.

I tucked the camera into my vest pocket so I could scoop her up. "Yes, I did see you! And I got it on camera to send to Mommy-ji and Doree. She's going to be so proud of you."

"Hy wanna go again!"

"No, that was the last time for today. We have to get home to get dinner and get ready for your party."

The excitement of having a real slumber party overwhelmed the excitement of more flying. "Uh-huh. We should do that. And I know the rules. Feet on the ground! And I promise to keep my shirt on *allll* night. Unless Rasa-ji takes hers off."

I chuckled and gave Rose an innocent look. "And is Rose going to take her shirt off?"

"Later, yeah." Rose caught my look and added, "but not until bedtime."

Wiley, Margot, and Fox met us by the Range Rover. Margot had our eggs, cheese, and lamb wrapped in newspaper for the ride home. We got the parcels stowed while Aparna had a farewell cuddle with Nacho and Frito.

"Saw your preacher friend on the news last night," Wiley said. "Some guys pulled out pistols during a church service and demanded she bring a friend of theirs back to life. Seems they needed him to find out where a bunch of drug money went."

"How'd that work out for them?"

"Not well. Your preacher buddy clapped her hands and said, "Lord, show them the burdens of their sins!" and *poof!* They were all yoked like oxen."

"Very nice," I said.

"All their guns vanished, too. She turned them into plows." He chortled, shaking his head. "I'd love to learn that spell."

"It is a nice touch." We exchanged hugs. "I'll tell her my hippy Pagan buddies approve."

Margot said, "Get her out here sometime. We'll get her dancing naked under the moon, preacher or not."

I had to laugh. "Harper already brought up the idea. She's coming out next month on a business trip and thought it would be a good way to keep her congregation on their toes. I'll let her know she's now been officially invited."

Wiley's eyebrows went up. "What's the occasion?"

Out of the corner of my eye I saw Fox perk up. I kept my gaze locked on Wiley. "There's a big interfaith conference on how to handle people with divine gifts of healing. Developing standards and practices, that sort of thing."

"Huh. So, is priestly malpractice considered a clerical error?"

Margot smacked Wiley with her fedora and pointed down the road. "Go. Now. Before you get him started."

"Yes, ma'am." I hopped in the car and we headed out before Fox could ask me anything.

Aparna insisted on watching the video of her flight three times on the way home, and each time she asked if I was going to send it to Manya. I was starting to run out of ways to promise I would take care of it first thing when she said, "Daddy-ji, Anna says the pony store has Mrs. Mullita-gawny! Can we go for my party?"

Rose looked back at her. "What's the magic word?"

Aparna pointed her finger at me. "*Imperio!*"

Rose and I cracked up. Good to see Ember was making sure Aparna got a classical education.

I glanced at her a moment and said, "We'll see, *Usagi-chan*. I have to talk to your friends' parents first. I'll let you know later."

"It would make me so much of happy..."

"Aparna, I said I'll let you know. That means you don't have to keep trying to convince me. Understand?"

I expected her to keep arguing, but she thought for a moment, then nodded. "Uh-huh." With that issue settled, she went back to her new favorite storybook and ignored me for the rest of the trip.

Obviously, I ranked somewhere below a bunch of anime ponies in the grand scheme of things. So much for thinking I was making progress in the Cool Dad department.

One of these days I wanted to have a few words with whoever decided raising children should work like coding a new game client on a live server full of paying players.

When we got home, Ember took charge of Aparna and whisked her off to finish cleaning her room. She wasn't that messy, actually; she was just used to servants cleaning up for her.

I watched them go and shook my head. Ember had a way of getting her to do things which I had yet to master. I left her to work her wiles on my darling angel and went upstairs to my office.

First thing, as promised, I called the other parents about hauling the girls off to get new plush flying cats. Since the Change, our neighborhood had become a lot more neighborly. We had the new neighborhood watch, very active social media accounts, and an online newsletter. We were even having some kind of social event at least once a month now.

The first event we went to as a family had been the Sixty Days Car Show and Barbecue, held to mark the two-month point since the Change. While I was showing off the Interceptor, Aparna sought out the dozen or so other girls her age and spent the day bonding with them over mutual pony fandom. That set the stage for tonight's party.

We'd invited all the girls she'd met at the barbecue, assuming several wouldn't be able to make it for some reason or another. As it turned out, all the Changed girls (two Gold Elves, one Gnome, an irrepressible Troll, and a Drow) were coming, but only one of the Human ones.

Two of the Human girls were seeing their father this weekend, and one was off with her family doing some Labor Day RV camping. I'd probably invite those three again.

All the parents liked the idea of getting some new plush, especially once I said I'd pay for everything. One mom even offered to help drive. Probably better than duct-taping urchins to the roof rack of our Range Rover.

Once that was settled and we had a reservation at the store, I emailed Harper with Margot and Wiley's invitation. I figured she'd accept; she wanted to come to the farm anyway.

Officially, I didn't know that Harper was reorganizing the church's businesses and intended to compensate Fox's family for the ranch. She could afford it now and wanted to clear her conscience.

I approved of the idea; I was just trying to avoid Fox so I didn't have to answer awkward questions. This was Harper's news to break, and I was staying out of it.

That wasn't the only change. My comment to Harper about the ethics of owning a firearm manufacturer had landed on fertile soil. Last month, the church divested of Angelic Arms. The new owner was (drum roll) Miss K, using capital from Llewellyn Industries and our own Rose Drake.

Between the paranoia about the Changed and Clarice Harrison's rising poll numbers, gun sales were skyrocketing. So were the calls for firearms safety. It was a perfect environment for the right product.

For that reason, Angelic would be going to market next year with pistols and rifles that would only fire for the verified owner and authorized guest users. Her first demo video (narrated by Gunny and starring Bo Breen's daughter Evelyn, a Marine marksman and silver medalist in biathlon) had already stirred up a lot of interest from law enforcement and Second Amendment advocates.

Geneva's yenta instincts were as good as she had promised; K was quite taken with the Dread Pirate she'd located. Morgan Skinner was full Drow, Earth-born to a refugee couple living in Gilead. He made his living as a repo agent while competing in mixed martial arts tournaments. Happily Ever After was working out pretty well for her. Sadly, despite my fervent urgings, K adamantly refused to consider hyphenating her married name to Tribble-Skinner.

Meanwhile, back in our neck of the woods....

We survived our excursion to Adopt-a-Bear and all the kids had a terrific time. I was ready to start shooting up liquid Valium by the time we left, but other than that I'd call it a success.

Back home, I got to make my one big contribution to the evening: grilling hamburgers and hot dogs for dinner. Once that was done, I was excused. No boys allowed, you know. I stayed in my office and did work stuff.

A little after midnight, I shut everything down and went to the kitchen for a snack. I figured the kids would be asleep, but obviously I knew nothing about little girls having sleepovers.

They were in the family room, gathered around the fireplace with the lights off, telling spooky stories. D'vorah, the Drow girl, was telling a story based on the 'B-17' segment of *Heavy Metal*. From the details, she must have seen the movie at least a few times. Obviously, she had older brothers.

She was a good storyteller, and the other kids were suitably terrified by the poor bomber pilot's gruesome fate. I almost applauded, but thought better of it.

Rose was up next. She looked around and said, "Well, my story is one I heard when I was about your age. It's not from around here, because I'm not from Earth. I'm in disguise, because I'm not Human at all."

Mary, the Gnome, raised her hand. "You look Human."

"It's a good disguise," Rose retorted. "I'm really a Dragon, and this story is a Dragon story. No one else on this planet has ever told this story before. Do you want to hear it?"

All the girls nodded and promised they'd keep it a secret—at least for tonight.

Rose leaned forward and said, "There is an old game dragon hatchlings play at parties, or when friends come to stay the night, or late at night when the adults are asleep. They gather around a lava pool with much giggling and whispering, until one of them declares 'this is serious!' and everyone tries to look solemn. One by one, they place treasured items from their hoards on the edge of the lava pool and look around, daring each other to place a more valuable item even closer to the glowing, molten rock. Once the last glittering bit of hoard is sitting by the lava, the hatchlings begin to quietly repeat a single name..."

Her voice dropped to a whisper. "Burnbones... Burnbones... Burnbones..."

"Deep into the molten rock they stare, daring the long-dead spirit to arise. Burnbones, the Dracolich. Burnbones, the Hoard Thief."

"The stories claim that he appears as a charred skeleton, wreathed in smoke. Smoldering embers fall from him as he moves, and his eyes are black, bottomless pits. Sometimes the hatchlings imagine they see him in the churning lava—and sometimes they actually do. He doesn't appear very often, for it taxes him greatly, but a valuable trinket is a strong lure and the occasional appearance ensures every new generation of hatchlings knows his name."

Rose leaned forward, curling her hands up like claws. "When he does appear, he erupts out of the lava and lunges for the most valuable hoard items and seizes them in his mouth before the hatchlings can move to reclaim them. Usually they're so frightened that they scamper backwards,

294

leaving all the offerings unprotected and he can claim them easily before withdrawing into the molten stone.”

“The cries of the hatchlings bring their parents, who listen to the frantic explanations with firm skepticism, then shoo the hatchlings to their lairs and leave them with threats of dire consequences if they don’t stop all this foolishness and get some sleep!”

Rose deepened her voice for that, sounding very pompous, and made a grumpy face. The girls burst into laughter, mimicking her and making faces in return.

Rose waited for the laughter to die down. “When morning comes, the hatchlings almost always decide that their imaginations got the best of them and that there is a logical explanation for the fact that their hoard items are missing. In time, they, like their parents, will forget the exhilaration and terror of these childhood tales. They may watch their children try the same game, and gently shake their heads.”

She leaned forward again, lowering her voice to a whisper. The girls leaned forward, too, straining to hear her. “Burnbones watches it all, and waits to be summoned again. He passes his time meditating upon his hoard, deep in the molten rock of his prison. He remembers every glittering gem, every biped-crafted sword, armor segment, tool, and piece of jewelry. He remembers every scale and spell. He remembers every rare and exotic item he claimed, every grave he ransacked and every corpse he desecrated to get them. He remembers the fury of the mob that followed him, and the searing agony of Helian spell and Lunus chain binding him deep within his hidden hoard treasury as it was slowly flooded, condemning him to live and burn forever in a hell of molten stone.”

Rose’s eyes turned red and started glowing. The girls gasped and clung to each other, eyes wide.

“Their fury and disgust meant nothing to him. His hoard was the biggest and the best, and he would be remembered forever for acquiring it.”

“So never leave anything too close to a fire, because you never know when Burnbones might...just...grab you! Rarggh!” Rose pounced, grabbing the girls and tickling them mercilessly.

Well, the party obviously had no need of me. I took two tumblers and a bottle of Glenlivet outside. One drink for me, the other for Sharon. I set hers across the table and raised mine in salute. “We did okay,” I whispered. “We made a beautiful little girl, Sharon. I promise, Manya will always be part of her life. So will your parents. They’re...not too bad, after all. And I will always take care of her.”

“Daddy-ji?”

I turned around. Aparna held her arms out, so I scooped her into my lap for a long hug. “Good night, *Usagi-chan*. Ready for bed?”

“Uh-huh.” She kissed my cheek. “Night-night, Daddy-ji.” Then she waved at the chair next to Sharon’s tumbler and added, “Night-night Mama-ji!”

I looked at the chair, too. For a moment, I thought I saw Sharon again, but no. The chair was still empty, still pushed up against the table. I shook my head and patted her on the back. "Did you want to start calling Mommy Sharon 'Mama' now?"

"Uh-huh!" She nodded emphatically. "She likes that better. She says she knows she's a freakin' ghost and doesn't need a reminder."

That sounds like Sharon, alright. "I like that better, too. I'll let Rose and Mommy-ji know, too. Why don't you go ahead and run back to your party?"

Aparna tugged at my hand. "Daddy-ji, you gots to come inside too. Mama-ji is singing her lullaby for us."

I hesitated for a moment. Aparna loved the video of Sharon singing, but the song was too energetic to lull a room full of kids to sleep.

Well, why not? Slumber parties are special occasions. "Sure, that sounds fun. Do you want me to set up the video?"

"No, she's ready."

While Aparna ran over to the electronics cabinet, I sat down on the couch next to Rose. "We'll never get them to sleep at this rate," she whispered.

I pulled her close and kissed her. "In the immortal words of Seven of Nine, 'we will adapt'."

Rose rolled her eyes, but nodded.

Aparna flopped down on her sleeping bag and started the video. The screen lit up with static for a moment, then went black. A moment later, a still frame of Sharon filled the screen.

My chest tightened. I closed my eyes and took a deep breath to steady myself. Call it ego, but I didn't want to cry in front of Aparna's friends. I opened my eyes again when Sharon started singing.

> *Of all the money that e'er I had,*
> *I spent it in good company...*

Our set must have a much better picture than Manya's; This time, I could see the foxes on the patio clearly. All...seven...of them.

That wasn't the only difference. Lady Vivien was playing a different harp, one with nylon strings. Her friend was playing a recorder, not uilleann pipes. And Sharon was singing this as a lullaby all the way through.

When she finished, Sharon blew the camera a kiss. "Sweet dreams, little angel. I love you, and I'll always be with you." The screen faded to black.

The living room was dark and quiet. All the girls were fast asleep. So was Ember, nestled under a pile of blankets, two cats, and her dragonette.

I looked at Rose and pointed to the television. *Should we...*

She shook her head. *Nope. I'm going to bed. So should you. You're cooking breakfast in the morning*

296

She had a point. I tiptoed out of the room and went to collect the whisky.

The bottle was down to the last pour. I emptied it into my tumbler but didn't drink. I just stood there, gazing out at Boulder without seeing it. In the back of my mind, I could still hear Sharon singing. I tried to shut it out, but even half a bottle of whisky wasn't enough to do that. Finally, I gave in and sang with her.

> *But since it fell unto my lot*
> *That I should rise and you should not*
> *I'll gently rise and softly call*
> *Good night and joy be to you all!*

I raised the tumbler, saluted, and drained it. Only after I set the empty glass down did I look at the tumbler I'd poured for Sharon.

It was empty. And upside down.

For a moment, I smelled Sharon's perfume and heard an old, familiar laugh. Then it was gone. I blew the night a kiss and took everything inside.

Rose made her way out of the family room and snuggled up to me. Holding her and watching Aparna, I felt enormous...contentment.

Adventurers fought for excitement. Or glory, or riches, or fame. Not so Heroes. Heroes fought for this. Home. Family. Peace.

Contentment.

Rose ran her finger along my cheek and stepped away. With a shrug, her nightgown slithered to the floor. She hooked it with one finger and went up the stairs, trailing the nightgown behind her. I followed.

So ends this tale. Good night, and joy be to you all.

Good night, and joy be to you all...

Acknowledgements

I'd like to thank Pam Gheysar, Mike Miller, and Velveeta the Cheese Queen for their services as beta readers. Your feedback was invaluable, and I deeply appreciate the work you put in to helping this story come to life.

Several folks were kind enough to take time out of their days to answer strange questions for me. This book would not have been possible without their help and I owe them a profound debt of gratitude:

Patricia and Elizabeth Yarrow, for their advice on Celtic harps and traditional music. Special thanks for the story of Liz and the foxes.

Rick Simmons and Virtrium, for allowing me to bring a few bits of Istaria into David and Rose's tale. Not only was my time on the Istaria content development team a great deal of fun, it had a profound influence on my writing.

Huntress, for her explanations and insights into nursing, hospital operations, and traumatic injuries. Remember, folks, clerics are not permitted to regenerate limbs, cure disease, or raise the dead without orders from an attending physician.

Credits

A Princess of Mars, by Edgar Rice Burroughs
Courtesy of Project Gutenberg

The Ballad of Roger Young, by Frank Loesser
Public domain under 17-1-105 USC

The Destruction of Sennacherib, by Lord Byron
Courtesy of Project Gutenberg

Hadith, Musnad Ahmad 12140, Sahih

Istaria: Chronicles of the Gifted content courtesy of Virtrium, LLC and used by permission.

Julius Caesar, by William Shakespeare
Courtesy of Project Gutenberg and PublicLiterature.org

King Lear, by William Shakespeare
Courtesy of shakespeare.mit.edu

The Mesnavi and The Acts of the Adepts, by Jelal-'d-din Rumi and Shemsu-'d-Din Ahmed, tr. by James W. Redhouse, 1881

The Parting Glass, Traditional
Courtesy of CSU-Fresno

Song of Myself, by Walt Whitman
Courtesy of Bartleby.com

About the Author

I grew up reading classical authors such as Verne, Burroughs, Wells, Haggard, and Lovecraft, often in conjunction with large doses of *Monty Python*, *Wild Wild West*, and *Hee-Haw*. My current influences include *Doctor Who*, *Girl Genius*, and *An Idiot Abroad*.

I began writing professionally as a member of the content design team for the MMORPG *Istaria: Chronicles of the Gift*ed. My first book, *Life With a Fire-Breathing Girlfriend*, was published in 2014.

I live in Denver with my wife, Noelle, and daughter, Alissa. The three of us can often be found prowling around Istaria, Wizard City, and the wilds of Azeroth. I also make occasional side jaunts to scavenge bits of ancient technology in the radioactive ruins of Las Vegas, Washington, and the Boston Commonwealth.

Find me on Facebook at:
https:// www.facebook.com/BryanFieldsAuthor

* * *

Did you enjoy *Born with Wings*? If so, please help spread the word about it. It's as easy as:

- Recommend the book to your family and friends
- Post a review
- Tweet and Facebook about it

Thank you,

Bryan Fields